A

A Complete History of the Marquis de Lafayette

SALZWASSER
VERLAG

Anonymous

A Complete History of the Marquis de Lafayette

Reprint of the original, first published in 1859.

1st Edition 2022 | ISBN: 978-3-37512-662-9

Verlag (Publisher): Salzwasser Verlag GmbH, Zeilweg 44, 60439 Frankfurt, Deutschland
Vertretungsberechtigt (Authorized to represent): E. Roepke, Zeilweg 44, 60439 Frankfurt, Deutschland
Druck (Print): Books on Demand GmbH, In de Tarpen 42, 22848 Norderstedt, Deutschland

A COMPLETE HISTORY OF THE MARQUIS DE LAFAYETTE,

MAJOR-GENERAL IN THE AMERICAN ARMY
IN THE WAR OF THE REVOLUTION.

EMBRACING

AN ACCOUNT OF HIS TOUR THROUGH THE UNITED STATES,

TO THE TIME OF HIS DEPARTURE,

SEPTEMBER, 1825.

BY AN OFFICER IN THE LATE ARMY.

COLUMBUS:
J. & H. MILLER, PUBLISHERS.
1858.

Lafayette

ceived an excellent education. In the year 1772, at the age of fifteen, he was enrolled among the Mousquitaires, a corps instituted for the protection of the royal person, and composed of young men of the most illustrious extraction. Previous to this time, he was made one of the pages of the queen of France. The mildness and affability of his manners soon attracted the universal esteem of his new comrades; and the immediate influence of royalty, in a short time, elevated him to the rank of a commissioned officer, a favour exclusively reserved for the most illustrious scions of nobility.

The Mousquitaires du Roi had for a long time been a costly establishment; and although such a noble guard was highly flattering to the dignity of the sovereign, yet the expense attending it was severely felt, and frequently regretted. The suppression of it had been repeatedly agitated; but no minister had yet been found sufficiently hardy to venture on a reform, which menaced him with the resentment of the most noble families of France. This instance of political fortitude was reserved for the Count de St. Germain, who enforced to Louis XVI. the considerable savings that might be applied to the effective marching battalions, from the reduction of a corps which was the offspring of pageantry. An edict was accordingly published, in the year 1775, for the suppression of the Mousquitaires.

Those brave men, whose courage had always been celebrated, received the news of their dismission with the deepest marks of sorrow and despair. Attached to each other by similarity of habits, and cemented in friendship by common dangers and services, they regarded the order which decreed their separation, with feelings of real and undisguised grief. M. de la Chaise, a veteran officer of tried resolution, and one of their commanders, fainted on receiving the fatal mandate; and the whole corps vented their sorrow in the loudest and most poignant exclamations. But the King and his ministers were inexorable—and, it is said, that the capital was not sorry to be delivered from a corps, whose impetuous and aristocratic spirit too frequently insulted the more humble class of citizens. In the year 1774, he married Anastasie, a daughter of the illustrious house of Noailles, celebrated for her virtues, courage, and conjugal affection. The history of female virtue and female heroism, presents nothing more rare in excellence than the life and character of Madame Lafayette. It will be found in the sequel, that she was worthy of the hero to whom she was united. Such characters, said Charles Fox, speaking of this admirable pair, should flourish in the annals of the world, and live to posterity, when kings, and the crowns they wear, must have mouldered in the dust. His union with the young Countess de Noailles increased the annual revenue of the Marquis de Lafayette, to two hundred thousand francs. At this time a general peace in Europe inflicted a painful restraint on his enthusiasm for military fame, and condemned him to a state of inactivity, which little accorded with his ardent and enterprising disposition. The enjoyments of affluence, and the luxuries of the court, were unable to subdue the spirit of his sires which animated his bosom. The same spirit which guided his gallant father to a soldier's death,* on the disastrous plains of Minden, glowed with equal purity and vigour in the breast of his noble descendant. He appeared at the French court to which his rank had called him, while yet a boy. Too young to be insensible to its pleasures, but too noble to be tainted by its corruptions, he obstinately refused a place, voluntarily offered to him, as the stepping-stone to such honours as courtiers eagerly solicit.† He had already, at the age of sixteen, felt and acknowledged another vocation.—The star of political liberty was, at that period, observed rising brightly

* The father of General Lafayette was killed at the battle of Minden It is a curious fact, that his death was occasioned by a shot from a battery commanded by the same General Phillips, to whom his son was opposed in Virginia, in the year 1781.

† Lady Morgan's France, p. 316.

in the west, and Lafayette was among the first who went forth from a distant land to worship it. At this period of his life, the Marquis de Lafayette was a noble looking man, notwithstanding his deep red hair. His forehead, though receding, was fine, his eye clear hazel, and his mouth and chin delicately formed; exhibiting beauty rather than strength. The expression of his countenance was strongly indicative of a generous and gallant spirit, mingled with something of the pride of conscious manliness. His mien was noble,—his manners frank and amiable,—his movements light and graceful. Formed both by nature and education, to be the ornament of a court, and already distinguished by his polished manners and attractive qualities, in the circle of his noble acquaintance, his free principles were neither withered by the sunshine of royalty, nor weakened by flattery and temptation.

Among the various nations of Europe, all more or less favourable to the American cause, and detesting the tyranny of England, none signalized themselves more than the French. The desire of vengeance, the hope of retrieving its losses, the remembrance of ancient splendour, the anguish of recent wounds, all stimulated the French government to side with the colonists in their struggles against oppression. The interest which France took in the contest, plainly indicated at its commencement, that the projects then in agitation in her councils would not long be concealed.

Exclusive of the national and hereditary inveteracy of the people towards the English, they believed them to be acting an unjustifiable part towards the Americans. Hence they considered themselves doubly authorized to assist the latter; and were prompted by motives of justice as well as of policy. In fact, the government only awaited the maturity of events, and a propitious occasion, openly to espouse our cause.—The nation was acquainted with the disposition of the ministry; and, as no people are more susceptible of impressions from those in power than the French, the cause of America found among them the most ardent and ingenious advocates.

The operation of many other causes concurred to the same effect. Although the people of France had been accustomed to live under a very absolute system of government, they have uniformly testified a particular esteem for such men, and for such nations as have valiantly defended their liberty against the usurpations of tyranny. When they are not led astray, and, as it were, transported by their exorbitant imagination, their character is naturally benevolent and gentle: they are always disposed to succour the oppressed, especially when they support their ill fortune with constancy, and endeavour to surmount it with courage. There is a national tendency in favour of great and glorious enterprises: such was the cause of America; and such were the general sentiments of the French toward them.

At this period, moreover, those writers who in all countries, but particularly in France, had treated on political subjects, had manifested themselves the advocates of a liberal mode of government, and thus the opinions prevalent at that time were extremely propitio is to civil liberty. Nothing can more evidently prove the spirit of that epoch, than the eager request for those writings, and the still more rapid dissemination of the principles they contained When the news of the commotions which agitated America arrived, in all social circles, as well as in numerous publications which daily appeared in France, the Americans were the objects of boundless eulogiums; their cause was defended by the most forcible arguments, and justified by a multitude of illustrious examples. If indeed, at the period when France, after the cession made by the republic of Geneva, had undertaken the conquest of Corsica, many were found among the French who professed themselves the apologists of those islanders, and ventured openly to condemn the determination of their own government to subdue them,—it may well be imagined that the partisans of America were much more numerous, and demonstrated an enthusiasm still more ardent. It would be difficult to describe the excessive joy,—the vast hopes that were excited by the convocation of the first American Congress. The names of the deputies were extolled to the skies: let them hasten (it was every where said,) to shake off the yoke of English despotism, to sever the bonds of servitude; let them establish civil liberty in their country; and let them serve as a perpetual example, that princes cannot without peril violate the fundamental law of their states, or attack with impunity the privileges and immunities of their subjects.* While Louis XVI., who had not long before mounted the throne, was not indifferent to the internal regulation of his own kingdom, he constantly directed his attention toward America; and watched with anxiety, the commencement and conduct of a contest which hourly became more important, and in the event of which, the humanity and interest of European powers were deeply concerned. Each day seemed to establish more firmly the jurisdiction of the states; their privateers overspread the seas; and Louis, while he professed to the court of London a strict neutrality, afforded to our vessels a secure refuge in his harbours, where the prize goods were bartered for the arms and ammunition so necessary for the support of our cause. The exultation of the French people had been openly and constantly proportioned to the success of the Americans. The princes of the blood and the chief nobility were eager to embark in the cause of freedom; and the prudence of the king and his most confidential ministers, alone restrained their ardour. The fatal events of the last war were still impressed on the mind of Louis XVI.; and he could not readily consent to expose his infant marine in a contest with a people who had so frequently asserted the dominion of the seas, and so lately broken the united strength of the house of Bourbon. Yet he was sensible that the opportunity of humbling Great

* Botta's War of Independence, vol. i, p. 204.

Britain ought not to be entirely neglected, and that some advantages should be taken of the existing commotions in America. Although all audience in a public capacity, was denied to Silas Deane and Dr. Benjamin Franklin, who had successively arrived at Paris as agents of the United States, still they were privately encouraged to hope that France only waited the proper opportunity to vindicate in arms, the freedom and independence of America.

In the mean-time the military preparations in France were diligently continued, the American cruisers were hospitably received into her ports; artillery, and all kinds of warlike stores were freely sold, or liberally granted to relieve the wants of the Colonists; and French officers and engineers, with the connivance of the government, entered into their service.* The king was not ignorant that the remonstrances of Great Britain, and the importunities of the agents of the United States would soon compel him to adopt some decisive line of conduct. He had been closely questioned by the English ambassador, Lord Stormont, respecting the warlike preparations which were diligently continued throughout the kingdom, and replied, that at a time when the seas were covered with English fleets and American cruisers, and when such armies were sent to the new world as had never before appeared there, it became prudent for him also to arm for the security of the colonies and the protection of the commerce of France. On the other hand, he was assailed by the entreaties, remonstrances, and address of Dr. Franklin, whose exertions for obtaining the powerful aid of the French government, were only equalled by his abilities in the prosecution of his duty.

"In judging of the past, from our knowledge of the events that have ensued," says Madame De Stael, "most people will be of opinion, that Louis XVI. did wrong in interfering between England and America. Although the independence of the United States was desired by all liberal minds,

* Gifford's Hist. France, 4to, vol. iii. p. 469.

the principles of the French monarchy did not permit the encouragement of what, according to these principles, must be pronounced a revolt. Besides, France at that time, had no cause of complaint against England, and to enter on a war wholly on the ground of the habitual rivalship between the two countries, was bad policy in itself, and more detrimental to France than to England: for France, possessing greater natural resources, but being inferior in naval power, was certain of acquiring additional strength in peace, and as certain of being weakened by a maritime war. M. Necker laid before the king the strongest motives for the continuance of peace, and he who has been charged with republican sentiments, declared himself hostile to a war, the object of which, was the independence of a people. He certainly wished every success to the noble cause of the colonists; but he felt on the one hand, that war ought never to be declared without positive necessity, and on the other, that no possible concurrence of political results could counterbalance to France, the loss she would sustain of the advantages she might derive from her capital wasted in the contest."*

Happily for America, and happily for the common cause of free and enlightened principles, the majority of the French people were not disposed to consider as a waste of capital those means which were employed in the defence of rational liberty, the humbling of a haughty nation, and the chastisement of a hereditary foe. The arguments of M. Necker proved unavailing: and the king decided for war. The motives for this measure were undoubtedly strong and the government was exposed to great difficulties in either alternative. The time was approaching when the words of Hume, in relation to Charles I., might have been applied to Louis XVI. He found himself in a situation where faults were irreparable; a condition too rigorous to be imposed on weak human nature. Whether it be admitted

* De Stael, Consid. French Revolution, vol. i. ch. vii. p. 88

or not, and it can hardly be denied that the success of the American revolution tended to the dreadful convulsions which overturned the throne of France, and filled the land with wailing and lamentations; it is certain that the French nation derived no advantage, and suffered serious injury from their participation in the contest. It was not, however, until the capture of Burgoyne in October, 1777, that the French government formally threw aside the vail which had but slightly covered their opinions and proceedings in favour of America. The success of the colonists on that occasion, was received at Paris with unbounded exultation. M. Sartine, who presided over the marine department, was impatient to measure the naval strength of France with that of Great Britain; and universal enthusiasm reigned throughout all classes of society. The queen, who had long favoured the applications of the agents of the United States, now espoused the cause with less reserve, and with increased ardour. The phlegmatic temper, and pacific disposition of the king were overborne by the reiterated zeal, imperceptible but weighty, of the numerous body of philosophers which pervaded every rank of life, by the suggestions of his ministers, and by the influence of his royal consort: and it was at length determined openly to acknowledge the independence of the United States of America.

The situation of Europe, at this juncture, was particularly favourable to the determination of the king of France. Differences between the court of Petersburg and the Ottoman Porte respecting the Crimea, threatened a revival of the hostilities* which had been so lately adjusted; and thus even if the empress were willing, precluded her from affording assistance to Great Britain. The flames of war had been rekindled between the houses of Austria and Brandenburg; Spain, by the family compact, was bound to accede to the designs, and to strengthen the arms of France; Por-

* Gifford's Hist. France, vol. iii. p. 474.

tugal, by her late treaty with Spain, had formed an intimate union with the house of Bourbon: while Holland, pursuing those pacific maxims which the policy of commerce dictates, avoided every overture which appeared likely to involve her in the war, which now extended to the principal powers of Europe, and transferred to her peaceful ports all the advantages of trade and neutrality. Louis XVI., thus satisfied that he had nothing to apprehend from the principal powers of Europe, devoted his whole attention to the approaching contest with the ancient rival of his kingdom.

His councils had been long suspended on the manner of procedure proper to be adopted with regard to America. The constant declarations of the British ministry appeared to be corroborated by the numbers of the Colonists that joined the royal army; a much more numerous body was known to have adopted a passive but suspicious neutrality; and the progressive steps by which they had arrived to a complete declaration of independence, accompanied in every stage by liberal offers of accommodation from the Colonists, and the most confident rejection of every measure short of absolute submission, tended to enforce an opinion in the cabinet of Versailles, that the great body of the Americans were not earnestly disposed to an irrevocable separation from Great Britain. But the contest daily assumed a more serious and effective form, and the private activity united with the address and sagacity of Dr. Franklin, removed every impression which retarded the decisive and effectual measures of France. Dr. Franklin and Silas Deane, who had hitherto acted only as private agents, were now publicly acknowledged as ambassadors from the United States to the Court of France; and, in the month of February, 1778, a treaty of amity and commerce was signed between the two powers. This treaty and the formal acknowledgment (by France,) of the independence of the United States of America, was communicated to the ministers of Great Britain, in the month of March, by the Duke de Noailles, ambassador to the Court of London; and the recall of Lord Stormont from Versailles was the signal for the commencement of hostilities.

But the spirit which prevailed throughout all ranks and denominations in France in favour of the Americans, could not be confined, or regulated by the slow and cautious rules of policy. It burst forth long previous to the formal acknowledgment of our rights by that government, and was chiefly manifested by rejoicings at the success, and sorrow for the failure of our arms. It was among the military classes that this ardour was eminently conspicuous. The Irish brigade, so famous for the services it had rendered to France, especially in its wars with Great Britain, furnished a number of brave officers to America. Nor were the other French regiments deficient in this spirit of general adventure in the cause of the colonies against the parent state. Numbers of the young nobility of France were eager to signalize themselves in the noble cause of liberty against oppression. Among others, Roche du Fermoy was in the army that acted against Burgoyne; Baron St. Ovary was a volunteer in the service; De Coudray, an officer of rank in the French army, was drowned in the Schuylkill a few days after the battle of Brandywine, in his eagerness to cross it in order to join the army of Washington, which was reported to be on the point of engaging, the Chevalier Duplesis Maudit displayed the greatest bravery at Germantown and Red Bank, and was assassinated at Port-au-Prince: the heroic gallantry of Lieutenant Fleury at Stony Point, can never be forgotten; De Buysson was not less brave; Baron de Kalb possessed a pure and disinterested patriotism, which led him to danger and a glorious death. Other parts of Europe also supplied our armies with brave and experienced officers, through whose assistance they daily improved in discipline and military skill. Germany in particular, a country that from the perpetual quarrels amongst its own sovereigns, and the many wars of which it had in latter times been the unhappy scene, abounded in military men, more than any other part of Europe, contributed her share of heroes for the defence of America.

It is a tribute of justice due to our French allies, to observe, that during the course of the revolution, they generally endeavoured to harmonize with our citizens, relinquishing on most occasions, their own modes and prejudices, to conform themselves to the manners and customs of America. The extent to which their desire to please and conciliate was carried, is exemplified in the following anecdote: General M'Intosh was presiding at a court-martial, and desirous of administering an oath to a French officer, inquired of what religion he was? he answered quickly, "The American, Sir;" thinking, undoubtedly, that it was a duty to conform, as much as possible, to the religious opinion of the people in whose cause he had drawn his sword. And this appears the more probable, because time being allowed for reflection, and the question varied by substituting "what faith" instead of what religion, he exclaimed, "c'est bien une autre affaire: Roman Catholique Apostolique, mon General."* It is almost needless to touch upon their bravery; they were Frenchmen, and enthusiastically attached to the opinions imbibed in favour of liberty and republicanism. Their intrepidity was exemplary, and gave them daily new claims to the admiration and gratitude of the people whose rights and properties they had pledged themselves to defend: some, however, acted from more ignoble motives. But among these, none were so conspicuous for the splendour of rank, the fascination of his personal qualities, and the purity of his political principles, as the Marquis de Lafayette. Born under a despotic regime, he saw nothing in his own country to employ a young and enthusiastic mind. North America—sorely oppressed, demanding justice in vain, her complaints rejected, her petitions unheeded, her murmurs disregarded—attracted his attention. She was be-

* Gorden's Anecdotes, p. 206.

ginning to feel the sacred impulse of liberty; she was stretching and unfolding her half-fledged wings, doubting her powers, dreading her adversary, and wavering between submission and despair. She was in the infancy of her strength, when Lafayette, animated with the glorious cause, left all the luxuries and indulgences of home, to cross the Atlantic, and offer himself to the Americans as a champion and a friend. Animated by the enthusiasm which generous minds are accustomed to feel for great enterprises, he espoused their cause with a partiality common to almost all the men of that time, and particularly to the French. He considered it not only just, but exalted and sacred: the affection he bore it was the more ardent, as independently of the candour of his character, he was of that age in which good appears not only good, but fair, and man not only loves, but is enamoured.*

When the destinies of America were tottering on the brink of destruction; when a triumphant enemy was overwhelming the Jerseys with deeds of desolation; when even the firmness of Washington was shaken, the young and gallant Lafayette resolved to cast his bread upon the waters, and mingle in a conflict which appeared almost desperate in the eyes of united Europe. He espoused the cause of this country, when it had not a single acting advocate beyond the waters of the Atlantic. At that period, the representations in France relative to the state of American affairs, were most deplorable, and sufficient to repress the most determined zeal. The army of Washington was represented as a mere rabble, flying before thirty thousand British regulars: nor was this far from the reality. The route and carnage at Brooklyn, and the consequent evacuation of Long-Island, had given, indeed, a gloomy aspect to the affairs of America. The continental troops had heretofore manifested a great degree of intrepidity, from a confidence arising from the persuasion of their superiority over the enemy. The

* Trotter's Life of Fox, p. 186. Botta's War Independ. book viii.

goodness of their cause, their early and habitual use of fire-arms, had been carefully inculcated and nourished by all their preceding experience. But when, by a course of evolutions, in which they imagined they perceived a great superiority of military skill, they found themselves encircled with unexpected dangers, from which no exertion could extricate them, their confidence in themselves and their leaders was greatly diminished, and the approach of the enemy inspired them with the apprehension that some stratagem was concealed, from which immediate flight could alone preserve them.* The subsequent negotiations, however fruitless, with Lord Howe, had also an evil effect in France, by demonstrating the desire of reconciliation still existing in the colonies.

The evacuation and capture of New-York greatly dispirited the American troops, and almost drove them to despair. The militia were impatient to return home, and almost totally disobedient to orders, deserting by half and even whole regiments. The battle of White-plains—the surrender of Fort Washington—the evacuation of Fort Lee—the gradual dissolution of the American army—the ineffectual attempts to raise the militia—the indisposition of the inhabitants to further resistance—the retreat of General Washington through New-Jersey at the head of less than three thousand men, one thousand of whom were militia, badly armed and clad, and almost without tents, blankets, or utensils for dressing their provisions; dispirited by losses and fatigue—retreating almost naked and barefooted, in the cold of November and December, before a numerous, well appointed, and victorious army, through a desponding country—the immense numbers that daily flocked to the British standard, for the purpose of making their peace and obtaining protection—the universal idea that the contest was approaching its termination, greatly supported by the contrast between the splendid appearance of the pursuing

* Marsh's Life of Washington, vol. ii. ch. 7, p. 453.

army, and that made by the ragged Americans who were flying before them, destitute of almost every necessary; all these causes contributed in Europe, almost to extinguish the hope of a successful issue to the struggles of America. But the confidence of Lafayette in the triumph of liberty, was, and it ever has been, that of a pious man in a future life. The first inducement that led him to embark in the cause of liberty and independence, has been related by the Marquis himself. While stationed in the citadel of Metz, and only eighteen years of age, the duke of Gloucester, who was then exiled from the court of Great Britain on account of his marriage, communicated to a select company, the information which he had received respecting the contest of the Americans. Lafayette was so strongly interested by this account, that he left Metz for Paris, where he became acquainted with Silas Deane, the first agent from America to France. At this time Doctor Franklin arrived at Paris, and after obtaining from him the best information concerning the state of the country, he was determined by his ardent love of liberty, to embark his life and fortune in the cause of American freedom. Thus inflamed with the desire to participate in the events which were echoed by all Europe, he communicated, about the close of the year 1776, his intention of repairing to America; and they encouraged him in that resolution. But when they were informed of the reverses in New-Jersey, they were compelled themselves almost to despair of the success of the revolution, and with an honourable sincerity, endeavoured to dissuade the Marquis from carrying his design into execution. They even declared to him that their affairs were so deranged by this unhappy news, that they were not able to charter a vessel for his passage to America.* "Now, then," replied the gallant nobleman, "is precisely the moment to serve your cause; the more people are discouraged, the greater utility will result from my departure; and if you cannot furnish me with a ves-

* Botta's Independence, vol. iii. p. 342.

sel, I will freight one at my own expense, to convey your despatches, and my person to the shores of America." And as he said he did. Nursed in the lap of luxury and ease, possessing a princely fortune, and ennobled by the most illustrious blood of France, he had unalterably formed the heroic resolution to abandon the comforts of home, the enjoyments of affluence, and the attractions of a court, to devote himself to the cause of that liberty, the love of which has decided every action of his life. Impelled by that ardour which arises from a liberal education and a native generosity of sentiments, he embarked in the cause of America, not from an enthusiasm, by the lukewarm and calculating, termed madness and youthful folly, but from a firm conviction that it was just and honourable. This determination on the part of so illustrious a personage, astonished the people of France, and excited universal attention and conversation. The court of France, either to save appearances and avoid giving umbrage to Great Britain, or really displeased at the proposed enterprise, prohibited his departure, and it is even asserted, that vessels were despatched with orders to arrest him in the waters of the West Indies. But resistance to the king's will on this occasion, was encouraged by the public applause, and it was hailed by universal approbation. Even at that moment, the seeds of the French revolution were beginning to germinate. When the royal authority has lost ground in public opinion, the principle of monarchical government, which places honour in obedience, is attacked at its basis.* Embarrassments served only to strengthen this resolution, and increase his youthful ardour and patriotism. According to the laws of France, he exposed himself by clandestine departure, to the loss of his whole property; and, if captured by the British on his passage to America, he was liable to a confinement of uncertain duration, without the most remote prospect of being exchanged. But no personal considerations could influence the conduct of that generous friend to

* De Stael Consid. French Rev. vol. i. ch 7, p. 89.

humanity, who to a certain degree, possessed the same perseverance in opinion, which distinguished the illustrious Washington. Tearing himself from the arms of his beloved wife, who was in all the bloom of youth, and from the circle of connexions to whom he was eminently endeared, he embarked at the early age of nineteen years in the vessel which he had purchased and equipped at his own expense, and steering wide of the West India Islands, safely arrived in South Carolina on the 19th of April, 1777.

What chequered scenes has Lafayette witnessed—what glory has he won—what miseries has he endured—since the following notice of his departure was published in a Paris paper of 1777:—

"*Paris, April 4th*, 1777.

"One of the richest of our young nobility, the Marquis de Lafayette, a relation of the Duke de Noailles, between nineteen and twenty years of age, has, at his own expense, hired a vessel and provided every thing necessary for a voyage to America, with two officers of his acquaintance. He set out last week, having told his lady and family that he was going to Italy. He is to serve as a Major General in the American army.—On the other hand the Count de Bulkley an Irish gentleman, who is a Major General in the French service, is going, with the leave of his majesty, to offer himself to the king of Great Britain, to serve against the Americans."

The Marquis landed on North Island in Winyau Bay, about sixty miles from Charleston, and was welcomed with the most cordial hospitality by the family of Major Benjamin Huger, an officer of great gallantry and high promise, who fell covered with wounds before Charleston, during Provost's invasion, while executing an important duty: to increase the calamity, he fell by friendly hands—the fire which destroyed him proceeding from the American lines. He remained a short time in this delightful retreat, but anxious to pursue the object of his voyage he soon removed to Charleston, under the guidance of his hospitable host. Admired by his entertainers, who felt deeply interested in his success, and whose sentiments in his favour increased with his rising fame, it is not surprising that a son of the family (the gallant Colonel Francis Kinlock Huger,) should have cherished that enthusiastic attachment to his character, which led to as noble an act of friendship and heroism, as adorns the page of chivalry.* On his very first landing in Carolina, in testimony of his respect and high admiration of the gallant defence made by General Moultrie, of the pass on Sullivan's Island, and charmed with the gallantry displayed by the troops on that occasion, he presented him with clothing, arms, and accoutrements for one hundred men. And well did they deserve this evidence of their valour—resolved to repel the foe, or nobly perish, the undaunted garrison received the tremendous fire of the British shipping with composure, and returned it with terrible effect, until valour accomplished what prudence had declared impracticable, and the retreat of the assailants adorned the brows of every individual concerned with laurels that can never fade, such were the circumstances under which Lafayette landed on our shores. Scarcely had he set his foot upon our soil before his gallant spirit mingled in enthusiasm with that of the brave warriors, whose brows were still contracted by the sternness of warfare, whose ears were still ringing with the shouts of battle, whose swords were yet reeking with the blood of their oppressors. The young hero met with the most cordial reception from Congress, who immediately accepted his proffered services and omitted no demonstration of the respect and esteem in which they held the person of a man, who had made the greatest sacrifices and exposed himself to danger in support of the tottering cause of America. His high rank, his influence at the court of Versailles, his frankness of manners, and zeal in the cause, soon secured him the unlimited respect of his own countrymen, and the universal

* Gorden's Anecd. p. 95.

esteem of the Americans. It is impossible to describe the affection with which he was regarded by them, and which was only surpassed by the love of their illustrious chief. To those who knew him, it was not a matter of wonder that he had discovered the secret of winning all their hearts. His deportment was dignified without pride; his manners gentle without apathy, frank without boldness, and courteous without servility. His zeal, activity, and enthusiasm in the cause of America, were wholly distinct from all the political views of co-operation with the wishes of his court, and when added to a sincere and uniform admiration of the greatest and best character of the age, completely endeared him to the American people. Of Lafayette it has been said by those who knew him well, that he was never spoken of without manifest tokens of attachment and affection.* Touched by this flattering reception, he resolved to exert himself to the utmost of his knowledge and ability, but he felt, and did not hesitate to confess the want of that practical knowledge, without which, the theoretical science of the soldier can seldom lead to glory or success.

With a generosity and modesty which delighted the Americans, he demanded no station in the army, would consent to receive no compensation, and requested permission to serve at first only as a volunteer. This generous conduct was the more pleasing, as the claims of some of the French who had entered the service, were so exorbitant that they could not be gratified, on the subject either of pay or of rank. Many of the foreign officers who assisted in the revolutionary war, had little in view but employment in the profession they had chosen; and, as few natives then possessed military skill, they found little difficulty in obtaining high commands. For their services, they deserved their wages, and if they were victorious in battle, they also deserved glory; but those who acted from these motives, had no claims on the *gratitude* of the American people. Fighting

* Chastelleux's Trav. vol. i. p. 103, note.

was their vocation, and for honour and emolument, they would have fought against liberty as readily as for it. The case of Lafayette was different,—he left an ample fortune to participate in all the privations of a people struggling for liberty.

The ambition by which he was actuated was honourable; and he has, by his subsequent conduct, proved the sincerity of his republicanism. It was Silas Deane who had encouraged these exorbitant expectations on the part of the French officers, by entering in France into such engagements with them, as could not be confirmed in America. The Marquis de Lafayette had also stipulated with Mr. Deane for the rank of major-general without emolument, and the honorary rank was conferred on him soon after his arrival in America, but without any immediate command. On the 31st of July, 1777, the following preamble and resolution was adopted by Congress:—

"*Whereas*, the Marquis de Lafayette, out of his great zeal to the cause of liberty, in which the United States are engaged, has left his family and connexions, and at his own expense, come over to offer his service to the United States without pension or particular allowance, and is anxious to risk his life in our cause.

"*Resolved*, That his services be accepted; and that in consideration of his zeal, illustrious family, and connexions, he have the rank and commission of major-general, in the army of the United States."

This noble philanthropist was immediately received into the family of the commander-in-chief, to whom he attached himself with all the ardour of youth. Washington felt for him, in turn, a warm and sincere friendship, and paved the way to bestowing on him a command in the army equal to his rank. It was here that the principles of liberty, which appear to have been almost co-existent with his birth, were judiciously regulated and fostered. Under the care and tuition of the venerated man of the age, whose adopted son he was, they grew with his growth, and strengthened with his strength. It was not long before the chivalrous ardour of the young hero was displayed upon the field of battle. At the battle of Brandywine, which occurred on the 11th of September, 1777, he evinced his gallantry and zeal, and first shed his blood in the cause which he had espoused with so much enthusiasm. In the year 1777, the British having in vain attempted to reach Philadelphia across the Jerseys by land, proceeded by sea to the Chesapeake, and on the twenty-fifth of August, landed near the head of Elk, to which place Sir William Howe marched with one division and the next day advanced his van to Gray's Hill, leaving General Knyphausen with three brigades at the place of landing. The whole force of the British army consisted of eighteen thousand men, in good health and spirits, trained to the service, admirably supplied with all the implements of war, and led by a general of experience and unquestionable military talents. On the twenty-fourth of August, Washington passed through Philadelphia, on his way to meet the enemy; and after stopping some short time on the Brandywine to refresh, and afford an opportunity of reconnoitering both the country and the enemy, the divisions of Greene and Stephen proceeded nearer to the Head of Elk, and encamped behind White Clay Creek. Although the real strength of the American army cannot be stated with certainty, the estimate of fifteen thousand made by Sir William Howe, did not probably exceed the reality; but it is an unfortunate fact attributable in some degree to the badness of their clothing and scarcity of tents, as well as of food, that the effective force, including militia, did not exceed eleven thousand.

General Maxwell being posted about three miles in front of White Clay Creek, was fallen in with, attacked, and routed, by a detachment under Lord Cornwallis, and retreated over White Clay Creek. The whole American army, except the light infantry, which remained on the lines, now retired behind Red Clay Creek, occupying with its left wing the town of Newport, situated near the Christiana, and on the great road to Philadelphia; its right extended a considerable distance up the creek to Hockesson township. On this ground General Washington thought it probable that the fate of Philadelphia and of the campaign might be decided; and therefore resorted to all the means in his power to encourage his troops, and stimulate them to the greatest exertions.

The enemy, reinforced by the rear guard under General Grant, advanced his main body by Newark, upon the right of the American encampment, and took post within four miles of that place, extending his left still further up the country. In the mean time, a strong column made a show of attacking in front, and after manœuvring for some time, halted at Milton, within two miles of the centre. Washington saw the threatened danger, and retired with his troops beyond the Brandywine, and took post behind that river, on the heights which extend from Chadd's Ford, in the direction of north-east to south-east. The militia, under the command of General Armstrong, guarded a passage two miles below the principal encampment of Washington, and the right wing extended some miles above, to guard other fords deemed less practicable. In this position, the American general awaited the movements of the enemy. Although the Brandywine, being fordable almost every where, could not serve as a sufficient defence against the impetuosity of the enemy, yet Washington had taken post on its banks, from a conviction that a battle was now inevitable, and that Philadelphia could only be saved by a victory. Besides which, the ill effect which the surrender of Philadelphia, without striking a blow, would have had on the public mind, demanded that a sacrifice should be made on the altar of public opinion. The protection of that city was deemed by all America, and especially by Congress, of such infinite magnitude, as to require the hazard of a battle for its attainment. Hence the general engagement sought by Howe, was not avoided by Washington.

Early in the morning of the eleventh of September the

whole British army was in motion. It was formed in two columns, the right commanded by General Knyphausen, and the left by Lord Cornwallis. It was the plan of General Howe, that the former should make repeated feints to attempt the passage of Chadd's Ford, in order to occupy the attention of the Americans, while the second should take a long circuit to the upper part of the river, and cross at a place where it is divided into two shallow streams.—Knyphausen advanced with his column, and commenced a furious cannonade upon the passage of Chadd's Ford, making all his dispositions as if he intended to ford it. The Americans defended themselves with gallantry, and even passed several detachments of light troops to the other side, in order to harass the enemy's flank. In this manner the attention of the Americans was fully occupied in the neighbourhood of Chadd's Ford. About eleven in the morning, Washington was informed of the movements of Lord Cornwallis, who had taken a road leading from Kennet's Square directly up the country, and had fallen into the great valley road, south of the Brandywine, and above its forks; they were then on their march toward Tremble's and Jeffrey's fords, which they passed without opposition, and then turning short down the river, took the road to Dilworth, in order to fall upon the right flank of the American army.

On receiving this information, Washington formed the most judicious, but bold plan to cross the river in person, with the centre and left wing of his army, and overwhelm Knyphausen by a furious attack;—justly reflecting that the advantage he should obtain over the right of the enemy, would amply counterbalance the loss that his own might sustain at the same time. In the critical moment when this plan was to be executed, the troops being in motion, counter intelligence was received, inducing a belief that the movement of the British had been only a feint, and that the column under Lord Cornwallis, after making demonstrations of crossing the Brandywine above the forks, actually marched down the southern side of that river, to re-unite itself with Knyphausen. Thus was prevented, by false intelligence, the execution of a measure which, if carried into effect, might have given a favourable turn to the events of the day.

But the uncertainty produced by this contradictory intelligence was speedily removed, and about two o'clock in the afternoon, it was positively ascertained that the column of Cornwallis, accompanied by Sir William Howe in person, was about to fall in great force upon the right wing. This was composed of the brigades of Generals Sullivan, Stirling, and Stephen, who, taking new ground, advanced a little further up the Brandywine, and fronted the column of the enemy. The division under General Wayne remained at Chadd's Ford, for the purpose of keeping Knyphausen in check, while Greene's division, accompanied by General Washington in person, formed a reserve, and took a central position, between the right and left wings.

The column of Cornwallis now arrived in sight of the Americans, and Sullivan, who commanded the right wing, drew up his troops on the commanding ground above Birmingham Meeting House, with his left extending toward the Brandywine, and both his flanks covered with very thick woods. The British, having reconnoitered the disposition of the Americans, immediately formed, and fell upon them with the utmost impetuosity; and about four o'clock in the afternoon, the action became equally fierce on both sides. For some length of time, the Americans defended themselves with great valour, and the carnage was terrible; but such was the emulation which invigorated the efforts of the English and the Hessians, that neither the advantages of situation, nor a heavy and well supported fire of small arms and artillery, nor the unshaken courage of the Americans, were able to resist their impetuosity. The American right, which was in some disorder, first gave way, and the light infantry, chasseurs, grenadiers, and guards, threw themselves with such fury into the midst of the republican battalions, that the route soon became general. The vanquished fled into the woods in their rear, pursued by the victors, who advanced by the great road toward Dilworth.—On the first commencement of the action, General Washington pressed forward with General Greene to the support of the righ wing. But, notwithstanding the rapidity of their march, (four miles in forty-two minutes,) he found it impossible to get up, before the route of that part of the army had become complete, the confusion wild and universal, and the enemy in full pursuit. General Greene, however, by a judicious manœuvre, checked the enemy, and secured the retreat of the fugitives. Having come to a defile, covered on both sides with woods, he drew up his men there, and again faced the enemy. His corps was composed of Pennsylvanians and Virginians, who defended themselves with gallantry, and their fire made such an impression, as, in addition to the approach of night, induced Sir William Howe, after dispersing them, to give over the pursuit.

When the right was found to be fully engaged with Cornwallis, General Knyphausen made preparations for attempting the passage of Chadd's Ford, in reality. It was defended by an intrenchment and battery. The Americans, under Wayne and Maxwell, made an obstinate resistance; but the works were forced, and intelligence of the defeat of the right being received, no further opposition was made in that quarter. Greene was the last to quit the field of battle, but, it being already dark, he also retired, after a long and obstinate conflict.

The whole army retreated that night to Chester, and the day following to Philadelphia. The loss sustained by the Americans in this action was estimated at three hundred killed and six hundred wounded. Between three and four hundred, principally the wounded, were made prisoners. The official letter of Sir William Howe stated his loss at one hundred killed and four hundred wounded. If the account be correct, the inequality of loss is to be attributed solely to the inferiority and miserable state of their arms, as the Americans sustained scarcely any injury during the retreat.—After this sanguinary battle, and a series of masterly manœuvres on the part of the two armies, the rich and populous capital of the confederation fell into the power of the royalists, and Lord Cornwallis entered Philadelphia on the twenty-sixth of September, 1777, at the head of a detachment of British and Hessian grenadiers.*

During the battle of Brandywine the French officers were extremely useful to the Americans, both in forming the troops, and rallying them when thrown into confusion. Among these the Marquis de Lafayette was particularly distinguished. Brave almost to a fault, and romantically so in the execution of orders, he exhibited on this occasion, full and early proofs of his undaunted bravery and military character. While he was endeavouring, by his words and example, to rally the fugitives, he received a wound in the leg, but continued nevertheless, to fulfil his duty, both as a soldier in fighting, and as a general in cheering the troops, and endeavouring to re-establish order. General Lafayette, with Lord Stirling, and Sullivan himself, (after the defeat of his division) fought with the body of troops which received the left column of Cornwallis, and it was not until the enemy were within twenty yards of them that they gave way, and threw themselves into the woods. Their post was the most important, and they made a long and gallant resistance. It was here that Lafayette was wounded in the left leg.† The baron St. Ovary, Captain de Fleury, and Count Pulaski, were also conspicuous for their cool courage and services during the engagement.

The British general, now in possession of Philadelphia, being compelled to relinquish the hope of supporting his army from the adjacent country, owing to the vigilance of the Americans, and the severe resolutions of Congress, subjecting to martial law and to death all those who should furnish the royal troops with provisions, applied himself with

* Botta's War of Independ. vol. ii. book vii.—Marshall's Life of Washington, vol. iii. ch. 3.—Ramsay's American Revolut. ch. 14.

† Chastelleux's Trav. i. 246.

diligence to the task of removing the obstructions of the Delaware, and opening a free communication with the fleet. To succeed in this operation, it was necessary to seize Mud Island, which was defended by Fort Mifflin, and the point of Red Bank, where the Americans had erected Fort Mercer. The former was commanded by Colonel Smith, and the latter by Colonel Greene. Colonel Donop, on the evening of the 21st of October, 1777, passed the Delaware with a strong detachment of Hessians, and arrived at a late hour, the following day in the rear of Red Bank. He attacked the fort with great gallantry, but the Americans retiring into the body of the redoubt, made a vigorous defence, and Colonel Donop being mortally wounded and taken prisoner, and his best officers either killed or disabled, the Hessians were severely repulsed, and retired with precipitation, with the loss of four or five hundred men. Much of the success of the day was attributed to the Chevalier Duplesis, a French officer, who directed the artillery with great ability and valour.—The attack on Fort Mifflin was more successful, notwithstanding the intrepidity displayed by the garrison: on the first attack they defended themselves with gallantry until night put an end to the engagement. The next day the British renewed the attack, in the hope that, under cover of their fire, the ships Augusta and Merlin, which had grounded, might be got off; the former, however, took fire and blew up; and the latter was hastily evacuated and laid in a train of destruction. The erection of works on Province Island, by the British, now decided the fate of Fort Mifflin: on the fifteenth of November, a furious cannonade was opened from the British fort and shipping, and at length, the American works being battered down, and the ditch filled up with ruins, their situation became extremely critical. Perceiving that the English were taking measures for storming the body of the fortress the following morning, and being sensible that it was no longer defensible, the stores were sent off, and setting fire to every thing that was capable of receiving it, they evacuated the place in the night, and withdrew to Red Bank.

It was now absolutely necessary, from the growing scarcity of provisions, as well as of firewood, to dislodge the garrison of Red Bank, and thereby wholly remove the impediments which obstructed the navigation of the Delaware. Cornwallis was accordingly despatched by lord Howe to the Jersey shore, with instructions to attack Fort Mercer in the rear. At Billingsport, where he was preparing to execute these orders, he was reinforced by a body of troops just arrived from New-York. Washington, being very desirous to preserve, if practicable, a position so well calculated to arrest the progress of the enemy, upon receiving intelligence of this movement, ordered Major-General Greene to pass, also, with his detachment into New-Jersey. It was hoped that he might not only be able to protect Fort Mercer, but obtain some advantage over Cornwallis. General Greene passed the Delaware, and landed at Burlington, accompanied by the enthusiastic Lafayette, eager, although his wound was not yet healed, to gather fresh laurels in the field. His division was to be reinforced by troops sent from the banks of the Hudson. The march was commenced; but general Greene abandoned the plan of giving battle to Cornwallis, when he learned the superiority in numbers which he had obtained by the junction of the reinforcement from New-York. Hence the commandant of the garrison, losing all hope of succour, and apprized of the approach of Cornwallis, evacuated Fort Mercer and Red Bank.—General Greene, with Lafayette, however, still continued in New-Jersey, and was joined by several corps sent by General Gates to the assistance of the army in Pennsylvania, among which was that of Morgan's Riflemen, become celebrated by a multitude of brilliant exploits. But Cornwallis had so fortified himself at Gloucester Point, that he was perfectly secure from any enterprise that could be made by general Greene. Washington now recalled General Greene.

fearful that Cornwallis, having accomplished the objects of his expedition, might suddenly re-cross the Delaware, and thus enable Howe, with all his forces, to attack the American army while divided. Greene, therefore, repassed the river, and joined the principal army at Skippach Creek; and similar considerations determined General Howe to direct the detachment of Cornwallis to rejoin him without delay. But the failure of the main object of the expedition, owing to the superior number and rapid movements of the British, did not prevent General Lafayette from evincing the same determined spirit and irresistible bravery, which characterised his conduct in the battle of Brandywine, On the 25th of November, previous to the evacuation of New Jersey, the rifle corps of Morgan, assisted by some detachments of militia under the command of Lafayette, gallantly attacked and routed a superior force of Hessians and British grenadiers. "The Marquis," said General Greene, speaking of this affair, "seemed to search for danger, and was charmed with the behaviour of his men."*

On this expedition, the mutual esteem conceived by Generals Greene and Lafayette, at the battle of Brandywine, and increased by a subsequent participation in toils and dangers, became cemented into a union of friendship and affection, which with the one lasted to his death, and with the other, exists to this day. After the full recognition of the independence of the American states, George Washington Greene, the eldest son of the general, was taken, in 1785, by the Marquis to France, and pursued his education under the care of his father's old and steadfast friend. When the revolution broke out in that country, his mother's apprehensions induced her to recall him; and he returned to Georgia, in 1794; he was all that the fondest parent could desire, but unfortunately was drowned in the Savannah river, a short time after his return.

After the gallant conduct displayed by him in New-Jer-

* Botta's War of Independence, vol. ii. book viii.—Johnson's Life of Greene, 4 to, vol. i p. 93, 94.

sey, the Marquis, who had hitherto served only as a volunteer, was invested by the commander-in-chief, with the command of a division of the army; an appointment which, on the first of December, 1777, was ratified by Congress, in the following words:

"*Resolved*, That General Washington be informed it is highly agreeable to Congress, that the Marquis de Lafayette be appointed to the command of a division in the continental army."

Notwithstanding the impetuous bravery, and almost rashness, which he had displayed, and although possessed of all the fire of youth, he conducted himself, when entrusted with a separate command, with a degree of caution and prudence that would have been creditable to the calm temper and circumspection of age.

General Lafayette was soon called upon by Congress to act in a more responsible station than he had hitherto done, as the commander-in-chief of an army destined to undertake a winter expedition into Canada. The manner in which the whole of this transaction was conducted on the part of the government, portrayed the power of that detestable cabal which had been formed for the destruction or degradation of the illustrious Washington. In the midst of the anxieties which almost overwhelmed him, in the commencement of 1778, he had the additional chagrin of finding that intrigues were in agitation against him. The impatient and the ambitious, attributed to his incapacity, the reverses of the two preceding years, in New-Jersey and Pennsylvania. The victories of Gates were enlarged upon, who was placed far above the commander-in-chief, and the heroic valour of American troops when led by a competent commander, was continually extolled. Private persons circulated these slanders; and discontent caused them to be repeated by men in office, until they found admittance into the midst of the army, into several of the state legislatures, and, finally, even into Congress itself. The main object of these machinations appears to have been to force Washington to retire in disgust from the army. The leaders of this combination, however, little concerned for the public good, but immoderately so for their own, aimed only to advance tnemselves and their friends at the expense of others.—But, supported by that elevated spirit, and by that firmness which no reverses of fortune could abate, the serenity which Washington enjoyed, was not even for a moment interrupted by these secret plotters; and he bore with composure the determination of Congress, matured in concert with the new board of war, and without any reference to his opinion, relative to the irruption into Canada which they had planned. It cannot be decided whether this ungrateful proceeding arose from the desire of Congress to show that they knew how to act by themselves, or whether it was adopted because they had really withdrawn from the commander-in-chief a portion of the confidence which they had placed in him in times past.* On the twenty-second of January, 1778, it was "*Resolved*, That an irruption be made into Canada, and that the board of war be authorized to take every necessary measure for the execution of the business, under such general officers as Congress shall appoint;" and on the following day, Major-General the Marquis de Lafayette, Major-General Conway, and Brigadier Stark, were appointed to conduct it.—Great advantages were anticipated from placing the marquis at the head of this expedition, because his character as a Frenchman of illustrious rank, rendered him more peculiarly qualified for the conquest of a province, recently attached to the French empire. But it was also surmised, that the authors of this scheme had it principally in view, by separating Lafayette from Washington, to deprive the commander-in-chief of the defence of so fond and faithful a friend.

Washington, without being at all consulted, received a letter from the president of the board of war, dated the twenty-fourth of January, enclosing one of the same date

* Botta's War of Independ, vol, ii. book 8.

to Lafayette, requiring his immediate attendance on Congress to receive his instructions. No other communication was made to the commander-in-chief, than to request that he would furnish Colonel Hazen's regiment, chiefly composed of Canadians, for the expedition; and, in the same letter, his opinions were asked respecting it. Without noticing the manner in which the business was conducted, and the unusual want of confidence it betrayed, orders were immediately given to Hazen's regiment, to march toward Albany; and the marquis proceeded to the residence of Congress. At his request, Major-General the Baron de Kalb was added to the expedition, as well as Lieutenant-Colonel Fleury.

The board of war counselled him, that, considering the length of the route into that country in an inclement season, he should be particularly attentive to have his men well clothed, and so supplied with provisions, as effectually to guard against any misfortune which might happen for want of these necessary articles; and that, in case he should fail in obtaining the forces which he might judge competent, or supplies sufficient for them, that he should carefully attend to those contingencies, and regulate his conduct according to the probability of success, without exposing his troops to any very great, or very apparent hazard. With these vague instructions, General Lafayette repaired in person to Albany, in order to take charge of the troops that were to be there assembled, and from whence he was to cross the lakes on the ice, and attack Montreal.—He now published a preparatory memorial addressed to the French Canadians, and calling upon them, by all the ties of allegiance, blood, religion, and country, as well as by the natural desire of recovering their freedom, to be ready to join and assist him;—and holding out all the severities of war to those, if any such there were, who, blindly perverse to their own interests, and forgetful of all those ties and duties, should in any manner, oppose the arms or impede the generous designs of their deliverers.

But the marquis found, in Albany, no preparation made for the expedition;—neither men, nor arms, nor munitions. Nothing that had been promised was in readiness: and he therefore abandoned the enterprise as totally impracticable. Congress soon after also determined on its relinquishment. On the second of March, the committee to whom the matter was referred, brought in the following report: "Whereas, it appears from authentic accounts, that difficulties attend the prosecution of the irruption ordered to be made into Canada, under the conduct of the Marquis de Lafayette, which render the attempt not only hazardous in a high degree, but extremely imprudent,—*Resolved*, That the board of war instruct the Marquis de Lafayette, to suspend, for the present, the intended irruption: and at the same time inform him, that Congress entertain a high sense of his prudence, activity, and zeal; and that they are fully persuaded, nothing has, or would have been wanting on his part, or on the part of the officers who accompanied him, to give the expedition the utmost possible effect." On the thirteenth of March, General Washington was authorized to recall both the Marquis de Lafayette and the Baron de Kalb;—but Conway, that wily and restless intriguer, was never again ordered to join the army.—At this time, the Marquis de Lafayette was only twenty years of age, and must have sensibly felt the attraction of a separate command; but his sound judgment, and singleness of heart prevented him from yielding to his passion for military renown, under circumstances where precipitation would have done so much injury to the cause which he had so zealously espoused. He found that if he advanced into Canada, the army he would be able to command would be in danger of experiencing the fate which had just fallen upon Burgoyne. Thus, by relinquishing the project at Albany, and conveying his free sentiments as to its practicableness to Congress, he not only received their thanks for the wisdom of his conduct, but afforded an example of firm and consummate prudence, which would have done honour to an experienced and veteran commander.

It is stated as a remarkable fact, that General Schuyler in November, 1777, addressed a letter to General Washington, containing a plan of attack on Canada, similar in its leading features to that which Lafayette was ordered to command in January, 1778. The young nobleman showed his instructions to General Schuyler, who discovered in them, his own plan, of which, he supposed, some other wished to claim the honour.*

To cover the country effectually on the north of the Schuylkill, and restrain, as much as possible, the parties detached in various directions from Philadelphia by the British who most generally effected their object, and returned before they could be opposed by the army lying at Valley Forge; to form an advance guard for the security of the main army;—and to be in readiness to annoy, if practicable, the rear of the enemy should they evacuate Philadelphia, an event which was speedily anticipated, the Marquis de Lafayette was detached, by General Washington, with an elite corps of rather more than two thousand men, and a few pieces of cannon, to take post near the lines. As this corps formed a very valuable part of the army, the instructions of the general recommended the utmost attention to its safety, and particularly advised him to avoid any permanent station, since a long continuance in one position would enable the enemy to concert their measures successfully against him. With this detachment, the marquis crossed the Schuylkill and took post at Barren Hill, on the morning of the eighteenth of May, about eight or ten miles in front of the army at Valley Forge. As soon as he arrived, he addressed the following note to Captain M'Lane, who commanded a light corps of observation charged with the arduous but honourable duty of watching the movements of the enemy, between the Delaware and Schuylkill rivers:

* Chastelleux's Trav. vol. i. p. 387.

"*Woods near Barren Hill Church,*
"9 *o'clock, A. M.* 18*th May,* 1778

DEAR SIR,

"I have just now received your letter, and wish you would come down immediately, that I might speak to you of several things. Inquire, if you please, if the people think there will be a market to-morrow? I wish, also, you would see if some man, to be depended on, and of credit with the enemy, would undertake a visit to the city for twelve guineas. Is it known toward the British lines, that a detachment has been ordered from our army?

"Your's

"M. DE LAFAYETTE

The argus-eyed M'Lane immediately waited on the general, and assisted him in taking every possible precaution to prevent surprise. His vigilance in securing his position, shows that the advantage obtained over the marquis, on this occasion, rested on grounds little understood, and wholly acquits him of want of caution. Lafayette, in person, guarded the most direct road to his position; Brigadier-General Potter, of the militia, was entrusted with the second; and patroles kept an eye on the third, which was the most circuitous. A spy, however, who had been formerly in the American army, and who still kept up his intercourse with his former comrades, and often visited Valley Forge, at this period maintained a correspondence with the enemy through the means of a messenger stationed at Frankford creek; and thus general Howe was apprized of the movement of the marquis almost as soon as it was made. Seizing, with avidity this favourable opportunity to overwhelm the youthful general, he resolved to make a vigorous effort to surprise and cut him off. So fully assured was he of success, that he is said to have invited many ladies to meet Lafayette at supper on the following day. In prosecution of the plan which he had formed, he sent General Grant, accompanied by Sir William Erskine, with five thousand select troops, by a forced night march, to turn the marquis' left and gain his rear, while General Gray, moving in concert by the Ridge Road, was to take possession of the heights near the falls of Schuylkill, and prevent his escape by fording the river at that place. About eight o'clock in the evening of the nineteenth of May, General Grant marched out of Philadelphia on the Germantown road, turned off at the Rising Sun tavern on the old York road, thus diverging from Barren Hill, and after passing Plymouth Meeting House, and White Marsh, he arrived at the position he was directed to occupy, about a mile in the rear of the marquis, between him and Valley Forge. He reached this point of destination about sunrise, and now believed that he had got the marquis in a *cul de sac*, and had nothing more to do but spring the net.

Captain M'Lane, who was posted in advance, and ever on the alert, could discover no indication of the enemy's movement on the eighteenth, nor before the night of the nineteenth. The British General, to mask his enterprise, had, by double guards, strictly interdicted all communication with the country; but the silence which this precaution occasioned, caused M'Lane to increase his vigilance. On the morning of the nineteenth, M'Lane was joined by Captain William Parr, of Morgan's rifle corps, an officer of distinguished bravery. With eighty men, and after night fall as was his custom, he advanced towards the enemy's lines, his evening patrole having reported every thing quiet; but, in crossing the country, he fell in with two of the enemy's grenadiers, who pretended to be deserters, from whom he learned that general Grant had marched at twilight with the grenadiers and light infantry on the Old York road, and that a body of Germans were preparing to march up the Schuylkill. These combined movements leaving no doubt on his mind that the marquis was the object of attack, he immediately set out for head quarters by the shortest route, after despatching Captain Parr across the country with the detachment, to get possession of Vandevin's Hill, with orders to oppose the column of the enemy which might advance on the Ridge Road, to the last extremity.

In the mean-time, General Gray, with a strong detachment, advanced along the south side of the Schuylkill, and took post at a ford, two or three miles in front of the right flank of Lafayette. The residue of the British army encamped on Chesnut Hill. Captain M'Lane reached Barren Hill about daybreak, and communicated the impending danger to Lafayette, who could hardly credit the report; but an express from Captain Parr's detachment, which had got possession of the heights of Schuylkill in season to engage general Gray's column and check its advance, and another, at the same moment, from an opposite quarter, giving information of the movements of General Grant soon brought sorrowful confirmation of his perilous situation. The manner in which the last mentioned information was conveyed, affords an instance of patriotic zeal, worthy of being recorded. In passing White Marsh, the noise of the British column awoke a Captain Stone of the militia, residing there, who, on making the discovery, jumped from a back window of his house, and ran naked across the country toward Barren Hill, until he was entirely exhausted: his report was then taken up and carried to the marquis, in the same manner, by Richard Burtleston, who resided near Plymouth Meeting House.

The Marquis now found himself in a state of extreme danger. Finding that he was turned, he justly concluded, like an experienced warrior, that the column marched against him would not be the first to attack, and that it would wait until the other was in readiness. In fact, General Grant, after marching, under cover of the night, nearly twenty miles in nine hours, was attending the movements of the column on the Ridge Road. At his position the roads forked; one branch led to the camp of Lafayette, less than a mile distant; the other went to Matson's Ford over the Schuylkill, at about the same distance. The retreat of Lafayette was thus cut off from every passage but Matson's Ford; and as the line from his position formed the base of an obtuse-angled triangle, it is obvious that his distance from it was much greater than that of the British.

General Lafayette now changed his front, and took a good position opposite the column of General Grant, having before him Barren Hill Church, and behind him the opening which served as a retreat. About this time his perilous situation was perceived by glasses from the camp at Valley Forge, and the whole army was put under arms to act as circumstances might require; and six alarm guns fired by General Washington, intended to give his detachment notice of the danger, served also to keep the enemy in awe, who imagined the whole American army was in march.—Nothing now remained but to retreat; and Lafayette, with a veteran composure, and with a promptness of decision so essential in moments of critical danger, took the only course which could have preserved his troops. He therefore advanced the head of a column toward Grant, as if to attack him, while the rear filed off rapidly toward the Schuylkill: this movement gained ground even for the front, which, while it advanced towards the enemy, also approached the river, and at the same time induced General Grant to lose time in order to prepare for battle. While this manœuvre was performing in the face of the detachment under Grant, a small party was thrown into the churchyard, which was surrounded by a wall, on the road toward General Gray, which also gave the appearance of an intention to attack in that quarter. By these dispositions, happily conceived, and executed with regularity, the marquis extricated himself and his party from the destruction which had appeared almost inevitable. The only road he could take made him approach the column of General Grant, and exposed him to be attacked by it in front, while Gray and the main body fell on his rear. In this situation, his own greatness of mind suggested to the young soldier the proper course to be pursued. Knowing that more honour was lost than time gained, in converting a retreat into a flight, he continued his march in a tranquil and regular order, and passed over at Matson's Ford without being intercepted by Grant, or sustaining a greater loss than nine men.—Considerable time was lost by General Grant, in making a disposition for the expected attack, during which delay, a corps of cavalry, that had formed the advanced guard on the march, took possession of a hill between the two roads leading from his position to Lafayette's encampment and to Matson's Ford. From this elevation the troops of Lafayette were first discovered on their retreat through the low, woody grounds which bordered the river. Information of this circumstance was immediately conveyed to General Grant, and his superior proximity to Matson's Ford is said to have been urged to him, and even pointed out, in the strongest manner; but, under a persuasion that these were only a part of Lafayette's troops, detached for some unaccountable reason, the general persisted in his resolution of advancing to Barren Hill, notwithstanding the strong remonstrances of Sir William Erskine against that measure. That post was fortunately concealed from view by intervening trees; otherwise the desertion of it by the Americans would have been perceived.

The British having advanced to Barren Hill church, and found the ground lately occupied by Lafayette abandoned, followed in his rear, and appeared at the ford just after the Americans had crossed it, as if by enchantment, with all their artillery. Finding Lafayette advantageously posted on the high and broken grounds which arose from the water's edge on the opposite side of the river, the British generals perceived that nothing further could be attempted against him, and returned to Philadelphia without having effected any thing. "The ladies," says Chastelleux, "did not see M. De Lafayette, and the generals themselves, arrived too late for supper."

General Grant did not escape censure, for having allowed the great advantage he had acquired, in gaining the rear of the American encampment unperceived, to slip through his hands unused. He might, with the utmost certainty, have reached Matson's Ford before the marquis, and thus have cut off the only retreat which remained for him. Lafayette would then have been compelled to seek for safety by flying toward the Delaware, and the army of Washington would have been consequently dismembered. Had General Grant pushed forward his troops without a halt;—had he, instead of keeping the road to Barren Hill, occupied the strong grounds at Matson's Ford, or those near to Spring Mills;—the American corps must either have fallen into his hands or been dispersed, and the remainder of the army placed in a situation of extreme danger. Had treason been triumphant,—had the rapidity of the enemy been more, or the military vigilance of Lafayette less,—a calamity would have fallen on the American army, which, while it deprived it of one of its brightest ornaments, would have defeated the operations of the approaching campaign, and either left the British general in undisturbed possession of the principal city of the union, or suffered the invading army to retreat without opposition through New-Jersey.

The conduct of Lafayette in this affair, was not only free from merited censure, but worthy of universal admiration; yet it was remarked, that the same degree of military talent was not discovered in guarding against the approach of danger, as in afterwards extricating himself from it. But the imputation which generally attaches to an officer, who permits an enemy to pass in full force unobserved, within a short distance of his flank, into his rear, is entirely removed by the fact, stated by Lafayette in his vindication, that the Pennsylvania militia were posted on his left flank, and relied on to guard the roads about White Marsh; but that, without his knowledge, they changed their position, and retired into the rear, leaving that important pass open to the enemy; who, moreover, had positive intelligence that these militia did not occupy the post assigned to them. The position he had taken at Barren Hill was almost impracticable in front and flank, and, warned by the monotorial voice of Washington, he had taken every possible precaution to secure it. A corps of observation was posted six or eight miles in advance, to watch the movements of the enemy, who practised every means to elude the vigilance of Captain M'Lane, but without success. The manner in which the young Frenchman outmanœuvred the experienced generals of Britain, and extricated himself from almost inevitable destruction in the face of seven thousand British regulars, produced a lively sensation of admiration throughout the army; and his conduct was for ever and triumphantly vindicated by the words of Washington, who applauded his "*well timed and masterly retreat.*"

During the advance of the British on this occasion, a laughable incident occurred, which, after the lapse of more than forty-six years, has been revived among the reminiscences which attended the affecting meeting of Lafayette with the venerable Colonel Willet of New-York. In the spring of 1778, the marquis sent to the latter officer, then stationed on the frontiers, for fifty young Indian warriors. These savages accompanied him to Barren Hill, and were placed in ambuscade, after their fashion, in the woods. Fifty English dragoons, who had never seen any Indians, marching at the head of a column, entered the wood where the savages were concealed, who on their part had never seen dragoons. Starting suddenly up, they raised a horrible yell, threw down their arms, and escaped by swimming across the Schuylkill The dragoons, on the other hand, equally astounded and terrified, turned about their horses, and did not recover their panic till they had got back to Philadelphia.*

* For accounts of the retreat from Barren Hill, *vide* Marshall's Wash. vol. iii. chap. viii. Stedman's Amer. War, vol. i. p. 420. Botta's War

The following notice of the affair at Barren Hill, published by the British after their return to Philadelphia, shows the manner in which they misrepresented many of the occurrences of the time; "Intelligence having been received, last Tuesday, that Mr. Washington and his tattered retinue had abandoned their mud-holes, and were on their way to Germantown, a detachment of British and Hessian troops went out to meet, and escort them into this city; but the rebels being apprised of their approach, fled back with precipitation to what they term their camp, determined to act no further on the offensive than might be consistent with their personal safety."

In the beginning of the year 1778, a general joy was diffused throughout the American community. The second of May was the day destined to carry their exultation to its utmost height, and to put the seal to the dismemberment of the vast and powerful British empire. On that day arrived, at Casco Bay, the French frigate La Sensible, which bore to Congress the treaties concluded with France. The Marquis De Lafayette, whose letters to France had no small share in producing this happy event, was among the first in the American army who received the welcome tidings of the treaty. In a transport of joy, mingled with tears, he embraced General Washington, exclaiming, "The king, my master, has acknowledged your independence, and entered into an alliance with you, for its establishment." The joy which spread from breast to breast, exceeded description. The name of Louis XVI. was in every body's mouth; every where he was proclaimed the protector of liberty, the defender of America, the saviour of the country. The several brigades at Valley Forge assembled by order of the commander-in-chief. Their chaplains offered up thanks to Almighty God, and delivered discourses suitable to the occasion. A feu-de-joie was fired, and, on a proper signal being

of Independ. vol. ii. book 8. Wilkinson's Memoirs, vol. i. pp. 829–833. Chastelleux's Trav. vol. i. p. 298.

given, the air resounded with "long live the king of France," poured forth from the breast of every private in the army.*

About the first of June, the three pacificatory commissioners from Great Britain, Carlisle, Eden, and Johnstone, arrived, with powers to give effect to the conciliatory acts of parliament, which had been proposed by lord North. The terms offered were such as America would, at one time, have most joyfully accepted; but that time was now passed. The union of the force of the two nations under one common sovereign, was a measure to which the government was no longer disposed, nor even at liberty to accede. A distressing war had eradicated all those affections which parts of the same empire should feel toward each other; the great body of the nation was determined, at every sacrifice, to maintain its independence; and the treaty with France had pledged them, by every principle of honour and national faith, never to consent to a re-union with the British empire. On reading the letter of the commissioners to Congress, some observations were found to be mingled with them, reflecting on the conduct of France. No sooner were they heard, than a violent clamour rose, many members exclaiming that the reading ought to be interrupted on account of the offensive language against his most Christian majesty. The words which produced this confusion were the following; "We cannot but remark the insidious interposition of a power, which has, from the first settlement of the colonies, been actuated with enmity to us both; and notwithstanding the pretended date, or present form, of the French offers to North America, it is notorious that they have only been made, because it was believed that Great Britain had conceived the design of an amicable arrangement, and with a view to prevent reconciliation, and prolong this destructive war." After animated debates, the further consideration of the subject was adjourned to the next sitting; but the question was agitated with equal vehemence, on the follow-

* Ramsay's Revolution, p. 381.

ing day. But, at length, Congress, having demonstrated by the warmth of this discussion the respect they bore to their august ally, and reflecting that a refusal to notice them might occasion discontents prejudicial to the state, determined to read the despatches of the commissioners.—But the high-minded and ingenuous Lafayette could not silently brook the aspersions which were cast upon his royal master. Indignant at the duplicity of the commissioners, who endeavoured so artfully to weaken the newly-formed connexion between France and America, he wrote a letter to the Earl of Carlisle, as the principal member of the commission complaining of the reflections cast upon his country, demanding reparation, and challenging that nobleman to meet him in the field. The noble lord, however, refused to grant, in a national concern, that satisfaction which he conceived ought to be exclusively confined to personal differences. This affair, however, served to display the spirit and zeal of the young marquis for the honour of his country; and it was no small addition to the mortification of the commissioners, to find themselves the objects of animadversion, in a private, as well as public capacity.* This conduct, which, on a common occasion, might have been considered as resulting from mere bravado on the part of a young officer, was in the present instance neither useless nor liable to that imputation. The Americans were not yet acquainted with the character of the French. They had been accustomed, from the prejudices of education, to consider them as less brave than the English, and it was useful to convince them that a Frenchman of high rank was not afraid to measure his strength with that of an Englishman. Besides, it in some measure, diminished the consequence of the commissioners, in the opinion of the people, and gave them a high idea of the courage and attachment of their new

* Marshall's Washington, vol. iii. p. 534.—Botta's War of Independence, vol. ii. p. 501, 2.—Andrew's American War, vol iii. p. 161.—Hist of France, vol. iii. p. 173.—Not. Biogr. sur le Gen. Fayette. p. 5.

allies. This action, in fact, greatly increased his popularity; and the most judicious men attributed it wholly to the ardour of a young hero, inflamed with the desire of gaining distinction by avenging the cause of his injured country. It cannot be denied that the Earl of Carlisle acted, as a commissioner, with propriety in refusing the challenge; but at the same time the Marquis De Lafayette obtained beneficial results by sending it.

These commissioners having brought positive and secret orders for the immediate evacuation of Philadelphia, Sir Henry Clinton, who had succeeded Lord Howe in the command of the British army, prepared to execute the orders of his government. On the eighteenth of June, 1778, the whole army passed the Delaware, and encamped at Gloucester Point on the Jersey shore. Clinton pursued his retreat slowly, passing through Haddonfield, Mount Holly, Slabtown, and Crosswick, to Allentown and Imlaytown, which places he reached on the twenty-fourth. He betrayed no symptoms of precipitation, but rather indicated a disposition for battle

Before Clinton left Philadelphia, General Washington had penetrated his design; and General Maxwell, with the Jersey brigade, was ordered over the Delaware to take post about Mount Holly, and to join Major General Dickenson, who was beginning to assemble the militia of that state, for the purpose of co-operating with the continental troops, in breaking up the bridges, falling trees in the roads, and otherwise embarrassing the march of the enemy. When authentic intelligence was received that the enemy had crossed the Delaware, a council of war was summoned to deliberate on the proper measures to be pursued. General Washington submitted to their deliberations whether it was proper, by harrassing the enemy's rear, to annoy him as much as possible, without, however, coming to a general engagement; or whether it was more advisable to attack him in front, and try the fortune of a decisive battle. A great diversity of opinion prevailed General Lee, who had lately been exchanged for Prescott, and whose military experience gave great weight to his opinions, was vehement against risking either a general or partial engagement. He maintained that, with the equality of force that existed, it would be "criminal" to hazard an action;—that it would be impossible to bring on a partial engagement, without the risk of its being made general, if such should be the choice of the enemy;—and that a general action ought not to be fought, unless the advantage was manifestly on the American side. He was also of opinion, that the superiority of the enemy in point of discipline was such, that the issue of an engagement would almost certainly be unfavourable; and that they ought to be content with following the enemy, observing his motions, and preventing him from ravaging the country. General Du Portail, the Baron De Steuben, and most of the foreign officers, maintained the same opinions, and thought that an action ought carefully to be avoided. The American officers appear to have been influenced by the counsels of the Europeans; for, of seventeen generals, only Wayne and Cadwallader were decidedly in favour of attacking the enemy. General Lafayette, however, without openly embracing it, appeared inclined to that opinion; and General Greene was also disposed to hazard more than the opinions of the majority would sanction. They were, in fact, the only two members of the board who expressed the opinions which appear afterward to have influenced the conduct of the commander-in-chief. They maintained that the country ought to be protected at all risks, and if it should prove necessary to that object, that duty enjoined them to hazard a battle; and that, if a favourable opportunity was afforded of attacking the enemy with effect, it ought not to be avoided;—in other words, that it was impossible to anticipate a decision. They could not bring their minds to endure the idea, that the enemy should retire with impunity during so long a march, and they believed that they had every thing to expect from soldiers, whose constancy had remained unsubdued by the rigour of the seasons, and the scarcity of every thing most necessary to life. They reflected, moreover, that the English army was embarrassed with the most cumbersome baggage, and they did not doubt that in the numerous defiles it would be compelled to thread, some favourable occasion would offer to attack with advantage. Nevertheless, the voice of the majority prevailed, not without evident dissatisfaction on the part of Washington, who remained steadfast in the opinion which he had formed.

On the same day that the British abandoned Philadelphia, the American commander moved from Valley Forge, and crossing the river at Coryell's ferry, on the twenty-second, took post at Hopewell. Sir Henry Clinton was now encamped at and round Allentown; and the main body of the American army was about five miles from Princeton. Notwithstanding the almost concurrent opinion of the general officers against risking an action, the Fabius of America, who, with a mind of uncommon firmness, combined an enterprising as well as cautious temper, indulged an anxious desire to adopt that measure. He therefore again assembled his general officers, and once more submitted to them the situation of the two armies. The same opinion respecting a general battle, that had been given the day before the movement from Valley Forge, was repeated; and the proposition was peremptorily and decidedly negatived. General Washington, however, still retained his inclination to engage the enemy, and finding himself supported by the private wishes of some officers whom he highly valued, he determined to take his measures on his own responsibility, and without calling another council. As soon as he discovered that the enemy were on their march toward Monmouth Court House, (not more than twelve miles from the heights of Middletown,) he determined that they should not escape without a blow. Major-General Dickenson with the Jersey militia, consisting of about one thousand men, and a brigade of continental troops commanded by Maxwell, now hung on their left flank toward the rear of the enemy;

General Cadwallader, with Jackson's regiment, and a very few militia, was entirely in their rear; and Colonel Morgan, with his regiment of six hundred men, was on their right. In pursuance of the opinion of the last military council, a detachment of fifteen hundred men, under Brigadier-General Scott, had also been marched to the lines. General Washington, having formed his decision, despatched General Wayne with a further detachment of one thousand select men to reinforce General Cadwallader. As the continental troops now in front of the main army amounted, at least, to four thousand men, and as the simultaneous action of the several detachments was of extreme importance, he deemed it proper to employ a major-general to collect and command them. This tour of duty Major-General Lee had a right to claim: but as he was openly and strongly against hazarding even a partial engagement, and expected that nothing further would be attempted than merely to reconnoitre the enemy, and restrain plundering parties, he showed no disposition to assert his claim, and very readily assenting to the private wishes of General Washington, that the command should be given to an officer whose views of the service comported more with his own, he yielded this important tour of duty to the Marquis De Lafayette. He was ordered to proceed immediately with the detachment, and to form a junction as expeditiously as possible with that under General Scott; to use the most effectual means for gaining the enemy's left flank and rear, and giving them every degree of annoyance. All the continental parties on the line were placed under his command, and he was directed to take such measures as would most impede the march of the enemy, and occasion them the greatest loss; for these purposes, he was to attack them as occasion might require by detachment, and, if a proper opening should be given, to act against them with his whole force. A letter was at the same time addressed to General Dickenson, placing the militia under the orders of Lafayette.

The marquis was young, generous, and brave; but notwithstanding his high qualifications, it was certainly an important trust to be confided to the captivating foreigner. Nothing is more dangerous than to hang with an inferior force upon a gallant enemy, never disinclined to draw his sword, and watchful to seize every advantage within his reach. But the discrimination of Washington was well justified by his conduct, not only on this occasion, but throughout the whole course of the war. The dispositions that he had made, and the orders which he had given, manifest very conclusively the intention and wish of the commander-in-chief. They could hardly fail to bring on an engagement. Wayne had openly espoused that measure, and Fayette, although he partially joined, in council, in the opinion against seeking a general action, had been in favour of a partial one; and would, therefore, if any proper occasion offered, certainly attack with his whole force, which would as certainly produce such measures on the part of the enemy, as would render it proper to support him with the whole army. He was accompanied too by Colonel Hamilton, who felt the strongest desire to signalize the detachment, and to accomplish all the wishes of the commander-in-chief. Immediately after sending this additional body of troops, the whole army moved to Cranberry, in order to be sufficiently near to support them. The advanced corps under Lafayette pressed forward, and took a position on the Monmouth road, about five miles in the rear of the enemy, with the intention of attacking them the next morning on their march; but it was found too remote, and too far on the right, to be supported in case of action, and orders were consequently sent to the marquis, to file off by his left toward Englishtown. These orders were executed early in the morning of the twenty-seventh of June.

No sooner had Lafayette marched toward the lines, than General Lee began to regret his resignation of the command of the advanced party. He perceived that, in the opinion of all the general officers, a greater importance was attached to this command than he had allowed it; and that his reputation was in danger of being somewhat impaired, by connecting his strenuous opposition to even a partial action, with his afterward declining the command of a very strong detachment, which, it was expected, would fall in with, and engage the rear of the enemy. He now therefore, solicited very earnestly for the command which he had before declined. To relieve the feelings of Lee, without wounding those of Lafayette, General Washington detached him with two other brigades to Englishtown, to support the Marquis. As senior officer, he would of course have the direction of the whole front division, which would now amount to five thousand men; but it was expressly stipulated, that if any enterprise had been already formed by Lafayette, it should be proceeded with, in like manner as if the commanding officer had not been changed. To this condition Lee acceded, and with two additional brigades, joined the front division of the army, now encamped at Englishtown. The whole van guard was placed under his command, leaving to Lafayette only that of the militia and light horse. The main army moved forward about three miles in his rear; Morgan's corps still hovered on the right flank of the British; and General Dickenson on their left.*

Sir Henry Clinton had taken a very strong position on the heights of Freehold, having his right flank in the skirt of a small wood, while his left was secured by a very thick one, and a morass running towards his rear: his whole front was also covered by a wood, and, for a considerable distance towards his left, by a morass. Descending from these heights towards Monmouth, there was a deep valley, three miles in length and one in breadth, broken with hills, woods, and morasses. General Washington finding this position unassailable, and knowing that it would be impossible to attempt any thing with a prospect of success if the

* Marshall's Washington, vol. iii. ch. 8.

enemy should reach the high grounds of Middletown, determined to attack their rear the moment they should move from the ground. This determination was immediately communicated to General Lee, and corresponding orders were also given to the rear division of the army.

In the mean-time, Clinton, seeing the enemy so near, and a battle inevitable, withdrew all his baggage from the rear, and passed it into the charge of the van, commanded by general Knyphausen, so that, while he endeavoured with the rear guard to keep the Americans in check, it might be conducted to a place of safety upon the hills of Middletown: he therefore retained in his encampment at Freehold several battalions of English infantry, both heavy and light, the Hessian grenadiers, and a regiment of cavalry; while Knyphausen, at daybreak on the morning of the twenty-eighth of June, descended into the valley with his convoy on his way toward Middletown. About eight o'clock Clinton also descended from the heights of Freehold, and took up his line of march in the rear of the front division. Washington, being promptly informed of all his motions, and apprehensive that the English would succeed in posting themselves in the mountains of Middletown, the distance being only a few miles, in which case it would have been impracticable to interrupt their retreat to New-York, despatched orders to General Lee to move on and attack the rear, "unless there should be powerful reasons to the contrary;" while Morgan and Dickenson were directed to descend into the valley upon the enemy's flanks in order to attempt the column of Knyphausen, encumbered with its long train of carriages and pack horses. Lee, having made the necessary dispositions to effect these orders, appeared on the heights of Freehold soon after the enemy had left them, and following the British into the plain, gave directions to general Wayne, to attack their covering party in the rear so as to halt them. In the meantime, he proposed to gain their front by a shorter road on their left, and entirely intercepting their communication with the line, to bear them off before they could be assisted. Before this plan was executed, Sir Henry Clinton had dispersed the militia under Dickenson, which infested his left flank, and perceiving that the Americans were descending with impetuosity to attack him, while Knyphausen, with the baggage, was exposed to the greatest peril in the defiles which continued several miles, instantly took the only resolution that could extricate him from the embarrassments of his position.

He determined to turn upon the Americans who menaced his rear, and to charge them with the utmost vigour, hoping to throw them into disorder by an unexpected attack, and thus compel them to recall to their succour the corps they had detached to intercept the baggage. Thus the English rear guard, commanded by Cornwallis and Clinton in person, and the American van guard, conducted by General Lee and the Marquis de Lafayette, advanced against each other, with a firm resolution to engage. The artillery began to play, and the queen's dragoons charged and routed the light horse of Lafayette. General Lee soon perceived himself to have been mistaken in the force which formed the rear of the British, and was also compelled to form his troops upon unfavourable ground, having behind him a ravine, which rendered his retreat extremely difficult in case of check, and which necessarily would impede the arrival of reinforcements to his aid. This was about ten o'clock; and while both armies were executing their preparatory manœuvres for action, general Scott, mistaking an oblique march of an American column for a retreat, and apprehensive of being abandoned, left his position and repassed the ravine in his rear. Lee, knowing the unfavourable position of his troops, directed the whole detachment to regain the heights they had passed. This country abounds with defiles of a peculiar sort: the valleys are cut by small rivulets with marshy grounds, difficult to man and horse, and impossible to artillery, except in particular spots. Persevering in his decision to join rather than recall Scott he continued to retire. During this retrograde movement some slight skirmishing ensued, in which very little damage was done on either side.

When the first firing announced the commencement of the action, the rear of the army threw off their packs, and advanced rapidly to the support of the front. Meantime the enemy had pursued Lee across the ravine, and pressed him hard before he had time to rally. In this critical moment, Washington arrived. As he approached the scene of action, he rode forward in total ignorance of Lee's retreat; and about noon, to his great astonishment and mortification, met the advanced corps retiring before the enemy, without having made a single effort to maintain their ground. Those whom he first fell in with, neither understood the motives which had governed General Lee, nor his present design; and could give no other information than that by his orders they had fled without fighting.—General Washington rode to the rear of the division, which he found closely pressed. He then met General Lee, to whom he spoke in terms of some warmth, implying disapprobation of his conduct. General Lee, instead of entering into that full explanation which his own honour, duty to his superior, and the good of his country, demanded, took offence at the manner in which he had been accosted, and replied unbecomingly. Such conduct, in an inferior officer, could not be brooked, and met, as it merited, marked disapprobation. In fact, the deviation of Lee from his instructions might have produced the most fatal effects.

It was now necessary, without delay, to arrest for a few moments the impetuosity of the English, in order to give time for all the corps of the rear guard to come up. The commander-in-chief, accordingly, ordered the regiments commanded by Colonel Stewart and Lieutenant-Colonel Ramsay, to occupy an important post on the left, behind a tuft of wood, and there to sustain the first efforts of the enemy. General Lee was directed to take proper measures, with the residue of his force, to stop the British column on that ground, and the commander-in-chief rode back himself to arrange the rear division of the army. Stung by the reproaches of his general, and stimulated by the point of honour, General Lee made extreme exertions to rally his troops, and disposed them on advantageous ground, where they defended themselves valiantly. But at length, overpowered by numbers, he, as well as Stewart and Ramsay, were compelled to fall back. Lee, however, brought off his troops in good order, and was directed to form in the rear, while the army moved on to battle. The check given by him to the enemy, afforded time to dispose the left wing and second line, to which Lafayette was now attached, of the American army, partly in a neighbouring wood, and partly upon a hill situated on the left, from which some pieces of cannon, which Lord Stirling had planted there, severely annoyed the enemy, and, with the aid of several parties of infantry, effectually put a stop to their advance. General Greene, who commanded the right wing, now took a very advantageous position on the right, and posted his artillery upon a lofty eminence, whence it cruelly infested the left wing of the enemy.

Finding themselves thus arrested, and so warmly opposed in front, the British attempted to turn the left flank of the Americans, but they were repulsed by the light infantry detached for that purpose. They then directed their efforts against Washington's right, which they endeavoured to surround; but overwhelmed by the artillery of Greene, they were soon compelled to retreat. At this moment, General Wayne was advanced with a body of infantry to engage them in front, who kept up so hot and well-directed a fire of musketry, that they drove the enemy behind the ravine, on the ground where the first halt had been made, and where the action had commenced immediately after the arrival of General Washington.—Victory was no longer doubtful; but the new position of the English was still formidable. Their flanks were covered by thick woods and deep morasses, while their front could only be reached through a narrow pass. Notwithstanding the fatigue of the action they suffered less, in killed and wounded, than their adversaries. In his official letter, Sir Henry Clinton stated his dead and missing at four officers and one hundred and eighty-four privates; and his wounded at sixteen officers, and one hundred and fifty-four privates. But the "stubborn fact" of burying the dead, manifests a great error in the official report of Sir Henry Clinton. Four officers, and two hundred and forty-five privates were buried on the field by persons appointed for that purpose; and some few were afterward found and buried, so as to increase the number to nearly three hundred. The loss of the Americans was eight officers, and sixty-one privates, killed, and about one hundred and sixty wounded.—Without doubt, Clinton, who claimed the victory, obtained his object,—security from further molestation, and the completion of his retreat. This, however, was not effected in the usual style of conquerors, but by decamping in the night, and seeking safety, near the place of embarkation, in a position secure from assault. Congress was highly gratified with the success which attended their arms at the battle of Monmouth. On the seventh of July, a resolution was unanimously passed, presenting their thanks to General Washington, and to the officers and men under his command, who distinguished themselves by their conduct and valour in the battle.—In this severe action, which terminated in a manner calculated to make a general impression favourable to the reputation of the American arms, General Lafayette displayed the utmost coolness and skill, and participated largely in the toils and dangers of the day. The venerable Colonel Willet, of New-York, in a letter written immediately after the action, in which he was personally engaged, makes the following remarks relative to the youthful hero: "I have been charmed with the blooming gallantry, and sagacity, of the Marquis De Lafayette, who appears to be possessed of every requisite to constitute a great General:" Colonel Willet was a volunteer aid to General Scott, of

Virginia, who commanded the light infantry, and in the commencement of the action, under the immediate orders of General Lafayette: hence, he enjoyed a favourable opportunity of observing and appreciating his conduct.*

The following extract from the "Historical Anecdotes of the Reign of Louis XVI," affords an epitome of the humanity and gallantry of the Marquis. During the Americau War, a General officer in the service of the United States, advanced, with a score of men, under the English batteries, to reconnoitre their position. His aid-de-camp, struck by a ball, fell at his side. The officers and orderly dragoons fled precipitately. The General, though under the fire of the cannon, approached the wounded man to see whether he had any signs of life remaining, or whether any assistance could be afforded him. Finding the wound had been mortal, he turned his eyes away with emotion, and slowly rejoined the group, which had got out of the reach of the pieces. This instance of courage and humanity took place at the battle of Monmouth. General Clinton, who commanded the English troops, knew that the Marquis De Lafayette generally rode a white horse; and it was upon a white horse that the general officer, who retired so slowly, was mounted. Clinton commanded the gunners not to fire. This noble forbearance probably saved General Lafayette's life, for it was he himself. At that time he was but twenty-two years of age.

Not long after the battle of Monmouth, General Lafayette was again selected for active service, and on the twenty-first of July, was detached with two brigades, to

* For accounts of the battle of Monmouth, &c. *vide* Marshall's Washington, vol. iii, chap. 8.—Andrews' Amer. War, vol. iii, p. 112.—H. Lee's Memoirs, vol. i, p. 58.—Johnson's Life of Greene, vol. i, p. 103.—Botta's War Independ. vol. ii, book x.—Ramsay's Revolution, p. 379—381.—Stedman's American War, vol. ii, ch. 22.—Mem. Histor. sur Lafayette, p. 6.

join General Sullivan, who had been appointed, in the preceding winter to the command of the troops in Rhode Island. Count D'Estaing having relinquished the meditated attack on the British fleet in the harbour of New-York, in consequence of the impracticability of passing the bar a Sandy Hook, an enterprise against the enemy at Rhode Island was concerted, by the combined forces of America and France. On the twenty-fifth of July, the French fleet arrived at Newport; and in the mean-time, directions were given to General Sullivan, to call on the New-England states to furnish, immediately, their quotas of militia; and to prepare magazines; to collect the boats necessary for a descent; to engage the best pilots; and to make himself perfectly master of the situation and strength of the enemy. General Greene was ordered, without delay, to Rhode Island, of which state he was a native, and where he possessed great influence, for the purpose of commanding under Sullivan.

General Pigot, who commanded in Rhode Island, had received considerable reinforcements from New-York, and the garrison now amounted to about six thousand effectives. The main body lay in Newport, which was strongly defended, and some small detachments occupied other works thrown up at the north end of the island, to prevent a descent from the adjacent continent. The American army lay on the main, about the town of Providence.

Soon after the arrival of D'Estaing, General Sullivan went on board the fleet, to concert a plan of operations for the allied forces. It was determined that their arms should be directed, as soon as possible, against Newport. According to the plan of attack, the fleet was to enter the harbour, and land the French troops on the west side of the island, while the Americans, at the same time, landed on the opposite coast, under cover of the guns of a frigate.

Thus they would be within the works which had been erected on the north end of the island for the purpose of preventing a descent from the continent. To be in readiness for the execution of this plan, General Greene marched with a detachment of continental and state troops, and some militia, to Tiverton, which lies on the east side of the East Channel: but considerable delay was occasioned by the slow arrival of the reinforcements of militia, which were deemed essential to the security of the enterprise; but as the militia of Massachusetts and New-Hampshire, who were principally volunteers, approached, Sullivan joined General Greene at Tiverton, and it was agreed that the fleet should enter the main channel immediately, and that the descent should be made the succeeding day.

Accordingly, on the eighth of August, all the preparations being completed, and the wind favourable, the French squadron entered the harbour of Newport, and coasting the town, discharged their broadsides into it, and received the fire of the batteries on shore: but little execution was done on either side.—The militia not arriving precisely at the time they were expected, Sullivan communicated to the French admiral the necessity of postponing the attack yet another day; but, finding next morning, that the British troops on the north end of the island had been recalled during the night, and fearful that they would return to them, he determined to take immediate possession of the works which had been abandoned. In conformity with this resolution, the whole army crossed the Sea-connet passage, at Howland's Ferry, on the ninth of August, and landed on the north end of Rhode Island.

On receiving information of this movement, D'Estaing highly resented the indelicacy supposed to have been committed by Sullivan, in landing before the French, and without consulting him. In addition to this cause of discontent, some previous difficulties, on subjects of mere punctilio, had been created. The Count D'Estaing was a land, as well as sea officer, and held the rank of Lieutenant-General in the French service. Sullivan, being only a Major-General, he had endeavoured to avoid a misunderstanding on this delicate point, by agreeing, in the first conference, that the Americans should land first, and afterward the French, to be commanded by D'Estaing in person. Either his own reflections, or the suggestions of others, afterward made the Count dissatisfied with this arrangement, and he insisted that the descent should be made on both sides of the island precisely at the same moment, and that one wing of the American army should be attached to the French, and land with them. He also declined the command in person, but requested that Lafayette should take charge of the French troops, as well as of the Americans attached to them.—The conduct of D'Estaing, on this occasion, was captious and assuming. As the command of the combined forces had been tendered to him, he ought to have accepted it, or not insisted on dictating with respect to that of the right wing. Although the high standing, unbounded popularity, and real merit of the Marquis de Lafayette, made every one willing to concede what he could with honour, yet D'Estaing's punctilious pretensions ought to have made him respect the rights and feelings of others. All conceded the propriety of delegating the command of the French troops to Lafayette; but when D'Estaing insisted that an entire division of the American army should act with them, and the command of the whole be given to the Marquis, he certainly carried his pretensions too far for one who had declined the chief command. At length, the French admiral was, with difficulty, prevailed on to consent that his demand should be reduced from one wing of the American army, to one thousand militia.—When, afterward, General Sullivan crossed over to the island before the time to which he had himself postponed the descent, and without giving previous notice to the Count of this movement, some suspicions were excited that the measure was taken with other views than those which were assigned. The French admiral was so much offended that he refused to answer Sullivan's letter the day which ought to have been appropriated to action, was passed in discussion; and this delicate and magnified point probably proved, in the end, the destruction of the whole expedition.

After reaching the island, General Sullivan hoped that the attack would be no longer delayed, when, on the same day, the squadron of Lord Howe appeared, which after communicating with General Pigot, came to an anchor off Point Judith. After a careful examination of the position of the French ships, the British admiral concluded, from various concurring causes, that he could entertain no hope of succouring the town. From the same causes, if the French admiral had been disposed to persist in the concerted plan of attack, and had not abandoned his station until he had afforded to General Sullivan all the co-operation in his power, there is good reason to believe that the town of Newport would have fallen into the hands of the allies. But the count D'Estaing, full of ardour and impatience, took advantage of a favourable change of wind to sail out of the harbour, in order to attack the enemy. Previously to his leaving port, he informed General Sullivan that, on his return, he would land his men as that officer should advise. Having stood out to sea, with the advantage of the weather-gage, which Lord Howe did not think it prudent to concede, the whole day was spent in manœuvreing. On the succeeding day, when on the point of engaging, the two fleets were separated and dispersed by a violent tempest, which lasted forty-eight hours, and rendered them both unfit for action The British squadron returned to New-York, for the purpose of refitting; and the French regained the harbour of Newport.

In the mean-time the militia had joined the army of Sullivan, which now amounted to ten thousand men. But General Lafayette objected to the commencement of any operations before the return of D'Estaing. He argued, that if measures were taken against the enemy without his co-operation, he would once more feel himself aggrieved; and therefore advised that the army should be advanced to a position in the neighbourhood of Newport, but not break ground until the Count should be in readiness to act in concert with them. Although it was extremely desirable to avoid whatever might give offence to the ally on whose assistance so much depended, yet time was considered of so much importance to an army which could not be long kept together, that this advice was over-ruled, and it was determined to open the trenches, and commence the siege immediately.

After surmounting the obstacles created by bad weather, and delay in the arrival of his stores and artillery, General Sullivan moved towards the lines, and encamped within two or three miles of the town of Newport. The succeeding morning, being the fifteenth of August, the siege was commenced, and continued, without any material circumstance, for several days. But the abandonment of D'Estaing had placed the American army in a very critical situation, because reinforcements might now be thrown, without interruption, into Newport, and not only defeat the enterprise, but render their retreat dangerous. On the evening of the nineteenth, their anxieties were momentarily relieved by the reappearance of the fleet.

The French admiral, however, immediately crushed the flattering hopes of the army, by communicating to General

Sullivan his intention, in pursuance of orders from the king, and with the advice of all his officers, of taking the fleet to Boston to refit. Success without the aid of the fleet, could not be hoped for; and the Americans had counted, with almost absolute certainty, on a brilliant termination of the enterprise. General Sullivan, reduced almost to despair by this determination, added entreaties to remonstrances, in order to dissuade D'Estaing from so fatal a measure. The Marquis de Lafayette and General Greene were directed to wait on him, with a letter from General Sullivan, remonstrating against the resolution he had formed, and to exert their utmost endeavours to induce him to change it. They, accordingly, besought him not to abandon the interests of the common cause; they represented to him the importance to France, as well as to America, of the enterprise commenced; they urged the certainty of carrying the garrison, if he would only co-operate with them for *two days;* that it could not be relinquished in its present stage without casting shame and reproach on the French and American arms, because the latter, confiding in the promised co-operation of the French fleet, had undertaken it with alacrity, and made incredible exertions to provide the requisite stores; that to be deserted in so critical a moment would have a very pernicious influence on the minds of the American people, and afford a triumph to the disaffected, who would not fail to exclaim against French faith, and animadvert on the fruit of such an alliance. They also urged the danger of carrying the fleet, in its present shattered condition, through the difficult navigation over the shoals of Nantucket; that it could be repaired more conveniently at Newport than at Boston; and that its present station afforded advantages over the harbour of Boston for distressing the enemy. Finally, they entreated the admiral, if any personal indiscretions had appeared in conducting the expedition, not to permit them to operate to the prejudice of the common cause. All was fruitless. The Count continued immoveable in the determination he had formed, and, on the twenty-second of August, set sail for Boston.

It was the opinion of Greene and Lafayette, that the principal officers on board the fleet were the enemies of D'Estaing, who, as a landsman, was unpopular among them as commandant in the navy. They therefore determined to thwart his measures, and prevent his achieving any brilliant exploit that might redound to his reputation. Hence, being unable, according to his instructions, to act in opposition to their unanimous opinion, he sailed from the island, although he would not otherwise have probably remained deaf to the arguments, and inexorable to the solicitations, of the commissioners.

When Greene and Lafayette returned to the army, universal indignation and dismay were excited; and the desertion of the French made a violent impression, and created loud clamours, throughout America. Sullivan, chagrined beyond measure, made yet another effort to retain the fleet, by despatching Lieutenant-colonel Laurens, in a swift privateer, to overtake the fleet, and deliver a letter to D'Estaing, remonstrating against his withdrawing from the enterprise, and pressing him, in any event, to leave his land forces. He was also charged with a protest, signed by all the general officers of the American army in Rhode-Island, except the Marquis De Lafayette, remonstrating against his departure in terms of great earnestness. D'Estaing was much displeased with the protest, and continued his voyage to Boston.

Sullivan now saw the fair prospect of acquiring distinction, and of rendering service to his country, escape from his grasp, by the desertion of his allies. The militia, who with so much zeal had hastened to join him, almost entirely disbanded, and the number of his army was reduced, in a short time, from nearly ten thousand men to about half that number, while the force of the enemy consisted of six thousand veterans. It was, therefore, determined to raise the siege of Newport, and to retire to the north end of the island, there to wait for events. He was thus anxious to hold the ground which he had gained, in the hope that D'Estaing might yet return in time to accomplish the object of the expedition. To endeavour to prevail on him to adopt this course, Generals Hancock and Lafayette set out for Boston;—the former to expedite the repairs of the vessel, and the latter to use the influence which his high rank and character gave him with the admiral.—The camp before Newport was broken up in great silence, in the night, and the army retired unobserved towards the works on the north end of the island. Early on the morning of the twenty-ninth, the retreat was discovered by the enemy, who immediately followed in two columns. A very warm action ensued, in which the English were repulsed with admirable resolution. The next day a cannonade was kept up by both parties, but neither thought proper to attack the other: the British were waiting for the reinforcements expected from New-York, and Sullivan had determined to withdraw his troops from the island. The American general, having received certain information that a large body of troops had sailed from New-York for the relief of Newport, crossed over his whole army to the main land, on the night of the thirtieth, without having created in the enemy, such were the judicious measures which he had taken, the slightest suspicion that he had contemplated the movement which was now completed.—Never was there a more fortunate retreat. The next day, Sir Henry Clinton arrived with his reinforcements, and with ships of war, which would probably have entirely cut off the retreat to the continent.

During this time the Marquis De Lafayette was in Boston endeavouring to conciliate the French admiral, and secure the return of his fleet as soon as it should be repaired; but, by great personal exertions, he rejoined the army just in time to have the charge of the rear guard, and to view the unfortunate issue of an expedition, undertaken not only with the fairest prospect of success, but which had been carried to the very threshold of a brilliant termination. The rapidity with which he travelled to the scene of danger as soon as he learned the retrograde movements of Sullivan, and the skill and bravery which he displayed in covering the retreat without the loss of a single man, elicited the approbation of Congress, who, on the ninth of September, 1778, adopted the following resolution :—

"*Resolved,* That Mr. President be requested to inform the Marquis De Lafayette, that Congress have a due sense of the sacrifice he made of his personal feelings in undertaking a journey to Boston, witn a view of promoting the interest of these States, at a time when an occasion was daily expected of his acquiring glory in the field, and that his gallantry in going on Rhode Island, when the greatest part of the army had retreated, and his good conduct in bringing off the pickets and out-sentinels, deserve their particular approbation."

Mr. Laurens, the then president of Congress, transmitted this flattering testimonial to Lafayette, with the following remarks :—

Philadelphia, Sept. 13, 1778.

SIR,

I experience a high degree of satisfaction in fulfilling the instructions embraced in the enclosed act of Congress, of the ninth instant, which expresses the sentiments of the representatives of the United States of America, relative to your excellent conduct during the expedition recently undertaken against Rhode Island.

Receive, Sir, this testimonial on the part of Congress, as a tribute of respect and gratitude, offered to you by a free people.

I have the honour to be, with very great respect and esteem, &c.

HENRY LAURENS.

To this well-merited communication, General Lafayette replied as follows :—

Camp, Sept. 23, 1778.

SIR,

I have just received the letter of the thirteenth instant, with which you have favoured me, and in which you communicate the honour that Congress has been pleased to confer by the adoption of its flattering resolution. Whatever sentiments of pride may be reasonably excited by such marks of approbation, I am not the less sensible of the feelings of gratitude, nor of the satisfaction of believing that my efforts have, in some measure, been considered as useful to a cause, in which my heart is so deeply interested. Have the goodness, Sir, to present to Congress my unfeigned and humble thanks, springing from the bottom of my heart, and accompanied with the assurances of my sincere and perfect attachment, as the only homage worthy of being offered to the representatives of a free people.

From the moment that I first heard the name of America, I loved her; from the moment that I learned her struggles for liberty, I was inflamed with the desire of shedding my blood in her cause;—and the moments that may be ex pended in her service, whenever they may occur, or in whatever part of the world I may be, shall be considered as the happiest of my existence. I feel more ardently than ever, the desire of deserving the obliging sentiments with which I am honoured by the United States, and by their representatives; and the flattering confidence which they have been pleased to repose in me, has filled my heart with the liveliest gratitude, and most lasting affection.

The desertion of Count D'Estaing, at the moment when Newport was about to fall into the power of the combined armies, greatly irritated the minds of the American community, and many began to entertain a loathing towards allies who seemed to forget all interests except their own. General Sullivan, goaded by chagrin and disappointment, of a temperament somewhat warm, and under the influence of a deep and just sense of injury, manifested the state of his feelings in the general orders issued on the twenty-eighth of August. "While," he remarked, "the General wishes them (the army) to place a proper confidence in him as their commander-in-chief, whose business it is to attend to their safety, he yet hopes the event will prove America able to procure that by her own arms, which her allies refuse to assist in obtaining." These expressions being understood to impute to the French nation an indisposition to promote the interests of the United States, wounded the feelings of the French officers, and added in no small degree to the resentments of the moment. The Count D'Estaing addressed a communication to Congress, in which his chagrin and irritation were but ill concealed, and in which he endeavoured to justify his conduct.

The discontent in New-England generally, but particularly in Boston, where the independent companies and militia had returned in excessive ill-humour, was so great as to inspire fears that even the means of repairing the French ships would be unattainable; and it was, in some degree, to guard against the mischief to be apprehended from the prevalence of such a temper, that Generals Lafayette and Hancock had repaired from camp to Boston. Congress, together with Washington, and every thinking man in the community, foresaw the fatal consequences that would ensue from an irreparable breach with their new ally, and took the most judicious and persevering measures to allay the ferment and restore confidence and harmony. That body directed General Washington to make every effort in his power to prevent the unwise protest of the officers of Sullivan's army from being made public, and General Greene, by his timely personal interference, arrested the despatches when on the point of being publicly submitted by the speaker to the assembly of Rhode Island, which General Sullivan had addressed to the Governor of that state, in the first moments of vexation and disappointment, and which complained bitterly of the conduct of D'Estaing, in terms calculated to increase the general discontent.

The Marquis de Lafayette experienced extreme anguish, which he communicated to Washington, at the injuries he supposed to be offered to his country, by the expressions of resentment which fell from the officers of the American army. But, in the expression of these feelings, while he showed his great sensibility wherever France was concerned, he also manifested the most unlimited attachment to the commander-in-chief. Washington laboured indefatigably to prevent the evils to be apprehended from the prejudices and resentments arising from the conduct of D'Estaing; and particularly exerted himself to calm the growing animosities found among the French and American officers. "I have not now time," he remarked in a letter to General Greene, "to take notice of the several arguments which were made use of, for and against the Count's quitting the harbour of Newport and sailing for Boston. Right or wrong, it will probably disappoint our sanguine expectation of success; and, which I deem a still worse consequence, I fear it will sow the seeds of dissension and distrust between us and our new allies, unless the most prudent measures be taken to suppress the feuds and jealousies that have already arisen. I depend much on your temper and influence to conciliate that animosity, which, I plainly perceive by a letter from the Marquis, subsists between the American and French officers in our service. This, you may be assured, will extend itself to the Count, and the officers and men of his whole fleet, should they return to Rhode Island, unless a reconciliation shall have taken place. The Marquis speaks kindly of a letter from you to him on this subject. He will, therefore, take any advice from you in a friendly way; and if he can be pacified, the other French gentlemen will of course be satisfied, since they look up to him as their head. The Marquis grounds his complaint on a general order of the twenty-fourth of August, and upon the universal clamour that prevailed against the French nation."

But notwithstanding the conciliatory measures adopted by the authorities of America, as well as by Count D'Estaing himself, the tide of popular feeling could not be entirely restrained. The conduct of the French officers, and even of the common sailors, at Boston, was truly exemplary. But this extreme circumspection did not prevent the occurrence, on the thirteenth of September, of a violent affray between some Americans and the French, which resulted in the death of the Chevalier de Saint Sauveur. The selectmen of the town, to allay the resentment of the French, showed themselves very solicitous to punish the offenders, and declared that the tumult was fomented by English sailors who had been made prisoners, and deserters from the army of Burgoyne. Tranquillity was restored; the Count

D'Estaing made no further inquiry into the affair; no offender was discovered; and the government of Massachusetts decreed a monument to be erected to Saint Sauveur.—The night of the sixth of the same month had witnessed a scene far more serious, at Charleston, South Carolina, between the French and American sailors. It terminated in a formal battle. The French were driven out of the city, and forced to take refuge on board their ships, from which they fired with artillery and musketry against the town. The Americans, on their part, fired upon the French vessels, from the adjoining wharves and stores. Many lives were lost on both sides. A reward of a thousand pounds sterling was offered to whoever should discover the authors of the tumult, but without effect.—Thus ended the riots of Boston and of Charleston, which were attributed, if not with truth, at least with prudence, to British artifice and instigation. Nothing can more clearly demonstrate the instability of public opinion than the occurrence of these disgraceful scenes. A few weeks before, the whole continent resounded with praises and gratitude to the king of France, as the saviour of the liberties of America, and now, by the conduct, whether right or wrong, of one of his officers, these favourable feelings were instantaneously converted into hatred and irritiation.

At length, provident and temperate measures triumphed, and a breach which threatened very serious consequences, was entirely made up. General Greene was successful in exerting his personal influence with Lafayette, which could be done more with the freedom and familiarity of a friend than that of Washington, although it certainly did not possess the same parental weight. Their combined endeavours were crowned with the success which was anticipated. The American officers, after the first ebullition of passion, were easily pacified; for theirs was a system of sacrifice for the good of the country.*

* For accounts of the expedition against Rhode Island, &c &c. *vide* Marshall's Washington, vol. iii. ch 9.—Journal's Congress, vol. 4, p

The failure of the plan of Congress for the invasion of Canada, to be conducted by the Marquis de Lafayette, did not change the wishes of that body, and after the commencement of hostilities between France and Great Britain, the subject was again taken up. Towards the autumn of 1779, and about the time that Lafayette obtained permission to return to France, a plan was completely matured for a combined attack, to be made by the allied forces of France and the United States, on all the British dominions on the continent, and on the adjacent islands of Cape Breton and Newfoundland. That nobleman was directed to transmit it to Doctor Franklin, the minister of the United States at the court of Versailles, with instructions to induce, if possible, the French cabinet to accede to it. Great reliance was also placed on the influence of the Marquis with his own government. Accordingly, this very extensive plan, prepared entirely in the cabinet, without consulting a single military character, was, for the first time, transmitted to General Washington, in October, with a request that he would enclose it by the Marquis de Lafayette, accompanied with his observations, to Doctor Franklin.

Washington was immediately and forcibly struck with the absolute impracticability of executing the magnificent plan already decided on by Congress, and in a very long and very serious letter to Congress, apologized for not obeying their orders in delivering the plan, with his observations on it, to Lafayette. He entered into a perfect investigation of all its parts, and demonstrated the mischiefs and dangers with which it was replete. Men recede slowly from favourite projects. Hence it was decided that eventual measures, at least, ought to be taken for the expedition. Besides which,

378;—Johnson's Life Greene, vol. i, p. 110—118.—Memoires Hist. su. M. de Lafayette, p 6, 7, 36, 38, 40.—Botta's War Independence, vol ii, p 545.

Congress probably felt, in some degree, committed by the conversations which had been held on the subject with Lafayette, and the minister of France. That body, therefore, directed General Washington to write to the Marquis, who had now departed for France, and to the American minister in Paris, relative to the adoption of eventual measures, in case an armament should be sent from France to Quebec. The Commander-in-Chief, however, whose objections to the proposed plan remained in full force, resolved not to open a correspondence for the purpose of soliciting the concurrence of France in an expedition to which he was firmly opposed. Requesting, therefore, a personal conference, he laid before them such satisfactory reasons for the opinions which he had adopted, that the expedition against Canada was entirely given up.—Thus was General Lafayette relieved from the necessity of urging to the French government the adoption of a plan, which promised little hopes of success, and left entirely free to pursue his solicitations for aid in a manner better adapted to promote the cause of independence.

In the month of January, 1779, the Marquis de Lafayette embarked at Boston, on a voyage to France, in the continental frigate Alliance. Ambitious of fame on another theatre, and anticipating a war on the continent of Europe, he was desirous of tendering his services to his king and his own country. But another principal object was to exert his influence in favour of the United States at the court of Versailles. He had witnessed and felt the mortifying embarrassments which environed the active promoters of the revolution, from a combination of causes, which could be best explained in personal and reiterated interviews with those who directed the policy of the French cabinet. Some fear, also, was entertained that unfavourable results might proceed from the fracas which occurred at Rhode Island, and the consequent excesses committed in Boston and Charleston.—

General Washington, from motives of real friendship, as well as political reasons, was very desirous of preserving Lafayette's connexion with the army, and of strengthening his attachment to America. He, therefore, in the following letter to the president of Congress, expressed his wishes that Lafayette, instead of resigning his commission, might have unlimited leave of absence, to return when it should be convenient to himself and might carry with him every mark of the confidence of the government.

Head Quarters, October 6, 1778.

SIR,

This letter will be presented to you by Major General Lafayette. The generous motives which formerly induced him to cross the ocean, and serve in the armies of the United States, are known to Congress. The same praise-worthy reasons now urge him to return to his native country, which, under existing circumstances, has a claim to his services.

However anxious he was to fulfil the duty which he owes to his king and country, that powerful consideration could not induce him to leave this continent, while the fate of the campaign remains undecided. He is, therefore, determined to remain until the termination of the present campaign, and takes advantage of the present cessation from hostilities, to communicate his designs to Congress, so that the necessary arrangements may be made at a convenient season, while he is at hand, if occasion should offer, to distinguish himself in the army.

At the same time, the Marquis, being desirous of preserving his connexion with this country, and hoping that he may enjoy opportunities of being useful to it, as an American officer, only solicits leave of absence, for the purpose of embracing the views which have been already suggested.

The pain which it costs me to separate from an officer who possesses all the military fire of youth, with a rare maturity of judgment, would lead me, if the choice depended on my wishes, to place his absence on the footing which he proposes. I shall always esteem it a pleasure to be able to give those testimonials of his services to which they are entitled, from the bravery and conduct which have distinguished him on every occasion; and I do not doubt that Congress will, in a proper manner, express how sensibly they appreciate his merits, and how much they regret his departure.

I have the honour to be, &c.

GEORGE WASHINGTON.

Some time after this flattering communication, the Marquis addressed a noble and generous letter to Congress on the same subject.

Philadelphia, October 13, 1778.

SIR,

However attentive I ought to be not to employ the precious moments of Congress in the consideration of private affairs, I beg leave, with that confidence which naturally springs from affection and gratitude, to unfold to them the circumstances in which I am, at present, situated. It is impossible to speak more appropriately of the sentiments which attach me to my own country, than in the presence of citizens who have done so much for their own. So long as I have had the power of regulating my own actions, it has been my pride and pleasure to fight beneath the banners of America, in the defence of a cause, which I may dare more particularly to call *ours*, as I have shed my blood in its support.

Now, Sir, that France is engaged in war, I am urged both by duty and patriotism, to present myself before my sovereign to know in what manner he may be pleased to employ my services. The most pleasing service that I can render, will be that which enables me to serve the common cause, among those whose friendships I have had the happiness to obtain. and in whose fortunes I participated, when your prospects were less bright than they now are. This motive, together with others which Congress will properly appreciate, induce me to request permission to return to my own country in the ensuing winter.

So long as a hope remained of an active campaign, I never indulged the idea of leaving the army; but the present state of peace and inaction leads me to prefer, to Congress, this petition. If it should be pleased to grant my request, the arrangements for my departure shall be taken in such a manner, that the result of the campaign shall be known before they are put in execution. I enclose a letter from his excellency, General Washington, consenting to the leave of absence which I wish to obtain. I flatter myself that you will consider me as a soldier on leave of absence, ardently wishing to rejoin his colours, as well as his beloved comrades. If, when I return to the midst of my fellow citizens, it is believed that I can, in any manner, promote the prosperity of America,—if my most strenuous exertions can promise any useful results, I trust, Sir, that I shall always be considered as the man who has the prosperity of the United States most at heart, and who entertains for their representatives the most perfect love and esteem.

I have the honour to be, &c.

LAFAYETTE.

Congress acceded, without hesitation, to the wishes of the Marquis. They knew that the confidence of America in him was well placed, and that he would use all his influence, at the court of Versailles, in her favour. Never, indeed, did a foreigner, whose primary attachments were to his own country, feel more anxious solicitude for the welfare of another, than was unceasingly manifested by this young nobleman for the United States.—On the twenty-first of October, Congress, in addition to the leave of absence which had been required, adopted the most flattering resolutions:

Resolved, That the Marquis de Lafayette, Major-General in the service of the United States, have leave to go to France; and that he return at such time as shall be most convenient to him.

Resolved, That the president write a letter to the Marquis de Lafayette, returning him the thanks of Congress for that disinterested zeal which led him to America, and for the services he hath rendered to the United States, by the exertion of his courage and abilities on many signal occasions.

Resolved, That the minister plenipotentiary of the United States of America at the court of Versailles, be directed to cause an elegant sword, with proper devices, to be made and presented in the name of the United States, to the Marquis de Lafayette.

A draught of a letter of recommendation to his most Christian majesty, the king of France, in favour of Lafayette, was also reported and agreed to.

According to the second resolution, these honourable evidences of the high character which he enjoyed in the estimation of the American community, were conveyed to the Marquis with the following observations, by the president of Congress:

Philadelphia, October 24, 1778.

SIR,

I had the honour to communicate to Congress, your letter soliciting leave of absence, and I am authorized by that body to express to you its thanks for the zeal you have shown in defence of the just cause in which it is engaged, and for the disinterested services you have rendered to the United States of America.—As a testimonial of the high esteem and affection which the people of these States entertain towards you, and as an acknowledgment of the bravery and military talents which you have displayed on many signal occasions, the representatives of the people, in Congress assembled, have directed the American minister at the court of Versailles, to present you with an elegant sword.

Enclosed you will find an act of Congress, of the twenty-first instant, authorizing these declarations, and granting you permission to return to France, and extending the leave of absence at your will.

I pray the Almighty to bless and protect you, and to guide you in safety to the presence of your friends, and to a happy meeting with your noble family.

I have the honour to be, &c.

HENRY LAURENS.

To this communication, the Marquis de Lafayette made the following reply:

Philadelphia, October 26, 1778.

SIR,

I have received your excellency's obliging letter, containing the several resolutions which Congress have done me the honour to adopt, and the leave of absence which it has been pleased to grant: nothing can afford me more happiness than the belief that my services have obtained its approbation. The glorious marks of confidence and satisfaction which I have received, at different times, from the representatives of America, although greater than my merits, cannot surpass the feelings of gratitude which they have occasioned. I consider the noble present which has been made to me in the name of the United States, as a most flattering honour, and my most ardent desire is speedily to employ that sword in their service, against the common enemy of my country and of its faithful and beloved allies.

May liberty, abundance, and concord, for ever reign in the United States: this is the ardent wish of a heart overflowing with unbounded zeal, love, and devotion, for this country, and with the highest respect and most sincere affection for its representatives.

Be pleased, Sir, to present to them my thanks, and accept for yourself the assurance of my respectful attachment.

I have the honour to be,

With profound veneration, &c. &c.

LAFAYETTE.

On the voyage to France, General Lafayette was exposed to new and unexpected dangers. It was found difficult, in Boston, to procure the complement of men necessary for the frigate Alliance, the national vessel appropriated to convey him to his own country: hence more than half the crew was composed of English sailors who had been made prisoners. Eight days before their arrival in Europe, a conspiracy was formed among the foreigners on board, the execution of which was prevented by the merest accident. Mistaking an American for one of their own countrymen, the English conspirators entrusted him with their secret, and offered him the command of the vessel, which, according to the proclamation of the king of Great Britain, (containing more policy than morality,) became the property of the mutineers. But the honest American revealed the plot to the officers only an hour previous to the time appointed for their general massacre. During this conspiracy and consequent confusion, the French and American sailors, without exception, made common cause against the English.

Thus this gallant nobleman returned to France, the leader of armies, the counsellor of statesmen, and the friend of philosophers, at the premature age of twenty-two years. The court and the people alike came forward to receive and welcome the young hero, who had reflected such credit on his country; who united the gay, gallant, fearless spirit of ancient chivalry, to the modern principles of philosophical liberty.

During this visit Doctor Franklin presented to him the sword ordered by Congress previous to his departure from America, which he accompanied with the following letter

Passy, August 24, 1779.

SIR,

The Congress, sensible of your merit towards the United States, but *unable adequately to reward it,* determined to present you with a sword, as a small mark of their grateful acknowledgment. They directed it to be ornamented with suitable devices. Some of the principal actions of the war, in which you distinguished yourself by your bravery and conduct, are, therefore, represented upon it. These, with a few emblematic figures, all admirably well executed, make its principal value. By the help of the exquisite artists France affords, I find it easy to express every thing but *the sense we have of your worth and our obligations to you.* For this, figures, and even words, are found insufficient.—I, therefore, only add, that, with the most perfect esteem and respect, I have the honour to be,

Your obedient servant,

B. FRANKLIN.

This sword was presented to the Marquis, at Havre, by the grandson of Doctor Franklin. On the four sides of the *coquille* are engraved representations of the battle of Monmouth, of the affair of Gloucester in New-Jersey, and of the retreat from Barren Hill, and from Rhode-Island: on one side of the handle, the Marquis is represented as wounding the British lion; and on the other as receiving a branch of laurel from America, under the form of a female, whose chains are broken. The pommel is, on one side, ornamented with the arms of Lafayette, and on the other with an emblem of America, represented by a crescent enlightening a half-civilized and half-cultivated country. On this part of the sword is also a figure of Fame bearing the arms of France, and a representation of the vessel in which he first came to America. The bow of the hilt bears the following inscription:

Presented by Congress to M. le Marquis de Lafayette.

The ardent zeal displayed by him in his solicitations to the French court in favour of the United States, merits the warmest gratitude of every American bosom. His temporary absence did not in the slightest degree diminish that passionate ardour for the promotion of American independence, which the affectionate attentions he had received, the enthusiasm of a soldier in the cause of those for whom he had made his first campaign, and by whom he had been highly distinguished, combined with a consciousness that he was substantially promoting the permanent interests of France, were all so well calculated to inspire in a young and generous mind, in favour of an infant people, struggling for liberty and self government, with the hereditary rival of his government. Being received at Versailles with every mark of distinction and favour, he employed all the interest he had acquired in impressing on the cabinet, the importance and policy of granting succours to the United States. His success was equal to the noble motives by which he was actuated. The court, governed by political expediency, endeavoured to feed the flame which consumed the strength of Great Britain; and little dreamed that from that flame a spark would proceed, which would eventually kindle the inflammable mass collected within its own bosom.*

Without any regular authority from Congress, the Marquis, taking upon himself the entire responsibility of those measures, employed himself assiduously in soliciting assistance in men, money, and clothing. In this favourite object, he was aided by the representations of the minister of

* Lady Morgan's France, book viii.—Marsh. Washington, vol. iv ch. 5.

France at Philadelphia; and the succours which he procured were various and important. He prevailed on the French court to embark heartily in the cause, and obtained from it a promise to despatch a formidable fleet and army to the ports of the United States. An extract from a letter written on the fifth of March, 1780, by Dr. Franklin to General Washington, will serve to show the estimation in which he was held by that sagacious philosopher and statesman: "I received but lately the letter your excellency did me the honour of writing to me, in recommendation of the Marquis de Lafayette. His modesty detained it long in his own hands. We became acquainted, however, from the time of his arrival in Paris; and his zeal for the honour of our country, his activity in our affairs here, and his firm attachment to our cause and to you, impressed me with the same regard and esteem for him that your excellency's letter would have done, had it immediately been delivered to me."

Having succeeded in his primary object, and finding no probability of active employment on the continent of Europe, Lafayette renounced the continued triumph afforded him by the universal homage and admiration of his countrymen, and once again crossed the ocean to resume his career of glory. In the latter part of April, 1780, he arrived at Boston in the royal frigate Hermione, Captain Le Touche. The day of his landing was one of public rejoicing. The inhabitants flocked to the shore to receive their generous defender, and he was conducted, amid the roar of cannon, the ringing of bells, and the enlivening strains of military music, to the house which the municipal authorities had prepared for his accommodation. The day was concluded by a brilliant display of fire-works in the public places. He escaped, as soon as possible, from the scenes of festivity, and the manifestations of public joy, which this cheering intelligence had occasioned, and hastened to head quarters, where he arrived on the twelfth of May. He was received with open arms, by General Washington, whose heart needed some such balm, for the affairs of America were not then in a prosperous train. The joyful news brought by this illustrious friend, buoyed up the spirit of the father of America. He brought with him the welcome tidings, that large reinforcements were immediately to be forwarded to the French army and navy. He announced that the troops were already embarked, and the ships that bore them on the point of sailing for America.

Congress received the noble Marquis with those marks of distinction and regard, to which his constant and indefatigable zeal in the support of their cause, as well as this last signal service, gave him such just pretensions. Having offered his services to that body on the thirteenth of May, the following resolution was immediately adopted:

" *Resolved*, That Congress consider the return of the Marquis de Lafayette to America, to resume his command, as a fresh proof of the disinterested zeal and persevering attachment which have justly recommended him to the public confidence and applause; and that they receive with pleasure a tender of the further services of so gallant and meritorious an officer."

The intelligence brought by him, gave a new impulse both to Congress and the state legislatures; and the lethargic slumber in which they seemed to be sinking, yielded to resolutions of the most vigorous complexion. His very return was grateful to the American people, and especially redoubled the ardour of the soldiers, who mutually incited each other to show themselves worthy of the allies they expected. They declared aloud that eternal reproach would be their portion, if, through a base and unmanly apathy, they should lose the glorious occasion now offered to them by this powerful co-operation of France. The Congress, and all the established authorities, as well as influential private citizens, neglected no means that could cherish and propagate this new enthusiasm; and their efforts had, in some measure, the desired effect. Thus the arrival of Lafayette was the signal of restoring confidence, of arousing the flagging spirit of the nation, and of reviving the authority, and giving fresh vigour to the measures of Congress.* About the middle of June, the Count de Rochambeau arrived at Rhode Island from Brest, with between five and six thousand select troops, and the Chevalier de Tornay with seven ships of the line, and several frigates.

Soon after the return of General Lafayette, he was appointed to command the van of Washington's army. His division was selected from the different corps: the first brigade was commanded by General Hand, with Colonels Van Courtlandt, Ogden, and Stewart;—the second by General Poor, with Colonels Shepherd, Swift, and Gimat. There was also a troop of horse attached to it, commanded by Colonel Henry Lee, as well as a major's command of artillery. Of all these officers then animated with the prospect of glory, and glittering in martial pomp, it is believed that all have descended to the tomb, but Generals Lafayette and Van Courtlandt.† In 1780, the Marquis de Chastellux, during his travels in America, visited the camp of Lafayette, in New-Jersey, which he found placed in an excellent position. It occupied two heights separated by a

* For accounts of his visit to France in 1779–1780, *vide* Mem. Hist. sur Lafayette.—Toulongeon, Hist. de France, tome i, appendix, p. 97.—Lady Morgan's France, p. 316.—Port Folio, vol. xix, p. 501, 2.—Botta's War Independ. vol. iii, p. 194.—Hist. France, vol. iii, p. 211.—Marsh. Life Washington, vol. iii, 531: iv. 237.—Thacher's Journal, p. 533.—Journal Congress, vol. iv, 446: vi, 49.

† We are, however, ignorant as it respects Colonel Gimat and the major commanding the artillery

small bottom, but with an easy communication between them. The river Totowaw, or Second River, protected its right; and the principal part of the front, and all the left flank, to a great distance, were covered by a rivulet flowing from the town of Paramus, and falling into the Totowaw. It was only twenty miles distant from York island. This vanguard consisted of light infantry, or what is the same thing, of a corps selected from the army. His troops made an excellent appearance. They were better clothed than the rest of the army; the uniform of both officers and soldiers, which was principally furnished at the expense of the Marquis, had a neat and military appearance, and each soldier wore a helmet made of hard leather, with a crest of horsehair. The officers were armed with espontoons, and the subalterns with fusils; the former were provided with short and light sabres, brought from France, and presented to them by General Lafayette. This select corps, he formed and modulated, according to his own wishes, and infused among them a spirit of pride and emulation. They were the pride of his heart;—he was the idol of their devotion. Deserving the highest confidence, and pronounced, by European veterans, to be equal to any corps in any country, they panted for some signal achievement, worthy of their own character, and worthy of the name of their illustrious commander. His dragoons were extremely well mounted, and did not shrink from meeting those of Great Britain, over whom they had gained several advantages; but they had never been numerous enough to form a solid and permanent body. Tarleton, indeed, discovered a vast difference between Lee's dragoons, and a surprised party of ill armed infantry and countrymen. But his *forte* was in the latter species of warfare: a forced march, a surprise, and a bloody gazette, are the records of *his* glory.*

When the first division of the French reinforcements arrived in July, 1780, they found the American force unpre-

* Chastellux's Trav. vol. i, 101—3, 123.

pared for active and offensive co-operation. Yet it was necessary for General Washington to communicate to the Count de Rochambeau, the system adopted for the residue of the campaign. The advanced state of the season forbad the idea of waiting for new levies, to execute his plan against New-York. Both the engagements of Congress and the interests of the United States, determined him immediately to forward to the French general and admiral; definitive proposals of co-operation, and pressed on all sides by a chain of difficulties, he resolved to hazard much, rather than forego the advantage to be derived from the aid afforded by France. The naval superiority of the French being ascertained, the general outlines of a plan for attacking New-York were drawn up, in which the fifth of August was named as the day on which the French troops should re-embark, and the American army assemble at Morrisania. This plan was committed to General Lafayette, who was authorized to explain fully to the Count de Rochambeau, the situation of the American army, and the views of the commander-in-chief; and to go more into detail, respecting the enterprise proposed, and others which were contemplated.

The arrival of Admiral Greaves at New-York, with six ships of the line, however, entirely reversed the superiority at sea, and this change of circumstances, of course prevented any other than an eventual plan for the campaign. The practicability of De Tornay's acquiring the naval superiority now depended on the arrival of the second division of his squadron from Brest, or a reinforcement from Count De Guichen, who commanded the French fleet in the West Indies. In the mean time, Sir Henry Clinton and Admiral Arbuthnot, formed a plan to attack the French fleet and army at Newport. Arbuthnot proceeded to Rhode Island and cruised off the harbour, while Clinton embarked six thousand chosen troops for the purpose of attacking Newport by land. But their designs could not elude the penetration of Washington. As it was impracticable to reach Rhode Island in time to unite the American troops with those of their ally, he resolved to collect all the force he could assemble, and making a rapid movement to New-York, attack that place during the absence of Sir Henry Clinton. Rapidly crossing the North River, he was in full march towards King's bridge with nearly ten thousand men, exclusive of militia, when the sudden return of Sir Henry Clinton, who had abandoned the expedition on learning the improved state of the fortifications on Rhode Island, defeated the hopes which had been formed of finding New-York weakly defended. The American army, accordingly, recrossed the Hudson, and took post near Orangetown.

Intelligence was now received that the second division of the fleet designed for the service of the United States, had been stopped by a British squadron which completely blockaded the port of Brest, and that the Count de Guichen, instead of coming to the American coast, had sailed for Europe. Admiral Rodney also arrived, in September, with eleven ships of the line and four frigates. This reinforcement completely disconcerted all the plans of the allies, and terminated the sanguine hopes which had been formed at the opening of the campaign.

In the mean time, the hostile armies in the neighbour hood of New-York continued vigilantly to observe each others motions. But while the British commander ap peared sunk in supineness, he meditated a deep and dark scheme, which, could it have taken effect in its full extent, would probably have brought the war to a conclusion, and have extinguished, for a time, the Independence of America. General Arnold had distinguished himself in the early attack on Quebec, and afterward maintained the high reputation which he had acquired there by a series of bold and enterprising exertions. Plunged by his profusion into pecuniary distresses, he endeavoured to extricate himself, by engaging in speculations which proved unfortunate, and taking a share in privateers which were unsuccessful. Possessing neither the strength of principle, nor the correctness of judgment, necessary to withstand the seductions to which his high station, as the commander of Philadelphia, exposed him, he committed gross extortions on the citizens, and peculated on the funds of the continent. Brought to a court martial, at the instigation of the executive of Pennsylvania, he was sentenced, on the twenty-sixth of January, 1779, to be reprimanded by the commander-in-chief. This censure alienated his unprincipled mind from the United States; entrusted with the most important command of West Point, in 1780, he basely permitted his pecuniary embarrassments, or resentments, to triumph over his fidelity, and entered into a close correspondence with the enemies of his country.—The particulars of this treacherous attempt, the unfortunate escape of Arnold, and the capture of Major Andre, are well known. Maledictions were heaped upon the former, and praises upon those who had arrested the latter. A board of general officers was convened to determine the fate of the gallant and unfortunate Andre: among its members, besides many distinguished American officers, were the Marquis de Lafayette and Baron Steuben, and they were called upon to determine in which character the prisoner was to be considered, and to what punishment he was liable.

To the feeling and generous heart of Lafayette, the stern performance of this distressing duty occasioned many severe pangs. The candour, openness, and magnanimity of Andre, made upon his mind the most favourable impressions; but he found himself compelled to unite in the decision which condemned to a disgraceful death, a young, brave, and accomplished officer, who united the polish of a court, and the refinements of education, to the heroism of a soldier. The court-martial, with the deep regret that was excited by his frank and noble demeanour, determined that he was a spy, and ought to suffer death. The general officers which composed it, lamented the sentence which the usages of war compelled them to pronounce; and perhaps on no occasion of his life, did Washington obey with more reluctance, the stern mandates of duty and of policy. The sympathy excited among the American officers by his fate, was as universal as is unusual on such occasions. On the second of October, 1780, the unhappy victim was executed at Tappan. When brought to the foot of the gibbet, he exclaimed, "And must I die thus!" He was answered, that it could not be otherwise. He did not dissemble his proud grief, and having past a few moments in prayer, he pronounced these words, which were his last; "Bear witness that I die as a brave man ought to die." Such was the just, but melancholy fate of a young man, deserving, in so many respects, a better destiny. Andre died with fortitude and dignity, his last hours soothed with every mark of attention and regard, and his execution accompanied by the tears of the very judges who pronounced it. Arnold lived "a recreant and most degenerate traitor," branded with infamy, the loathsome object of scorn, and regarded with contempt and detestation by the honourable, the generous, and the brave, who could never forget that he was a sordid villain, first the slave of his rage, then purchased with gold, and finally secured from the gallows by the blood of one of the most accomplished officers in the British army.

The events of the campaign of 1780, although by no means adverse, had disappointed the sanguine expectations which attended its commencement. But although unmarked by any memorable event, the American General had succeeded in keeping the enemy shut up in New-York. This state of inactivity little accorded with the martial spirit and desire of distinction, which animated the Marquis de Lafayette. In October, 1780, when Greene was appointed to the command of the southern department, many gallant spirits earnestly solicited to be enrolled under his banners. Among these were Colonel John Laurens, literally the "*chevalier sans peur et sans reproche*," Colonel Christopher Greene, the hero of Red Bank, Doctor M'Henry, then aid to General Washington, Major Lee, the celebrated partisan, and finally, Lafayette. On the tenth of November, 1780, the Marquis addressed the following letter to General Greene:—

MY DEAR FRIEND,

As soon as your letter from head-quarters came to hand, I hastened to make an answer to the several articles it contained, and was greatly disappointed to hear you were gone before it could reach you. For my friends, my dear Sir, I have no different feelings from those which I experience for myself. I therefore feel for you as I would on my own account, were I appointed to command the southern army. You will, I confess, have great difficulties to struggle with, the worst of them all will, I fear, be the article of provisions. But, on the other hand, defeats are expected from that quarter. It was yet more the case before Ferguson's affair.* Could it have been properly agreeable for the public welfare, I wish this affair had been postponed. Indeed. my friend, if I feel for you on account of the obstacles which you will have to encounter, I, on the other hand, cannot help foreseeing a great deal of personal glory which you are entitled to hope. But whatever might have been hereafter the case; whatever bad chances, (and in our profession chance is something,) a malignant fortune might throw in your way,

* Major Ferguson was defeated by a body of militia, at King's Mountain on the seventh of October. Upwards of eight hundred British were made prisoners, and two hundred and twenty-five killed or wounded.

believe me, my dear Sir, my friendship as well as my esteem for you, are founded upon such a basis as cannot be shaken by any run of good or ill luck, which may subject you to the praise or the blame of common opinions. In all cases, I am heartily willing to have my fate united to yours; and by this junction of stars, to have my little share in any thing, good or bad, that may happen to the troops under your command.

As soon as we enter into winter quarters, I shall the more freely ask the General leave to join you; as, by that time, letters from France will have convinced us that my presence at head-quarters is not, for some months, useful to his purpose of co-operation. By the first of January, at furthest, and sooner, I hope, I intend to be with you, and to consecrate to the country I early loved, under a General I have long marked out as my friend, the efforts of my zeal, and of any thing, by nature or acquisition, I may be worth in the military service. Hamilton has told me that you have conversed with him on the manner of being employed that you thought most agreeable to me.* Though by my temper and principles, I am bound to accept of any thing, and cheerfully to act upon any scale that a superior officer thinks fit for me, I cannot help acknowledging your kindness, and frankly tell you, you are not mistaken in believing that the command of a flying camp, composed of the horse and light infantry of your army, will better please me than the honourable, but less active command of a wing. As I am sure that my friend Lee will apply for being attached to me, I beg leave to support the motion of that officer, whom I love, and in whom I greatly confide, both for counsel and execution.

* This letter was written by the Marquis in English.

In case the dispositions of the enemy make you wish that I should repair to such or such any particular place, I will, on the least hint from you, ask leave from the General to fly there with the greatest despatch.

LAFAYETTE.

On the twenty-ninth of December, General Greene communicated to the Marquis the deplorable situation in which he was placed, and the little prospect of distinction which existed in the southern department. "It is now," he said, "within a few days of the time you mentioned of being with me. Were you to arrive, you would find a few ragged, half starved troops, in the wilderness, destitute of every thing necessary for either the comfort or convenience of soldiers." "Indeed, my dear Sir, the department is in a most deplorable condition, nor have I a prospect of its mending. The country is almost laid waste, and the inhabitants plunder one another with little less than savage fury. We live from hand to mouth, and have nothing to subsist on but what we collect with armed parties. In this situation, I believe you will agree with me that there is nothing inviting this way, especially when I assure you our whole force, fit for duty, that are properly clothed, and properly equipped, does not amount to eight hundred men." "Your professions and assurances of friendship are very flattering and soothing to my feelings. I wish my situation and future prospects afforded something more inviting and worthy your attention, that I might have an opportunity to indulge your wishes and gratify your feelings. But I fear this department is to be the great Sarbonian bog to the American armies, and particularly to the general officers."

The distresses and privations which awaited him in the south produced no effect whatever on the resolution which

Lafayette had adopted. But he did not reach the southern army. After obtaining the permission of the commander-in-chief, he had proceeded as far as Philadelphia on his way to join General Greene, when he was called upon to assist in the negotiation then going on with the French minister to forward the concerted co-operation of the French fleet in the West Indies, which finally resulted in the capture of Cornwallis After terminating this important affair, he immediately resumed his journey, and had advanced as far as Petersburg, when he was recalled to take the command of the expedition against Arnold in Virginia.

In the month of December, 1780, the traitor Arnold, now a Brigadier-General in the British service, was despatched from New-York, with about sixteen hundred men, and landed at Westover on the fourth of January, which is distant on James River, about one hundred and forty miles from the Capes of Virginia. The next day he entered Richmond, where he ravaged both public and private property. Afterward, proceeding slowly down the river, followed by Baron Steuben, he destroyed several mills on his way, and established himself on the twentieth at Portsmouth, where Steuben, finding himself unable to force the position, stationed his troops in such a manner as to confine him to the narrowest possible limits. During this expedition, devastation had been extended, under Arnold's direction, until even his greedy appetite was cloyed, and his revengeful heart sated. As if he coveted to couple the name of bandit with that of traitor, he carried fire and sword wherever he went. Washington, not less surprised than mortified at the tidings from Virginia, bestowed his immediate attention upon that quarter. He addressed himself to Rochambeau, commanding the land forces of his Most Christian Majesty, and to Monsieur Destouches, admiral of his squadron in the American seas, urging them to seize the present moment for inflicting a severe blow on the common enemy. Providentially, the French possessed, at this moment, the superiority on the sea, the British having suffered severely in a storm off Long Island. The French Admiral sent an inefficient force to the Chesapeake under M. de Tilly, who, discovering his inability to execute the expected service, immediately returned to Newport.

In the mean-time, General Washington had detached the Marquis de Lafayette, with a corps of twelve hundred light infantry, drafted from the lines of New-England and New-Jersey, for the purpose of marching to the head of Elk, there to embark for that part of Virginia which was become the theatre of action, under convoy of a French frigate which he expected to obtain from the admiral. The commander-in-chief himself hastened to Newport to use his personal exertions to facilitate the execution of the enterprise; and it was determined that a detachment of the French army, then in readiness, should be embarked under the Count de Viominil. Two days after the fleet had sailed, it was followed by the British admiral, and a partial engagement ensued off the Capes of Virginia, which continued about an hour. A council of war was called the next day, and it being decided that it was unadviseable to renew the action, the French vessels returned to Newport.

During these operations, General Lafayette had embarked his detachment at the head of Elk, and proceeded with it to Annapolis, in Maryland, where he waited for a frigate from the French squadron to convoy it to Virginia. The rencontre of the fleets, and the return of the French admiral to Newport, having rendered the object of the expedition unattainable, Lafayette re-embarked his detachment, and returned to the head of Elk, where he received orders to join the southern army.

Thus Arnold escaped from, probably, the most imminent danger in which he had ever been involved. Had the

French forces reached the Chesapeake unopposed, the British must have fallen, and the American traitor would have expiated his atrocious crime on a gibbet. So persuaded was Washington that this was now the probable termination to his infamous life, that he instructed the Marquis de Lafayette not to admit any stipulation, in his surrender, for his safety, and forbade the smallest injury to the person of Arnold; his object being to bring him to public punishment, agreeably to the rules and regulations established by Congress for the government of the army.

Sir Henry Clinton, sensible of the vulnerable condition of Arnold, hastened the embarkation of a considerable body of troops, under Major General Phillips, consisting of two thousand men. This powerful reinforcement debarked at Portsmouth on the twenty-sixth of March to the great joy of Arnold, whose apprehensions during the preceding three weeks had been unceasing and excruciating.—General Phillips, on his arrival, took command of all the British troops in Virginia, and had the decided superiority over any force that could be brought against him. Having occupied himself in completing the fortifications of Portsmouth, as soon as that object was effected, he prepared for offensive operations.

The arrival of Phillips changed the destination of Lafayette, to whom the defence of Virginia was now committed. At the head of Elk, he received an express from the commander-in-chief, announcing the sailing of Phillips, directing him to proceed to Virginia to take the command of the troops collected and collecting for its protection, and urging him to prevent, if possible, the meditated descent of that general or his junction with Cornwallis. He, accordingly, prepared to execute these orders, and as the command of the bay by the British rendered it hazardous again to attempt the passage to Annapolis, the line of march was taken up for Baltimore, ascending the east side of the bay.

The troops under his command had been taken chiefly from the eastren regiments, and had imbibed strong prejudices against a southern climate. The service on which they were detached, was not expected to be of long duration, and they were consequently unprepared for a campaign in a department where no relief from the most pressing wants could be procured. When they marched from the head of Elk, it was the early part of the month of April, and the north winds still blew keen. The half naked soldiers became sullen and intractable. The states on whom the duty devolved had neglected to clothe them, and the United States had neither money nor credit to supply the deficiency. In a letter to General Greene, the Marquis gave an interesting and exculpatory account of the sufferings of his soldicrs, whom he was obliged to punish with one hand, and relieve with the other. Such had been the necessity for secrecy and despatch, when they were ordered off from New Windsor in the state of New-York, that they were hurried away under an impression that they were proceeding on a march of a few days. The consequence was, that even the officers were destitute of money, clothing, and every thing that could contribute to cleanliness and comfort. When they arrived at Trenton, they were crowded on board of shallops, and passing down to New Castle, were landed and marched across the isthmus to the head of the Elk. Here they began to take a deliberate survey of their situation, and, at this time, their murmurs were suppressed only by the suggestion of a short and rapid expedition against Arnold. On their retrogade march, they were still contented, for they were approaching the depository of their wives, and of the few little comforts which their encampment had afforded them.—Money had also been transmitted to head quarters by the State of Massachusetts, for the pay of her troops; and present sufferings were forgotten under the enlivening prospects of approaching enjoyments. But every hope was blighted when the countermanding orders arrested their progress. Without tents,—for many, even of the officers, slept in the open air;—their shoes worn out,—their hats lost in their repeated voyages;—in a state (as the Marquis expresses it,) "of shocking nakedness."—not the least particle of baggage attending their march,—no provision made for a protracted absence from their wives and families, many of whom had joined them and been left at their winter quarters;—murmuring at being thus hurried off, without notice to prepare for the service they were entering upon;—reasonably fearing that their destination was to serve in a climate which they dreaded,—and supported by the general pity which their case excited;—such was the temper of his army, that many of the officers assured the Marquis, that it would speedily be reduced to one half by desertion. Facts supported the assertion, for thirteen out of one company deserted in a single day.—To add to the general distress, a nauseous and contagious disease generally produced, and always aggravated, by a want of cleanliness, had nearly overspread the whole camp; and naked and exposed and kept in motion, as the soldiers were, the ordinary remedies could not be applied for their cure, with safety to their general health. Desertion cannot, for any cause, be pardoned in an army: but it is impossible to view such a complication of distresses in a camp, without admiring the passive merit which could resist the impulse to desert.

But the firm and generous spirit of the Marquis de Lafayette triumphed over these difficulties, and his energetic appeals to the honourable principles of his soldiers,—principles on which the feelings of his own bosom taught him to rely—were crowned with success. His purse was as open as his heart. As unmindful of money as he was ambitious of fame, he resolved, by a noble and generous act, to conciliate his troops, and strengthen them in the good disposition of the moment. Such were his zeal and public spirit,—such the confidence and respect of the people,—that at a time, when the credit of Congress was so low that nothing could be obtained on its promises, he was able to borrow, on his private credit, ten thousand dollars from the merchants of Baltimore, with which he purchased shoes, linen, spirits, and other articles of immediate necessity, for his detachment: And it is not unworthy of notice, that every fair hand in Baltimore was promptly set in motion, in preparing his purchases for immediate use.

The following extract from a letter to General Greene from Mr. M'Henry, the president of the Baltimore board of war, exhibits the arduous situation and noble liberality of the Marquis at this time:

"*Baltimore, April* 16, 1781.

"While I admire your policy, I have more than once pitied the Marquis'* situation. His troops passed here yesterday, discontented almost to general desertion;—destitute of shirts, and proper equipments, and in most respects, unprovided for a march. You know the Marquis: He has been with us but two days; but, in this time, he adopted an expedient to conciliate them to a degree, which no one but himself would have thought of. To-day, he signs a contract, binding himself to certain merchants of this place, for above *two thousand guineas*, to be disposed of in shirts, overalls, and hats, for the detachment. Without these the army could not proceed; and with these, he has managed to reconcile them to the service. He is also bent upon trying the power of novelty on their minds, by giving to the march the air of a frolic. His troops will ride in wagons and carts, from Elkridge landing

* In speaking of Lafayette, the comprehensive term "*the Marquis*,' was universally used, and as universally understood.

to the limits of this state, and how much further he will continue this mode of movement, depends on Virginia."

In a letter from the Marquis to General Greene, on the same subject, he observes: "As our brave and excellent men (for this detachment is exceedingly good,) are shockingly destitute of linen, I have borrowed from the merchants of Baltimore a sum on my credit, which will amount to about two thousand pounds, and will procure a few hats, some shoes, some blankets, and a pair of linen overalls, to each man. I hope to set the Baltimore ladies at work for the shirts, which will be sent after me, and the overalls will be made by our tailors. I will use my influence to have the money added to the loan which the French court have made to the United States, and in case I cannot succeed, bind myself to the merchants for payment, with interest, in two years."

Great and just was the eclat acquired by the Marquis De Lafayette on the occasion. His cotemporaries appeared at a loss which most to admire, his ingenuity, magnanimity, decision, or engaging urbanity. By these happy expedients, tranquillity and discipline were once more restored to his command; and every wagon or cart that could be procured, being put in requisition, the troops were rapidly hurried forward to Richmond. The novelty and relief pleased the soldiers; the increasing distance from their homes diminished the facility of desertion; the baggage and artillery were left to follow on; and the time thus gained was barely sufficient to check the advance of General Phillips. As Lafayette entered Richmond, the British army made its appearance at Manchester, on the opposite bank of James River.*

During this time, the inroads of Philips and Arnold into

* Johnson's Life Greene, Vol. II. chap. 12, p. 38—51. Marsh. Washington—Vol. IV. chap. VIII, p. 523, 424.

Virginia were signalized by devastation and pillage.* Embarking about two thousand five hundred men, Philips had ascended James River and landed below Petersburg. The next day he occupied that city, after some slight skirmishing with a body of militia under Baron Steuben, amounting to only one thousand men, and pursuing the usual marauding system, he burned the ware-houses stored with tobacco, and all the vessels lying in the river. Every thing valuable was destroyed, and the wealth of this flourishing town, in a few hours disappeared. Prosecuting this war of devastation, the gallant commanders separated in search of tobacco-houses, and re-united their divisions on the route to Manchester, a small village south of James River, and within view of the metropolis.—Here the tobacco-war was renewed, great quantities of that article being found in the ware-houses. Nothing now remained on the south side of James River, below the falls, for the firebands of these ruthless invaders; all the tobacco, and every thing else that was valuable, within reach, were burnt, or conveyed on board their ships.—It was necessary to cross to Richmond, or lay aside the torch.

But the opportune arrival of General Lafayette, on the preceding evening, after a forced march of two hundred miles, put an insuperable bar to the project of taking the capital, and Richmond, in which a great proportion of the military stores of the state were then collected, was saved for the present, from the desolations of the enemy. At this place the Marquis formed a junction with the Baron Steuben, and found himself at the head of about one thousand regulars, two thousand militia, and sixty dragoons, while the British force consisted of nearly four thousand veteran troops. A singular coincidence now presented itself to the public eye. The father of Lafayette had fal-

* During these predatory excursions, the destruction, in the single article of tobacco was enormous; it amounted to about ten thousand hogsheads.

len at the battle of Minden, by a shot from the artillery, then commanded by General Philips. This fact is noticed by the Marquis De Lafayette in a letter to General Greene, touching his continuance in the command of Virginia. "I will now only mention, that General Philips' battery, at Minden, having killed my father, I should have on objection to contract the latitude of his plans." At the same time General Lafayette modestly solicited to be confirmed in his command. As the direction of the military operations in Virginia had been delegated to Steuben, while Lafayette was designed for a command in the main army, the Baron had expressed the most serious chagrin at being superseded, at the very moment when an opportunity presented itself for active service. To give umbrage to either of two officers whom he valued so highly, would have been, to General Greene, the subject of very great regret: all his address was necessary to manage so as to continue Lafayette in command, without disgusting a man whose zeal and fidelity had rendered him such important services. But Steuben had become unpopular in Virginia, and every thing was to be expected from the strong public partialities in favour of Lafayette, and the high opinion justly entertained of his capacity as a soldier. Greene addressed the Baron as a friend, a man of understanding, and a zealous advocate of the cause and the latter submitted with a magnanimity and self denial, which furnish not the least of his claims to the gratitude of America.*

Not thinking it advisable to attempt the passage of the river, Philips marched back to Bermuda Hundred, a point of land at the confluence of the James and Appomattox rivers, destroying in his way property to an immense amount. At that place he re-embarked his troops, and fell down as far as Hog Island, which he

* Johnson's Greene, Vol. II. p. 52.

reached on the fifth of May. The Marquis de Lafayette followed cautiously on the north side of the river, until he reached the head waters of the Chickahominy, one of the branches of James River, behind which he took post, at the distance of eighteen miles from Richmond:—here he remained until Philips, by the command of Cornwallis, began to re-ascend the river, for the purpose of forming a junction at Petersburg.

General Lafayette now hastened back to Richmond; but having, on his arrival, been informed that Lord Cornwallis was marching northward, and that General Philips was again disembarking his army at Brandon, the seat of Benjamin Harrison, Esq. on the south side of the river, he was persuaded that a junction of the two armies was intended, and hastened to take possession of Petersburg before Philips could reach that place. In this design, however, he was anticipated. The British general advanced with equal rapidity, and being nearer to Petersburg, reached it first. Disappointed in this design, Lafayette encamped a few miles below Richmond, where he exerted himself to increase the ability of his army, by diminishing his baggage, establishing system and punctuality in its several departments, and introducing throughout the most rigid discipline.

The taking possession of Petersburg on the ninth of May was the last exploit of General Philips. He had been attacked by a fever some days before, the progress of which was so rapid, and its symptoms so malignant, that it baffled all medical exertions, and put a period to his life on the thirteenth of May. As an officer, he was universally admired; and his military career, previous to his command in Virginia, had been filled with glory. But the friends of his fame have great reason to regret that he did not die three weeks sooner. By this event the command of the army devolved on Arnold.

Lord Cornwallis had moved from Wilmington on the twenty-fifth of April, and proceeded toward Halifax on the river Roanoke, preserving, as a brilliant contrast to the maraudings of Philips and Arnold the country from devastation, and private property from spoliation. During the tedious progress from Cape Fear to the Roanoke, he met with no interruption, and reached Halifax without at all disturbing the general torpor which prevailed throughout the country. At this place the restrained licentiousness of the unprincipled burst forth in shocking outrage upon the defenceless citizens, alike disgraceful to the British arms, and degrading to the name of man. But Cornwallis, on learning these enormities, acted according to his natural humanity and moderation, and commanded Colonel Tarleton to dismount his dragoons, (who, with characteristic ferocity, had been the fit actors in the atrocious outrages that had been committed,) and to form them in such order as might be convenient for the inspection of the inhabitants who were requested to designate the principal villains. A sergeant and one private being pointed out, and accused of rape and robbery, they were conducted back to Halifax, tried by martial law, condemned to death, and immediately executed.

Lord Cornwallis, leaving Halifax, passed the Roanoke, and detached Colonel Tarleton with his legion to the Meherrion, to take possession of the fords across that river;—Lieutenant General Simcoe, with the queen's rangers being at the same time sent forward by Arnold to the Not toway, for the like purpose. No interruption was attempted against either detachment, all the force assembled for the protection of the State being with Lafayette in his position near Richmond; and Lord Cornwallis, passing those rivers, entered Petersburg on the twentieth of May, when he took the general command of all the British forces.

The British General now determined on a vigorous plan of offensive operations. After being reinforced by two British regiments, and two battalions of Anspach troops from New-York, under General Leslie, his immediate object with his overwhelming superiority, was to bring the Marquis De Lafayette to an action, which could not fail to terminate in his defeat. The field-force under Cornwallis was not less than eight thousand; more than double of that acting under Lafayette. Besides which, his strength in horse, amounting to four hundred dragoons, and seven or eight hundred mounted infantry, added vastly to his superiority. Lafayette's force, in the camp below Richmond, did not exceed four thousand, of which three-fourths were militia. Baron Steuben, with six hundred levies, was ordered to the point of the fork, the depot of most of the remaining military stores; and Brigadier General Wayne, with the Pennsylvania line, now reduced to eight hundred, was on his march from the northern army to unite with Lafayette.

Lord Cornwallis, for the purpose of bringing his enemy to action, immediately put his troops in motion on the twenty fourth of May, and passing the James River at Westover, attempted, by turning the left flank of the American army, to get in its rear. Lafayette was in no condition to risk an engagement. The native ardour of his temper, and the reluctance with which he exposed himself to the charge of giving up the country without even an attempt to save it by an action, required all the vigilance of his judgment, to restrain him from hazarding more than his present situation would justify. The main and immediate objects which it was now his duty to effect, were the security of the public stores, the preservation of his small army for future service, and a junction with the Pennsylvania line. As Lord Cornwallis passed James River, the Marquis De Lafayette abandoned Richmond, after removing all the most valuable military stores, and fell behind the Chickahominy river, in the direction toward Fredericksburg, for the double purpose of favouring the contemplated junction with General Wayne, and of covering the manufactory of arms in the vicinity of Falmouth.

Lord Cornwallis followed with zeal and rapidity, and crossing the Chickahominy at Bottom Bridge, manifested his determination to force Lafayette to battle before his junction with General Wayne. He was so entirely confident of success against his young antagonist, that he imprudently remarked in a letter, which was intercepted, "*the boy cannot escape me.*" But a combination of talents and skill defeated all the energies of physical power, and the gallant "boy" escaped to give new evidences at Yorktown, of his generosity and modesty, by declining to receive the sword of the captured Cornwallis himself.

Lafayette moved with so much celerity and caution as to convince Lord Cornwallis of the impracticability of overtaking him, or of preventing his junction with General Wayne. Before the British army reached the Chickahominy, he had passed the Pamunkey, the southern branch of York River. Finding that the distance between his adversary and himself daily increased, Cornwallis halted, and turned his attention to objects of less magnitude. He accordingly, made two considerable detachments from his army while encamped in the county of Hanover; one for the purpose of destroying the magazines at the Point of Fork, then under the protection of Baron Steuben with his raw levies, and the other, for seizing the members of the general assembly convened at Charlotteville, a small town on the western bank of the Rivannah, a northern branch of James River. Simcoe, who commanded the first, by the rapidity of his march, as well as the precipitate retreat of the Baron, succeeded in destroying the military stores; and Colonel Tarleton, who led the detachment against Charlotteville, was equally successful in destroying the stores at that place: but nearly all the members of the legislature made their escape. In the mean-time, Lafayette continued to retreat, and to keep up his communication with the north, passed the Rapidan, the southern branch of the Rapahannoc. The movements of the two armies had thrown Lord Cornwallis completely between Marquis de Lafayette and the military stores which had been transported from Richmond up James River, and deposited principally at Albemarle old court-house. The British general therefore directed his march toward that place.

Lafayette had now effected a junction with the Pennsylvania line, consisting of eight hundred men under General Wayne. Emboldened by this reinforcement, he lost no time in recrossing the Rapidan, and moving toward the enemy. He arrived and encamped within a few miles of the British army, when they were yet more than a day's march from their point of destination. Cornwallis was willing that his antagonists should proceed on the experiment of preserving the stores at Albemarle old court-house, and continued in his position convenient to his adversary's presumed route, with a detachment to fall upon him in his progress. Thus, in the opinion of Cornwallis, he was effectually cut off from the route by which alone he could reach the objects which he was hazarding every thing to secure. Never was disappointment more complete than that of the British commander, when, on the morning of the fifteenth of June, he found his youthful foe in his front, strongly reinforced, and occupying a position from which he could not be easily forced, and would not be tempted. Lafayette's discernment and activity had completely baffled his views. He discovered, and opened in the night, a road which was nearer to Albemarle, but had long been disused, and crossed the Rivannah before Cornwallis was acquainted with his having reached it. Then, taking post behind Mechunck's creek, he sat down on the direct route from the British camp to Albemarle, The following is the modest account given of this masterly movement, by the author of it: " In the mean-time, the British army was moving to the Point of Fork, with intention to strike our magazine at Albemarle old court-house. Our force was not equal to their defence; and a delay of our junction would have answered the views of the enemy. But on the arrival of the Pennsylvanians, we made forced marches toward James River, and on our gaining the South Anna, we found Lord Cornwallis en camped some miles below the camp of Fork. A stolen march, through a difficult road, gave us a position upon Mechunck creek, between that of the enemy and our stores, where, agreeably to previous appointment we were joined by a body of riflemen."

The expedition against Albemarle was now relinquished, and the British General drawing in his van corps, fell back, on the ensuing day, toward, Richmond. This movement was the means of exciting considerable surprise, as, notwithstanding the junction of Wayne, and the succeeding reinforcement of riflemen under Lord Cornwallis continued to possess a decided superiority of force, both with respect to quality and number. By some it was attributed to the difficulties which he apprehended near the mountains, when even a victory might be attended with no decisive consequences: hence he chose to transfer the war to the lower country, the face of which appeared more favourable to his views. But the change in his conduct is now known to have been owing to orders from his superior.

Fabius Maximus Quintus, when warring against Hannibal, avoided open action, but successfully and continually harassed him by counter-marches and ambuscades and all those difficult manœuvres which distinguish the experienced and calculating commander. There is no other mode by which an inferior force can act with efficacy against an enemy both numerically and scientifically superior. Hannibal sent word to Fabius, that "If he was as great a captain as he would be thought, he ought to come into the plain and give him battle." Fabius coolly replied, that "if he was as great as he would be thought, he would do well to force him to fight." Such were precisely the relative situations of the Marquis de Lafayette and the enemy. The former gained every thing by avoiding a general action, which would inevitably have resulted in his total destruction, while the latter found himself incessantly harassed, his power to destroy restricted, and his progress retarded and endangered by the rapid movements, indefatigable vigilance, and masterly military skill of General Lafayette.

As soon as the retreat of Lord Cornwallis was ascertained, General Lafayette put his army in motion, and followed with undiminished circumspection, taking care to keep the command of the upper country, and to avoid a general engagement. He held his main body between twenty and thirty miles in the rear of the foe, and explored his front and flanks with his cavalry and riflemen. On the fifteenth of June, the British general reached Westham, without making a single effort to strike his following enemy, and on the subsequent day, entered Richmond, where he halted. General Lafayette took a strong position on Allen's creek, in the county of Goochland, twenty-two miles from Lord Cornwallis After a few days, the latter resumed his march, and entered Williamsburg on the twenty-fifth of June.

On the eighteenth of June, while in his camp above Richmond, the Marquis de Lafayette was joined by Baron Steuben with his corps of levies, amounting to between five and six hundred. His army was now increased to four thousand men, of whom two thousand one hundred were regulars; but only one thousand five hundred were veteran troops Still, however, Cornwallis was superior in number by a third, and his army was composed entirely of veterans furnished with a powerful and well mounted cavalry, who had spread terror as well as desolation through the country, and had greatly intimidated the militia.

During the retreat of the enemy to Williamsburg, no attempt was made by either general to disturb the other; a game, of all others, the most to be desired by General Lafayette, as the campaign appeared to be wasting without any improvement by his superior foe. He merely caused his light parties to press on their rear, which was covered by a strong corps under Major Simcoe. That officer was overtaken by Colonel Butler about six miles from Williamsburg, to which he was proceeding from the destruction of a few boats and stores on the Chickahominy. A sharp action ensued which was attended with loss on both sides; but the Americans were compelled to retire by the approach of the whole British army, which had moved on hearing the first fire, to shield Simcoe. Lafayette claimed the advantage in this recontre, and stated the enemy's loss amounted to sixty killed, and one hundred wounded.

After this skirmish, the Marquis encamped about twenty miles above Williamsburg, in a secure position near James River, interposing the Chickahominy between him and the enemy.

Intercepted letters had disclosed to Sir Henry Clinton the designs which were meditated against the seat of the British power in the United states, and he, becoming alarmed for the safety of New-York, required the return of a part of the troops in Virginia. Lord Cornwallis, supposing himself too weak, after complying with this requisition, to remain at Williamsburg, resolved to pass James River and retire to Portsmouth. He accordingly left that city on the fourth of July, having decided to cross at James City Island, and encamped along the river, having his right covered by a pond, and the centre and left by swamps. On the fifth and sixth, a small number of troops, and all the baggage, artillery, and munitions, were transported across the river, and Cornwallis intended to have passed his army on the seventh.

The morning after the evacuation of Williamsburg, Lafayette put his army in motion, with the intention of falling upon the rear of the enemy, when a major part of his army should have passed, or was passing the river Crossing the Chickahominy, he pushed his best troops within eight miles of the British camp, On the morning of the sixth, he prepared to advance, believing that the hour was at hand for striking the meditated blow, as he had been accurately informed of the passage of troops on the fourth, and the continued crossing and recrossing of the boats ever since. All the intelligence which was received by General Lafayette concurred in the representation that the greater part of the British army had already passed over into the island of Jamestown, in the night, and every appearance was calculated to countenance the opinion that had been formed.

But Lord Cornwallis suspected the design of Lafayette, and was confident that the opportunity afforded by his crossing James river, would be seized with ardour by his youthful antagonist. He heard with pleasure that the American forces were drawing near, and adopted proper measures to encourage their advance. The British light parties were all drawn in, their troops were held compact, covering as little ground as possible in their march and in camp, and the piquets, which lay close to the encampment, were ordered to fall back with the appearance of alarm and confusion, as soon as they should be seriously attacked.

General Lafayette had detached some riflemen and militia to harass the outposts of the enemy, while he advanced at the head of the continental troops, in order to cut off their rear, should the intelligence he had received of the passage of the main body, be well founded. The enemy's piquets were briskly attacked, and losing some of their men, killed, wounded, and taken, fell back in confusion upon the legion-horse, drawn up in their rear. Emboldened by this successful onset, the Americans continued to advance, and took post in a ditch, under cover of a rail-fence. After a keen conflict of some minutes, they fell back upon general Wayne, who was formed in close order in an adjacent wood. That brave officer, who commanded the van-guard, now discovered the whole British army in order of battle, moving out against him. A retreat was impossible, and the boldest, had become the safest measure. Advancing rapidly, he made a gallant charge on the British line, with his small detachment, not exceeding eight hundred men, and the warm action which ensued, was kept up with great spirit for several minutes.

Lafayette, who arrived a little before sun-set, began soon to apprehend that the expected covering party would turn out to be the British army, and determined, by reconnoitring to judge of the enemy's strength from his own observation. He soon became convinced that his apprehensions were well founded, and immediately hastened to draw off his troops. On his return, finding Wayne closely engaged, and his flanks nearly enveloped, he directed him to retreat, and form in a line with the light infantry, then drawn up about half a mile in the rear. This was instantly executed through the favour of a dark night, with the loss of two field pieces, the horses attached to them being killed. The whole army then retreated the distance of six miles, when Lafayette, finding that the enemy did not pursue, encamped for the night.

No pursuit was even attempted by Cornwallis, who returned, immediately after the battle closed to his camp. The night, the nature of the country, broken with woods and marshes, but especially the suspicion that the retreat was a stratagem of the American general, to draw him into an ambuscade, induced the British commander to decline all pursuit. In the course of the night he crossed over into the island, and soon after proceeded to Portsmouth, in order to embark the troops, which Clinton expected at New York. Lafayette retired with the greater part of his army, having dismissed all his militia, to the forks of York river, where it was permitted to repose itself, all active operations having ceased. During the action near Jamestown, his person was greatly exposed, and he had a horse killed under him.*

Thus terminated the summer campaign of lord Cornwallis, in Virginia. He was at the head of an army completely fitted for the arduous scenes of war, warmly attached to their commander, proud in its knowledge of its own ability, and ready to encounter every difficulty and danger. On the other hand, the inferiority of Lafayette in numbers, in quality, in cavalry, in arms and equipment, was very great and well known.—Although, says Marshall, no brilliant service was achieved by this young nobleman, the campaign in Virginia enhanced his military reputation, and raised him in the general esteem. That, with so decided an inferiority of effective force, and especially of cavalry, he had been able to keep the field in an open country, and to preserve a great proportion of his military stores, as well as his army, was believed to furnish unequivocal evidence of the prudence and vigour of his conduct.

The omission of lord Cornwallis to compel Lafayette manœuvring in his face in an open country, to battle, is inexplicable. Such an event, with his vast superiority of force, would have proved the ruin of the American army, which was frequently and unavoidably in situations where no military skill could have prevented a general engagement. The American general, says an actor in those scenes, had great difficulties to surmount, as well as to guard against his formidable foe, pressing him on his retreat. Wayne, directing his most efficient aid, was far to his right; and the baron Steuben, with the Virginia levies, was as far on his left. The public stores were deposited in several magazines accessible to the enemy; and the great body of the inhabitants below

* For accounts of this action, Vide, Marshall's Washington, Vol. IV, p. 440, 1, 2. Botta's American War, Book XIII. H. Lee's Memoirs, Vol. II, 222--231. Ramsay's Revolution, p. 550. Mem. Histor. sur. M. de Lafayette, p. 18. Thacher's Journal, p. 530.

the mountains were flying from their homes, with their wives, their children, and the most valuable of their personal property, to seek protection in the mountains. The state authorities, executive and legislative, like the flying inhabitants had been driven from the seat of government, chased from Charlotteville; and, at length, compelled to interpose the Blue Ridge between themselves and the enemy, to secure a resting place at Staunton.

In this period of gloom, of disorder, and of peril, Lafayette was collected and undismayed. With zeal, with courage, and with sagacity, he discharged his arduous duties, and throughout his difficult retreat, was never brought even to array, but once, in order for battle. Invigorating our councils by his precepts; dispelling our despondency by his example; and encouraging his troops to submit to their many privations, by the cheerfulness with which he participated in their wants, he imparted the energy of his own mind to the country, and infused his high toned spirit into his army.* His efforts were crowned with success, and the young Frenchman, with the judgment, skill, and prudence of a veteran, seared the laurels of that British general, who, in the north and in the south, in the cabinet and in the field, had stood pre-eminent,—the bulwark of great Britain—the terror of America.

No American ought to pass over the interesting occurrences of this period without reflecting, that the defence of the great state of Virginia, and with it, of all the states in the Union, was conducted with consummate fidelity and skill, by two foreigners, whom the voice of Providence had called to our aid from countries almost unknown to us, and from nations which, until that time, we had regarded only with feelings of hostility.†

Cornwallis, when he reached Portsmouth, proceeded with diligence to embark the troops destined for the defence of

* H. Lee's Memoirs, Vol. II, page 233.

† Johnson's Life Greene, Vol. II, p. 58.

New-York: in the meantime, however, he received countermanding orders, directing him to return to Williamsburg, to retain all the troops he had with him, and instead of Portsmouth, to establish the intended post at Old Point Comfort. The principal causes which determined general Clinton to embrace this new resolution, were the arrival from Europe of a re-enforcement consisting of three thousand Germans, and his desire to open a passage by way of Hampton and the James River, toward that fertile and populous part of Virginia which lies between the James and York rivers: The report of the engineer and navy officers, appointed to examine Old Point Comfort, was unfavourable, and lord Cornwallis, coinciding in the same opinion, selected York and Gloucester, not far above the mouth of York River, instead of the former place.

York town is a port of entry, and post-town, of Virginia, and the capital of York county. It is agreeably situated on the south side of York River, which is here contracted to the breadth of a mile, and confined by very high banks, close under which vessels of the largest burden may ride with safety. On the opposite, or left bank, of the river is situated Gloucester, a smaller town, built upon a point of land projecting into the river. A marshy stream flowing on the right of Yorktown; and in front of the place, for the distance of a mile, the ground is open and level. As the spot which proved the terminating scene of the revolution, its name will be revered by posterity, while liberty has an advocate, and reason and humanity, a friend.

Before the twenty-third of August, 1781, the whole British force had concentrated in the position of York and Gloucester. With a regular army of more than seven thousand men, lord Cornwallis had retreated to the sea-coast before one of not more than two thousand, three hundred, regulars; he had first crowded the transports which had been sent from New-York, with his troops, then re-landed them, and finally, breaking up from Portsmouth and Norfolk, took up his head-quarters at York-town. Upon this ground, he applied his attention to intrench himself in the strongest possible manner, and pressed forward, with zeal and assiduity, the completion of his fortifications.

As soon as Lafayette received intelligence of the new position taken by Cornwallis, he re-crossed the Pamunkey, and took post in the county of New-Kent. He had no intention of attacking the enemy, because, at that period, his force did not admit of it; but he was disposed, at least, to harass them, to repress their excursions, and to prevent their foraging in the country. In the defence of Virginia, with which he had been entrusted by Washington, he had acquitted himself in the most satisfactory and masterly manner; sometimes by his manœuvres, holding the greatest British general in America, in check,—sometimes combating him with vigour—he had now conducted him to a place, where he might hope to be assisted by the powerful French fleet that was expected on the American coast.

At a conference held between Washington and Rochambeau, the siege of New York had been resolved upon by the two generals, who agreed that it was necessary to wrest from the English that shelter which, from the commencement of hostilities to the present hour, had been so favourable to their interests. All the movements of the combined armies were, from that time, directed toward this object.—But it is not our province particularly to detail the causes which led to the relinquishment of that plan, and transferred the principal scene of war to the state of Virginia. Suffice it to say, that the arrival of the German re-enforcements at New York, the great strength of the garrison, the failure of the states in filling up their battalions and embodying their militia, and, especially, recent intelligence from the count de Grasse, that his destination was fixed to the Chesapeake, made a total change in the plan of the campaign. General Washington had entertained apprehensions, early in the month of August, that he would be unable to accomplish his favourite object, and took the precaution of placing himself in the most convenient condition to march to Virginia, should he be compelled to abandon the design on New-York.—Never was a game better played when the commander-in-chief at length made his final decision to march against Cornwallis. Notwithstanding he had changed his plan, he resolved to nourish the fears of his adversary for New-York, by a series of the most spirited demonstrations, so that he might not penetrate his real design, and throw obstacles in the way of its accomplishment. The various stratagems practised to deceive sir Henry Clinton perfectly succeeded; and that general, full of apprehensions for the safety of New-York, was indefatigable in multiplying its defences.

The change in the plan of operations, which had before been suggested to Lafayette as probable, was now communicated to that nobleman, as certain; and he was requested to make such a disposition of his army as should be best calculated to prevent lord Cornwallis from saving himself by a sudden march to Charleston. He also addressed the governor of Virginia, urging him to exert all his powers in preparing certain specified aids of men, provisions, wagons, and implements, which the conjuncture demanded. The most positive intelligence was soon received by Lafayette, that lord Cornwallis intended to penetrate, with his army from York to South Carolina, by land, and that in consequence of the arrival of the French fleet, he was about moving from York to James River, and was getting his boats across from Queen's creek to the College-landing, to go from thence to James-town, and then crossing James River to Cobhams, to proceed from that place to South Carolina. These indications of a movement to the south were immediately communicated to general Greene, who, in order to counteract it, crossed the Santee river on the twelfth of September, and despatched orders in every direction for the collection of reenforcements. General Lafayette and governor Burke had been long on their guard against this movement. The former moved to the bank of James River to counteract it; and Muhlenburg was thrown across the river to place himself in lord Cornwallis' front;—not with the hope of resisting him in his progress, but with a view to precede him, and by destroying all the means of subsistence and transportation, to impede his progress until he could be overtaken by a force competent to cope with him.*

Upon the first intelligence of this movement of Cornwallis, the most animated measures were adopted by governor Burke, to co-operate with Muhlenburg. Every boat on the Roanoke, Neuse, and Meherrin, were secured under guard or destroyed; every crossing place guarded, and crossed by abatis, and the militia were ordered out *en masse.* The whole state of North Carolina, from the Dan to the sea-coast, appears to have been set in motion by this active governor.

Lord Cornwallis had provided a number of boats, transportable on wagons, in the nature of pontons; and the reasons which led to the relinquishment of his project of retreat southwardly, are easily deducible from the occurrences of the day. The French fleet arrived in the Chesapeake on the first of September; a few days after, the British fleet, under admiral Greaves, made its appearance, and count de Grasse stood out of the Chesapeake, and engaged him, having first furnished an accession of strength to Lafayette, which put it in his power to advance upon, and alarm, his adversary. This was the period of the attempt of lord Cornwallis to escape into Carolina, and also of its relinquishment. The arrival of the French fleet suggested the movement; its departure delayed it, until he found himself environed with difficulties. Below him, he saw the whole country in arms to oppose his retreat, whilst Greene waited in the south to receive him on the point of the bayonet; above him, Lafayette watched his opportunity of striking when he should expose

* Johnson's Life Greene, Vol. II. chap. XVI, p. 243. *et seq.*

his flank: toward the ocean, the face of the bay was covered with the fleets of France, and Washington was advancing to seize him in his toils. Yet, it was not until the thirtieth of September, that he found himself entirely hemmed in on the south, and compelled to cover himself beneath the shield of his entrenchments.

On the thirtieth of August, the count de Grasse arrived in the Chesapeake with twenty-eight sail of the line and several frigates. As soon as he anchored, he was boarded by an officer from Lafayette, announcing his situation, and that of the enemy. In consequence of this information, he immediately detached four ships of the line to block up York River, and employed some of his frigates in conveying the land forces, brought from the West Indies under the command of the marquis de St. Simon, up James River, to form a junction with Lafayette at Williamsburg. These troops were principally drawn from the garrison of St. Domingo. and amounted to three thousand, two hundred men. General Lafayette was extremely gratified by being re-enforced with so considerable a number of his own countrymen, and at the increasing prospect of being able to render important services to a cause in which he had engaged with such noble and inextinguishable ardour. He had, moreover, felt some disquietude relative to his position. He was apprehensive that Cornwallis, perceiving the circle that was traced around him, would profit of the superiority which he still possessed, and by falling upon, and overwhelming him, escape into the Carolinas.—On the twenty-fifth of August, the count de Barras sailed from Newport, Rhode Island, with eight ships of the line, and fourteen transports laden with heavy artillery and military stores, proper for carrying on a siege, and formed a junction with de Grasse on the fourteenth of September, in the Chesapeake.

On the fifth of September, a British fleet, commanded by admiral Greaves, appeared off the Chesapeake bay. Orders were immediately given by de Grasse for the ships to slip their cables, and leaving their anchorage ground, severally to form the line as they should come up. An indecisive engagement took place, and neither admiral could claim the victory. For five successive days, the hostile fleets continued in view of each other, and as the French generally maintained the wind, it was in the power of de Grasse at any time to renew the engagement. But the capture of the British army in Virginia, was an object of too much importance to be put in hazard by an action, which might have lost the command of the Chesapeake. He was sensible of his advantages, and would not refer to the caprices of fortune, the decision of events which he considered himself as already certain of controlling. He fought for the undisturbed possession of the Chesapeake, and this was yielded by the enemy's return into port. A chief object, moreover, was to cover the fleet of count de Barras, expected from Rhode Island, whom, on his return, he found safely anchored in the Chesapeake, having passed the British squadron in the night.*

In the mean time general Washington prepared to execute the new plan of operations which he had formed. On the nineteenth of August, the whole American army was put in motion, and on the twentieth and twenty-first, the troops crossed the Hudson, and proceeded by forced marches through New Jersey, to Trenton upon the Delaware. The allied army pressed its march with all possible despatch; and the van division, when it reached Elkton on the northern extremity of the Chesapeake bay, embarked in transports collected for its conveyance. The centre division continued its march to Baltimore, where it also embarked; and the remainder of the troops, and some of the baggage, proceeded by land through Alexandria and Fredericksburg.

General Washington, attended by the count de Rocham-

* Botta's American War, Vol. III, Book XIII, p. 382, 3. H. Lee's Memoirs, Vol. II. Chap. XXXIV. p. 317—320. Marshall's Washington, Vol. IV. Chap. IX, p. 470—472.

beau and the chevalier de Chastelleux, reached Williamsburg, the head-quarters of Lafayette, on the fourteenth of September, and proceeding immediately to Hampton, went on board the *Ville de Paris*, where the plan of the siege was concerted with count de Grasse.—The gallant Lafayette now had a fresh opportunity of exerting his personal influence in favour of the land in defence of whose liberties he had shed his blood. De Grasse, having received information that six ships of the line, under the command of admiral Digby, had reached New York, considered it certain that the British fleet would be induced, by this addition to its strength, to attempt every thing for the relief of lord Cornwallis. Thinking his present situation unfavourable for a naval combat, he designed to change it; and communicated to general Washington his intention to leave a few frigates, to block up the mouths of James and York rivers, and to put to sea with his fleet in quest of the enemy. If they should not have left the harbour of New York, he proposed to block them up in that place. The commander-in-chief was exceedingly alarmed at this communication. Such a measure would have exposed to the caprice of fortune, an event of infinite importance, which was now reduced to almost certain calculation. The marquis de Lafayette was accordingly despatched on board the Ville de Paris, with a letter dissuading count de Grasse from so dangerous a measure: but it is believed that, without the interference and personal application of the marquis, the French admiral would have persevered in carrying into execution a design, which might have given to the enemy, during his absence, a temporary naval superiority in those waters, and the army of Cornwallis might then, with the loss of his artillery, and a few men, have been placed in perfect security. When we consider that the capture of Cornwallis sealed the destinies of the union,—that his escape would have protracted the war, and entirely changed the prosperous aspect of public affairs—and that a long series of bloodshed and desolation would have been thereby renewed,—we must regard this happy exercise of personal influence and persuasive talent, as one among the brightest acts in his American career of glory.

The last division of the allied army landed in the neighbourhood of Williamsburg, on the twenty-fifth of September, and the whole force being now collected, it moved, on the twenty-eighth, in four columns, toward York-town, and sat down about two miles in front of the enemy. The next day the right wing, consisting of Americans, extended further to the right, and occupied the ground east of Beaver-dam creek; while the left wing, consisting of the French, was stationed on the west side of that creek. In the course of the night, lord Cornwallis withdrew within his inner lines, and the subsequent day, the abandoned ground was occupied by Washington, ready to open trenches, whenever the ordnance, and other requisite implements, arrived at camp. Notwithstanding his indefatigable exertions, their transportation was not completed before the sixth of October. In the mean time a rigid blockade of the post of Gloucester was instituted by general Choise, after a sharp skirmish, which resulted in the defeat of the British.———

On the night of the sixth of October, the first parallel was commenced within six hundred yards of the British lines, and as every man observed profound silence, no discovery of the operation took place before the return of daylight, by which time the trenches were in such forwardness as to cover the men. Before the tenth, several batteries and redoubts were completed along the fosse, many of them mounted, which, opening in succession, dismounted and silenced a number of the enemy's guns, and demolished their works in different places. When all the batteries on the first parallel were completed, the fire, on the eleventh and twelfth, became so heavy, that it tore in pieces most of the enemy's batteries, dismounting their ordnance in every direction. The shells and red hot balls reached even the ships in the harbour where the Charon, of forty-four guns, and three transports, were entirely consumed.

Washington now continued to urge his operations, and, on the night of the eleventh, opened his second parallel, within three hundred yards of the British lines. The same order was given, commanding silence, which was strictly observed, and the trench was nearly completed before the dawn of day. Notwithstanding the unexampled rapidity with which the siege was conducted, and the unexpected condition in which he now found himself involved, lord Cornwallis, relying on succour from New-York, determined, with unappalled courage, to maintain his lines. He endeavoured to arrest the progress of the besiegers by a deluge of bombs and balls, and during the three succeeding days, which were devoted to the completion of the second parallel, and of the batteries constructed in it, the fire of the garrison became more destructive than at any other time.

Two redoubts, advanced three hundred yards in front of the enemy's works, flanked the second parallel, and directed their fire with severe effect. It was necessary to possess these redoubts, and Washington determined to silence them with the bayonet. To avail himself of the spirit of emulation existing between the troops of the two nations, the attack of the one was committed to the Americans, and of the other, to the French. The American detachment composed of light infantry, was commanded by the marquis de Lafayette, who conducted the assault in person, and the baron de Viominil led the grenadiers and chasseurs of France, against the redoubt, which, being farther toward the British right, approached rather nearer to the French lines. Major Campbell, with sixty men, defended the first, and lieutenant-colonel Johnson, with one hundred and seventy men defended the latter, redoubt. On the fourteenth of October, as soon as it was dark, the two detachments marched with equal firmness to the assault. The attack was extremely impetuous. On its success depended, in a great measure, that of the siege.

Relying entirely on their bayonets, the Americans advanced with unloaded arms, and rushed to the charge with so much ardour, that they did not allow the sappers time to remove the abatis and pallisades. Passing over them, they assaulted the works with irresistible impetuosity on all sides at once, and entered them with such rapidity, that their loss was inconsiderable, and the enemy, astonished at so much audacity, was instantly overpowered. Major Campbell, a captain, an ensign, and seventeen privates, were made prisoners; eight privates were killed, and a few escaped. On the part of the Americans, one sergeant and eight privates, were killed; and one lieutenant-colonel, four captains, one subaltern, one sergeant, and twenty-five rank and file wounded.—The redoubt upon the left made a more formidable resistance; but the intrepidity of the assailants was irresistible, and it was carried with the bayonet. The commandant escaped; eighteen men were killed; and forty-two, among whom were a captain and two subaltern officers, were made prisoners. The loss of the assailants was very severe, being about one hundred in killed and wounded.

The humanity of the conquerors was equal to their courage. Notwithstanding the recent horrid and barbarous outrage committed at Fort Griswold, in Connecticut, where the greater part of the garrison was murdered in cold blood by a detachment under the command of the apostate Arnold, who reduced the town of New-London to ashes, and where the sword surrendered by the commanding officer of the fort, colonel Ledyard, was immediately plunged into his bosom,—notwithstanding these diabolical deeds, the irritation which they produced had not so far subdued the humanity of the American character as to induce retaliation. Not a man was killed except in action. "Incapable," said colonel Hamilton in his report, "of imitating examples of barbarity, and forgetting recent provocation, the soldiery spared every man that ceased to resist." Nevertheless, Mr. Gordon, in his History of the American war, states, that orders were given by Lafayette, with the approbation of Washington, that every man in the redoubt, after its surrender, should be put to the sword. This charge is absolutely false. These sanguinary orders, so repugnant to the character of Washington, and of Lafayette, were never given. There is no trace of them among the papers of the commander-in-chief; and colonel Hamilton, whose participation in the enterprise assures his perfect knowledge of every material occurrence, has publicly contradicted the statement.*

Washington was highly gratified with the splendid termination of this double assault, which was no less useful to the allies than it was honourable to their arms. He remarks in his diary, that "the bravery exhibited by the attacking troops was emulous and praiseworthy. Few cases have exhibited greater proofs of intrepidity, coolness, and firmness, than were shown on this occasion." The orders of the succeeding day expressed a high sense of the judicious dispositions and gallant conduct of both the marquis de Lafayette and the baron de Viominil, and conclude in the following manner: "The general reflects, with the highest degree of pleasure, on the confidence which the troops of the two nations must hereafter have in each other. Assured of mutual support, he is convinced there is no danger which they will not cheerfully encounter,—no difficulty which they will not bravely overcome."

Nothing could exceed the vigour with which Washington now urged on his operations: before daylight the two redoubts were included in the second parallel; and by five in the afternoon some howitzers, which had been placed in them, were opened on the besieged.

The situation of Cornwallis was now become desperate: he perfectly foresaw that when the besiegers should have opened the fire of the batteries of their second parallel, all means of resistance would be at an end. The greater part

* Marshall's Life Washington, Vol. IV, Chap. IX, p. 486. *note.* Garden's Anecdotes, p. 308.

of his artillery was dismounted, broken, or otherwise disabled; the walls were crumbled into the ditches, in a word, almost all the defences were razed. He therefore resolved by a vigorous sortie, to retard, as much as possible the completion of the batteries in the second parallel. A detachment, accordingly, sallied from the town, on the night of the sixteenth of October, who made themselves masters of two batteries, guarded by French troops. But they were furiously charged by the Vicomte de Noailles, who drove them before him into the town, and the few cannon which they had hastily spiked, were soon rendered fit for service.

Cornwallis now found himself reduced to the alternative of surrendering, or of attempting his escape. Incapable of submitting so long as such an event could possibly be avoided, he proposed, with profound secrecy, to pass his army in the night to Gloucester, garnishing the works with his convalescents, and leaving behind his baggage of every sort, his sick, wounded, shipping, and stores. He intended, after cutting to pieces, or dispersing the troops which invested Gloucester, to force his way through Maryland, Pennsylvania, and New-Jersey, and form a junction with the army in New York. In prosecution of this bold and desperate attempt, he passed over, early in the night, the first division of his army to Gloucester, the other division being ready to embark for the same shore as soon as the boats returned. But the decree of Providence rendered his plan abortive. A violent storm of wind and rain suddenly arose, and forced the returning boats down the river, considerably below the town. Day appeared before they reached their destination; and the forenoon was occupied in bringing back the troops which had passed.

On the seventeenth, the second parallel was completed, and the besiegers opened a tremendous fire from all their batteries, showering the bombs copiously, even into the river. The enemy's defences were every where falling under the destructive fire; and Cornwallis, being sensible that his position was no longer tenable, and preferring the lives of his brave troops to the honour they might have acquired in a murderous and desperate assault, sent a flag to Washington, proposing a cessation of arms for twenty-four hours, and that commissioners might be appointed on both sides for settling the terms of capitulation. Two hours only were granted; and this armistice resulted, after a series of negotiations, during which the suspension of hostilities was prolonged, in the final surrender by lord Cornwallis, on the nineteenth of October, 1781, of the posts of York and Gloucester Point, with the garrisons which had defended them, and the shipping in the harbour with their seamen, to the land and naval officers of America and France.*

It is stated† that Cornwallis, struck with the persevering skill and gallantry of Lafayette, of which he was a feeling and competent judge, requested, as a favour, that he might treat with, and surrender his army to him alone; but general Lincoln was appointed to receive the submission of the royal army, precisely in the same manner as his own had been conducted, about eighteen months before.

General Lafayette, ranked among the most active and intrepid of the general officers at the siege of York-town, and promoted with unceasing perseverance the completion of the glorious scheme, to which his efforts had so long been directed. In the orders issued the day after the capitulation, he was particularly mentioned by the commander-in-chief: and when we consider the long series of dangers and skilful manœuvres, by which he finally conducted Cornwallis into the toils of Washington, we must justly bestow upon the youthful warrior, a large portion of the glory which at-

* The articles of capitulation were digested by lieutenant colonel Laurens, and the viscount de Noailles, of the allied army, and colonel Dundas, and major Ross, on the part of the British. It is remarkable, that while colonel Laurens was drawing up these articles, his father was closely confined in the Tower of London, of which lord Cornwallis was constable. By this singular combination of circumstances, his lordship became a prisoner to the son of his own prisoner.

† Mem. Histor. et Pieces Authent. sur M. de Lafayette, p. 8, 9.

tended the extermination of the British flag from the shores of the Union.

The news of this glorious and important victory created transports of joy from one extremity of the Union to the other. The remembrance of past evils was universally lost amid the most brilliant anticipations. The firm establishment of independence was no longer doubted; and every one looked forward with confidence to the fast approaching termination of their toils and privations. In all parts of the United States, solemn festivals and rejoicings celebrated the triumph of American fortune, and the downfall of that of the enemy. The names of Washington,—Rochambeau,—de Grasse,—Lafayette,—resounded every where. The provincial assemblies, the universities, the literary societies, addressed to them, the sincere homage of their felicitations and admiration.—Congress united the authority of its decrees to the unanimous acclaim of the people. It addressed thanks to the generals, as well as to the officers and soldiers of the victorious army. It ordained that a marble column should be erected at York-town, adorned with emblems of the alliance between the United States a[illegible] the king of France, and inscribed with a succint narra[illegible] of the surrender of Cornwallis. Nor did they stop here. Desirous that the chiefs of the allied forces should carry with them into retirement, some of the trophies of their prowess, they presented to Washington, two of the standards taken from the enemy; to admiral de Grasse, two field pieces; and a like number to general Rochambeau. They repaired in a body to the Dutch Lutheran Church, to return thanks to Almighty God, for the recent victory; and issued a special proclamation appointing the thirteenth day of December, as a day of general thanksgiving and prayer, on account of so signal an interposition of divine Providence.*

* For accounts of the siege and surrender of York, *vide* Marshall's Washington, Vol. IV, Chap. IX, p. 485.—498. Ramsay's Revolution, p, 559—562. Thacher's Journal, p. 536. Johnson's Greene, Vol. II, p. 64, 66, 243, 5. H. Lee's Memoirs, Vol. II. p. 245 246, 307. 375 Andrew's

Soon after the surrender of York, the personal influence of Lafayette was again called in requisition by the commander-in-chief. In a letter addressed to the count de Grasse, Washington had urged every argument to prevail on him to give his aid to an expedition against Charleston. To enforce the representations contained in his letter, he repaired on board the admiral's ship, the Ville de Paris, in company with Lafayette; and on his return, left that nobleman for the purpose of using his influence in support of the request which had been made. But all was unavailing; and de Grasse conclusively replied, that "the orders of his court, ulterior projects, and his engagements with the Spaniards, rendered it impossible for him to remain on the coast, during the time which would be required for the operation." The marquis, however, obtained his consent to convoy a detachment of two thousand Americans to Wilmington, and to cover their landing. This corps, which was destined to re-enforce the army of general Greene, was put under the command of Lafayette, with orders to possess himself of Wilmington, situated fifteen miles up the Cape Fear, which was still held by the British, and thence to march to the southern head-quarters. As the time of embarkation approached, the admiral found it necessary to recede from this engagement, from the necessity of being in the West Indies at a certain time, and the American commander was thus deprived of the advantage to be derived from the facile and expeditious conveyance of his re-enforcement as at first arranged.*

Preparations were accordingly made for marching them by land. But Lafayette was once more arrested in his southern progress. Negotiations for peace soon demanded his

American War, Vol. IV. 194, 5. Stedman's American War, Vol. II. Notice Biograph. p. 6. Garden's Anecdotes, p. 307, 308. Botta's Amer. War, Vol. III, p. 374, 401, Port Folio, Vol. XIX, p. 502. Toulongeon, History de France, Vol. I, Append. p. 97. Mem. Hist. sur M. de Lafayette, p. 8, 9. 20, 34.

* H Lee's Memoirs, Vol. II, p. 370, 1. Marshall's Washington, Vol IV. p, 500. 1.

presence in Europe, to lend to the American cause the aid of his industry and zeal. Apprehensions were entertained that France was not ardent in her wishes for peace; and the influence and intelligence of the marquis, it was thought, would contribute to the support of the American negotiation. Previous to his departure from York-town, he issued his last affectionate orders to his favourite corps of infantry, in which are contained the following expressions: "In the moment the major-general leaves this place, he wishes once more to express his gratitude to the brave corps of light infantry, who, for nine months past, have been the companions of his fortunes. He will never forget, that with them alone, of regular troops, he had the good fortune to manœuvre before an army, which, after all its reductions, is still *six times superior* to the regular force he had at that time."

In the month of November, 1781, general Lafayette proceeded to Philadelphia, where he was hailed with joyful acclamations, and received the most flattering marks of gratitude and respect from the inhabitants. To whatever quarter he directed his steps, he was accompanied with the admiration and applause of the people; and his journey was one perpetuated scene of joy and festivity.

The field for military operations was now very much contracted; important negotiations were pending in Europe, both with regard to supplies and peace; and the marquis, believing that he might more effectually serve the cause of America by his presence beyond the Atlantic, again obtained leave to embark for France. The credit which he possessed at the court of France, and the use which, from his avowed attachment to the United States, he would probably make of it, induced congress to add to the resolutions which expressed their sense of his meritorious services, others, requesting their ministers in Europe to confer with him on the situation of American affairs, and to employ his assistance in accelerating such supplies as might be afforded by his most christian majesty. In granting his request for leave of absence, congress, on the twenty-third of November,

Resolved, That major-general the marquis de Lafayette have permission to go to France; and that he return at such time as shall be most convenient to him.

That he be informed, that on a review of his conduct throughout the past campaign, and particularly during the period in which he had the chief command in Virginia, the many new proofs which present themselves of his zealous attachment to the cause he has espoused, and of his judgment, vigilance, gallantry, and address, in its defence, have greatly added to the high opinion entertained by congress of his merits and military talents.

That he make known to the officers and troops whom he commanded during that period, that the brave and enterprising services with which they seconded his zeal and efforts, and which enabled him to defeat the attempts of an enemy far superior in numbers, have been beheld by congress with particular satisfaction and approbation:

That the secretary of foreign affairs acquaint the ministers plenipotentiary of the United States, that it is the design of congress that they confer with the marquis de Lafayette, and avail themselves of his information relative to the situation of public affairs in the United States:

That the secretary for foreign affairs further acquaint the minister plenipotentiary at the court of Versailles, that he will conform to the intention of congress by consulting with, and employing the assistance of, the marquis de Lafayette, in accelerating the supplies which may be afforded by his most christian majesty, for the use of the United States:

That the superintendant of finance, the secretary for foreign affairs, and the board of war, make such communications to the marquis de Lafayette, touching the affairs of their respective departments, as will best enable him to fulfil the purpose of the two resolutions immediately preceding:

That the superintendant of finance take order for discharging the engagements entered into by the marquis de Lafayette, with the merchants of Baltimore, referred to in the act of the twenty-fourth of May last.*

Ordered, That the superintendant of finance furnish the marquis de Lafayette, with a proper conveyance to France:

That the secretary for foreign affairs report a letter to his most Christian majesty, to be sent by the marquis de Lafayette.

In addition to these testimonials of the love, gratitude, and confidence, of the national legislature, he was furnished by the great Robert Morris, superintendant of finance, with a most flattering letter to his excellency, Benjamin Franklin, minister in France, dated the twenty-seventh of November, 1781, of which the following is an extract:

"Sir,

"The marquis de Lafayette who is about to sail for France, will have the honour to deliver this letter, and, consistently with the acts of congress of the twenty-third instant, I must request you to communicate it to him; and, from time to time, to take his aid in the prosecution of the business which I must recommend to your particular attention. The affairs

* This resolution refers to the supply of shoes, &c. procured by the marquis on his private credit in Baltimore, in the month of April. On the twenty-fourth of May, 1781, congress adopted the following resolutions:

Resolved, That congress entertain a just sense of the patriotic and timely exertions of the merchants of Baltimore, who so generously supplied the marquis de Lafayette, with about two thousand guineas, to enable him to forward the detachment under his command:

That the marquis de Lafayette be assured that congress will take proper measures to discharge the engagements he has entered into with the merchants.

From these resolutions, it would appear that the marquis merely acted as the agent of congress; and no one would imagine from their tenor, that that body had not sufficient credit to procure the loan, and that Lafayette, accomplished it on his private responsibility.—It would have been more noble to have acknowledged the obligation, and voted to the marquis the thanks which he deserved. It might have wounded the self-pride of members, as individuals, but would have exalted the national legislature.

of my department are of a nature not to require concealment: but even if that were not the case, I have such perfect confidence, as well in the prudence of the marquis, as in his attachment to this country, that, the acts of congress out of the question, I should feel a pleasure in making him acquainted with my views and wishes. Indeed, I expect that his zeal and activity will go far in smoothing the way towards the accomplishment of those objects which your excellency has to solicit."

In the month of December, 1781, he embarked for Europe, accompanied by the affections and regrets, and loaded with the gratitude, of the American people.

The affection which the marquis bore toward the illustrious Washington was as pure and as holy, as that of a lover towards his mistress. Far from presuming to endeavour to scale the height upon which Washington stood,—a height inaccessible to any other man;—far from attempting to divide with him the wonder and veneration of the world;—he looked up to him only as a father and a friend, and as a model, which though he would never equal, he might yet copy at a distance. During the intrigues that were in agitation against his revered patron, in the year 1778, which had for their object the deposition of the commander-in-chief, Lafayette, like another Patroclus, buckled on his armour in defence of his Achilles, who disdained to notice the malignant attacks of those restless spirits, whose only aim was the aggrandizement of themselves and their friends at the expense of others. As to general Conway, who was the most busy actor in the cabal, and one of the most wily and inveterate intriguers that had passed from Europe to America, the marquis de Lafayette, and, led by his example, all the other French officers of distinction regarded him with contempt, and seldom deigned to notice him at all. This Conway, after puffing himself off as an officer of great consequence, obtaining, by the lowest artifices, the appointment of major-general, displaying his total want of military science—exhibiting his cowardice by skulking into a farm-house at the battle of Germantown,—and resigning his commission because he was too much despised to be employed—was shot in a duel by general Cadwalader, for having dared to indulge too freely in unbecoming expressions regarding the commander-in-chief. Believing his wound to be mortal, he retracted, in a letter to general Washington, dated the twenty-third of July, 1778, all the falsehoods which he had circulated against him; but, recovering from his wound, he returned to France, covered with ignominy. The whole junto were soon desirous of burying their ambitious schemes in oblivion.—The most affectionate attachment indeed existed between general Lafayette and the commander-in-chief, beneath whose banners it was his delight to serve. The language of Washington, respecting his adopted son, was, "this nobleman unites to all the military fire of youth, an uncommon maturity of judgment."

The influence, the fortune, and the blood, of the marquis de Lafayette, were all devoted to the service of America. He was engaged in her cause, either in a political or military capacity, during almost the whole course of the war. When he was not animating his brave followers in the field of battle, or disciplining them in the camp, he was unfolding the comprehensiveness and soundness of his understanding in the cabinet, or pressing, at the court of France, with all his influence and eloquence, the policy and necessity of supporting the efforts of struggling America. His very soul burned with the spirit of enterprise; and he manifested a disinterestedness and devotion in the cause of freedom, which should ever be admired and applauded by a grateful people. Possessed of unshaken patriotism, integrity, and humanity, and of those cardinal virtues which characterise real greatness of soul, he always discovered, both in design and execution, those traits of genius, and that intuitive knowledge of tactics, which designate the great man, and the successful warrior. It was no ordinary mind that could lead its pos sessor, in the very outset of life, in the spring-tide of worldly joy, to sacrifice all the common charms of existence, to the higher claims of a laudable ambition. Many of those who flocked to our shores were tempted by the hope of gain: but the principles which guided Lafayette from all the comforts of life to the wilderness of the western world, were as pure as the cause, in support of which, his sword now leaped from its scabbard. Congress was elated, encouraged and flattered by an auxiliary of such high rank, of so much spirit, and such great promise, and were not deceived in the expectations which they formed of the future services of this "noble phænomenon."—The perseverance of the marquis through so many discouraging vicissitudes, and his noble generosity in seasons of peculiar distress, show him in a great and elevated point of view, having few parallels in history. Had he arrived on our shores, a poor and needy adventurer, a ready hireling in any cause where pay and plunder might have been expected,—had he merely, with a fleeting enthusiasm, hastily engaged in the American cause as a quixotic crusader, for some momentary feat of chivalry,—he would have ranked with the ordinary class of adventurers, found in all ages and countries in time of war. As such, he would have shrunk from the appalling scenes exhibited by a starving, naked, and retreating army;—he would have fled from the delays and vexations attending the tardiness of the different states in supplying their quota of men and money; or probably, joined in the mutinies and desertions so frequent during the revolutionary war. But he was governed by motives too exalted and powful to be depressed even by disastrous campaigns, unremitted vigilance, and arduous service, from year to year, in watching and opposing a well disciplined and powerful enemy.* His love of liberty burned too fiercely to be extinguished or diminished, either by perils or privations.

"On seeing the marquis," says Chastelleux, "one is at a

* Short Biography, Lafayette, p. 8.

loss which most to admire, that so young a man should have given such eminent proofs of talents, or that a man so tried, should give hopes of so long a career of glory." He was the true disciple of Washington, gifted with those rare endowments, and that pre-eminence of character, which distinguished the heroes of antiquity. He endured calumny with the calmness of a stoic, and sustained misfortune with the resignation of a christian, and the firmness of a man. His courage was only equalled by his humanity; and he gained universal praise for his benevolence and compassion, in visiting and administering relief to the wounded soldiers. Although arms were his vocation, his professional duties were always tempered with humanity; and he preferred the lives of his brave soldiers, to the chance of decorating his brows with blood-stained laurels. When he was re-enforced, in Virginia, by three thousand, two hundred Frenchmen, under the marquis de St. Simon, he was strongly urged by that nobleman, and admiral de Grasse, to attack lord Cornwallis. But he steadfastly resisted their entreaties, and declined the opportunity of covering himself with the glory which a victory would have obtained. Wishing that blood might be spared, he quietly awaited the arrival of generals Washington and Rochambeau from the north, with a force adequate to look down the opposition of despair itself.

From his easy, affable, and engaging manners, Lafayette was particularly endeared to the officers and soldiers under his command; they admired, loved, and revered him, as their guide and support when in peril, and their warmest friend when in perplexity and trouble. He was beloved, indiscriminately, by the whole army, not only for that amiable disposition, and those charming manners, but for his great gallantry, and ardent attachment to his country. The confidence and affection of the troops, were, to him, invaluable possessions, and well acquired riches, of which no one could, and no one desired, to deprive him; and he always expressed, by his air and countenance, that he was happier in receiving his friends at their head, than at his estate in Auvergne. The influence and consideration which he acquired among the political, as well as the military body, were highly flattering to a young man of his age ; and it is confidently asserted that his private letters have frequently produced more effect in arousing the lethargy of some of the states, than the strongest exhortations of Congress. In short, he possessed, in so high a degree, the character of an accomplished and perfect soldier, as to gain the confidence of his superiors, the affection of his equals, and the respect and veneration of all who served under him. It is no trifling compliment to say, that next to the commander-in chief, and the intrepid Greene, no general stood higher in the public favour, or more constantly commanded the admiration of the army than Lafayette.

Nor did his solicitude for the *public* welfare of America bound his exertions ; for he was ever ready to aid our fellow citizens when distressed in Europe ; and oftentimes even without being called upon. Some he rescued from poverty, by opening to them his purse ; others, he counselled and defended. His protecting arm stretched itself beyond the Pyrenees and snatched the indiscreet American, either from the fangs of the officer of the customs, or from the dark and unforgiving tribunals of the inquisition. His succour unhappily came too late on one of these melancholy occasions ; and his letter, on that subject, to the late Samuel Breck, esquire, dated in Paris, second June, 1785, is an additional evidence of the correctness of his feelings and the goodness of his heart :

" As soon as your letter came to hand," the marquis writes, " I addressed the count de Florida Blanca, the Spanish prime minister, in behalf of Mr. H. Enclosed you will find his answer, and also the copy of an account given to Mr. Carmichael, whereby I was much affected to hear poor Mr. H. is no more. For fear of disgusting the minister with the application, I had, in some measure, refrained from exposing the horror I feel for the hellish tribunal; but it was superfluous; and I beg you will assure Mr. H's friends that I am heartily sorry not to have it in my power to give them a more agreeable account."*

On the twentieth of April, 1787, a fire was discovered in a malt-house, in Beach-street, Boston, which consumed about one hundred buildings, sixty of which were dwelling houses: in fact, the greater part of the south end of the town was destroyed. As soon as the melancholy news reached Paris, the benevolent Lafayette desired his friend and correspondent, the late Samuel Breck, esquire, of Boston, to draw upon him for *three hundred pounds sterling*, and to distribute that sum among the indigent sufferers. This noble charity, so characteristic of the munificence and goodness of that excellent man, was of the greatest benefit. It served to give bread and shelter to many reduced and houseless families, and, coming in aid of other donations, was one of the principal means of restoring them to their lost comforts. Boston did not then, as at the present day, abound in men of wealth. The alms of its inhabitants were limited by their narrow means; and that town, which now contains so many secure and magnificent edifices, was then built of such combustible materials, that almost every accidental fire ended in a destructive conflagration.† This donation deserves more particular notice, on account of the final adieu which Lafayette had, in all probability, bade to America; as well as from the circumstance, that all his affection for this country was accidentally awakened, amid the great public concerns of France, which then demanded and engrossed his attention by the perusal of a newspaper containing an account of the destruction and distress occasioned by the fire.

The benevolent perseverance with which he pursued the claim of the widow of a revolutionary officer, for the long period of eight years, is not only an evidence of his attachment to this country, and more especially to those who la-

* Port Folio, Vol. XIX, p. 504.
† Port Folio, Vol. XIX, p. 504.

boured with him in the cause of independence, but bespeaks a heart not given to every man. It is gratifying to add, that the claim was brought, by his unremitting and voluntary exertions, to a final and favourable close.—The natural bias of his mind is even developed in the names of his children. His only son bears the distinguished name of George Washington, and his only daughters, in remembrance of "the theatre of his toils and of his glory," those of Virginia and Carolina.

At La Grange he was always accessible to Americans; and his eye kindled whenever he spoke of America. "Why cannot you come and live among us," said a visiter,—"to lay down your bones among a people who owe you so much, and whose latest descendants, will venerate your ashes?"—Lafayette pointed to his grandchildren around him—he made no other reply. They were among the strongest ties which bound him to France.

"You are now in America," he said once to an intelligent Virginian.—"America?"—"Yes; this room is what I call America." His guest looked around him, and beheld every where scattered the tokens of his country: maps of the different states—the portraits of our distinguished men,—of Washington, Franklin, Henry, &c. &c.—American books—and the electrical machine, with which the great Franklin had made so many experiments, and which he had given, as a mark of his respect, to this noble Frenchman.

The people of the United States, fully apprised of the high obligations which they owe to Lafayette,* have practically and triumphantly refuted the pretended dogma of the ingratitude of republics, not only by the spontaneous effusion of affection and veneration which has burst forth from the whole mass of the people, but by the more formal acts of their representatives. On the third of March, 1803, the national legislature passed "an act to revive and continue in force, an act in addition to an act, entitled an act in ad-

* A grand dinner was given to general Lafayette, at the University, Charlottesville, Virginia, on the fifth of November, 1824. On this occasion, an address, by the venerable Mr. Jefferson, was read, which

dition to an act regulating the grants of lands appropriated for military services, &c. &c."

Section 4th. And be it further enacted, that the secretary of war be, and he is hereby, authorised to issue land-warrants to major general Lafayette, for eleven thousand, five hundred, and twenty acres, which shall, at his option, be located, surveyed, and patented, in conformity with the provisions of an act, intituled an act regulating the grants of land appropriated for military services, and for the society of the United Brethren for propagating the gospel among the heathen, or, which may be received, acre for acre, in payment for any of the lands of the United States, north of the river Ohio, and above the mouth of Kentucky river."

The name of Lafayette will continue to be preserved not only in the hearts, but in the laws of the American people: as given to various portions of our territory, it will serve to recall to remembrance the services of him who bore it, when century upon century have been buried in the "dark backward and abysm of time," and when the deeds and virtues of their forefathers shall appear to our posterity, like the bright glories of Rome in her best days, to those who now dwell upon the earth. In all parts of the union, we find the name of Lafayette mingled with the very existence of the republic. In North Carolina, there is a district, one hundred miles in length, and fifty in breadth, called Fayette, in

contains the following remarks. From his official station at the court of France, he is undoubtedly the best judge, now living, of the value of the marquis' services at the period of which he speaks:—"I joy, my friends, in your joy, inspired by the visit of this our ancient and distinguished leader and benefactor. His deeds in the war of Independence, you have heard and read. They are known to you, and embalmed in your memories, and in the pages of faithful history. His deeds, in the peace which followed that war, are perhaps not known to you; but I can attest them. When I was stationed in his country, for the purpose of cementing its friendship with ours, and of advancing our mutual interests, this friend of both was my most powerful auxiliary and advocate. He made our cause his own, as in truth it was that of his native country also. His influence and connexions there, were great. All doors of all departments were open to him at all times; to me, only formally, and at appointed times. In truth, I only held the nail,—he drove it. Honour him, then, as your benefactor in peace, as well as in war.'

which is situated the flourishing town of Fayetteville. In Pennsylvania, there is a county called Fayette, thirty-nine miles long, and twenty-nine broad; and there is another in Kentucky of the same name. There are, also, the town of Fayette in Kennebeck county, Maine, and the township of Fayette, in Alleghany county, Pennsylvania.

The mark of respect and honour shown to the marquis by the legislature of Pennsylvania, in giving to a newly erected county, the name of Fayette, was communicated to him in the following letter from the governor of the state:

"SIR,

"The general assembly has lately erected a considerable part of this state into a county, under the name of *Lafayette;* and the government of it is about to be organized under this new denomination.

"The proclamation of this law has caused me the liveliest satisfaction, as a testimonial of the respect in which you are held by my fellow citizens. My satisfaction will be greatly increased when I learn, that this evidence of the general feeling which your talents and conduct have inspired, has proved agreeable to you.—As governor of this state, it might, perhaps, be proper for me, at this time, to detail to you the reasons that have induced the legislature to award this extraordinary mark of their esteem;—but common language would be inadequate to express my feelings. Moreover, the high idea which we entertain of your character will not permit me to dwell upon that subject. Let the world judge of the merits of your deeds, and the justice of our gratitude. You have been the defender of our liberty: and "the legislative assembly, while they enjoy that liberty, congratulate themselves with the idea, that your name will be henceforth inscribed on the various judicial acts which will continue to be the record, and evidence, of its existence."

To this flattering communication, Lafayette returned the following reply:

'Sir,

"I received your excellency's letter of the sixth of March a short time previous to my departure from France; and I congratulate myself on the prospect of having the honour of personally presenting the tribute of my gratitude to the legislative assembly of this state. The slightest marks of its consideration could not fail to prove extremely flattering to me; but the honour which it has deigned to confer, by giving my name to one of the counties of the state, is so distinguished a proof of its esteem, that I want words to express my gratitude.

"So long as I have had the happiness to be acquainted with this state, its civil and political rights have been dear to me; and I confess that I am sensibly affected with the thought that my name will be united to the administration of laws, whose spirit is so favourable to the rights of human nature.

"I pray your excellency to present to the legislative assembly, the tribute of my lively gratitude and profound respect, and, at the same time, to receive my particular acknowledgments, for the polite and obliging manner in which you have been pleased to communicate the honour which that body has conferred upon me."

General Lafayette arrived in the beginning of the year 1782, in his native country, where he was received with universal respect and admiration. His reception at court was extremely flattering; and wherever he went he was greeted with the same enthusiasm and popular favour that always accompanied his steps in America. The heroic wife of the marquis participated in the homage universally offered to her illustrious consort;—a homage which, from her subsequent conduct, could not have been too affectionate and respectful. *Instar omnium:* a short time before his death, Voltaire was invited to a numerous party at the house of the duke de Choiseul, where he was received with the usual applause which attended him wherever he went. Perceiving the marchioness de Lafayette among the ladies, he kneeled down at her feet, and bestowed the most flattering eulogiums on her husband, who was then in America: madame received this homage with affecting modesty, and embarrassment, mingled with joy. The venerable old man, at the close of his life, experienced the happiness and honour of announcing the return of M. de Lafayette to his native country.* After remaining a short time in Paris, honoured and respected by the court, and almost idolized by the people, he visited his estates in Tourraine; and afterwards proceeded to the courts of many of the German princes, where he received extraordinary marks of the admiration which his political and military conduct had diffused over Europe. He brought even to the court of the Cæsars, as he had done to the pavilions of Versailles, the spirit of a pure and antique attachment to liberty, with the graces of a gallant soldier, and accomplished gentleman; and he was received by Joseph the second, and Frederick the Great, with flattering distinction.

In September, 1782, Lafayette arrived at Pottsdam, anxious to behold the great man who had so long attracted the attention of the world. When Frederick was advised of the arrival of general Lafayette, he invited him to Sans Soucie without delay, where the despot and the defender of liberty, frequently entered into long and interesting conversations. The stern, unbending, and tyrannical Frederick, not only expressed his admiration of Washington and Lafayette, but presented the marquis with his miniature set in diamonds; on this occasion, he remarked, that he hoped this trifling memento would sometimes recall him to recollection. It was in accompanying the king of Prussia to his reviews, that he had an opportunity afforded him of close observation of the military genius of that royal tactician, with which he doubtless enriched his own experience.

From the time of his landing in Europe, Lafayette had incessantly continued his customary exertions in favour of

* Mem. Historiques, p. 118, 119.

America, and he was extremely anxious to accelerate the ratification of the treaty between Great Britain, France, and America, provisional and preliminary articles for which, had been signed, with regard to America, on the thirtieth of November, 1782, and, as they respected France, on the twentieth of January, 1783. At the same time, he strenuously represented to the French government, the evils which might flow from a relaxation in their exertions, and the necessity of compelling Great Britain to consummate a peace, by giving greater and renewed aid to the American cause. His exertions in favour of this country, which he considered a paramount duty, were so valuable and unceasing, as to call forth the particular approbation of congress. On the tenth of April, 1783, it was "*Resolved,* That congress are satisfied with the reasons which have prevailed with major-general the marquis de Lafayette, for his stay in Europe, and his consequent absence from his command in the army of the United States; and have a high sense of the new proofs he has exhibited of his zeal in the cause of the said states, and of his constant attachment to their interests and welfare."

In a long and feeling letter to general Washington, written immediately after his return from the north of Europe, Lafayette exhibits at once his warm affection for the "man of the age," his correct view of the political situation of the United States, and the necessity of a more stable and efficient form of government. In communicating the occurrences at the courts he had visited, and especially at that of Prussia, whose aged and distinguished monarch, uniting the acquirements of the scholar, with the most profound skill in the art of war, could bestow either literary or military fame, he dwelt with enthusiasm on the plaudits which were universally bestowed on his military patron, and paternal friend. "I wish," he remarked, "the other sentiments I have had occasion to discover with respect to America, were equally satisfactory with those that are personal to yourself, I need not say that the spirit, the firmness with which the revolution was conducted, have excited universal admiration; that every friend to the rights of mankind is an enthusiast for the principles on which those constitutions are built;—but I have often had the mortification to hear, that the want of powers in the congress, of union between the states, of energy in their government, would make the confederation very insignificant." "By their conduct in the revolution," he added, "the citizens of America have commanded the respect of the world; but it grieves me to think they will, in a measure, lose it, unless they strengthen the confederation; give congress power to regulate their trade; pay off their debt, or at least the interest of it; establish a well regulated militia; and, in a word, complete all those measures which you have recommended to them."*—Such were the opinions of the best and wisest men of the time; and they resulted in the formation of one of the noblest, and, I trust, most durable monuments of human sagacity and political wisdom to be found in the records of history.

Cabinet negotiations, although, from a sense of duty, so long patiently endured, could now no longer restrain the enterprising courage and spirit of Lafayette. He had been appointed adjutant general to count d'Estaing, an officer grown grey in naval combats, who commanded the French fleet at Cadiz, on board of which were eight thousand French and Spanish troops destined for America. He immediately proceeded to Cadiz, to join this powerful expedition, and was about to set sail in quest of new triumphs, and fresher glories, when the sailing of the fleet was arrested by the news of peace.

As soon as he received this welcome intelligence from Mr. Carmichael, minister of the United States (although not then acknowledged,) at the court of Madrid, the noble hearted Lafayette, with characteristic benevolence, resolved to adopt the most effectual measures to prevent the unneces-

* Marshal's Life of Washington, Vol. V. p. 73.

sary effusion of blood. He immediately applied to the count d'Estaing, requesting him to furnish a fast sailing vessel for the purpose of conveying his despatches, containing the intelligence of the conclusion of the treaty of peace, to America. This request was complied with; and the good ship *Triumph* was soon cleaving her way over the waters of the Atlantic, bearing, to a lacerated country, the healing balm of peace. It was on the afternoon of Sunday, March twenty-third, 1783, when the Triumph cast anchor before the city of Philadelphia, and great and joyful was the sensation which spread itself over the city on the evening of that day. She arrived before the official, or any other account of the peace had been received. The humanity of giving the earliest possible advice of this event—the lives that were saved by the consequent cessation of hostilities, greatly enhances the debt of gratitude due to Lafayette, from the people of the United States.*—The letter of the marquis to congress dated fifth February 1783, accompanied by a copy of an order from the count d'Estaing, directing the cessation of hostilities by sea. Congress according to the following abstract from the journals, proceeded, without delay, to take these important communications into consideration:

"*Monday, March 24th*, 1783.

"A letter of February fifth, from the marquis de Lafayette, announcing a general peace, and a copy of orders given by the count d'Estaing, vice-admiral of France, to the chevalier du Quesne, commander of the corvette Triumph, despatched from Cadiz the sixth of February last, for the purpose of putting a stop to all hostilities by sea, being laid before congress and read;

"*Resolved*, That the agent of marine be, and he is hereby, directed, immediately to re-call all armed vessels cruizing under commissions from the United States of America."

* This strong claim upon our gratitude has not been noticed in the commendations so deservedly bestowed on the marquis.

At a subsequent period, a bust of the marquis was placed, by the legislature of Virginia, in a niche of the wall of a spacious area in the centre of the capitol of that state, near the fine marble statue of his adopted father.

No sooner was the independence of America established, and tranquillity once more restored to Europe, than the marquis applied himself with increased attention, to the commercial relations of France and America, which had for some time occupied his thoughts. His exertions in 1783 and 1784, principally related to certain free ports in France, in favour of American vessels, a grant, which he endeavoured successfully to prove to the French government, would be equally beneficial to both countries. The perseverance and ability with which he prosecuted this scheme, insured its success, and its precise nature may be gathered from the following letter of the minister de Colonne, in answer to a memorial on the subject:

Versailles, January 9th, 1784.

Sir,

I have communicated to the king, the observations contained in the memorial which you transmitted to me, relative to the commerce of America, and those which you made at our last conference.

I am authorised to announce to you, that it is the intention of his majesty to grant to the United States, the ports of L'Orient and Bayonne, as free ports, and besides these, those of Dunkirk and Marseilles; the first of which enjoys absolute freedom, and the other is restrained in the exercise of that freedom, only with regard to tobacco, which is there subjected to a duty. The Americans may, from this moment, send their vessels to those four ports, where they will not meet with any kind of difficulty. You may, if necessary, explain what is meant by free ports, agreeably to the signification thereof, given by M. de Vergennes, in his letter of the twenty-ninth of June last.* The Americans will find above all at Dunkirk, all the facilities they can desire for the sale of their leaf-tobacco, their rice, their timber, and other merchandise, as well as for the purchase of what they want, such as linens, woollens, brandy, &c. It is proposed to establish stores and magazines there, which shall be well supplied, on terms very advantageous for their commerce. I have given orders to the farmer general to treat, in preference, and at a reasonable price, for the purchase of the tobaccos of North America; and, moreover, the United States will be as much favoured in France, in matters of commerce, as any other nation. The complaints which they may make to you, or which Mr. Franklin, and the other American ministers, which I would be very glad to see, may transmit to me on their behalf, shall be examined with great attention, and government will not suffer them to experience any kind of vexation. Every possible precaution will also be taken to prevent the sending out bad merchandise, which, if it has hitherto taken place, can only be attributed to the avarice of some merchants of the lowest order. I intend immediately to examine what relates to the customs and duties which are injurious to commerce. This is an important subject and requires great attention.—In fine, Sir, you may rely

* The following is the letter alluded to by M. de Colonne:

Versailles, June 29th, 1783.

SIR,

I have received the letter you did me the honour to write on the seventeenth of this month. You desire to know what is meant by a free port.

By this term, Sir, we mean a place to which all merchandises, as well foreign as domestic, may be imported, and from which they may be freely exported. You will judge, Sir, by this definition, that all the merchandises of the North, without exception, may be imported into L'Orient, and exported from it, by the Americans. In a word, L'Orient will be reputed foreign with regard to France, as far as respects commerce. The prohibitions and duties on foreign merchandises, will take effect only in case any person desires to introduce into the interior part of the realm, the merchandises subjected to the one or the other.

I have the honour to be &c.

DE VERGENNES.

M. the marquis de Lafayette.

that I shall be always disposed, as well as Mons. the marshal de Castries, and Mons. the count de Vergennes, to receive and listen with attention, to the demands and further representations which you shall think proper to make in favour of the commerce of America.

I have the honour to be, &c.

De Colonne.

M. the marquis de Lafayette.

P. S. The ports of Bayonne and L'Orient, will be made similar to that of Dunkirk, with regard to entire freedom.

The succeeding extracts from the official letters of the superintendant of Finance, not only demonstrate the untiring zeal of Lafayette for the service of this country, but the importance that was attached to the commercial privileges which he obtained in her favour:

Mr. Morris to the president of congress, transmitting the observations of Lafayette on the commerce between France and the United States.

April 16, 1784.

"The masterly manner in which the marquis has treated a subject, certainly foreign to his former habits and views, merits great applause, and will, I doubt not, procure that approbation from Congress, which will be to him a grateful reward, for his zealous and dexterous exertions to promote the interests of America."

Mr. Morris to the president of Congress, enclosing certain letters from France.

May 19, 1784.

"Congress will see, from these papers, new instances of the affectionate zeal and industry of that nobleman in the service of the United States. The grateful sense which they entertain of these services, will be, to him, a pleasing gratification, and I shall find it my duty, in acknowledging his letters, to assure him of their favourable dispositions, and to solicit his farther exertions."

Mr. Morris to the marquis de Lafayette.

September 30, 1784.

"Accept, I pray you, my thanks for the services you have rendered to America, and be persuaded of my warmest wishes for success to all your subsequent pursuits."

Mr. Morris to the president of Congress.

September 30, 1784.

"The unexampled attention to every American interest, which this gentleman has exhibited, cannot fail to excite the strongest emotions in his favour, and we must, at the same time, admire the judgment which he has shown in the manner of his applications, as well as the industry in selecting proper materials. There can be little doubt that his interest, at his own court, must always prove beneficial to this country, while the same cordiality shall continue which now subsists between him, and the venerable plenipotentiary now resident at Passy."

In the beginning of 1784, an interesting correspondence took place between Robert Morris and the marquis de Lafayette, relative to the Isle of France, in which the superintendant of finance endeavoured to procure the establishment of a free port on that island. It was thought that great advantages would accrue to both nations from the adoption of that measure, and that it would be the means of establishing, at that port, the most extensive and useful commerce with India, that had ever before existed. The Americans, it was supposed, would find it particularly beneficial, because they might trade freely and without risk to such port;—and the French, because they would undoubtedly furnish all those articles of India goods which American vessels would otherwise go in search of, to India, or procure from other nations.

"This," said Mr. Morris, "will form an object of near twenty millions of livres annually; or, calculating both the export and import cargoes, it will amount to about thirty millions; and, consequently, cannot be less than five millions clear advantage to France. And if it be considered that this is so much taken from her commercial rival, we may estimate it as being an object of ten millions annually." "I consider it as almost certain," he adds, "that America would find it more advantageous to trade with that port, than to go on to India And hence I draw one very strong inference, that we should not only be, by that means, brought into a closer political connexion with France, but that France would hold a much larger share of all our other commerce, than she would without such an establishment."

The services rendered by Lafayette, and the privileges that he obtained, in relation to the commerce of America, strongly excited the gratitude of her citizens and rulers. Congress, on the third of May, 1784, "*Resolved*, That a letter be written by the president to the marquis de Lafayette, expressing the high sense which Congress entertains of his important services, relative to the commerce of France and these United States, and particularly to free ports; that there is every reason to expect mutual and permanent advantages from these liberal measures adopted by his most Christian majesty, and that an extension thereof to his West India colonies will, in the opinion of Congress, increase those advantages, and produce the most salutary effect."

It is proper, in this place, to notice the benefits conferred by Lafayette on that portion of the American community, engaged in the whale fisheries, during the years 1784 and 1785. Addressing himself to the ministry of Louis XVI, he obtained from them in favour of a company of merchants, to be instituted in Boston, the exclusive privilege of furnishing free of duty, sixteen thousand quintals of oil to M. Sangrain, contractor general for lighting the cities of Paris, Versailles, &c. &c. who agreed to enter into a contract with a company, to be formed in America, to purchase that quantity of whale oil, of three qualities; one half of the first quality, one quarter of the second, and one quarter of the third, deliverable at Havre, Nantz and Bordeaux;—the value of each kind to be fixed by the current price of the port, at the time of delivery. After the establishment of the price, payment was to be made by M. Sangraîn, in articles of the growth and manufacture of France, according to invoices to be furnished by the American company's agents, and to the full value of the oil imported;—the price of these articles to be regulated in the same manner as that of the oil.

These proposals were signed by M. Sangrain at Paris, on the seventh of May, 1785, and immediately delivered to, and forwarded by, the marquis, to the United States. He had laboured with great assiduity to procure the total exemption of duties on whale oil, but without success; because the French government had directed their attention to the encouragement of the fisheries in vessels of their own nation. The following extract from his letter, however, to Samuel Breck, esquire, of Boston, will show that, with regard to the sixteen thousand quintals already mentioned, he was completely successful; at the same time, it is an evidence of the singleness of his heart, and the simplicity of his style:

"*Paris*, *May* 13*th*, 1785.

"MY DEAR FRIEND,

"In consequence of our conversations, I have endeavoured to obtain an exemption of duties upon whale oils, but it could not be done, because the French ministry are this very moment encouraging that fishery. I, therefore, took another way, and made a bargain, which you will find the more advantageous, as I have obtained from M. de Calonne, a total exemption of duties,—national—foreign—of every kind whatsoever—for the three American vessels who will carry this invoice of oils. You easily can conceive that the favour could not be granted for more than one invoice. It is very important that it be of a good nature; but I have put in the bargain that the residue, i. e. the most precious part, might be left out. I very much wish Wadsworth and you may undertake it, as I think there is a profit to be made. The passports, I will send by the next packet. Mr. Adams is to show you, and Mr. Wadsworth is to send you by express, the copy of the proposals. So much for one time; but am not so sanguine for the future, except this invoice is very satisfactory, and the national attempt does not meet with success.

"I worked very hard to bring this about; and am happy at having, at last, obtained a point which may be agreeable to New England, and the people of Boston. I wish they may, at large, know I did not neglect their affairs; and, although this is a kind of private bargain, yet as it amounts to a value of about eight hundred thousand French livres, and government have been prevailed upon to take off all duties, it can be considered as a matter of importance."

On the twenty-eighth of June, M. de Calonne officially announced to the farmer general and to M. de Lafayette, the total exemption from duty on the specified quantity of oil, if imported previous to the first day of June, 1786—the proceeds of the oil to be invested in the produce or manufactures of France.

These continued and valuable marks of his affection for this country could not fail to make a general and lasting impression on the minds of the American community. No wonder, then, that his progress through the United States in the year 1784, resembled, in its best features, a Roman triumph. We cannot omit, in this place, as connected with the subject which has just been treated upon, the singular mode of testifying their gratitude, adopted by the inhabitants of Nantucket, who had become extremely impoverished by the long war, by which their common means of subsistence had been totally destroyed. This novelty is described in the following letter, dated Nantucket, nineteenth September, 1786, and published in the New Plymouth Gazette of the twenty-seventh of the same month.

"Although separated from the continent, the inhabitants of this island have nevertheless, participated with their fellow citizens, in the just tribute of gratitude which the great services rendered by M. the marquis de Lafayette to the United States have obtained. As wise, as useful, and as enlightened in peace, as he was brave and skilful in war, he has endeavoured still closer to draw together two nations, already united by policy and reason. To accomplish this object, he has devoted his attention to those commercial ties which might prove mutually advantageous. With the view of establishing our commercial relations on a solid and permanent basis, and of affording to us the means of paying for the merchandise which we are desirous of exporting from France, he has obtained the privilege that our whale oil (which, with our flocks, constitutes our sole riches) shall pay no other duty than that of the Hanseatic towns : this generous concession on the part of the French government, has conferred upon us an extraordinary benefit, as it revives our discouraged industry, and establishes us on this island, the land of our fathers, from which the new order of things would otherwise have compelled us to emigrate. Penetrated with gratitude for so signal a service, the inhabitants of Nantucket, in corporation assembled, *voted and resolved*, That each of them should contribute the milk afforded by his cow during the space of twenty-four hours ; that the whole quantity thus obtained should be manufactured into a *cheese weighing five hundred pounds ;* and that the same should be transmitted to the marquis de Lafayette, as a feeble, but not less sincere, testimonial, of the affection and gratitude of the inhabitants of Nantucket."*—We trust that the present generation will not imitate their fathers, by preparing a second grand vaccine jubilee.

In the summer of 1784, Lafayette urged by his strong public and private attachments, and by the urgent entreaties of his American friends, prepared again to visit the transatlantic theatre of his toils and glory. He longed once more to em-

* Mem. Hist. pp. 117, 118.

brace his friend and patron, the illustrious Washington, who had earnestly joined in the general invitation, and who, having retired to the shades of private life, thus feelingly described his happy situation, to his adopted child. "At length, my dear marquis, I have become a private citizen on the banks of the Potomac; and, under the shadow of my own vine, and my own fig-tree, free from the bustle of the camp and the busy scenes of public life, I am solacing myself with those tranquil enjoyments, of which the soldier, who is ever in pursuit of fame,—the statesman, whose watchful days and sleepless nights are spent in devising schemes to promote the welfare of his own, perhaps the ruin of other countries, as if this globe was insufficient for us all,—and the courtier, who is always watching the countenance of his prince in the hope of catching a gracious smile,—can have very little conception. I have not only retired from all public employments, but am retiring within myself, and shall be able to view the solitary walk, and tread the paths of private life, with heartfelt satisfaction. Envious of none, I am determined to be pleased with all; and this, my dear friend, being the order of my march, I will move gently, down the stream of life, until I sleep with my fathers."

On the first of July, 1784, the marquis embarked at Havre on board of the packet ship Courier, and arrived at New-York on the fourth of August.*

* The particulars of Lafayette's tour through the United States in 1784, are principally derived from a work, entitled, "Memoires Historiques et Pieces Authentiques sur M. de Lafayette, Paris, l'au second (1794) 12mo. pp. 303;" which contains a mass of miscellaneous matter relative to the marquis. His visit to this country is minutely described, by M. de Crevecœur, in not less than sixty-three pages, which embrace the various addresses presented to Lafayette, together with his reply to each. We have made these observations and acknowledgments, to avoid the suspicion that we are indebted to the book of general Holstein for our account of the marquis' visit. As the general has published nearly a literal translation from the Memoires Historiques, and no reference is made to that work, we might very readily, and, indeed, almost certainly, without this explanation, have fallen under the imputation of having pilfered from the pages of Holstein. It has been our pleasure to enter more into details, and to alter the phraseology of our authority, but the resemblance is still very apparent.—*Vide Mem. Hist. p.* 51—114.

The visit of Lafayette to America in 1784, may be ranked among the most interesting events of his life. He now crossed the ocean to behold the glorious fruits of the toils and dangers in which he had participated. He had gone forth as a sower to sow: but his seeds fell neither by the way side, where the fowls came and devoured them up;—nor upon stony places, where they were scorched by the sun and withered away;—nor among thorns, which sprung up and choked them. But "they fell into good ground, and brought forth fruit, some a hundred fold, some sixty fold, some thirty fold. Who hath ears to hear, let him hear."—He found America free, united, and independent, enjoying, after a long, calamitous, and uncertain war, the uninterrupted blessings of peace. Surrounded by his old associates in arms, who had now beaten their swords into plough-shares, and their spears into pruning hooks, he might well have exclaimed, in the language of the psalmist, "Behold, how good and how pleasant it is for brethren to dwell together in unity: it is as the dew of Hermon, and as the dew that descended upon the mountains of Zion."

No sooner had the news of Lafayette's arrival spread itself over the city, than all the officers who had served with him or under his command, and the citizens who were acquainted with him during the war, abandoned their usual occupations, and hastened to behold again their fellow soldier and friend, and to welcome him to their shores. The next day, he was invited to a splendid entertainment, where the officers appeared in their uniforms, which had been long cast aside, but were now resumed in honour of the occasion. Uninterrupted joy and cordiality enlivened this friendly and paternal festival; for it was the first repast that Lafayette made in America, after the acknowledgment and full establishment of her independence.

Having passed a few days in New-York, he departed for Philadelphia, where he was preceded by the happy news of his arrival from Europe. At some distance from the city, he was met by a numerous escort, consisting of the officers who had served in the continental army, the officers of militia, and a great number of citizens who received him with the most ardent tokens of gratitude. The ringing of bells, and the thunder of cannons, announced his entrance into Philadelphia. Not only the streets; but the doors and windows of the houses, were crowded with spectators, and all the public places resounded with acclamations—After visiting the governor, he was escorted to his rooms in the City Hotel, where he partook of a splendid supper: in the evening, a general illumination took place. On the day after his arrival, generals Wayne, St. Clair, and Irwin, were deputed by the corps of officers, to congratulate him on his arrival, and offer him their respects, in the name of the Pennsylvania line. But it was not only from his friends, his acquaintance, and the different societies of the city, that he received the most flattering and energetic addresses. The legislature of Pennsylvania, as soon as they were informed of his arrival, appointed a committee, consisting of one member from each county, to present him with the following

ADDRESS.

The representatives of the freemen of the state of Pennsylvania, offer you their most affectionate congratulations on your safe arrival in Philadelphia, and welcome you in the name of the state. Enjoying the blessings of liberty and peace, we contemplate, with peculiar delight, those distinguished characters who braved the dangers of the ocean, to unite in our struggle against oppression, and to aid us in bringing our revolutionary war to a happy termination. We consider you as the first among those illustrious men ;—your example and your zeal, animated and encouraged even our own citizens, and you did not depart from us until the object of our wishes was accomplished. Receive, sir, this mark of our gratitude for the numerous services that you have rendered to this country, both in the cabinet and the field. May your abode in America be as pleasing to you, as to a nation which can never forget the brilliant conduct, and distinguished talents, of the MARQUIS DE LAFAYETTE.

To this address the marquis replied in the following terms:

I deeply feel the flattering testimonial of approbation, with which I am honoured by the legislature of Pennsylvania. My reception in this city,—the remembrance of the great obligations which I owe to this state,—the beautiful spectacle created by the return of peace and plenty,—all concur at this time, in augmenting my happiness.—I sensibly acknowledge, gentlemen, your goodness in recalling my feeble efforts to your remembrance;—and I, also, recollect the impression which your zeal, your patriotism, and your perseverance, at that time, made upon my mind.

Now that the great work is accomplished, let us mutually congratulate ourselves on the federal union which the peace has cemented, and upon which, the importance, the power and the riches of this beautiful country, rest: that union is the bond which will continue to preserve brotherly love and reciprocal friendship among the citizens of the states.—I shall be happy to receive the commands of this republic, at every period of my existence, and in whatever part of the world I may be: my zeal for its prosperity is only equalled by my gratitude and respect.*

Desirous of speedily accomplishing one of the principal objects of his voyage, and of enjoying the heartfelt happiness of again beholding his illustrious patron and friend, he left Philadelphia on the fourteenth of August—slept at Baltimore the next night—and on the nineteenth, arrived at Mount Vernon, and rested beneath the roof hallowed by the presence and the virtues of Washington.

* These documents being translated from the French, as well as some others which are to be found in this volume, some variation from the phraseology of the originals, no doubt, exists; but the sense is in no wise altered. The originals were not at hand.

When we reflect upon the principal events in the lives of these two illustrious men;—the difference in their ages and countries;—the distance which separated them from each other;—the circumstances which brought them together;—the importance of the scenes through which they had passed; the glorious success of their courageous efforts;—the mutual anxiety again to embrace each other;—the tender and truly paternal esteem of the one, and the respect, admiration, and filial attachment, of the other;—when we reflect upon all this, we find that every thing contributed to stamp this interesting interview with a sublimity of character, which had no prototype in the annals of man.*

After having passed twelve happy days at Mount Vernon, the remembrance of which have long been faithfully cherished by Lafayette, he proceeded to Baltimore, where he arrived on the thirty-first of August. One impulse alone appeared to animate every mind, and immense crowds flocked to offer to him the tribute of their gratitude and affection. An address was presented to him by a committee consisting of the principal inhabitants, in the name of the citizens of Baltimore; and he was honoured with a civic festival, at which more than three hundred individuals were present.

It would be necessary to translate all our thoughts and feelings to the days of the revolution, to abstract ourselves as it were, from the present to the past,—to be able to appreciate the remarkable and almost miraculous ascendency, which this young man, then in his twenty-eighth year, had obtained over the minds of all classes of society. This influence even extended to the allied nations of Indians, with whom he had frequently treated during the war; and he was so well known to the members of congress, who had just been deputed to negotiate a treaty of peace with those savages at Fort Schuyler, that he was invited to join in their deliberations.

* Memoires Historiques, &c. p. 63.

In consequence of this invitation, he returned to New-York, on the twelfth of September, where he remained three days previous to the continuance of his route to Albany.—The day after his arrival, the corporation of the city unanimously admitted him to all the rights of citizenship, and appointed a committee to present to him the diploma in a golden box, accompanied with a suitable address. Major-general M'Dougal, at the head of the officers of the continental army, also presented him with an expressive and affectionate address, and invited him to a superb entertainment. On the following day, he was placed at the head of a table, around which were seated the greater part of the respectable citizens and strangers.

On the twentieth of September, he embarked on the Hudson, accompanied by numerous individuals who were anxious to witness the approaching ceremony, and proceeded to Fort Schuyler, to participate in the "talk" with the Indians. He addressed them with his usual eloquence and skill, pointing out the advantages of peace, and the certain destruction that awaited them, if they persisted in ravaging the frontiers. The words of *Kayewla*, for such was the Indian title of Lafayette, were received with satisfaction and gratitude, even by the untutored savage, "Father!" replied one of the Mohawk chiefs, "we have heard thy voice, and we rejoice that thou hast visited thy children, to give to them good and necessary advice: thou hast said that we have done wrong in opening our ears to wicked men, and closing our hearts to thy counsels. Father! it is all true; we have left the good path; we have wandered away from it, and been enveloped in a black cloud. We have now returned, that thou mayest find in us, good and faithful children. Father! we rejoice to hear thy voice among us; it seems that the Great Spirit has directed thy footsteps to this council of friendship, to smoke the calamut of peace and fellowship, with thy long-lost children."

After returning to Albany, and visiting the famous battleground of Saratoga, Lafayette proceeded toward Boston, in accordance with the pressing invitations that he had received. In passing through Connecticut, he was met at some distance from Hartford by a great number of its principal inhabitants, who escorted him into the town, amid the roar of cannon, and the acclamations of the people. The civil authorities addressed him on behalf of the citizens, and expressed the real pleasure which his return had universally produced: they also invited him to a grand public dinner. Some time after, when the town of Hartford was incorporated, the new municipality, at their first meeting, conferred on him, as well as his son, all the rights of citizenship.

From Hartford, he directed his course to Worcester, in the state of Massachusetts, and from thence to Watertown, about seven miles from Boston, where he was met by the officers of the old continental army, and escorted to the hotel. On their march toward Boston, they were met by a body of troops, bearing the flags of America and France. who saluted their distinguished visiter with thirteen guns: soon after, a great number of citizens joined this military escort. The procession was now formed in the following order: 1. The pioneers. 2. A company of artillery and of independents. 3. Drums and fifes. 4. Full military band. 5. The marquis de Lafayette, accompanied by the count Grandehain, commander of the royal frigate La Nymphe, the chevalier de Caraman, who attended him from France, and major-general Knox. 6. The officers of the Massachusetts line. 7. M. de Letombe, consul-general of France. 8. Citizens in carriages. 9. Last division of officers.—His approach was proclaimed to the citizens of Boston by the firing of cannon and the ringing of bells, and an immense multitude poured forth to welcome the hero; the streets through which he passed were filled with spectators, as well as the doors, windows, and even the roofs, of the houses. When he entered State-street, a second salute of thirteen guns was fired, and the shouts and acclamations of the multitude were unceasing, until he arrived at his lodgings. Having presented himself in the balcony to gratify the loud and reiterated wishes of the people, he returned thanks to the citizens with his usual affability. The proper authorities relighted the lamps of the city on the evening of this memorable day, for the first time since the conclusion of the war.

The day after his arrival, general Knox presented him with an address in the name of the continental officers of the Massachusetts line, to which he made a modest and affectionate reply.

The state government, being desirous of affording a distinguished evidence of their gratitude and esteem toward the marquis, selected the nineteenth day of October, celebrated as the anniversary of the capture of Cornwallis, to confer new public honours on their illustrious guest. In consequence of previous arrangements, the governor of the state the president of the senate, the speaker of the house of representatives, the executive council, and the members of the two houses, assembled in the great hall of audience, to congratulate him on his happy arrival in America. When M de Lafayette was introduced, the governor, in eloquent and impressive terms, testified the high esteem and gratitude entertained for him by the state of Massachusetts, the remembrance of which could never be effaced.—The report of this ceremony having spread itself over the city, all the neighbouring streets were completely crowded with people, and it was with great difficulty that a lane was formed by the military through the multitude, to the City Hotel. When this was effected, Lafayette appeared, accompanied by the governor, the members of the legislature, the old continental officers, the clergymen of different sects, and the principal citizens, who escorted him into the great saloon of the hotel where an entertainment had been prepared for five hundred persons. Thirteen arcades were thrown across the bottom of the saloon, emblematical of the thirteen states of the Union: Lafayette was seated beneath the centre arch, from which a fleur-de-lys was suspended. After dinner, thirteen patriotic toasts were drunk, and each one celebrated by thirteen guns stationed in the market-place. When the health of general Washington was pronounced, a curtain, placed behind M. de Lafayette, immediately fell, and disclosed the portrait of that great man, encircled with laurels, and decorated with the flags of America and France. Lafayette arose, and steadfastly regarded it with a mixture of tenderness, pleasure, and surprise. For a few moments he gazed in silent admiration, when a voice exclaimed, *Long live Washington!*—the effect was electrical; the name of the gallant chieftain of liberty resounded from all parts of the room, and the shouts of *Long live Washington!* were drowned amid peals of applause and enthusiastic acclamations.—On the same evening Mrs. Hayley gave a grand ball, accompanied with splendid fire-works, in honour of Lafayette, and her house was brilliantly illuminated. The legislative assembly granted him the privilege of assisting in their sittings, which he frequently made use of during his stay in Boston.

After remaining a few days, he proceeded to visit the towns of Salem, Cape-Anne, Marblehead, Beverly, and Newburyport, and then proceeded to Portsmouth, the capital of New-Hampshire, where a great number of his old military comrades had retired to enjoy repose in the bosom of their families. Wherever he went he was greeted with affectionate addresses and public entertainments: his entrance into, and departure from, the towns on his route, were announced by the merry ringing of bells, the loud roar of cannon, and the acclamations of grateful multitudes; and these evidences of national affection and gratitude were the more precious, as they bore the marks of an energetic zeal and friendly sincerity, rather than of pomp and ostentation.—When the address of the inhabitants of Marblehead was concluded, the orator perceiving that M. de Lafayette appeared astonished at the great number of women mingled with the male citizens who had been deputed to offer him their congratulations, remarked; "These are the widows of those who have perished in the revolutionary war, and the mothers of children for whose liberty you have contended on the field of battle.—They are now here in the places of their husbands, many of whom were once known to you.

Lafayette now returned to Boston, and, in a few days, proceeded to Providence, where he met with the customary honours. He was invited to a grand entertainment, by the governor, deputy-governor, members of the legislature, and principal citizens, and presented with addresses both by the government and the officers of the army.

After visiting Newport, the scene of his active exertions in the summer of 1778, he returned to Boston, and embarked in the royal frigate La Nymphe for the mouth of York River, in Chesapeake Bay. Lafayette now approached the theatre on which he had displayed the full powers of his military greatness,—where he had united the bravery of youth, with the circumspection of the veteran,—and where he had baffled the manœuvres, restricted the operations, and finally, entangled in inextricable toils, one of the most brave and celebrated generals of Europe.—The inhabitants of Williamsburg came to the shore to receive the gallant youth who had saved a part of their territory from British devastations, and escorted him into the city, where he was received with almost indescribable marks of enthusiasm and love. He became the guest of the brave general Nelson; and, the next day, received the congratulations and addresses of the city-corporation.

On the morning of the eighteenth of November, the marquis entered Richmond, where Washington had arrived three days before, a city which, by a long and extraordinary forced march, he had once saved from pillage and destruction.—Never was reception more cordial, or more demonstrative of affection and respect, than was given to these beloved personages. The house of delegates, immediately on its meeting, came to the following resolution: "The house being informed of the arrival, this morning, of the marquis de Lafayette in this city, Resolved, *nemine contradicente*, that a committee of five be appointed, to present to him the affectionate respects of this house, to signify to him their sensibility to the pleasing proof, given by this visit to the United States, and to this state in particular; that the benevolent and honourable sentiments which originally prompted him to embark in the hazardous fortunes of America, still render the prosperity of its affairs an object of his attention and regard; and to assure him, that they cannot review the scenes of blood and danger through which we have arrived at the blessings of peace, without being touched, in the most lively manner, with the recollection, not only of the invaluable services for which the United States at large are so much indebted to him, but of that conspicuous display of cool intrepidity and wise conduct, during his command in the campaign of 1781, which, by having so essentially served this state in particular, have given him so just a title to its particular acknowledgments. That, impressed as they thus are with the distinguished lustre of his character, they cannot form a wish more suitable, than that the lesson it affords may inspire all those whose noble minds may emulate his glory, to pursue it by means equally auspicious to the interests of humanity."

And a committee was appointed, of Mr. Henry, Mr. Madison, Mr. Jones, (of King George,) Mr. Matthews, and Mr. Brent.

An address like this, proceeding from an assembly adorned by the virtues, the abilities, and the eloquence, of a Henry and a Madison, could not have failed to impress the heart of the marquis de Lafayette with feelings of almost inexpressible delight. And, accordingly, in his feeling reply, he expressed, in appropriate terms, his thanks for the flattering favour which they had conferred on him, and for the constant partiality and unbounded confidence of Virginia towards him, in the most trying times. "I need not add,' said he, "what my sentiments must be in Virginia, where step by step have I so keenly felt for her distress,—so eagerly enjoyed her recovery. Our armed force was obliged to retreat, but your patriotic hearts stood unshaken; and while, either at that period, or in our better hours, my obligations to you are numberless, I am happy in this opportunity to observe, that the excellent services of your militia were continued with unparalleled steadiness. Impressed with the necessity of federal union, I was the more pleased in the command of an army so peculiarly federal, as Virginia herself freely bled in defence of her sister states.—In my wishes to this commonwealth, gentlemen, I will persevere with the same zeal, that, once and for ever, has devoted me to her. May her fertile soil rapidly increase her wealth—may all the waters, which so luxuriantly flow within her limits, be happy channels of the most extensive trade—and may she in her wisdom, and the enjoyment of prosperity, continue to give the world unquestionable proofs of her philanthropy, and her regard for the liberties of all mankind."

Washington and Lafayette now returned together to Mount Vernon; and, for some time, they were fully occupied in honouring with their presence, the entertainments given by the citizens of Alexandria and Annapolis. The house of assembly, of Maryland, which met in the latter city, hastened to testify their high respect and gratitude toward such illustrious individuals, by an eloquent address, that flowed directly from the heart; and the splendid festival which followed, was rendered yet more interesting, by the presence of Henry Laurens, formerly president of congress.

At Annapolis, Lafayette received the last embraces and paternal benedictions of Washington: and took an affectionate farewell of the numerous friends who had assembled in that city.

After passing through Baltimore and Philadelphia, he arrived on the eighth of December at Trenton, where congress was then sitting, to take leave of that body. The next day he received the congratulations, and address, of the legislature of New-Jersey, who appointed a committee to welcome him in the name of the state. On the ninth of December, congress, desirous of manifesting, in the strongest manner, their esteem and regard for their distinguished guest,

Resolved, That a committee, to consist of one member from each state, be appointed to receive the marquis, and, in the name of congress, to take leave of him. That they be instructed to assure him, that congress continue to entertain the same high sense of his abilities and zeal to promote the welfare of America, both here and in Europe, which they have frequently expressed and manifested on former occasions, and which the recent marks of his attention to their commercial and other interests, have perfectly confirmed. That, as his uniform and unceasing attachment to this country has resembled that of a patriotic citizen, the United States regard him with particular affection, and will not cease to feel an interest in whatever may concern his honour and prosperity; and that their best and kindest wishes will always attend him.

Resolved, that a letter be written to his most Christian majesty, to be signed by his excellency, the president of congress, expressive of the high sense which the United States, in congress assembled, entertain of the zeal, talents, and meritorious services, of the marquis de Lafayette, and recommending him to the favour and patronage of his majesty.

On the thirteenth of December, Mr. Jay, chairman of the committee thus appointed to receive and take leave of the marquis, reported, that on the eleventh instant, they received him in the congress chamber, and took leave of him according to the instructions which they had received;—that they communicated to him the purport of the resolutions of the ninth,—and that he, thereupon, made the following answer:

SIR,

While it pleases the United States in congress, so kindly to receive me, I want words to express the feelings of a heart which delights in their present situation, and the bestowed marks of their esteem.

Since I joined the standard of liberty, to this wished-for hour of my personal congratulations, I have seen such glorious deeds performed, and virtues displayed, by the sons of America, that, in the instant of my first concern for them, I had anticipated but a part of the love and regard which devote me to this rising empire.

During our revolution, sir, I obtained an unlimited, indulgent, confidence, which I am equally happy and proud to acknowledge; it dates with the time, when, an unexperienced youth, I could only claim my respected friends' paternal adoption. It has been most benevolently continued throughout every circumstance of the cabinet and the field; and, in personal friendships, I have often found a support against public difficulties. While, on this solemn occasion, I mention my obligations to congress, the states, the people at large, permit me also to remember the dear military companions, to whose services their country is so much indebted.

Having felt both for the timely aid of my country, and for the part she, with a beloved king, acted in the cause of mankind, I enjoy an alliance so well rivetted by mutual affection, by interest, and even local situation. Recollection ensures it. Futurity does but enlarge the prospect; and the private intercourse, will, every day, increase, which independent and advantageous trade cherishes, in proportion as it is well understood.

In unbounded wishes to America, sir, I am happy to observe the prevailing disposition of the people to strengthen the confederation, preserve public faith, regulate trade, and, in a proper guard over continental magazines and frontier posts, in a general system of militia, in foreseeing attention to the navy, to ensure every kind of safety. *May this immense temple of freedom ever stand a lesson to oppressors, an example to the oppressed, and a sanctuary for the rights of mankind!* and may these happy United States attain that complete splendour and prosperity, which will illustrate the blessings of their government, and for ages to come, rejoice the departed souls of its founders.

However unwilling to trespass on your time, I must yet present you with grateful thanks for the late favours of congress, and never can they oblige me so much as when they put it in my power, in every part of the world, to the latest day of my life, to gratify the attachment which will ever rank me among the most zealous and respectful servants of the United States.

LAFAYETTE.

Lafayette now returned to New-York, where the frigate La Nymphe was prepared for his reception, and after remaining ten days in that city, he embarked at Whitehall, on the twenty-fifth of December, 1784, accompanied on board by the governor of the state, the officers of the army, the French consul, and a number of the citizens, who now reiterated their affectionate adieus. The flag of the United States waved over the forts on the battery, which saluted him with thirteen guns: and the frigate returned the same number, the moment he stepped on board.

Such was the closing scene of a visit, as novel, as it proved pregnant in instructive truths, and as honourable to the two nations of France and America, as it was to the marquis de Lafayette.

We have already mentioned that George Washington Greene, the eldest son of general Greene, accompanied him to France, and pursued his education under the marquis' care, until the revolution broke out in that country.—Lafayette also took with him a young Indian, named Otsiguette, prince, and heir-apparent, of the Oneidas, a nation well known for their persevering attachment to the American cause. At this period, he was wholly in a rude and uncultivated state: but, after some years instruction in France, his proficiency in speaking, reading, and writing the French and English languages, and in other acquirements, promised much usefulness to his nation. But, after his return in the summer of 1788, he soon became dissipated, and more savage than ever, and died in a short time.

Many of the states enacted laws to naturalize the marquis de Lafayette and his male descendants. In the year 1784, November session, the legislature of Maryland passed an act for that purpose, breathing the warm and strong feelings of those who knew him well, and speaking a language to which the heart of every American responds in sincere and cheerful accordance.—Connecticut was the second state in the union, that offered, without solicitation, these noble and flattering privileges to a foreigner. The general assembly of Massachusetts also passed a special act of naturalization in favour of the marquis and his family: an honour which is thus acknowledged by him, in a letter to the late Samuel Breck, esquire, of Boston, with whom he enjoyed reciprocal and uninterrupted friendship, until the period of his decease: "To be naturalized a Massachusetts-man, as well as my posterity, will be one of the most honourable, and the most pleasing circumstances of a life which is for ever devoted to love and to serve your country." Virginia, and, it is believed, some other states, enacted similar laws, but his unlimited zeal for the glory and prosperity of the United States, and his ardent affection for the people, had long before naturalized him in the heart of every lover of liberty.—During his visit, the colleges of Harvard and Princeton conferred on him the honorary degree of Doctor of Laws; and he is also a member of the American Academy of Arts and Sciences, the American Philosophical Society, and other learned institutions.

The resolution of the legislature of Virginia, placing the bust of Lafayette in the capitol of that state, has already beer mentioned. The following is an extract of a letter relating to that bust, dated seventeenth September, 1786, from Mr. Jefferson, minister plenipotentiary of the United States, to the Prevot des Marchands, and municipality of Paris: "The legislature of Virginia, in grateful acknowledgment of the services of major-general the marquis de Lafayette, have resolved to place his bust in the capitol of that state.—Their intention of erecting, in the country to which they owe his birth, a monument to those virtues which he possesses, and a memorial of those sentiments with which he has inspired them, have encouraged them to hope that the city of Paris will consent to become the depository of a second evidence of their gratitude.—Charged by the legislature with the execution of the resolution which they have adopted, I have the honour to solicit the Prevot des Marchands, and the municipality of Paris, to accept the bust of that brave officer, and to place it in a situation where he may ever continue to call forth the homage, and attest the admiration and love, of the allies of France."

Soon after this letter was received, the baron de Breteuil, minister and secretary of state, for the department of Paris, informed the Prevot des Marchands and municipality, that the king, to whom the proposition had been submitted, approved of the erection of the bust by the city. In consequence of this permission, the corporation met on the twenty-eighth of September, 1786, and Mr. Short, formerly a member of the council of Virginia, (Mr. Jefferson being confined by indisposition to his house,) attended at the Hotel-de-Ville, to present to them the bust of the marquis, together with a letter from Mr. Jefferson, and a copy of the resolutions adopted by the legislature of Virginia. M. le Pelletier de Morfontaine, counsellor of state and Prevot des Marchands having stated the object of the meeting, the documents relating to it were read by M. Veytard, the chief clerk; after which the attorney general, M. Ethit de Corny, a member of the American Cincinatti, pronounced a suitable discourse, in which he depicted, with eloquence and animation, the various services which M. de Lafayette had rendered in North America, the confidence reposed in him by the army, and the affection of the people toward that celebrated commander. By virtue of his official station he gave the necessary directions for the formal acceptance of the bust, which was placed in one of the halls of l'Hotel-de-Ville.—This novel and interesting ceremony produced the most delightful impressions on the minds of the spectators: and a gentleman present happily applied to the marquis de Lafayette, the words of Tacitus, *fruitur fama.** "*Frangas non flectas,*" would have been equally applicable.†

We have now detailed the services rendered by Lafayette to the United States, the glory which he obtained, and the well-merited honours that were bestowed on him by a grateful people. And, while a sentiment of public virtue continues to animate the human mind, the name of LAFAYETTE will be enthusiastically venerated as dear to liberty, to true glory, honour, and humanity.

Europe now became the theatre on which the marquis de Lafayette continued to devote his time and talents to the accomplishment of those objects, which he believed conducible to the happiness and welfare of his fellow-creatures. An indefatigable activity in the cause of all that is great or good, united the efforts of Lafayette to those of Malesherbes, for the amelioration of the condition of the French protestants, and he obtained a decree in their favour in the assembly of the Notables, in 1787. At the same time he espoused the interests of the Batavian patriots, and devoted his powers and fortune to the gradual emancipation of the blacks. At a subsequent period, fifteenth May, 1791, he demanded, and obtained, a decree permitting men of colour to the rights of citizens.—While the court of Versailles protected the Bar-

* Mem. Historiques, p.114.—116.

† This bust was subsequently *broken* to pieces by the Jacobins or their satellites; but the original could never be made to *bend* beneath oppression or tyranny.

bary corsairs, he opposed the measure at home, and assisted Jefferson in his league against that piratical band, so long the shame and scourge of Europe.—In this manner did Lafayette unite his philanthropic feelings with those which existed in various and widely separated countries. It is a remarkable circumstance, says Madame De Stael, that throughout the world, wherever a certain depth of thought exists, there is not to be found an enemy to freedom. From one end of the world to the other, the friends of freedom maintain communication by knowledge, as religious men by sentiments; or rather knowledge and sentiment unite in the love of freedom, as in that of the Supreme Being. Is the question, the abolition of the slave trade, or the liberty of the press, or religious toleration?—Jefferson thinks as Lafayette; Lafayette, as Wilberforce; and even they who are now no more, unite in the holy league. Is it then from the calculations of interest, is it from bad motives, that men so superior, in situations and countries so different, should be in such harmony in their political opinions? Without doubt, knowledge is necessary to enable us to soar above prejudices; but it is in the soul also that the principles of liberty are founded;—they make the heart palpitate like love and friendship,—they come from nature,—they ennoble the character. One connected series of virtues and ideas seems to form that golden chain described by Homer, which, in binding man to Heaven, delivers him from all the fetters of tyranny.*

We are now arrived at the commencement of a revolution, which, on the one hand, was hailed as the harbinger of universal freedom, and called "the most stupendous fabric of human wisdom and virtue that ever had been erected," and on the other, was pronounced "the most tremendous chaos that ever the united wiles and strength of insanity, backed by the profoundest combinations of wickedness, had made

* De Stael French Revolution, vol. iii. p. 403, 410.—Lady Morgan's France, p. 317.

of human society;" and, say the advocates of the last opinion, it was the more destructive, because the men who undertook it, if they had not the prudence which knowledge can bestow, had all its ingenuity, and employed their vivacity in more speedy demolition than ever before was imagined by man.—It is not our province, at present, to examine the course and conduct of the French revolution, abstracted from its connexion with the life of Lafayette. It is, however, proper to observe, that the beginning of it bore a character entirely distinct from that which marked its subsequent frantic and sanguinary scenes. At the first period of that extraordinary event, it was almost universally admired. When the Bastile was destroyed, who did not rejoice at the approaching emancipation of the French?—In considering the affairs of France at that period, we find that four classes of men existed in that country. The first grand division was into royalists and republicans; the royalists were subdivided into those who were advocates for the ancient despotism, and those who were the advocates of a limited monarchy:—the republicans also were divided into those who wished for a popular form of government by a representative assembly, and those who, professing democratic principles, established the tyranny which for a season prevailed. The latter class, deriving all their ideas of government from clubs, soon sunk under the furious tyranny of that authority; and, without minutely tracing the progress of the revolution, it is only necessary to remark, that from it sprung the ruffians who ruled over France, and deluged that unfortunate country with blood.—In which of these classes or descriptions of men, are we to seek for Lafayette?—Most undoubtedly in that which favoured the establishment of a limited monarchy, and of which he was a distinguished member.—The eminent men who exerted themselves in the dawn of the revolution, acted from the most pure and patriotic motives: they were alike the enemies of anarchy and the friends of rational freedom. If their political acts were, in some cases, erroneous, the fault was unintentional;—if they led to fatal results, it arose not from any actual criminality attached to the measures, but from the use that was made of them. It may be admitted that the first constitution of France was so unskilfully made, that it contained principles of self-destruction, and must have terminated as it did; but then it must be observed that those who formed it, did it from error of judgment;—that, among them, there were men of the best intentions;—and that, in forming it, they adopted a wise and efficient plan, although their country had not the good fortune to make it effective. Among the promoters of this scheme, and one of the first in the consideration of the constituent assembly, was the marquis de Lafayette. At that time, his principles and actions were consonant with the general feelings of all good men who heard of them: but the course which the revolution took, when guided by the Jacobin party, and the enormities committed under the mask of liberty, soon produced a revolution in public sentiment. The re-action was as powerful as the original excitement, and resulted, as usual, in the formation of opinions founded in extremes. Every thing that sounded like liberty was now reprobated, every thing criminal was attributed to it, and every actor in its support denounced;—while every thing done by despots was admired and extolled, as if kings alone had an exclusive privilege or patent, to commit crimes.—Many, influenced by the consequences of the French revolution, viewed with equal enmity those men who, from the most laudable motive, joined in the measures for obtaining a free constitution for France, and those who rendered these measures abortive, by involving the country in anarchy, and drenching it in blood. With equal discernment might Hampden be confounded with Cromwell, or Russell or Sydney with Titus Oates. To charge the dukes of Rouchefoucault and Liancourt, Monsieurs de Lally-Tolendal, Mounier, Clermont-Tonnerre, Malouet, Lafayette, and many others, whose views were to reform the abuses of an arbitrary government, and establish a limited monarchy as in any respect accessary to the bloody scenes which were acted in the course of the revolution, is in the highest degree absurd. If such reasoning were admitted, Luther would be proved to be the author of the massacre of St. Bartholomew; because, unless he had attempted to detect the abuses of popery, and brought about the reformation, there would have been no protestants to massacre.*

But according to the view given by those who, from policy or fear, have slandered the character of Lafayette, it would appear that he was a prime instigator of, and principal actor in, the worst and most atrocious enormities committed during the revolution. It would seem that, almost exclusively to him, the French nation owed the origin of *sansculottes*—the prostration of religion—the deification of the goddess of Reason—the invention of the guillotine, or "national razor"—the monstrous horrors of *feux-de-file*, *noyades*, and *fusillades;* of "patriotic curtailing," and "*lanterning*"—the shouts of *Vive la Montagne! Vive la liberte!* Vive la nation!—A la Force! A l'Abbaye! A la mort!—the curse of domiciliary visits—the massacres of the Septembrisers—the "*bonnetsrouges*" of the female "furies of the guillotine"—the frantic yells of the regicides, and mangling butchers of madame de Lamballe, the bands of *Sanguinocrats* and *Montagnards;*—and, in a word, all those many and varied horrors which attended the French revolution, and which seemed to be a summary of all that had ever before taken place in the world. But what is the fact? While these atrocities were committed, Lafayette was immured in the dungeons of a despot, for having dared to endeavour to stem the torrent of Jacobinical fury, and prevent the perpetration of crimes at which human nature revolts: in flying from the fury of self-created tyrants, he fell into the power of legal, but not more merciful, despots. We are prepared not only to show that he had necessarily no agency, direct or indirect,

* Moore's View of France, vol. i. 288, 9.—Parliament. Chron. vol. ix. 643, 668.—Quarterly Review, vol. xxviii. 273, 5.

in crimes committed after the insurrection of the populace on the twentieth of June, 1792, but that he uniformly used every exertion, and even risked his life, in the support of order and law, previous to that period. On the nineteenth of August, 1792, Lafayette was compelled to abandon an ungrateful country, in order to save himself from the exterminating fangs of the Jacobins. The insurrection of the tenth of August, accompanied by a forcible entrance into the Tuileries, the massacre of the king's guards, and the suspension of his power, although it took place previous to the actual retirement of Fayette from the French territory, was totally unknown to, and unsuspected by him, distant as he then was from the capital. The massacres of September, the formal abolishment of royalty, the execution of the royal family, and the long train of judicial murders and monstrous barbarities, committed during the reign of terror, and the complete ascendancy of the Jacobins, all took place subsequent to his emigration; and were not less odious to him than to every real friend of virtue and humanity. If we follow him in every step he took, from the commencement of the revolution down to the moment that he withdrew himself from the Jacobin club, whom he detested for their popular excesses, and their usurpation of power, we should find in him a steady friend to peace, to order, general tranquillity, and happiness; a supporter of the existing law; a fixed foe to anarchy and confusion. We venture to challenge the strictest scrutiny into his conduct during the whole of these trying scenes, in which he was engaged in common with every other Frenchman; and we are confident that he would be uniformly and constantly found to have been the undeviating friend of the law, as established, and the promoter of the peace and happiness of his countrymen.*

A variety of causes conspired to shake the foundation of a throne upheld by the veneration of fourteen centuries, and to threaten the downfall of a prince, the successor of sixty

* Parliament. Chron. vol. ix. 643, 644.

eight kings. The grand primary and pre-disposing cause of the revolution, originated in the disorganization of the finances, which excited the clamours of the people;—the spirited and eloquent protests of the parliaments, the impotent vengeance of the prince, and finally, an appeal to the states-general, awakened the multitude from their lethargy, and prepared the catastrophe that so speedily ensued. Besides these excitements, the liberties and prosperity of England, which flourished under its free constitution, could not be contemplated without producing a powerful effect. From various causes, the great body of the army, hitherto the bulwark of the monarchy and the scourge of the people, participated also, in some measure, in the general disaffection. The French soldiery were soon taught that they had hitherto mistaken the object of their glory: they learned to distinguish between the monarch and the monarchy; they were impressed with the great and important lesson,—that allegiance and protection are reciprocal duties, and that true patriotism consists in serving our country alone.*

"The revolution," madame de Stael remarks, "must be attributed to every thing, and to nothing; every year of the century led to it by every path." It is not our duty to tread them.—The American revolution was, without doubt, accessary to that which occurred in France. It is difficult to suppose that so many thousand officers and soldiers had visited and fought in behalf of the rights of America, without being imbued with something of a kindred spirit. There, they beheld a new and happy nation, among whom the pride of birth and the distinctions of rank, were alike unknown; there they, for the first time, saw virtue and talents and courage, rewarded; there they viewed, with surprise, a sovereign people fighting, not for a master, but themselves, and haranguing, deliberating, dispensing justice, and administering the laws, by representatives of their own free choice. On their return, the contrast was odious and intolerable;—they

* Wars of the French Rev. vol. i. Introd. sect. 5.

beheld family preferred to merit, influence to justice, wealth to worth; they began to examine into a constitution in which the monarch, whom they were now accustomed to consider as only the first magistrate, was every thing, and the people, the fountain of all power, merely cyphers; and they may well be supposed to have wished, and even languished for a change.*

In fine, the people being left entirely destitute of redress or protection, the royal authority paramount and unbounded; the laws venal; the peasantry oppressed; agriculture in a languishing state, commerce considered as degrading; the public revenues farmed out to greedy financiers; the public money consumed by a court wallowing in luxury; and every institution at variance with justice, policy, and reason;—a change became inevitable in the ordinary course of human events; and, like all sudden alterations in corrupt states was accompanied with temporary evils and crimes, that made many good men look back on the ancient despotism with a sigh. But, at this period, the cry of liberty resounded in every direction from Paris, the city where the revolution was engendered, to the Alps, the Pyrennees, the plains of Flanders, the borders of the Channel, and the shores of the Mediterranean and the Atlantic.†

The heroic Lafayette could not fail to attract the attention of his countrymen at this important period;—a period pregnant too with men of extraordinary parts. Yet vast as was the genius of many of those who stept forth to regenerate the ill-fated land, and actuated, as they were, by motives and systems of the most opposite kind, they all united in fixing the marquis in the foremost rank. Actuated exclusively by the love of his country, his motives have, however, been alike calumniated by the emigrants and the Jacobins; to whose selfishness and personality, his example and his influence were equally opposed: and, while the family of Louis XVI. rejected his proffered assistance, in distrust of his ex-

* Wars French Rev. vol. i. Introd. xlii.
† Wars French Rev. vol. i. Introd. liv.

ertions in the cause of freedom, he was already marked out for destruction by the clubs, for his strenuous attachment to constitutional monarchy. The spirit by which he was governed, cannot be better displayed, than in his reply to the eager enthusiasm of the mob, when, in the day of his brightest popularity, the ever-memorable fourteenth of July, he exclaimed to those who pressed around him, "*Aimez les amis du peuple, mais reservez l'aveugle soumission pour la loi, et l'enthousiasme pour la liberte.*" (Love the friends of the people, but remember submission to the laws, and enthusiasm for liberty.) When the march of the revolution was interrupted, and its objects frustrated, by the intrigues of faction and the fury of democracy, Lafayette opposed himself steadily to the colossal and disorganizing power of the Jacobins: "Que le regne des clubs," he exclaimed, "aneanti par vous, fasse place au regne de la loi." (May the reign of the clubs, annihilated by you, give place to the reign of the law.)*

The minister, De Calonne, fully sensible that the finances of the kingdom could never be placed on a solid basis, but by the reformation of what was vicious in the constitution of the state, was at the same time convinced that something more was necessary to give weight to this reform, than the royal authority. He perceived that the parliament was neither a fit instrument for introducing a new order into public affairs, nor would submit to be the passive machine for sanctioning the plans of a minister, even if those plans were the emanation of perfect wisdom. An assembly more dignified and solemn in its character, and which should consist, in a greater degree, of members from the different provinces of the kingdom, was necessary to give force and efficacy to his proceedings. The true and legitimate assembly of the nation, the states-general, had not met since the year 1614; and was, moreover, a meeting which a despotic sovereign could not but regard with apprehension. Another assembly had been occasionally substituted instead of the states-

* Lady Morgan's France, p. 317.—Port Folio, vol. xix. p. 504. 5.

general; and as it consisted of a number of persons from all parts of the realm, chiefly selected from the higher orders, and nominated by the king himself, it had been dignified by the title of *the notables.* This assembly had been convened by Henry IV, and again by Lewis XIII, and was now once more assembled by the authority of Lewis XVI. The proclamation for assembling the notables, who consisted of one hundred and four members, was issued on the twenty-ninth of December, 1786, and that body first met on the twenty-second of February, 1787, when M. de Calonne submitted his long expected plan of reform.

The notables were divided into seven different bureaux, or sections, over each of which a prince of the blood presided. Every question was to be decided by the majority of the sections; and thus the minister contrived that forty-four suffrages should constitute a majority of the whole; which, by a skilful disposal of his creatures, he reasonably expected to secure. But all his precautions were in vain; it was impossible to conceal the monstrous deficit of one hundred and ten millions of livres.*

Lafayette was a member of the opposition party. The law prescribed a certain age for the admission of members, but he was elected and admitted, although some months younger than the requisite time, the law being suspended in his favour. In this assembly, he appealed against the mighty mass of abuses in the criminal jurisprudence of the state; but they were not effectually attacked until the meeting of the constituent assembly. He was the first to raise his voice for the suppression of state-prisons, and *lettres-de-cachet,* which were described as being the common instruments of concealed views, and private revenge; the monarchy was stated to be degenerated into actual despotism, through the nefarious abuse of the king's authority by ministers in the application of those lettres; and it was boldly asserted, that no Frenchman had any security for his liberty, while *lettres-*

* Gifford's History France, 4to, vol. iii. 532.

de-cachet were permitted to have the effect of laws, and were considered as necessary and essential parts of government.—Lafayette also supported the cause of the protestants, particularly in a memorial presented to the king during the session of the notables in 1787, which led, in a great measure, to the edict in their favour introduced on the nineteenth of November, 1787, and registered by the parliament on the twenty-ninth of January, 1788. "A portion of our citizens," said M. de Lafayette, "who unfortunately do not profess the catholic religion, find themselves condemned to a kind of civil death. The bureau is too well acquainted with the heart of his majesty not to be convinced that his majesty, (wishing to extend the love of religion among all his subjects, of whom he is the common father, and knowing that truth will support itself, while error alone requires constraint,) unites the benevolent spirit of tolerance to the other virtues which have attracted the love of the nation. The bureau, therefore, hastens to present to his majesty its earnest solicitations, that that numerous portion of his subjects may no longer be suffered to groan under a system of proscription, equally opposed to the general interests of religion, to national industry, population, and all the principles of policy and morality." As a powerful opponent of the plans of the minister, he demanded a reform in the government, and supported his opinions by four memorials, which particularly embraced the miserable state of the finances, and the absolute necessity of introducing a more efficacious system of finance, and which he submitted to the bureau, or section, over which M. le Compte D'Artois presided. Much excitement was occasioned by the demands of Lafayette relating to the public economy, and the count D'Artois particularly expressed his disapprobation of the course pursued by the marquis. The king having objected to the memorials which, at various stages of their deliberations, had been transmitted to him by the notables, because they wanted the signatures of the memorialists, M. de Lafayette, whose patriotism was as active and pure as his courage and abilities had been useful to America, requested permission to read another memorial signed by himself, at the same time, praying M. the count D'Artois to present it to his majesty, as coming from him alone. The bureau unanimously agreed to hear the memorial, but before it could be read, Lafayette found himself placed in a very delicate situation. The count D'Artois declared that, in the very first phrase, it appeared to him, to be too personal and emphatic. Under these circumstances, it required more than ordinary presence of mind, united with the most disinterested patriotism, not to be confused or intimidated. M. de Lafayette betrayed no symptoms of fear, but frankly replied to his royal highness, *that he possessed by birth the right of laying his representations at the foot of the throne.* He was promptly supported by M. de Castillon, who addressed Lafayette nearly in the following terms: "I undertake to assure you, in the name of the notables of this bureau, what none will, I believe, disavow, that your appeal is just;—that we all consider it our duty zealously to support it;—and that this bureau will unite with you in obtaining a redress of the grievances of which you complain." Another of the members highly excited by his enthusiasm, exclaimed to Lafayette, "Your exploits in America have already exalted you to the rank of heroes; but it is especially at this time that you merit that glorious title."—M. de Lafayette interrupted these flattering remarks, and addressed himself to the president, the count D'Artois, in energetic language, condemning the monstrous system of stock-jobbing that had been so fatally practised; proposing a close and general examination into the royal receipts and expenditures; and exhibiting the disorder of the finances, and wanton waste of the public revenue. "I repeat," he concluded, "with renewed confidence, the remark, that the millions which are dissipated, are collected by taxation, and that taxation can only be justified by the real wants of the state;—that the millions abandoned to peculation or avarice, are the fruits of the labour, the tears, and perhaps the blood, of the people; and that the computation of unfortunate individuals, which has been made for the purpose of realizing sums so heedlessly squandered, affords a frightful subject of consideration for the justice and goodness which, we feel convinced, are the natural sentiments of his majesty."*

During the second session of the notables, who met on the sixth of November, 1787, he proposed, and ably advocated, the convocation of the states-general. "*Quoi!*" said the timid courtier, the count D'Artois, "*vous faites la motion des etats-generaux?*" "*Et meme mieux que cela!*" (What!—you make the motion of the states-general!—And better even than that,) replied Lafayette.—At the earnest entreaty of the new minister of finances, (M. Necker,) the king reluctantly consented to the convocation of the states-general, whose powers and popularity would overshadow his authority, and whose jurisdiction would confine within narrow limits, the ample prerogative he had inherited from his predecessors. The meeting of that celebrated assembly was at length fixed for the first of May, 1789. The whole nation appeared to be electrified by the event: popular meetings were held, and addresses presented; and the principles of liberty victoriously diffused themselves through every part of the kingdom. The attention of all Europe was fixed on this great meeting, and the fifth of May, 1789, on which it actually occurred, after a lapse of one hundred and seventy-five years, will be long memorable in the annals of France: and it was, indeed, a day of festivity to the whole nation.

Lafayette was chosen deputy to the states-general, without opposition, by the nobility of Auvergne, and he took his seat in that body supported by public opinion. The states-general were composed of three different bodies;—the nobility, the clergy, and the tiers-etats, or commons. During the contests which occurred with res ect to the mode of vo-

* Port Folio, vol. xix. 505.—Annual Reg. xxxi. p. 4, 6.—Mem. Historiq. p. 133—151.

ting by orders, or by poll, a question which soon involved the national representatives in faction and dispute, Lafayette held himself in reserve, and, although he fully united with the unanimous voice of the three orders in favour of a constitution, liberty, the assumption of natural rights, and the protection of the public treasure, and afterwards placed himself in the first rank in constitutional enterprises, he did not then speak on the occasion.

After a long contest relative to the mode of voting, and after the states-general, at the termination of five weeks, found themselves in the same inactive state as at first, the tiers-etats, or commons, resolved to emerge from this criminal inactivity; to make a last effort for a union of the orders; and, should that fail, to form themselves into an *active assembly* for the despatch of business. On the thirteenth of June, they accordingly proceeded to the call of the deputies, including those of the privileged classes. Not one of the nobility appeared, and but three of the clergy: the latter were, the next day, followed by five more of their brethren. At length the deputies of the people, finding themselves supported by the public opinion, proceeded, on the seventeenth of June, 1789, to the daring step of assuming to themselves the legislative government; and, on that memorable day, they announced themselves to the public by the since celebrated denomination of the *national assembly*.*

We must now confine ourselves to those parts of the history of the French revolution, in which the marquis de Lafayette was a principal or conspicuous actor.

The sitting of eleventh July, 1789, drew the public attention still more particularly towards Lafayette, and from that day, may be dated the immense power which he acquired. It was on that day, that he addressed the constituent assembly, and proposed a declaration of rights, nearly similar to that which the Americans placed at the head of their constitution, after conquering their independence. The English,

* Hist. Revol. in France, vol. i. p. 56, 7.

likewise, after excluding the Stewarts, and calling William III. to the crown, made him sign a bill of rights, on which their present constitution is founded. But the American bill of rights being intended for a people where there were no re-existing privileges to impede the pure operation of reason, there was a propriety in prefixing a declaration of the universal principles of political liberty and equality, altogether in conformity with the state of knowledge already diffused among them. In England, the bill of rights did not proceed on general ideas; it confirmed existing laws and institutions.—The French declaration of rights of 1789, contained the best part of those of England and America; but it would have, perhaps, been better to have confined it, on the one hand, to what was indisputable, and, on the other, to what would not have admitted of any dangerous interpretation. There can be no doubt, says Madame De Stael, that *distinctions in society can have no other object than the general good; that all political power takes its rise from the interest of the people; and that men are born and remain free and equal in the eye of the law;*—but there is ample space for sophistry in so wide a field, while nothing is more clear or undoubted than the application of these truths to individual liberty, the establishment of juries, the freedom of the press, popular elections, the division of the legislative power, the sanctioning of taxes, &c. &c.*

The three different plans of a declaration of rights, which principally engaged the attention of the assembly, were submitted by Lafayette, Mounier, and the Abbe Sieyes. Mounier was a literary man, and of great abilities, and his project was preferred; but, in fact, it was very little different from that first offered by Fayette; all the originality of it was due to his first speech on that subject. In its clearness and simplicity the scheme of Lafayette greatly resembled the celebrated American declaration. In offering it to the consideration of the assembly, he made the following memorable discourse:

* Consider. French Rev. vol. i. chap iii, p. 273.

" Although my powers have taken from me the right of voting among you, I ought nevertheless to offer to you my opinion. The labour of making a declaration of rights has been presented to you, as a primary object,—a declaration which is undoubtedly indispensable. It is not founded on ideas merely metaphysical, but on the very basis of society. It is necessary to recognise the rights which are engraven on every heart.—Yet, it appears to me, that this declaration ought to be restricted to the rights of man, and of man living in society.—I will have the honour of submitting to you the first model of this work; but I am far from demanding its adoption: I merely request that copies of it may be circulated among the different *bureaux*." He then proceeded to establish two practical advantages which would result from a declaration of rights. The first was to call forth the sentiments which nature had stamped on the heart of every man, but which receive new force when they are recognised by all; and this development, he maintained, was so much the more interesting, as a nation, to love liberty, only required a knowledge of it: " to be free," said he, " they have only to desire it."—The second advantage anticipated, was to unfold and declare those truths from which every institution ought to emanate, and to become, in the labours of the national representatives, a faithful guide which would steadfastly direct their attention toward the true source of natural and social right.—He insisted that the principal merits of a declaration of rights consisted in truth and precision; that it ought to declare what all the world knew, and felt; and that that opinion alone had induced him to sketch the digest which he was now about to submit for their consideration, in the hope that it might lead other members to produce better plans, to which he would willingly give his support.—M. de Lally Tolendal then rose in support of the motion, and observed, " All the principles which it contains are sacred,—its sentiments noble and sublime; and the author of it now speaks as eloquently of liberty, as he has gallantly de fended it."—The following project of Lafayette, was then read:

"Nature has made all men free and equal: the distinctions which are necessary for social order are founded alone on public good.

"Man is born with inalienable and imprescriptible rights; such as the unshackled liberty of opinion, the care of his honour and life, the right of property, the complete control over his person, his industry, and all his faculties: the free expression of his opinion in every possible manner; the worship of the Almighty; and resistance against oppression.

"The exercise of natural rights has no other limits than those which are necessary to secure their enjoyments to every member of society.

"No man can be submitted to laws which he has not sanctioned, either himself, or through his representatives, and which have not been properly promulgated and legally executed.

"The principle of all sovereignty rests in the people. No body, nor individual, can possess any authority which does not expressly emanate from the nation.

"The sole end of all government is the public good. That good demands that the legislative, executive, and judicial, powers, should be distinct and defined; and that their organization should secure the free representation of the citizens, the responsibility of their deputies, and the impartiality of the judges.

"The laws ought to be clear, precise, and uniform in their operation, toward every class of citizens.

"Subsidies ought to be liberally granted; and the taxes proportionally distributed.

"And, as the introduction of abuses, and the rights of succeeding generations, will require the revisions of all human institutions, the nation ought to possess the power, in certain cases, to summon an extraordinary assembly of deputies, whose sole object shall be to examine, and correct, if it be necessary, the faults of the constitution,"*

Such was the foundation on which the celebrated declaration of rights, passed in the month of August, 1789, was formed. In the course of the long debate which it occasioned, M. de Lafayette pronounced that far-famed sentence, which has been so often repeated, and so variously expounded,—"*Insurrection is the most holy of duties.*"—It might have been expected that Lafayette would be considered criminal, for wishing to establish not only the freedom of his own country, but universal liberty, by the enemies of all revolutions, and by all those who love better *quietum servitium quam periculosam libertatem*;—it might have been especially expected, that foreign governments, which consider their subjects as the property of their family, or of their particular order, would have distorted the application of this maxim to all cases, instead of restricting it to opposition against *unjust oppression*;—but that rational and sensible men should, in order to render the expression reprehensible, have endeavoured to generalise it, is truly in itself a most unjust, illiberal, and oppressive act. It is a reproach which ought never to have been uttered in any other place than at the portals of the prison of Olmutz.†—The sentiments of Lafayette on this subject, are, in fact, as universal as liberty; because where they are not cherished, liberty cannot exist. It was especially in Great Britain that this axiom was subjected to the vilest opprobrium; and the political writers of that country continue, in the face of justice and honour, to hold it up in its distorted features, as a lasting blemish upon the character of Lafayette.‡ What opinion, then, ought such men to form of their own parliamentary representatives who did not pretend to oppose or deny the same axiom, still more emphatically pronounced by Mr. Courtney in the house of

* Memoires Historiques, p. 168—173. † Toulong. Hist. de France. tome i. Pieces Justicatives, page 140. ‡ Vide Quart. Rev. vol. xxviii. p. 293, &c.

commons?* He justly and eloquently declared, that he considered democratic insurrections as useful; that they could last but a short time, and, like hurricanes and thunder-storms, they cleared the stagnant atmosphere. "I would rather," he exclaimed, "be tossed about in the wildest blasts and tempests of democracy, than breathe for an hour the still and pestilential breath of despotism."—Happily for the universal cause of liberty, there is now scarcely a bosom that does not respond to these sentiments, from our inland oceans, to the southern verge of America:—and a whole hemisphere is ready to exclaim, in the words, and according to the meaning of Lafayette, that *Insurrection is the most holy of duties.*

At this period, the court was making military preparations which seemed to announce the intention of dissolving the assembly by force. Orders had been, for some time, issued to collect a large body of troops; and as the French soldiery could not now be depended on, foreigners were preferred to the national regiments. Thirty-five thousand men were already cantoned in the neighbourhood of the capital, and twenty-thousand more were expected. These, connected with other formidable preparations, produced a general agitation among the citizens of Paris, and excited them to commit many outrages. Lafayette now zealously supported the motion of Mirabeau for the removal of the troops, and, on the tenth of July, an address to that effect was presented to the king. On the fifteenth, the sovereign appeared in the assembly, and announced that the troops were ordered back: this was the beginning of the emigration. In the course of these proceedings, Lafayette demanded an immediate declaration of the responsibility of ministers, and the recall of M. Necker; and the assembly accordingly resolved unanimously; "That M. Necker, and the rest of the late ministry, carried with them the confidence and the regret of the assembly; that they would not cease to insist on the removal of the troops; that no intermediate power can exist between

* Parliamentary Chronicle, vol. ix. p. 668. March 17, 1794.

the king and the representatives of the nation; that the ministers and agents of authority, civil and military, are responsible to the people for their conduct; that the present ministers and counsellors of his majesty were personally responsible for the impending calamities, and all those which might be the consequences of their advice; that the assembly having placed the public debts under the safeguard of the honour and loyalty of the French nation, no power has a right even to pronounce the word *bankruptcy;* that they persisted in all their former decrees; and that these minutes should be presented to the king, and the late ministry, and committed to the press.

From the twelfth to the fifteenth of July, Paris had been the unhappy scene of commotion, of terror, and of bloodshed. The revolution which occurred at this time, was professedly occasioned by the dismissal of M. Necker. The fourteenth of July, although marked by assassinations on the part of the populace, was yet a day of grandeur: the movement was national; no faction, either foreign or domestic, would have been able to excite such enthusiasm. All France participated in the feelings which, on that day, caused the destruction of the bastile; and the emotion of a whole people is always connected with true and natural feeling. The most honourable names, Lafayette, Bailly, Lally, were elevated by public opinion;—the silence of a country, governed by a court, was exchanged for the sound of the spontaneous acclamations of all the citizens. The minds of the people were exalted; but, as yet, there was nothing but purity in their souls; and the conquerors had not yet had time to contract those haughty passions from which the strongest party in France is scarcely ever able to preserve itself.*

The enthusiasm and the fury of the people were so great, that the bastile, the citadel of Paris, with its seemingly impassable ditches, and its inaccessible towers and ramparts, covered with a powerful artillery, was in a short time car-

* De Stael, French Revolution, vol. i. p. 239

ried by storm. Thus fell, in less than four hours, a castle, which had menaced France for nearly as many ages; and which an army, commanded by the great Conde, had formerly besieged, in vain, during three-and-twenty days.—The demolition of this famous fortress was the epocha from which the partisans of French liberty dated their regeneration.—Lafayette largely contributed to the fall of that celebrated engine of tyrannical power. During the laborious sessions of the national assembly which succeeded the disgrace of M. Necker, it was thought that the age and infirmities of the president, the venerable archbishop of Vienne, would scarcely allow him to exercise so difficult an office without the assistance of a younger person; and the marquis de Lafayette was, therefore, unanimously nominated vice-president. In this capacity he presided over the sittings of the assembly on the nights of the thirteenth and fourteenth of July.—All lovers of rational freedom, of all nations, rejoiced in the destruction of the bastile, if they condemned the atrocities which, in a moment of frenzy, were committed by the populace, and which Lafayette did all he could to prevent. The key of the building was afterwards sent by him, as a present, and a pledge of his unshaken principles, to general Washington; and it is now preserved, in a glass case, in the hall of Mount Vernon. In testimony of his services on the occasion, the contractor who had undertaken to tear down the bastile, presented to him the first stone that was removed; and not long after, while Lafayette was conducting general Paoli over its ruins, he received from the same hands, the last stone of its dungeons.*

The appearance of the monarch in the assembly, on the fifteenth of July, his affectionate and conciliatory address, his grief at the disturbances which had occurred in the capital, his disavowal of any meditated attack on the persons of the deputies, and his orders for the immediate removal of the

* Mem. Hist. p. 263.—De Stael, French Rev. i. p. 236.—Port Folio vol. xix. p. 505.—Hist. French Rev. i. p. 74.

troops from the vicinity of the metropolis, produced the happiest results. An expressive silence first pervaded the assembly, which was soon succeeded by a burst of applause and acclamation. These feelings became general throughout Versailles, and the people flocked around the palace with shouts of loyalty and exclamations of joy. The assembly immediately appointed a deputation to convey the happy intelligence which they had received to the metropolis. An interesting spectacle now presented itself to the citizens of Paris. The deputation, consisting of eighty-four of the most distinguished members of the assembly, with Lafayette at their head, approached with the evidences of the sovereign's love toward the people, accompanied by an immense crowd, who covered the road from Versailles to the capital, and loaded them with blessings, and the most unequivocal proofs of affection. On their arrival at the Hotel-de-Ville, the marquis de Lafayette, and other principal members, addressed the people. From this place they adjourned to the church of Notre Dame, where *Te Deum* was sung in celebration of the happy return of peace* accompanied with liberty. In the evening the deputies returned to Versailles.

A further distinction now awaited the disciple of Washington; and his services to the state, his disinterested patriotism, and his abilities, pointed him out to the citizens as the only man fit to be entrusted with the important commission of general, and commander-in-chief, of the national guard. The establishment of a *garde nationale* was a very great benefit derived from the constituent assembly; because no liberty can exist in that country where arms are borne only by soldiers, and not by citizens. The selection of a proper commander was at that time of the greatest importance: a vast army of citizen soldiers gave to Lafayette their united and unsolicited suffrages; and he was, on the sixteenth of July, elevated to a rank, worthy, as M. Rabaut remarks, of the friend of Washington, and which finally placed him at

* Hist. French Rev. i. 85.

the head of a greater body of troops than had ever been commanded by one man since the days of Xerxes. To govern the enthusiasm that animated this newly emancipated people, required a temperate conduct; a middle line of behaviour partaking neither of extreme indulgence nor extreme severity. Lafayette's disposition and experience both concurred to make him, under these circumstances, at once a popular and efficient leader with the soldiery; for, whenever he had to do with *them* alone, he could execute the laws and prevent excesses: but he was unable at times, to restrain the populace, whose barbarity occasioned disgust and horror. He possessed, at the same time, the entire confidence of the Parisian guard, and the public esteem, which his high qualities demanded. The faculty of animating the courage, or rather the hearts, of his soldiers, was natural to him. His simple, popular, and attractive manners, joined with his youthful and animated exterior, to please the multitude.—Better calculated to rule over the tumults of factions, than govern in the cabinet, he possessed all that was necessary for commencing and guiding a revolution;—the brilliant qualities of military activity, and undaunted courage in public commotions.—In the important operation of organising the national guard, the plan adopted by him was simple and excellent. He apportioned the city of Paris into six districts, and a commandant was created for each. The districts elected their military officers, and the right of electing a commander-in-chief was vested in the districts at large.

On the seventeenth of July, the king, with a degree of courage and patriotism which does honour to his character, and in spite of the consternation of those who were apprehensive for his safety, and of others who were apprehensive of their own, resolved to visit Paris, in order, by his presence, to calm the disquietudes of the people. The militia of Versailles composed his only guard until the procession arrived at the Seve, where they were relieved by the national guard of Paris, with Lafayette at their head. On their arrival at the Hotel-de-Ville, the king solemnly confirmed the election of the marquis de Lafayette to the command of the guards. He received, from the hands of the mayor, the national or tri-coloured cockade, which had been instituted by Fayette; and when he showed himself to the people, decorated with this badge of patriotism, their joy could no longer be restrained:—the shouts of *Vive le roi!* which had before been scarcely heard among the cries of *Vive la nation!* filled the whole atmosphere, and resounded from one extremity of the city to the other.*

The royal visit to Paris was the signal for the dispersion of the ministry. But of all who were connected with the court, none was more odious than M. Foulon, who had long been hated by the people, for his unfeeling tyranny, and his insatiable avarice. By rapacity and extortions, he had risen from a very low situation in life, to the acquisition of immense riches; and he had boasted "that if ever it should be his good fortune to be minister, he would make the people live upon hay." He attempted to escape, but was pursued and detected by his own vassals, and on the twenty-second of July brought back to Paris, with a bundle of hay at his back, in allusion to the language which he had employed in expressing his contempt for the people. Judges were appointed to try this miserable victim, but the impatience of the multitude could ill brook the forms of justice; he was forced from the guards; the cord of a lantern supplied the instrument of execution; his body was dragged through the kennels; and his head, with the mouth full of hay, was carried through the streets, to the eternal disgrace of the capital.—M. Berthier, who had married the daughter of M. Foulon, was implicated in the fate of his father-in-law. Unhappily for him, he arrived in Paris the very evening on which the mob had imbrued their hands in the blood of his relation; his death was, therefore, inevitable. The head of the unfortunate Foulon was thrust into his carriage, and he was com-

* Hist. French Rev. i. 87, 88.

pelled to salute it. He was at length dragged to the fatal lamp-iron, where a cord was already prepared for him ; but despair inspired him with courage, and snatching a bayonet out of the hands of one of his guards, he attempted to defend himself, if not from death, at least from ignominy,—and fell, pierced with innumerable wounds. His head was also cut off, and carried about with that of M. Foulon.

The murder of these two magistrates has formed the basis of an accusation against Lafayette as ungenerous, as it is false and unjust. He is said not only to have connived at, but participated in, the atrocities committed on that occasion ; not only to have purposely sent the unfortunate victims to prison under a feeble escort, and given orders to that guard " *to do no violence to the people*," but to have been actually one of the most sanguinary personal actors in their death and mutilation. " Such," says Playfair, " was the commencement of the reign of liberty and justice ; such was the beginning of the administration of M. Bailly as mayor, and M. de Lafayette as commander ; with such a people, such a mayor, and such a commander, it was not to be wondered if the human character grew worse, and if peaceable men began to wish to be out of the kingdom."* If Lafayette, observes the same writer, sanctified insurrection, the people did it every justice in the execution.—" Never, never," said Mr. Windham, in the house of commons, " shall be forgotten his gross and criminal conduct in July, 1789. What figure did he make at the head of the national guards, when he allowed Berthier to be torn in pieces by the mob, after he had thrown himself under his protection ? It might be said that he acted under the influence of terror :—but why did he yield to such a feeling ? He could not have had a more glorious death than if he had fallen on that day."—On the seventeenth of March, 1794, when general Fitzpatrick submitted to the house of commons, a motion in favour of Lafayette, then a prisoner in the dungeons of Olmutz, Mr. Burke remarked that " the

* Hist. Jacob. vol. i. 176.

present was the most extraordinary application he had ever heard of: it was made for the author of so many horrors, which seemed to be a summary of all that had ever before taken place in the world !—*Altera editio multo brevior et emendatior.* And of all these horrors," he continued, "there was no circumstance of barbarity, (except the murder of the king and queen,) more atrocious than the massacre of Foulon." This member had even the effrontery to repeat the mad expressions of the Abbe Foulon, a son of the murdered magistrate,—"I'll be revenged of Lafayette; it was he that had my father murdered; it was *he who tore out and devoured his heart !*"—"I would not," concluded the consistent statesman, "debauch my humanity in supporting an application like the present, for such a *horrid ruffian.*"—Other members supported the groundless assertions of their leaders. One of them, (Mr. Jenkinson,) affirmed that he was in Paris at the time, when it was generally acknowledged that he could, if he pleased, have prevented many of the circumstances so much reprobated; but he was unfortunately followed by Mr. Stanley, who observed, that *he* also was in Paris at the time, and must, in justice to the unfortunate Lafayette, declare, that he not only did every thing in his power to prevent the circumstances that had happened, but risked also his own personal safety.*

Now, it is abundantly testified, that Lafayette endeavoured, in vain, to rescue the unfortunate Foulon and Berthier from the murderous grasp of the populace. But his authority, his entreaties, and his tears, were disregarded; and the laws of the new government, as yet too feeble to restrain these atrocities, were unhappily often violated in his presence, by the licentious inhabitants of the suburbs. In the case of Berthier, it was in vain that M. Bailly, the mayor, opposed his utmost eloquence to the fury of the multitude; in vain the commander-in-chief, Lafayette, prostrated himself on his knees to entreat that the popular cause should no

* Parliamentary Chronicle, ix. 663, 667: xvi. 406.

no more be defiled with blood. " *Numerous as the escort*" of the unfortunate man was, they were soon dispersed, and he was put to death.* A monster of inhumanity, a dragoon, plunged his hand into his reeking entrails, tore out his heart, fixed it on the point of his cutlass, and carried it about as a trophy. His comrades were so disgusted with his barbarity, that they determined to fight him successively, till by his death they had removed the dishonour which it fixed upon their corps: he fought, and was killed the same evening.— This, doubtless, was the ground-work of the fable, taken by Mr. Burke from the lips of a mad Abbe.

It was no crime in M. de Lafayette to be unable to restrain the fury of a Parisian mob; it was a violent tumult which no exertion could avert. Although his authority sometimes proved inadequate, he let no opportunity pass without exerting himself in favour of good order and submission to the law, even at the hazard of his own existence. But it is necessary, in vindicating the character of Lafayette, to afford a true statement of Foulon's case, which the records of the national assembly enable us to do.—When M. Foulon was brought before the assembly, he was accompanied by the mob, who were clamorous for revenge. Several of the members offered, in vain, to deliver themselves up as hostages, and be personally responsible, for M. Foulon; and when all means of restraining the impatience and fury of the multitude had failed, loud shouts and acclamations announced the arrival of M. de Lafayette. On his entrance, he placed himself by the side of the president, and the late tumult was succeeded by the most profound silence. He immediately addressed the multitude, and it would be difficult to describe the power of his discourse, mingled as it was, with consummate skill, and the most simple and energetic traits of eloquence. " I am known to you all," said he; " you have appointed me your commander; a station which while it confers honour, imposes upon me the duty of speaking to you

* Hist. French Rev. 2 vols. in one. Philadelphia, 1794, vol. i. p. 90.

with that liberty and candour which form the basis of my character. You wish, without a trial, to put to death the man who is before you: such an act of injustice would dishonour you;—it would disgrace me—and, were I weak enough to permit it, it would blast all the efforts which I have made in favour of liberty.—I will not permit it. But I am far from pretending to save him, if he be guilty: I only desire that the orders of the assembly should be carried into execution, and that this man be conducted to prison, to be judged by a legal tribunal. I wish the law to be respected;—law, without which there can be no liberty; law, without whose aid I would never have contributed to the revolution of the new world, and without which I will not contribute to the revolution which is preparing here. What I advance in favour of the forms of law, ought not to be interpreted in favour of M. Foulon. I am free from suspicion as it regards him; and perhaps the manner in which, on several occasions, I have expressed myself with relation to his conduct would alone deprive me of the right of judging. But the greater the presumption of his guilt is, the more important is it that the usual formalities should be observed in his case: so as to render his punishment more striking, and, by legal examinations, to discover his accomplices. I, therefore, command that he be conducted to the prison of L'Abbaye St. Germain."

M. de Lafayette took this popular ground, in urging the detention of the criminal, as the only probable means of rescuing him from the power of the mob. His discourse made a great and favourable impression on those who were within the hearing of his voice; and they assented, by their tokens of applause, to his being conducted to prison. But this sentiment did not extend to those whose furious cries for vengeance sounded from the extremity of the hall. The unhappy Foulon, whether in testimony of his innocence, or by a mechanical movement, clapped his hands in token of approbation, at the proposal of imprisonment. A general exclamation was immediately raised,—" They are conniving at his guilt; they wish to save him."—The victim attempted to speak, but the following words only could be distinguished :—" *Respectable assembly! Just and generous people!—I am in the midst of my fellow citizens—I fear nothing.*"—These words produced an effect entirely different from what might have been expected. The frenzy of the people redoubled its fury: an individual cried out, " Why should you judge a man who has been condemned for thirty years?"—Three different times did Lafayette harangue the people, and each time his discourse produced a favourable effect. It is impossible now to know what the result would have been, when shouts more terrible than had yet been heard, arose from the square of the Hotel-de-Ville. At the same moment, a number of voices from the extremity of the hall, exclaimed, that the populace from the Palais-Royal, and the faubourg St. Antoine, had arrived to carry off the prisoner. The most horrible cries now resounded through the passages of the Hotel-de-Ville : a fresh mob pressed against that which already filled the hall; the whole mass moved together, and rushed impetuously toward the chair in which Foulon was seated, without regarding the intercessions of Lafayette, who continued, in a loud voice, to order him to be conducted to prison.—But the miserable man was already in the hands of the populace, who conducted him uninjured from the hall: a few minutes after, it was announced that the mob had hung him to a lamp-iron in front of the Hotel-de-Ville.*

Is it just to charge Lafayette with this atrocious act, committed by an infuriated mob, in the very presence of the whole national assembly?—Certainly not;—and history owes to him this justice, that after the fourteenth of July, when the bastile was destroyed, these two murders were the only ones, during his command, in which public rage could not be suppressed. Many others were personally prevented by

* Mem. Historiq. p. 184—9.—Proces-verbal des Seances et Deliberations de l' Assemb. Nat. &c.

him, and in this benevolent object he frequently exposed himself to great danger; for the people could not perceive why that which was committed on the fourteenth should not always be permitted; and they considered all those as enemies who opposed their will. But Lafayette was too brave, too humane, too noble, to think of danger in the performance of his duty. For example, an instance of his generous intrepidity occurred on the nineteenth of May, 1790. On that day an unfortunate man was charged with stealing a sack of oats. Some soldiers of the national guard took him immediately under their protection, and were conveying him as a prisoner to the Chatelet; but the populace, wishing to inflict summary justice, tore him from the soldiers, and were in the act of beating him to death with their clubs, when the marquis de Lafayette happened to pass by the horrible scene. He plunged instantly into the thickest of the mob, and in despite of their outcries and menaces, seized the person who had begun the tumult, and conducted him with his own hands to the Chatelet. He next delivered the unfortunate man from the mob; and, exhorting them to disperse, and conduct themselves like orderly citizens, had the happiness to see the tumult entirely suppressed, and the people return to their houses, full of the praises of the man who had so intrepidly rescued them from their own frenzy, and prevented their contaminating themselves with human blood.*

In times of peace, we ought to estimate public men according to the good which they do; but in revolutionary storms, we ought also to consider the evil which they prevent: and certainly, at that period, Lafayette prevented a great part, we may almost say all, of the evil that was not committed. Moreover, the massacres of Foulon and Berthier occurred but a few days after his appointment to the head of the guards, and before he had, or could have, introduced a proper system of discipline.—His indignation and sorrow were extreme, at the commission of acts which sul-

* Hist. French Rev. vol. i. p. 187.—Mem. Hist. p. 265, Pref. p. xiv

lied the first moments of his command. Filled with horror and disgust, and exasperated by this contempt of all authority, he determined at once to resign his office of commander-in-chief; and this determination he immediately conveyed, in the following letter, to M. Bailly, mayor of the city of Paris:

SIR,

Summoned by the confidence of its citizens to the military command of the capital, I have uniformly declared, that in the actual state of affairs, it was necessary, to be useful, that confidence should be full and universal. I have steadily declared to the people, that, although devoted to their interest to my last breath, yet I was incapable of purchasing their favour by unjustly yielding to their wishes. You are aware, sir, that one of the individuals who perished yesterday was placed under a guard, and that the other was under the escort of our troops, both being sentenced by the civil power to undergo a regular trial. Such were the proper means to satisfy justice, to discover their accomplices, and to fulfil the solemn engagements of every citizen toward the national assembly and the king.

The people would not hearken to my advice; and the moment when the confidence which they promised, and reposed in me, is lost, it becomes my duty, as I have before stated, to abandon a post in which I can be no longer useful.

I am, with respect, &c. &c.

LAFAYETTE.

On the receipt of this intelligence, universal consternation reigned in the assembly. The members rose *en masse*, and with M. Moreau de Saint-Mery at their head, proceeded in a body to M. de Lafayette. With a disorder which their highly excited feelings produced and justified, they surrounded him on all sides, exclaiming with one voice, that the safety of the city depended on his preserving the command.—Lafayette replied, that the public good itself appeared to demand his retirement; that the bloody and unlawful acts of the preceding day, and his total incompetency to prevent them, had too plainly convinced him that he was not the object of universal confidence; that he did not possess that authority which could alone prevent or depress such tumults, and which confidence alone could give; that the flattering and affecting conduct of the electors was well calculated to shake his resolution; and that he would attend at the assembly, to concert upon the measures best adapted to the existing state of affairs, and to the promotion of the public good.– He at length yielded to the solicitations of his fellow-citizens, and resumed the command, hoping that he might be the means, (as he assuredly was,) of preventing still more dreadful disorders.* Indeed, it was not long before this hope was realized. On the fifth of August, M. de La Salle, acting under the orders of Lafayette, was sought for, and threatened with instant death, by a mob of forty thousand ruffians, from whom he had the good fortune to escape. They were awaiting his return from the country at the Hotel-de-Ville, and a miscreant had mounted the lamp-post with a new rope in his hand, where he remained, while a crew of banditti broke into the Hotel-de-Ville, and ascended even into the clock, in quest of the marquis de Salle. The coolness and serenity of the marquis de Lafayette appeared to increase with the tumult and danger. In the mean time, he gave secret orders, and arranged every thing for the public safety, by the agency of a faithful officer. At length, when he was satisfied that every thing was right, he suddenly arose, and addressing himself to the committee who had sat with him the whole evening, he observed, "You are fatigued, gentlemen, and I also am fatigued:—let us retire;—the Greve is completely free, and I give you my word that Paris was never in a more perfect state of tranquillity."—On looking from the windows, nothing was to be seen of the mob who had so lately filled

* Mem. Hist. p. 194—7.—Hist. French Revolution, p. 92.—Annual Register, vol. xxxi. p. 255.—Not. Biog. p. 8.

the square; it was entirely occupied by soldiers of the national guard, drawn up in most excellent order, who had been gradually introduced by the marquis, and by this means, without tumult or trouble, expelled their opponents.*

On the eighth of September, 1789, Lafayette proposed to the meeting of the commune of Paris, to send a deputation to the national assembly, then sitting at Versailles, to demand an immediate reform of the criminal jurisprudence, as far, at least, as respected its most prominent abuses; to require that the accused should have the assistance of counsel; that the proceedings of the examination should be public; that the witnesses should be publicly confronted with the accused; and that the documents employed against him should be freely communicated.—Even this step, although urged by all the influence of Lafayette, was not taken without considerable hesitation, so little was public opinion formed, at that time, on this important point. It was, however, with these advantages that the baron de Bezensal and M. de Favras met their trial; and already were the benefits of the change duly appreciated. The fact that, amid all the tumults and jealousies of a revolution, the *only person put to death for political offences from this period to the tenth of August*, 1792, that is to say, before the proscription of the author of the fact, will stand as an imperishable monument to the memory of Lafayette.—At that time the use of torture still subsisted: the king had indeed abolished only the rack before trial; but punishments, such as straining on the wheel, and torments similar to those which, during three days, were inflicted on Damiens, were, in certain cases, still admitted. Urged by the influence of Lafayette and his party, the constituent assembly abolished even the name of these judicial barbarities. M. de Lafayette, from the time that he was placed at the head of the armed force of Paris, declared to the magistrates of that city, that he could not take upon himself to arrest any one, unless the accused were to be provi-

* Historv of the French Revolution, i. p. 116.

ded with counsel, a copy of the charge, the power of confronting witnesses, and publicity given to the whole procedure. And it was in consequence of this demand, equally liberal and rare on the part of a military man, that the magistrates asked and obtained from the assembly, that those precious securities should be in force, till the establishment of juries should prevent all anxiety about the equity of decisions.*

The fifth and sixth of October, 1789, were two of the most memorable days of the revolution, when the populace marching from Paris to Versailles, compelled the king and royal family to remove to the capital. Nor is the epocha less important in the life of Lafayette, because, if the accusations which have been heaped upon him relative to his conduct during that insurrection, were not susceptible of entire refutation, he would indeed appear on the page of history, as the "horrid ruffian" which Mr. Burke pretended to consider him.—An unfounded report that the king was about to remove to Metz;—his refusal fully to sanction the proceedings of the assembly which had overturned the feudal system; an ill advised entertainment given in the castle of Versailles, denounced by Petion under the name of a plot:—and particularly, and more immediately, the scarcity of bread in the metropolis;—were the principal causes which produced the sanguinary and disgraceful scenes of the fifth and sixth of October. The commotion began among the women, and the progress of discontent was rapid and frightful. Hundreds of the most licentious and daring of the rabble, chiefly women, collected from the markets and public halls, armed with staves, pikes, and every weapon that their blind fury could supply, poured from their dark and secret lurking places. They surrounded the Hotel-de-Ville with fearful cries, forced open the doors, and possessed themselves of the arms Their numbers were soon swelled to several thousands, by successive and motley groups of both sexes, furnished with

* Lady Morgan's France, Appendix, i. p. xiii.—De Stael's Consid. vol. i. ch. iv. p. 275, 6.

fusils and pistols, swords and poniards, lances and hatchets, and dragging two pieces of cannon. At length they took the road to Versailles, compelling all whom they met to enlist under their banners. Terror and dismay preceded their van; and the frantic crowd, intoxicated with rage and liquor, precipitated themselves on Versailles. Presenting themselves with loud cries and imprecations at the doors of the assembly, they were permitted to enter, and the benches were instantly occupied by a crowd of women, covered with dust and sweat, deaf to reason, inflamed with liquor, and insatiate of blood. With menacing gestures, and tumultuous cries, they demanded bread for themselves, and for Paris; and the assembly, dismayed by the imperious voice of the insurgents, sought only to avert destruction by the most degrading compliances.—A deputation, consisting of the president, fifteen deputies, and twelve women of the dregs of Paris, entered into the royal presence, and described the distress of the capital. The monarch answered in the language of sensibility, and with every assurance of prompt and effectual succour. The report of the female deputies was far from satisfying their impatient companions, and the ferocious multitude directed their disorderly steps toward the castle, where the garde-du-corps, from the defection of the militia of Versailles and the regiment of Flanders, beheld themselves alone, and without resource, exposed to the headlong torrent. The hostile fury of the mob soon burst upon them, and many of them were severely wounded—About ten o'clock at night, Lafayette arrived, at the head of the national guards of Paris, amounting to eighteen thousand men. He first presented himself to the national assembly, and assured the president both of his own pacific intentions, and of those of his followers. He then passed to the royal presence, where he repeated the same assurances, and after making the necessary arrangements, he again returned to the castle, and communicated to the king the welcome tidings of public tranquillity. It was now about two o'clock in the morning, and his majesty, oppressed by fatigue, prepared to retire to rest. The marquis impressed by the deceitful quiet that prevailed, then hastened to the national assembly, and assuring them of his reliance on the fidelity of his army, he retired for the purpose of procuring the repose so much needed after the exertions which he had made.—But sleep seemed to have recruited the strength without allaying the rage of the insurgents. About six o'clock in the morning, the frantic crowd rushed, with discordant cries, and sanguinary menaces, on the hotel of the gardes-du-corps. The doors were forced; fifteen of the guards were made prisoners by the multitude; and the rest fled to the palace, eagerly pursued by their blood-thirsty enemies. The courts of the royal residence were filled with the banditti, and two of the body guards were murdered near the iron-railing: a third was slaughtered on the marble stair-case; and the resistance made by the household troops being overcome, the insurgents rushed forward to the apartments of the queen, who escaped almost naked through a private passage. On the first intelligence of these events, Lafayette hastened to the scene with the rapidity of lightning; the militia of Paris rallied at the well known voice of their commander; they flew to his support; and their united efforts wrested from the populace several of the gardes-du-corps, whose fate had been deferred to render it more lingering and cruel. He also introduced into the castle a considerable body of the national troops, and by his well-timed and noble exertions, preserved the lives of the royal family, and restored peace to the palace. By his advice, the king consented to the demand of the multitude for his removal to Paris, and appeared with the queen, in an open balcony, to signify his acquiescence. On the same day, the royal family departed from Versailles for Paris, accompanied by a crowd of frantic women, still staggering under the debauch of the preceding night, and still stained with the blood which they had wantonly shed. These were surrounded by a host of men, the refuse of a vast and luxurious capital, two of which, with their arms naked and bloody, displayed aloft on their pikes, the heads of two of the gardes-du-corps, whom they had inhumanly massacred. The royal family followed, continually exposed to the insults of a licentious rabble, who incessantly reproached them as the authors of that scarcity which the hand of Providence had inflicted.*

The whole conduct of Lafayette on this memorable occasion, both at Paris and at Versailles, has been employed by his enemies, or, what is the same thing, by the enemies of free principles, to vitiate his character; and it becomes our duty to defend it.—It is said that he did not adopt proper precautions in Paris to allay the ferment; and that, "whatever were his motives," he contented himself with simply haranguing the soldiery, and recommending patience and forbearance, when they demanded to be led to Versailles. "The national guards," says a late writer, "who had lately chosen Lafayette for their commander, assembled; and insisted upon being led to Versailles, to fetch the king to the capital. Lafayette, unprepared for this demand, hesitated; but the municipal council ordered him to march. He obeyed. Never was there such conduct as this, on the part of a man who professed himself an apostle of honest liberty. He consulted a body that had no legal authority in the state; and, by their orders, he led, against his sovereign, a band of disorganised troops who had openly declared their intention of making him their captive. It may be said that there was danger in disobedience. But had not M. Lafayette learned in America that danger is honourable? and did he march with his soldiers, as their prisoner, or their chief?—as the minion or the slave, of faction?"† "Lafayette," says Mr. Playfair, 'went literally guarded as a prisoner by his own troops, and apparently with the greatest reluctance. Two American gentlemen, friends of Fayette, met this cavalcade: he seemed to them to be in a state of great consterna-

* History of France, 3 vols. vol. iii. p. 468—489.
† Quarterly Review, vol. xxviii. p. 289, for 1823.

tion, and having stopped his horse only an instant as they passed by, one of the national soldiers took him by his bridle instantly, and with an oath, forced him to advance."*—But if the conduct of Lafayette, according to his calumniators, was factious and cowardly in Paris, at that time, it was afterwards savage and ferocious: and, as the projector of, and accomplice in, the insurrection, he well deserves the execrations of every honest man. It has been asserted, where Lafayette's services to the royal family could not be denied, that the principle on which those services were performed, was self, and his own particular aggrandisement; that every other consideration was secondary in his mind; and that he had ambition enough to wish, and to endeavour, to be the first man in the kingdom, and resolution enough to stick at nothing to procure him this pre-eminence;—affecting the maxim of a tyrant borrowed from a poet, "that if wrong and robbery were excusable, it was on the score of empire." "The proof of these charges," says the same writer, "is drawn chiefly from the general tenor of Lafayette's conduct; and from a design which he had planned of seizing the government, on the fifth and sixth of October, 1789, with the aid of monsieur D'Orleans, who, as the tool of Lafayette, it was intended should have murdered the royal family at Versailles, by his myrmidons, and then be put to death in his turn by the commander-in-chief at the head of the national guards, who were to revenge the king's murder. The field would then have been open for Lafayette, to have proclaimed himself protector. Two things are, it is said, certain, that the duke of Orleans was at Versailles on the fifth, in disguise, and that Lafayette, after having promised to protect the king, retired to a corner incognito, on a pretext of writing to the national assembly."† This undoubtedly was a very magnificent, very ambitious, and very bloody plan on the part of general Lafayette: and it actually wants no other

* Playfair's History of Jacob. i. p. 203, and Note.
† Letters from Paris in 1792, vol. ii. 292—3.

quality but truth, to make it very decisive: but other writers will not even allow him the credit of being able to conceive it. "The duke of Orleans," say the quarterly reviewers, "was unquestionably the principal mover, of the insurrection; but how far another agent, Lafayette, was concerned in it, though none can doubt the wicked part he played, is more difficult to determine. That the duke of Orleans aspired at being appointed lieutenant-general of the kingdom, and eventually at the crown, is what cannot now be doubted." "Of a different character was Lafayette, both in disposition and intention. This nobleman, descended from an ancient family of Auvergne, exhibited a lamentable disproportion between his faculties and his ambition. All the errors of his life are derived from an overrated apprehension of his own abilities. With unbounded desires and contracted views, an imagination always exaggerated, yet always barren; a judgment always unsound, yet always confident; he thought that great ends could be attained by petty means, and that political perfection could be accomplished by such agents as himself. Of all the men of the revolution, the duke of Orleans not excepted, he possessed the least understanding; and, with the exception of Necker perhaps, he attributed to himself the greatest talents. The same defect was in his heart, as in his mind, and the same misconception of its powers; for, with the utmost chilliness of soul, he conceived himself to be enthusiastic, and almost imagined that he felt. In the war for American independence, he had shown himself the knight-errant of republicanism; and the necessity which he thought incumbent upon him, to maintain the reputation he had acquired there, imposed upon him duties which he had not the faculty to support. He had been the friend of Washington; indeed the first foreign friend which the cause of liberty had given him. He had reaped some reputation, and the renown of his exploits, which certainly did not surpass the average of those performed by any gallant officer, outstripping his return to France, unfortunately represented him as a hero. But his fame was too much for him to sustain; and happy had it been if he had prudently submitted to sink under it. Rather than this, however, he chose the fatal honour of introducing into a nation long corrupted, long monarchical, long luxurious, the notions he had imbibed, with little comprehension, among a people newly created, agricultural, laborious, and thinly dispersed over a wide territory. In America, he might still have been respected as the pupil of a great and good man. In Europe, he appeared only as the awkward imitator of a patriotism which he did not understand. The justness of his political views may be appreciated by the perseverance with which he endeavoured to introduce Pennsylvanian simplicity under the arcades of the Palais-Royal. He was most happily named by Mirabeau, a Grandison-Cromwell. Lafayette could never have aspired to the crown—neither would he have consented to assist the duke of Orleans in his project of usurpation. Visions of popularity still more abstract than those of Necker, tormented him; and he became a steady opponent of the court, without enrolling himself under the same banners with Mirabeau and Sieyes. Hence it was that, although the Orleanists, as well as Lafayette, were great agents on these days, their motives were unlike; and while both tended to one object, the destruction of the power of the sovereign, both laboured with different views and hopes."* To the truth of this tirade of abuse, we oppose the whole life and character of Lafayette, drawn as it is, from authentic and creditable sources. Bare assertions from such a quarter do not particularly demand refutation; but we expose their fallacy the more willingly, as it affords the opportunity of placing new laurels in the chaplet of his fame —To proceed with our extracts: a historian remarks that "from the reputation he had hitherto enjoyed, vigilance and activity were at least to be expected; and from the military power vested in his hands, and from the confidence which

* Quarterly Review, vol. xxviii p 285—7.

had been fondly attached to his conduct, he alone was capable of restraining the blind fury of the populace. Yet," he continues, " whether from contempt or design, he seemed to persevere in supine indifference: we have already observed with what inattention he received the address of the grenadiers; and though their disposition promised consequences the most fatal, yet no precautions were taken, no orders given, no posts occupied. It appeared as if the marquis was willing to enhance the merit of his services, and to suffer Versailles to be reduced to the last extremity before he appeared to its relief."*—Mr. Windham, (then secretary at war,) observed, in the British parliament, that Lafayette's conduct on the memorable fifth and sixth of October, in which there was clear and evident matter of condemnation, with the fate that subsequently attended him, ought to be an eternal lesson to all those who, actuated by similar motives of guilty ambition, would bring ruin on their country. " When at the head of the national guards," said he, " did he lead them as was his duty, to the relief of his king? If he had not done so, what excuse could be offered for him? Would it be said that he acted under the impression of terror for himself?—If so, would they insist upon that as an excuse? or would they say, that he ought not to have risked his life? A soldier, honoured with such rank and favour, commanding the guards, could not have fallen in a nobler cause. He ought, even though certain of death, to have encountered it in discharge of his duty, and expiated, in some sort, the great calamities his ambition had occasioned. His own excuse was, that he had no command over the guards; but what could be said of a man, who, having declared that he had no command over troops, continued nevertheless along with them. He should have retired, and in repentance endeavoured to atone for the ruins he had made. But no:—it was well understood what part he played, and what end he had in view."†

* Hist. France, 3 vols. vol. iii. p. 480—1.

† Parl. Chron. vol. xvi. p. 406, December 16, 1796.

The proceedings of the marquis at Versailles, his inattention to the safety of the royal family, and his shameful neglect of duty, also afford abundant food for the palates of the malevolent. "After having amused the king," said Windham, "with a promise that there was no danger, which threw him off his guard; after the palace had been forced, and the royal family in danger;—he appeared. Lulled into security by his promises, the king and queen had gone to rest; the mob burst so suddenly into the palace, that her majesty was obliged to escape undressed. Lafayette said, that no farther violence would be offered; but when called for, was not in town. For how much mischief was he not answerable?" Mr. Windham "would not say, for he did not believe it, that Lafayette wished entirely to destroy the king, or to erect a republic in the place of the monarchy, but that he wished to lower the king to a state of dependence on himself, and to be like Trinculo in the Tempest, vice-roy over him."* "On the first intelligence of these disastrous events," (the attack of the palace,) says a prejudiced writer, "the marquis de Lafayette quitted his bed, and endeavoured to atone by his activity, for his former credulity and negligence: his splendid promises of security were now converted into reproaches; and shame succeeded to misplaced confidence. As he pressed with hasty steps toward the castle, he beheld on every side, the fatal effects of his own imprudence."†— "The first step of Lafayette, on arriving at Versailles," according to the Quarterly Review, whose principles are properly appreciated in this country, "was to tranquillize the assembly, on the presence of the national guards, *since he was at their head;* and afterwards to offer his services to the king, to whom he said, 'Sire, votre majeste n'a pas de plus fidele serviteur que moi? (Sire, your majesty does not possess a more faithful servant than myself.) These exploits achieved, the hero of French liberty diffused the like tranquillity among meaner mortals; and like Morpheus, shook his poppies over

* Parl. Chron. vol. xvi. p. 407.

† History of France, 3 vols. vol. iii. p. 486.

all he saw. After sending the king and royal family to sleep, he sent the vigilant Mounier to sleep, together with the whole national assembly, and every man who should have waked; and then retired to rest himself. Was this treachery? Was it imbecility, in the man who had bivouacked with Washington? And did he suppose that the duke of Orleans, with his sixty thousand mad and drunken partizans, was sleeping by his side?—Be that as it may, the assault began just two hours after this faithful and intrepid commander of the national guard had distributed his opiate. One of the gates of the castle had been unaccountably left open. A small portion of the mob introduced themselves, through this passage, to the staircase leading to the queen's apartments; and shortly afterwards, the attack became general."* "Again; as soon as the king learned that the wish of his subjects was that he should go to Paris, he resolved upon complying. The king announced his compliance from the balcony; and the queen herself confirmed it, by giving her hand publicly to Lafayette, who, after allowing sufficient leisure for the perpetration of much evil, had, some time before, fortunately started from his ominous repose."†

Those charges, which are worthy of observation, may be arranged under three general heads. First, the conduct of Lafayette in Paris, previous to the march of the militia to Versailles; secondly, his neglect of duty, and criminal supineness at Versailles; and lastly, his agency in planning and fomenting the insurrection, with the duke of Orleans and others. We believe that we are able, considering the limits to which we are now restricted, to produce a refutation of all these charges, so true and triumphant, as to baffle even the crafty sophistry of the Quarterly Review.

In the first place, the conduct of Lafayette in Paris was precisely that which every man of principle, placed in his situation, would have adopted. Could his voice alone restrain the simultaneous movement of the whole population

* Quarterly Review, 1823, vol. xxvi. p. 289, † Ibid 290.

of the city? Could he singly have opposed a famished and ferocious mob, much less the whole militia of Paris, of whom he was, indeed, the commander, but who unanimously resolved, with, or without a leader, to proceed to Versailles? Without a single soldier of the regular army at his command, was he alone to stem a torrent, which the royal, and constituted, authorities, together, were unable to resist? Would it have benefitted his own fame, or his country, if he had madly rushed on ruin, and sacrificed his life, at a moment when its preservation was of the last importance to the very existence of the royal family?—These are questions which, when truly answered, serve to reflect additional honours on the character of Fayette; and in so doing, we do not rest on mere assertions, but on the testimony of those whose credit is not to be impeached, and who, as eye-witnesses of the events which they describe, have rescued the fame of Lafayette from the calumny of factions, and the false aspersions of political foes.

At the commencement of the insurrection, when the numerous mob, composed chiefly of women, repaired to the Hotel-de-Ville, where a few of the committee of the *Commune* were assembled, M. Gouvion, aid to general Lafayette, and lieutenant-general, endeavoured, at the head of the national guard, to prevent their entrance; but the soldiers, swayed either by gallantry, humanity, or disaffection, gave way, and permitted them to pass. They then, with horrid imprecations, demanded bread and arms; exclaimed with violence against the pusillanimity of the men; and threatened the lives of the whole committee, and particularly of M. Bailly, and the marquis de Lafayette. Having penetrated the magazine of arms, the universal clamour was to proceed to Versailles, and all endeavours to resist the fury of the mob were vain; and for the best of all reasons, the want of means. Unfortunately the fanaticism was communicated to the grenadiers, who formed a part of the national guards. They not only declared that "they would not turn their bayonets against the poor women who came to ask for bread," but intimated an inclination themselves to proceed to Versailles Their spokesman declaimed loudly against the committee of subsistence, against the gardes-du-corps, and concluded, "that the people were miserable, and the source of evil was at Versailles; that they must go and find out the king, and bring him to Paris." The marquis de Lafayette reasoned, insisted, and threatened, but the tumult increased from all quarters. at length, though the national guard appeared not in the most tractable disposition, the mayor and municipality conceived it to be the only means of preventing mischief at Versailles, to permit their departure, with their commander at their head. The marquis, therefore, received an order to depart for Versailles.*—Experience had shown with what rapidity all Paris was inflamed, up in arms, and embodied, when the citizens imagined that public safety was endangered. No power could resist an assemblage of women, and the dreadful declarations of mothers, that they had not bread to give to their children. This, in fact, was the spring which put in motion all the deeds performed that day. "Meanwhile," says M. Rabaut de Saint-Etienne, an actor in, and victim of, the revolution, "the citizens also were desirous of bringing the king to Paris. Assembled in arms, they expressed their wishes in a manner which showed that they were determined to be obeyed. In vain did M. de Lafayette, who seemed astonished at the idea of doing violence to the king, endeavour to allay this fermentation; he himself became the object of their menaces. He required an order from the city council; the order was given, and he sat out."† Playfair, an inveterate enemy both to Lafayette and his liberal principles, remarks, that he "hesitated to obey those whom he expected to command, but was forced to comply by the unanswerable argument of the lantern, which was just ready within a few yards of his house, and which, it is not to be doubted, would have

* Hist. Rev. in France, 2 vols. in one, vol. i. 133—4, Philad. 1794.

† Hist. Rev. in France, by St. Etienne, p. 95—6. Transl. Dublin 1792.

been employed,"* After the first body of insurgents had departed from Paris, "a second army of Amazons," says another writer, "was preparing to follow the first, who were with much difficulty dispersed by Lafayette, the national guards telling their general that they could not fire upon, or use any force, against their fellow-citizens who were asking for bread. At the same time, the rage for going to Versailles was now become general, and so strongly infected the national troops, that they rather commanded than desired their officers to lead them thither. Upon this occasion, some of the grenadiers told Lafayette, without reserve, that understanding the king was an idiot, there was no doubt but matters would go on much better by the appointment of a council of regency. Lafayette, who seemed astonished at even the idea of offering any violence to the king's person, or laying any restraint upon his inclinations, with respect to residence, endeavoured to allay this fermentation, and temporized with the troops as long as possible; but they becoming every instant more outrageous, and at length directing their menaces against himself, he and his principal officers were compelled to submit to the demands of the soldiery: but, in order to legalize his proceedings as much as he could, he first required and obtained an order from the mayor and council of Paris, to lay before the king the uneasiness of his people."†

"At the very first alarm," says Toulongeon, "Lafayette repaired to the Hotel-de-Ville, where the grenadiers of the guards vehemently urged him to conduct them to Versailles. His long resistance was useless; and six grenadiers, deputed from the six companies of grenadiers, addressed him as follows; 'General, we do not believe you to be a traitor, but that you are betrayed by the government. Our committee of subsistence are either guilty of malversation, or incapable of executing their functions, and they ought to be changed. The people are miserable, and the source of the evil is at Versailles. It is necessary to bring the king to Paris. We

* History Jacob. vol. i. p. 203. † Annual Reg. 1790, vol xxxii. p. 43.

cannot turn our arms against women who are demanding bread. We are determined to go to Versailles, and exterminate the gardes-du-corps, and the regiment of Flanders, who have dared to trample under foot the national cockade.' M. de Lafayette, having said and did every thing that he could, to prevent their departure, at length requested orders from the civil authority: and it is important to observe that he expressly received them as "cedes a la force des circonstances." (Obeyed from necessity, owing to circumstances.)*

The whole of Lafayette's conduct, both at this time and previous to it, proves his sincerity in endeavouring to allay the popular ferment. When a riot was excited, some time before this period, by a very turbulent and seditious man of the name of St. Huruge, who proposed this very measure, that the king and the national assembly should be appointed to reside in Paris, it was greatly owing to the spirited exertions of Lafayette, that the mob which this man had assembled was dispersed, and St. Huruge himself, with several other agitators, seized and sent to prison; and "there can be no doubt," says Moore, "that the present insurrection would have had a similar termination, if the national guards had been equally obedient on this occasion as on the former." The national guards assembled before the Hotel-de-Ville, were so determined on this expedition to Versailles, and so irritated at Lafayette's persevering endeavours to dissuade them, that a large body of them declared that they would no longer have him for their commander, and actually proposed to M. Dogni, Intendant-des-postes, to accept the chief command instead of Lafayette, and to lead them to Versailles, declaring that they would follow his orders in all respects. He, however, positively refused. Seeing that, at all events, they were decided on going, and being utterly unable to oppose their decision by force, M. de Lafayette at length said, that if the municipality would give him an order for that purpose, he would go at the head of the national guards to

* Hist. de France, par Toulongeon, tome i. page 134, Paris, 1801.

communicate to the king the distresses of the capital, and the grievances of which they complained. Having obtained the order, he set out for Versailles, four or five hours after the motley band of males and females had taken the same route.*

Happy, indeed, was it, as we shall now proceed to show, that Lafayette was thus induced, from circumstances to alter his determination. Had not his all-commanding voice been heard at Versailles, the royal family would, beyond all doubt, have fallen victims to the ferocity of the mob. No other man could have guided the national guards, for no other man possessed so large a share of their confidence and affection. Whatever threats they may have uttered, and however ready some of them may have been, in the frenzy of the moment, even to immolate their commander, yet every other of their actions in which he was personally interested, during the period of his command, when ruled by reason, demonstrated the ardent love they bore him. If the Parisian guard, as in case of his refusal they certainly would have done, had marched to Versailles without Lafayette at their head, they would have, if not actually joined the mob, at least like the Versailles guard, remained passive: and in either event the destruction of the royal family, and the massacre of its few but brave defenders, would have been inevitable.

However insubordinate the Parisian guards may have been previous to their departure from the capital, it is clearly demonstrated by subsequent events, that they afterwards subjected themselves fully to the orders of their beloved commander. He now appeared to them in a new character; not as the opponent of their designs, but as the bearer of their complaints from the commune of Paris to the king.— The policy of this measure is too obvious not to satisfy, with respect to his motives, all those who are not interested in defaming Lafayette. It was an easy and pretty plausible assertion, taking care, however, to omit the *rationale*, that the

* Moore's View French Rev. vol. i. 287–9.

general headed the insurgents as the organ of communicating their grievances to the sovereign; while, in fact, it was only done so as to regain the confidence which rage had momentarily weakened, and as the lesser evil, to assure himself of obedience from those under his command, and to prevent greater evils by restraining a spirit which his presence alone could effect. That he possessed perfect command over his troops, is proved by his causing them, on the route, to swear fidelity to the king and to the laws. For, notwithstanding the absurd tales of Mr. Playfair, and the arithmetical calculations of others, whereby the time necessary to administer an oath to so large an army, and the number of square feet necessary for the said army to stand upon while undergoing the ceremony, are nicely computed, the fact is not the less true.* Indeed, while some inimical writers deny it altogether as affording too strong a proof of the marquis' power over the soldiery, and especially of his pacific and loyal intentions, others adduce it as an evidence of his guilt, and of his desire to procrastinate the arrival of succour to Versailles!—"The national guard," says De Stael, "marched with order, was obedient to its commander, and expressed no wish but that of bringing the king and the assembly to Paris."†

It was midnight when the Parisian army arrived at Versailles; and whatever alarm an expedition, the object of which they knew not, might have occasioned in the breasts of the deputies, it was soon removed by the conduct of Lafayette, who presented himself to the national assembly with every appearance of respect and submission. He lamented the disorders and jealousies which had compelled him, against his judgment, to march at the head of the national guards to Versailles; expressing at the same time his hope and belief, that an apology from the gardes-du-corps, and their adoption of the national cockade, would produce an oblivion of the

* Toulong. Hist. de France, vol. i. p. 135.—Ann. Reg. vol. xxxii. p. 51–2.—Hist. of France, 3 vols. vol. iii. p. 482.

† Consider. French Rev. vol. i. p. 340.

past, and a good understanding in future.—The weather was cold; and it continued to rain with violence. The soldiers took refuge in taverns, coffee-houses, under porticos, wherever they could rest, and find shelter. Refreshments were distributed among them; and an appearance of good humour inspired hopes that all danger of tumult was over for that night at least. When Lafayette perceived this, he gave such an account of this apparent tranquillity that the king and queen retired to rest. After having made the necessary arrangements, appointed different guards, and placed sentinels where he deemed it necessary, he again entered the national assembly, and gave them the same assurances that he had given the king. The members accordingly dispersed, convinced of the general pacific disposition; and, at about five in the morning, the marquis himself, after having visited all the posts, and found every thing perfectly quiet, retired to his quarters to write to the municipality of Paris, and to snatch a few hours repose.*—Madame De Stael, who was not only in Versailles, but in the palace, at the time, observes that "M. de Lafayette entered the palace, and crossed the hall where we were, to go into the king. Every one surrounded him with ardour, as if he had been the master of events, while the popular party was already stronger than its leader. M. de Lafayette," she continues, "seemed perfectly calm; he has never been seen otherwise; but his delicacy suffered by the importance of the part he had to act:—*to insure the safety of the palace, he desired to occupy the posts of the interior;—the exterior posts only were given to him.* This refusal was natural, as the body-guards ought not to be removed; but it had almost been the cause of the greatest misfortunes.—M. de Lafayette left the palace, giving us the most tranquillizing assurances. At five in the morning, he thought that all danger was over, and relied on the body guards, who had answered for the interior of the palace. A

* Moore's View, vol. ii. p. 9, 10.—Etienne's Rev. p. 99.—Hist. French Rev. 2 vols. in one, vol. i. p. 159

passage which they had forgotten to shut, enabled the assassins to get in. A similar accident proved favourable to two conspiracies in Russia, at times when vigilance was at its height, and when outward circumstances were most tranquil. It is, therefore, absurd to censure M. de Lafayette for an event that was so unlikely to occur. No sooner was he apprized of it, than he rushed forward to the assistance of those who were threatened with an ardour which was acknowledged at the moment, before calumny had prepared her poison."*

"It has been asserted by M. Lafayette's enemies," says Moore, "that he affected to retire to rest, knowing that the palace was to be attacked, that he might not be thought to have any part in the horrid attempt which took place during his absence. But whatever blame he may be charged with for not taking more effectual means for guarding the palace, or for giving way to the desire of rest at such a period, the excessive fatigue, both of mind and body, which he had undergone, precludes the suspicion of affectation; and his conduct, from the moment he was awaked, as well as his general behaviour and character through life, must satisfy the candid and impartial, that the accusation is unjust, and that he had not the least notion when he retired, that the castle would be attacked.—Notwithstanding some scenes of confusion which no activity could prevent, the manner in which he suppressed the great insurrection in the Champ-de-Mars, on the seventeenth of July, and the state of tranquillity in which Paris was kept during the whole time that M. Lafayette had the command of the national guards, compared with the horrid scenes that were acted there after it was entrusted to others, afford reason to believe, that it would have been fortunate for the royal family, and for France, that he had continued in that command; in which case, the insurrection of the tenth of August would not have happened; or, if it had, the issue would probably have been different, and the massacres in September would certainly have been prevented."†

* Consider. French Rev. vol. i. p. 340, 1.—† Moore's View, vol. ii. p. 10, 11

The palace was attacked soon after day-break, on the sixth of October, and it was evident that the orders of Lafayette, in guarding the external courts, were ill-obeyed. It is of the first importance to repeat, that he had required the command over the posts of the interior, which request was refused. The internal regulations of the castle would not admit of his interference:—the day before the attack, it would have been universally condemned as an abuse of his power. This etiquette was so sacred, that no one even entertained the idea of permitting any innovation.* The national guards were merely permitted to occupy the exterior posts; the Swiss guards occupied all the posts toward the gardens; and, by express order, the gardes-du-corps alone were reserved for the interior posts of the castle. It was impossible for Lafayette to change these orders, without employing an authority which, owing to circumstances, would have been considered as an abuse of power. On the evening of the fifth none of the events of the sixth could have been expected except by those who planned them; and it is still more probable that the enterprise was concerted during the night.—In fact, order was so little established in the interior of the castle,—the event was so little expected,—and every thing was so little changed from the usual system, that, according to daily custom, the posts of the gardes-du-corps were merely commanded by the brigadiers or quarter-masters in ordinary.†

Thus was the marquis de Lafayette actually excluded from the palace, which, say his enemies, ought to have been his post during the night. This apparent neglect of a duty which he was not permitted to fulfil, is the only point of blame, that has ever, on this occasion, been urged against him with any degree of confidence. "The truth was," said general

* The respect in which it was held may be gathered from the following anecdote:—When Lafayette arrived, during the tumult, and after rapidly passing through the apartments, arrived at the entrance of the king's chamber, he was stopped by the proper officer, who observed "le roi *vous accorde les grandes entrees.*"

† Toulong. Hist. tome i. Pieces Justif. 120–1.

Fitzpatrick, "that having conceived an opinion that he had perfectly restored tranquillity, and provided for the safety of the royal family, and having been *sixty hours without sleep*, and fifteen actually on watch, worn by the weather and the turbulence of the multitude, and exhausted with fatigue, he suffered himself to be persuaded to throw himself, undressed as he was, on a bed, to get some repose for an hour or two. The mob, during this interval, renewed their attack; and his enemies asserted, that he had retired with a view to suffer this renewal;—a calumny which every circumstance tended to refute. Instantly upon his being informed of this second outrage, he again went to repress their violence, and succeeded. If we look at him afterwards, we constantly see him the defender of good order and the law, the opposer of tyranny and oppression, from whatever quarter it arose."*

As soon as the marquis de Lafayette heard of the attack, he started from his bed, mounted his horse, and having summoned a company of grenadiers, conjured them to accompany him to the palace, and save the royal family from assassination, and the French name from lasting infamy. They arrived as the ruffians were attempting to force the king's apartment, to which the queen had fled for safety. Nothing but instant death was expected by the royal company. Suddenly, however, the tumult seemed to cease—every thing was quiet; and a moment after, a gentle rap was heard at the door. The gardes-du-corps refused to open it: "Admit us," cried the grenadiers, "we have not forgotten that you saved us at Fontenoy." In an instant the apartment was filled with the Parisian guard, who grounded their arms.—"We come," said their commander, "to save the king;"—and turning to such of the gardes-du-corps as were in the apartments—"We will save you also, gentlemen; let us from this moment be united."†

Unfortunately the national guard arrived too late to pre-

* Parl Chron vol. ix. p. 645.

† Toulong. Hist. tome i. p. 144.—Hist. Rev. France, vol. i. p. 140.—Moore's View, vol. ii. p. 12.

vent all the mischief. Two of the gardes-du-corps were murdered by the mob, before the troops could be rallied.—From the first moment of the alarm, the marquis de Lafayette had even exceeded his usual activity. He appeared in every quarter :—" Gentlemen," he exclaimed to the Parisian soldiers, " I have pledged my word and honour to the king, that nothing belonging to him shall receive injury. If I break my word, I shall be no longer worthy to be your commander." Animated by him, the Parisians forced their way in every part, through the almost impenetrable mass, surrounded the gardes-du-corps, and placed them in safety under their own colours.*—Fifteen of these body-guards, who having opposed the first entrance of the mob into the palace, had been surrounded and overpowered, were still in the hands of those savages, who were preparing to put them to death. "*Grenadiers!*" cried Lafayette to his soldiers, "*souffrierz-vous donc que de braves gens soient ainsi lachement assassines?*" (Grenadiers! will you then suffer those brave men to be assassinated in so cowardly a manner?)—The victims were rescued, and immediately conducted into the palace, while Lafayette endeavoured to soothe and mollify the populace.† This glorious act was performed in the courts, and beneath the windows of the palace. In the record of those moments of murder and rage, it is delightful to recite deeds which are an honour to humanity.‡ " In the next hall," says madame de Stael, describing the scene at the castle, " the body guards were embracing the national guards, with that warmth which is always inspired by emotion in great emergencies: they were exchanging their distinctive marks, the national guards putting on the belt of the body-guards and the body-guards the tri-coloured cockade. All were then exclaiming with transport, *Vive Lafayette!* because he had saved the lives of the body-guards, when threatened by the populace."§

* Hist. Rev. France vol. i, p. 141.—† Moore's View, ii, 13.—‡ Toulong. Hist. i. Pieces Justif. p. 121.

§ Consider. French Rev. vol. i. 342.

Thus, with his own hand did the gallant general rescue fifteen of the king's guard, whom the populace had marked for destruction. And no fact can be more clearly established that it was to Lafayette that all the royal family of France owed their existence for one hour after the attack on the castle. For some time after that event, before their passions had gained the mastery over recent recollections, all parties, without exception, agreed, that, at that dreadful period, the king, his family, and the whole court, owed their safety to the devoted zeal with which Lafayette fulfilled his numerous duties. The evidence of this fact is overwhelming; it cannot be overthrown; it proceeded from the lips of the queen herself, who at least could not be suspected of partiality in favour of the services rendered by Lafayette, on that day: she never afterwards refused to acknowledge the obligations which gratitude exacted; and she never contradicted, nor denied the truth of, her triumphant expression, "*Nous lui devons la vie ce jour-la.*" (On that day we owed our lives to him.*)

The king's mind was greatly affected with the death of the guards who had fallen in his defence; and, notwithstanding all the assurances of Lafayette, while he walked through his palace accompanied and protected by the general, he was making continual inquiries respecting them. The king, accompanied by the queen, with the dauphin and princess royal at her side, having shown himself in a balcony, loud cries of *Le roi a Paris !—le roi a Paris !* (the king to Paris !) mingled with menaces, arose. His majesty retired, and after having conferred with Lafayette, re-appeared, and signified his intention of going immediately to the capital. In fact, he had no choice left: it would not, perhaps, have been in the power of M. de Lafayette himself, to have saved the

* Toulong. Hist. tome i. Pieces Justif. 121—2.—Parliament Chron. vol. ix. 645. The "queen," said general Fitzpatrick, "had publicly declared that it was to him she owed her life; of this there are in London, at this hour, persons ready to bear testimony they heard that unfortunate princess say so."–Ibid. vol. xvi, 415.–Moore's View. ii. p. 12, 13.

lives of the royal family, had he refused.—The acquiescence of the king in their demand was received with shouts of joy by the people. At this moment, Lafayette approached the queen, and inquired with respectful hesitation, if it was her intention to accompany the king. "Yes," she replied, "although I know the danger." "Madame," said he, "are you resolved?"—"I am."—"Condescend, then, to appear in the balcony, and permit me to accompany you."—"Without the king!—have you observed the threats?"—"Yes, madam, but venture to confide in me."—Lafayette then conducted her majesty to the balcony. It was a delicate and dangerous step;—but the danger was less, than to permit the queen to depart for Paris without reconciling her to the people.—The noise and agitation of the mob would not permit the voice to be heard; it was necessary to speak to the eyes of the multitude. Lafayette approached, and kissed the hand of the queen, in the sight of all the people. This action first created general astonishment; but it was soon interrupted, and the silence was broken by loud acclamations, and cries of *Vive la reine! Vive le general!*—The king in a state of apprehension, had followed the queen, and remained in the back ground: observing the success of her appearance he said to Lafayette, cannot you do something for my guards?" "Sire!" replied the hero, "command one of them to advance." He did so; and Lafayette, taking off his own cockade, placed it in the cap of the guard, and embraced him. In a moment the air resounded with loud cries of "*Vive les gardes-du-corps.*"*

The royal family proceeded to Paris on the same day, and the tokens of joy manifested by the citizens on their return, was, in a great degree, owing to the exertions and popularity of Lafayette.

From the detail which has been faithfully and necessarily given, it is not absolutely requisite to disprove further, the assertion, that M. de Lafayette was connected with the duke

* Moore's View. ii, p. 15.—Toulong. Hist. tome i. p. 146–7.

of Orleans in fomenting the insurrection. The ill terms on which he was with D'Orleans is sufficient of itself to clear him of this accusation. No two men were less likely to be in intimacy with each other. Their characters were directly opposite: Lafayette was indefatigable in the pursuit of renown; disinterested, brave, and generous:—qualities never attributed to the character of the duke D'Orleans. Even Playfair admits, in exaggerated language, that "Lafayette was become his mortal enemy." The sending of the duke of Orleans out of the kingdom, by Lafayette, is also a triumphant vindication from the charges of his enemies. It must be remembered that nothing could exceed the indignation of Lafayette, at the unexpected disobedience which he experienced from his troops on the fifth of October. All the mutual ties which should unite a general and his army, seemed at once dissolved. He well knew that their disobedience and mutiny did not originate with themselves, but were produced by the machinations of the cabal, of which Mirabeau was, at least, the ostensible head, and the duke D'Orleans the real father. Against the latter, therefore, he justly directed his indignation: for, whatever his private political views might have been, there certainly was nothing farther removed from them, or which he abhorred more, even in idea, than that the duke of Orleans, through any convulsion, or change of circumstances, or under any denomination, of regent or otherwise, should ever be placed at the head of public affairs. The views of the cabal were now thoroughly seen through, and they had consequently lost all influence, weight, and confidence, in the assembly; and rumours were circulated which represented the duke of Orleans as harbouring criminal designs upon the crown, or the regency at least. M. de Lafayette had for some time perceived that the national guards were not so ready and cheerful in their obedience to his orders, as formerly. The rabble, also, were uncommonly tumultuous. The duke of Orleans was strongly suspected of being the author of these excesses, and of the mutinous disposition of the national guards. He was not more odious to the court than to Lafayette, and would have been arrested, had it not been judged imprudent to venture on so decisive a measure, in the present circumstances. Another plan less likely to create popular commotion, but which it was thought, would have all the good effect of arresting him, was adopted. M. de Lafayette settled the business like a soldier with little ceremony, but peremptory effect. In a short and sudden conference with the duke, he informed him, in a few words, that his presence in France was, at this juncture, incompatible with the good of the nation; that England, where he was well acquainted, was deemed the country most fitting for him to retire to; that a passport from the king was ready for him; and that, to cover the matter, he should be apparently sent to execute a private commission from his majesty. The mandate was so peremptory, delivered with such firmness, and accompanied with an air of such decisive authority, that the duke, surprised and subdued, shrunk under its effect; and, every thing being prepared, was despatched to England. "There was probably something," says Moore, "very powerful in M. Lafayette's *manner*, which convinced the duke so suddenly of the expediency of this journey; for, in the *expressions* he used, there appears to have been nothing very persuasive." It is stated by others, that the duke made some objections to the measure, and that, at a meeting on the subject held at the office of the minister for foreign affairs, he remarked to Lafayette, "My enemies pretend that you possess proofs against me."—"They are rather my enemies who say it," replied the general, "If I were capable of producing proofs against you, you would have already been arrested."*

We have deemed it a duty to transgress our limits in describing the part acted by the marquis de Lafayette, on the fifth and sixth of October, and to particularize a conduct

* Toulong. Hist. tome i. Pieces Justif. p. 122.—Consid. French Rev. i. 349, 350.—Hist. Rev. i. 146.—Etienne's Rev. 102. Annual Reg. xxxii. 61, 62—Moore's View, vol. ii. p. 89, 90.

which, so far from deserving the opprobrium which has been cast upon it, is a beautiful and brilliant display of the noblest qualities of a noble soul.* In the official report subsequently made to the *Commune* of Paris, the committee observed, that 'it was their duty to commence with the highest eulogiums on the commander-in-chief, not only on account of his well known courage, prudence, and firmness, but also of his patriotic devotion, which caused him to brave murmurs and menaces, in order to restrain the multitude within the bounds of duty, and guide with wisdom an impetuous torrent which had burst from its banks."† The princess Elizabeth also joined her testimony in favour of Lafayette. Nearly two years after the sixth of October, she heard it remarked, that, in case of a counter-revolution, it was intended to produce against Lafayette, a letter written by him on that day. Warmed with indignation at so unjust a design, she caused him to be made acquainted with it, and advised him to withdraw the document from the Hotel-de-Ville, where it was deposited. Lafayette, touched with the generosity of the princess, replied, "that he had written nothing which he feared to make public."‡

The national assembly soon followed the king to Paris, and on the day of their first sitting were waited on by the mayor, and Lafayette, at the head of a deputation from the municipality, with the congratulations of the capital; in return for which M. Bailly and Lafayette received a unanimous vote of thanks from the assembly, for the zeal, vigilance, activity, and patriotism, which had distinguished their conduct during the late troubles. In the answer to their address, the president observed, in allusion to Lafayette,—"That hero is a philosopher whom the interests of mankind

* As an additional proof that Lafayette had no participation whatever in creating this insurrection, it is stated, that letters from him to D'Estaing, dated in September, indicative of some approaching, or apprehended danger, were communicated to the municipal committee of Versailles, who accordingly demanded an additional regiment to protect the town.—*Annual Reg.* vol. xxxii. p. 42.

† Mem Hist. p. 190. ‡ Toulong. Hist. Pieces Justif. p. 121.

alone called into the field of glory, and who, beneath the banners of an illustrious warrior who can never be forgotten, seemed like him, to prize the lessons of a modern Lycurgus, as much as, and perhaps more than, the laurels of the triumphs which founded the liberty of Philadelphia."*

Towards the close of the year 1789, the marquis de Favras was accused of a conspiracy, the object of which was to massacre M. de Lafayette, M. Bailly, and M. Necker, and convey the king, with or without his consent, to Peronne. He was subsequently condemned, and executed on the nineteenth of February, 1790; and the first day of his trial afforded another opportunity to the commander-in-chief, in the display of his duty. The mob then endeavoured riotously to assemble; but they were dispersed by the masterly conduct of Lafayette, and the city was thereby restored to perfect tranquillity.

In the month of January, 1790, the baron de Bezenval, the Swiss general, was tried and acquitted by the court of chatelet; but before the sentence had been declared, nothing could exceed the rage and indignation of the populace, when they became convinced of the certainty of his acquittal. They resolved to exercise the right of summary and executive justice, by forcing the prison in which Bezenval was confined; and exhibiting in his person a memorable and bloody instance to mankind, of that inexorable justice by which they were guided. The twelfth of January was fixed on for the execution of this design; and the expectations and cruel hopes of the rabble were elevated to the highest pitch But they were not able, in their present state, to conduct schemes of this nature with that secrecy which is so necessary to their success. Bailly, Lafayette, the chatelet, the national assembly, and, in a word, every part of government, became masters of the whole design, and all adopted such measures as seemed best calculated for its prevention or defeat. Lafayette, in particular, acted with great vigour,

* Mem. Hist. p. 165-6 7.

diligence, and effect. But, although the immediate designs of the plotters were thus overthrown, yet the capital continued in a state of great disorder for two or three days.—Cabals and meetings were continually taking place, and all the past indications of mischief were renewed, and seemed to appear in stronger colours than usual. Mischiefs of every kind, and accompanied with every degree of horror and ruin, were generally expected; and even those who were best informed, anticipated some great, and probably dreadful event. But Lafayette, by a vigorous act of exertion put an end to the combustion in Paris. With his militia, he suddenly surrounded, at night, a body of eleven hundred of the insurgents, who were assembled in the Champs Elysees, of whom he made two hundred prisoners; the rest being so terrified that they seemed to consider themselves fortunate in escaping with their lives. This put a stop for the present, to nocturnal meetings, as well as to riots by day.*

On the twenty-second of May, 1790, after a long and stormy debate during several sittings, the national assembly decreed that " war could not be declared but by a decree of the legislative assembly, predicated on the formal and necessary proposition of the king, and afterwards sanctioned by his majesty." On this occasion, which brought forward all the talents of the assembly, M. de Lafayette opposed the absolute right of the king to declare war, but maintained that a division of the power would be more conformable to the true constitutional principles of liberty and monarchy, more calculated to keep at a distance the scourge of war, and more advantageous to the people.—In concluding his opinions on this subject, which were of course less popular than those which vested the whole power in the legislative assembly, Lafayette made the following noble remark;—" I have believed that I could not better pay the immense obligations which I owe to the people, than in not sacrificing to the fleet-

† Ann. Reg. vol. xxxii, p. 124–5, 6.—Toulong. Hist. vol. i, p. 187.

ing popularity of a day, the opinions which I considered as most useful in promoting their good."*

On the seventh of June, general Lafayette afforded a signal proof of the disinterestedness of his principles, when some anxiety was either felt, or feigned, at his command over so vast an army as the whole national guard of the kingdom. He mounted the tribune, and proposed a decree that no individual should command more than one department of the national guards at a time; and this, too, when fourteen thousand deputies of four millions of armed citizens were about to entreat him to become their chief. It is such traits in the life and character of a man which ought especially to be recorded.†

Lafayette had, since its establishment, uniformly declared himself against the Jacobin club‡ and its projects. With Bailly, the mayor of Paris, he had organised an opposing club, and the victory between the two parties was doubtful for more than a year and a half. The position in which Lafayette was placed during the contest, was extremely embarrassing and dangerous. He was obliged to oppose the unprincipled purposes of the Jacobins, without retreating toward the principles of the ancient despotism; and it is greatly to his honour, that he did it most faithfully and consistently. When, therefore, on the twentieth of June, 1790, a proposition was suddenly made in the convention to abolish all titles of nobility, La Fayette, true to his principles, rose to second it. This proposition emanated from a member of the minority of the *noblesse*. A short discussion followed. Lafayette observed that the suppression of titles was a necessary consequence of the constitution which had been adopted. "What!" exclaimed M. Foucault, who opposed the motion, "would you deprive man of the most powerful, and the most noble motive, of emulation?—What would you

* Mem. Hist. p. 197-8, 9.—Toulong. Hist. i, 208.

† Biog. Not. p. 9.—Toulong. i. 214.—Mem. Hist. Pref. xv.

‡ The first meeting of this club was held on the sixth of October, 1789.

do, for instance, if there were no titles, with the man whom Henry II. created, according to the words of the patent, "noble and count, for having saved the state?" "I would omit," replied Lafayette, "the words *created a count*, and insert only that *he had saved the state*."—It was attempted to preserve the title of *seigneurs* for the princes of the reigning family, but Lafayette opposed it, in the same genuine spirit of liberty which had dictated his first opinion.—From this time, Lafayette renounced the title of marquis, and has never since resumed it. Since the restoration of the Bourbons, indeed, and the revival of the ancient nobility, there has been sometimes an affectation among the ultra royalists of calling him by his former title; but he has never recognised it, and is still known in France only by the address of general. At least, if he is sometimes called otherwise there, it is not by his friends. On the seventh of February, 1824, he was summoned as a witness in the trial of madame Chauvet, the wife of a person condemned to death, as an accomplice with general Berton, but who fled to England.—After the accusation was read, the first witness called was the "marquis de Lafayette." General Lafayette immediately rose, and observed, that since the decree of the constitutional assembly, of June, 1790, he had ceased to bear the title of marquis. The clerk of the court, by the order of the president then called M. de Lafayette, the father, and M. de Lafayette, the son, who had been also summoned.*

At length the constitution of a representative monarchy, which Lafayette's exertions had, from the first opening of the assembly, been consistently devoted to establish, was prepared; and all were desirous that it should be received and recognised by the nation in the most solemn manner. A great public ceremony was, therefore, resolved on, and the day selected as most appropriate for the occasion was the fourteenth of July, 1790, the anniversary of the destruction

* North Am. Rev. No. xlvi. p. 160.—Hist. French Rev. i. 192.—Toulong. Hist. i. 217.—Nat. Gaz. March 17, 1824.

of the bastile. The king, the national assembly, and the people, were then to take an oath to maintain the cause of liberty and the constitution; for although the latter was not yet completed, yet the principles which it declared sacred had obtained universal assent. The Champ-de-Mars, in front of the military school, was chosen for the grand national solemnity. In the midst of this extensive plain, an altar was erected, for the purpose of administering the civic oath; and round it, an immense amphitheatre was thrown up, of a league in circumference, and capable of containing four hundred thousand spectators. The entrance into the Champ-de-Confederation, (as it was now called,) was through triumphal arches: the king's throne was placed under an elegant pavilion in the middle, and on each side of it were seats for the members of the national assembly. Two thousand workmen were employed upon this immense labour: but the citizens of Paris, fearing lest the preparations should not be completed at the appointed period, flocked from every quarter to assist in the undertaking. Not only the military but the clergy, and even the ladies, lent their cheerful assistance. Women of the first rank were seen joining the crowd of voluntary labourers; and young women of every denomination were daily seen tripping to the field with their gowns tucked, and belts of the national ribbon around their waists. There the lover wrought by the side of his mistress, enlivened by her smiles, and encouraged by the tune of Ca Ira.*

The day preceding the intended celebration, a deputation from the whole of the national guards in the kingdom, paid their homage to the national assembly and the king. M. de Lafayette was at its head. In addressing the national assembly, Lafayette, among other things, remarked, that the national guards of France now came to offer the homage of their respect and gratitude; that the nation desired liberty and demanded a constitution; but that they might have ex

* North Am. Review, No. xlvi. p. 160-1.—Moore's View vol. ii. p 90-1.—Hist. French Rev. vol. i. 195.

pected it in vain, if the enlightened will of the assembly had not created the power entrusted to the national guards, and if their united and harmonious efforts had not reinstated the order which the first movements of liberty had destroyed. "Gentlemen," he exclaimed, "you well knew the necessities of France, and the will of Frenchmen, when you destroyed the gothic fabric of our government and laws, and respected only their monarchical principle: Europe then discovered that a good king could be the protector of a free, as he had been the ground of comfort to an oppressed, people.—The rights of man are declared; the sovereignty of the people acknowledged; their power is representative; and the bases of public order are established. Hasten, then, to give energy to the power of the state. The people owe to you the glory of a new constitution: but they require and expect that peace and tranquillity which cannot exist without a firm and effectual organization of government.—We, gentlemen, devoted to the revolution, and united in the name of liberty, the guarantees alike of individual and common rights and safety; we, called by the most imperative duty from all parts of the kingdom, founding our confidence on your wisdom, and our hopes on your services,—we will bear, without hesitation, to the altar of the country, the oath which you may dictate to its soldiers.—Yes, gentlemen, our arms shall be stretched forth together, and at the same instant, our brothers from all parts of France, shall utter the oath which will unite them together. May the solemnity of that great day be the signal of the conciliation of parties, of the oblivion of resentments, and of the establishment of public peace and happiness.—And fear not that this holy enthusiasm will hurry us beyond the proper and prescribed limits of public order. Under the protection of the law, the standard of liberty shall never become the rallying point of licentiousness and disorder. Gentlemen, we swear to you to respect the law which it is our duty to defend,—we swear, by our honour as freemen;—and Frenchmen do not promise in vain."—The address of

Lafayette to the king evinced the same regard to royal, and national rights. "Sire," said he, "in the course of those memorable events which have restored to the nation its imprescriptible rights, and during which the energy of the people, and the virtues of their king, have produced such illustrious examples for the contemplation of the world, we loved to hail, in the person of your majesty, the most illustrious of all titles,—chief of the French, and king of a free people.—Enjoy, sire, the recompense of your virtues, and let that pure homage, which despotism could not command, be the glory and reward of a citizen-king. You have desired that we should possess a constitution founded on liberty and public order. All your wishes, sire, shall be accomplished; liberty we have secured, and our zeal is the guarantee of public order." Lafayette concluded with these remarkable words: "The national guards of France swear to your majesty, an obedience which shall know no other limits than those of the law, and a love which shall only terminate with their existence." The reply of the king was extremely circumspect and affectionate; "Repeat to your fellow-citizens, that it would have been my desire to speak to them all, as I now speak to you. Say to them, that their king is their father, their brother, their friend, that he cannot be contented without their prosperity, great without their glory, rich without their property, nor unhappy without they are afflicted."*

The day of vast and universal expectation at last arrived. The king, the court, the clergy, the national assembly, a deputation of military from the eighty-three departments, and a body of people amounting to above four hundred thousand souls, were assembled in the magnificent amphitheatre of the Champ-de-Confederation. The king had been appointed, for that day only, supreme and absolute commander of all the national guards in France. He named Lafayette as his delegate to perform the functions; so that he was not only commander-in-chief of the national guards of Paris, but high

* Toulong. p. 219, 220.—Mem. Hist. p. 203, 207

constable of all the armed men in the kingdom; which was, probably, a greater number than had ever before been in any kingdom in the world. At this time he occupied a most important station indeed; the eyes of the whole world were fixed upon him. Having the military command over six millions of men, and holding in his hands the power of the monarchy, a boundless influence, and a devoted army might have carried him successfully to the highest grade of power. In a word, on him reposed the destinies of France. This was the crisis of his reputation; and from his course at that time, his friends and enemies imbibed their opinions of his character. There was but one course for Lafayette to pursue, and that was the support of liberty, of constitutional monarchy, and of public tranquillity; and he always held, as it were, a magnanimous neutrality between the different parties, when their projects went beyond the laws of justice and moderation. After mass was celebrated by M. de Talleyrand, then bishop of Autun, M. de Lafayette dismounted from his white charger, and approached the king to receive his orders, who delivered to him the form of the oath prescribed for the national troops. "Is it not Tacitus who remarks," says a writer of that period, "speaking of Agricola, that nothing heightens the brilliancy of a throne more than to see bending before it, the person of a man who possesses a bold and noble soul, and who, although yet in his youth, can boast of many triumphs?" M. de Lafayette, as the representative of the nation, took the oath first, at the altar which had been erected in the midst of the arena. When he left the foot of the throne, where he had for some time stood, and moved toward the altar, the trumpets began to sound, and while he ascended its steps, a vast band of martial music continued to play. Every eye of the immense mass was turned on him; every hand was raised to join in the oath he uttered. It was, no doubt, one of the most magnificent and solemn ceremonies the world ever saw; and, perhaps, no man ever enjoyed the sincere confidence of an entire people more completely than

Lafayette did, as he thus bore the most imposing part in these extraordinary solemnities.—In the view of the multitude who filled the immense circus around, he laid the point of his sword upon the bible which was on the table of the altar, and raising his hand toward heaven, the music ceased; a universal stillness ensued; and he pronounced the oath: "We swear to be for ever faithful to the nation, to the law, and to the king; to maintain, to the utmost of our power, the constitution decreed by the national assembly, and accepted by the king." The conclusion of this ceremony was announced by the discharge of artillery, the reiterated shouts of *Vive le roi! vive la nation!* the clanging of arms, and the flourishes of warlike instruments;—and the immense multitude, who witnessed the oath, united in it with loud and long acclamations.—Similar oaths were then taken by the president of the national assembly, and the king.*

Lafayette was, on this day, the grand object of popular affection: he inspired the national guards with an exalted devotion. The oath, and the man who pronounced it, excited a strong feeling of confidence. The spectators felt an intoxication of delight: the king and liberty seemed to them, at that time, completely united. For Lafayette, it was an epoch pregnant with difficulties. The part he played caused him to be closely watched by all parties; but his conduct removed all cause for uneasiness, and preserved to him his high rank and consideration. The throne feared him; and he had been useful to the throne; but confidence could never be established between him and the king; and mutual advantages were lost, because they never dared to assist each other.—But, if the political opinion of Lafayette had been different, his power would have fallen to the ground if he had ventured to oppose the feeling of the day. Ideas, not individuals, were then all-powerful. A limited monarchy has always been the true wish of France, but, as madam

* Stael. Consid. Rev. i. 376—Hist. French Rev. i. 194.—Moore's View ii. 93-5.—Toulong. Hist. i. 222, 3, 4.—Mem. Hist. 199. 203, 207.—North American Review, No. xlvi. p. 161, 2

De Stael has well observed, the last movement of a truly national enthusiasm was displayed at this federation of 1790. The Jacobins were constantly gaining power, and the revolution was falling more and more into the hands of the populace. Notwithstanding the good intentions of many who took the oath, the ceremony has been considered as the grandest and most extensive act of perjury that heaven and earth have ever witnessed. But Lafayette himself, under all circumstances, remained strictly faithful to his oaths; and now defended the freedom of the king, as sincerely as he had ever defended the freedom of the people. Every subsequent act proved his sincerity: every day his situation became more dangerous. He might have taken great power to himself, and so have been safe. He might have received the sword of constable of France, which was once worn by the Montmorencies, but he declined it: or he might have been generalissimo of the national guards, who owed their existence to him, but he thought it more for the safety of the state that no such power should exist.*

Previous to the confederation, the duke of Orleans desired leave to return and assist at this august ceremony, adding, that if the assembly should not think it necessary to deliberate on the subject, he should consider that as a permission for his return. The assembly immediately cast their eyes toward Lafayette, who ascended the tribune and explained his motives for having advised the departure of the duke.—The reasons, he added, in his opinion, did still exist, though he saw nothing to make him apprehensive, at present, for the public safety. The assembly then passed to the order of the day, which was construed into a permission, for his returning to Paris, where he accordingly arrived on the eleventh of July, and after first renewing his civic oath in the national assembly, assisted personally at the confederation.†

* North American Review, No. xlvi. p. 161.—Consid. French Rev. vol. i. 376.—Toulong. tome i. 227–8.

† Moore's View, ii. 89, 90.—Hist. French Rev. i. 195, 196.

Three days after the federation, Lafayette received a most flattering and affectionate address from the national guards of France, signed by more than twelve hundred commandants, captains, officers, and privates, belonging to all departments of the kingdom. "The more," observed these deputies of four millions of soldiers, "you perform for the public benefit, the less you desire to receive rewards; you have refused the homage about to be offered from the grateful hearts of your fellow-citizens; you endeavour to escape from our zeal and our eulogiums; and you have afforded the striking example, that a truly great man can never believe that he has performed enough for his country.—The deputies of the national guard of France, retire under the fear that they will be unable to appoint you their chief; they respect the constitutional law which arrests the impulse of their hearts; and the fact that you yourself originated that law—that you yourself prescribed limits to the expression of our gratitude—ought for ever to cover you with glory. But if you cannot be our chief, you will ever be our friend, our guide, and our model: accustomed to behold in you, one of those heroes who have principally contributed to the success of the revolution, we will never forget the great example which you have shown us; and, should it be possible that, at a future day, any attempt shall be made to abuse our love of liberty,—should it be possible that that love, so pure in its principle, shall give any hopes to the partizans of disorder,—be firm and encouraged: millions of men are armed for the defence of the constitution; millions of men to partake in your dangers.—As representative of the nation, be, sir, always near the legislative assembly, as the pledge of our zeal in the execution of its decrees."*

It is a pleasing part of the duty of the biographer, to record the numerous examples, which shed so much lustre on the pure and disinterested principles of Lafayette. That truly great man steadily resisted the entreaties of the muni-

* Mem. Hist. p. 292.

cipality of Paris, which required him to accept the compensation legally granted to him as the commander of the national guard. In September, 1790, the president of the Commune, at length addressed a letter to Lafayette, in which he declared and reiterated in the most positive manner, that it was the intention of the assembly no longer to permit him to refuse the indemnity which was legally and unavoidably his due, for the immense expenditures which he had been obliged to make in the eminent situation which the public voice had entrusted to him :—that the assembly requested, and (as authoritative expressions on their part could not be disagreeable to him who had uniformly supported their authority,) it understood, that he would receive the necessary indemnities. " You may be generous," it concluded, " but the city of Paris cannot possibly be ungrateful. You have created its felicity —it cannot involve you in ruin."—To this letter, general Lafayette made the following reply :

GENTLEMEN,

Permit me, while I positively declare that I have received nothing, either directly or indirectly, from the municipality nor the executive, to add, that I receive a sweet and sufficient compensation for the trouble occasioned by fulfilling the duties of the distinguished situation to which I have been called by the voice of the people, in the kind and flattering professions with which you have ever deigned to honour me. I do not affect a false generosity, in persisting in my refusal : I would be disposed, not only to accept, but to demand, to solicit, from the people, in whose cause I have devoted my fortune and my life, indemnity for my expenditures, if my fortune did not raise me above want.—*It was considerable ; it has sufficed for two revolutions ; and if a third should occur, for the benefit of the people, it shall belong wholly to it.*

LAFAYETTE.

A deputation was then appointed to wait on the commander-in-chief: he remained firm, but respectful in his refusal.

His second reply contains sentiments ennobling to human nature. "I will observe, gentlemen," said he, "that in this moment of troubles, it is difficult to regulate the expenditure of the commander-in-chief. If my personal situation required pecuniary aid, I would have demanded it: and I beg you to believe, that I do not attach more importance to refusing, than to accepting it. But, at a time when so many citizens are in want, and so many expenses are necessary, it is repugnant to my feelings uselessly to increase them. My fortune is sufficient for the rank I hold.—After this declaration, gentlemen, I confine myself simply to the request, that the one hundred thousand livres added for the current year, to the forty thousand crowns, may contribute to the comfort and relief of those who have most severely suffered for their country." In the same communication, he declared that the compensation of the commander-in-chief, fixed at one hundred and twenty thousand livres, was excessive, and ought to be diminished.*

The society of Jacobins, one of the most powerful engines recurred to during the French revolution, was now beginning to dictate laws to the assembly itself. "From the moment," says madame De Stael, "that we admit into a government, a power that is not legal, it invariably ends by becoming the strongest." The Jacobin clubs, (for there were no less than twenty thousand *affiliated* clubs in France,) were organised as a government more than the government itself: they passed decrees; they were connected by correspondence in the provinces, with other clubs not less powerful; and, finally, they could be considered only as a mine, always ready to blow up existing institutions, when opportunities should offer But its incendiary motions and outrageous proceedings, and the equivocal characters of many of the ruling members, had cast an indelible stain on a society which, after efficaciously and usefully counterbalancing the influence of the court, was now likely, at no distant period, to endanger the fabric of

* Mem. Hist. p. 178—184.

national liberty. M. de Lafayette and his partizans would not, therefore, consent to go to a club, whose leaders scarcely concealed their wishes to dethrone the king, and either nominate a new dynasty to the throne, or erect a republic on its ruins. To balance the influence of the Jacobin club, they instituted a rival society under the name of the "club of 1789," in which the friends of order and liberty were expected to meet. The principal leaders of this club, on its establishment, were Lafayette, Talleyrand, the dukes de Rouchefoucault, and Liancourt, the two Lameths; and many other celebrated orators, patriots, and politicians. When they became more numerous, they were better known by the title of *Feuillans*, from the convent of that name, in which they assembled. Their former associates, the Jacobins, perceiving them to be formidable, affected to wish for a reunion, and accordingly sent a deputation for that purpose; but the Feuillans decidedly rejected the proposition; a circumstance which their rivals well knew how to turn to their advantage, and soon found means not only to render them suspected by the people, but even, at length, to annihilate them as a deliberative body. These two formidable societies evinced a rooted hatred to each other. The friends of order and of the constitution, were unable to resist the intolerant spirit which soon involved France in blood and calamity; and when, at last, the monarchy was dissolved, the blood of the advocates of liberty flowed on the same scaffold that had received the victims of aristocracy; and the founders of the republic began to proscribe each other with an envenomed rancour, that admitted neither of compromise nor of mercy. Lafayette himself became the victim of Jacobinical fury, and of the free and rational principles, which caused him steadily to oppose the growing power of the Jacobin society.*

In the beginning of the year 1791, the spirit of sedition seemed to augment every moment, and would no doubt have

*. Consid. French Rev. i. 398—Stephen's Hist. Wars French Rev. i. Introd. cix.—x.

produced very dreadful effects, had it not been for the steady conduct of Lafayette, and the national guards acting under his orders. It is impossible to unfold the motives of every insurrection which occurred during the revolution. Some, which were begun in consequence of premeditated plans, failed, from the error or weakness of the conductors: some arose from mere accident, independent of any regular scheme, and became formidable from being considered as the result of profound design and extensive conspiracy. On the twenty-eighth of February, 1791, the jealousy and dissatisfaction of the public were unfortunately increased by a rumour which prevailed, that the castle of Vincennes was intended to replace the Bastile. It is uncertain whether this idea originated with the rabble, or was suggested by men who had some view in it, which afterwards failed: but, on the day mentioned a large body of men set out from the Fauxbourg St. Antoine, with the avowed intention of destroying the castle of Vincennes. This mob was led by Santerre, a brewer of that suburb, who had endeavoured to supplant Lafayette in the good graces of the people: indeed, being a coarse, rough, man, he seemed more fit for the confidence of men, whose professed aim it was to level all distinctions, and who, therefore, required a commander who was hearty in the cause of anarchy. Santerre commanded a division of the national guard, and the riot of Vincennes served to show the two parties in their proper colours. Lafayette, the superior officer, opposed himself to the demolition, and Santerre opposed himself to Lafayette. A detachment of national guards which had been immediately sent to the spot, and drawn up for the protection of the castle, became, from their artful remonstrances and entreaties, more disposed to assist than to repel the rioters. Lafayette, having heard that the work of destruction was begun, and the troops passive, repaired in person to Vincennes, expostulated with the soldiers, and brought them to a sense of their duty. He then ordered them to attack the rabble without firing on them. Sixty were seized, and the rest dispersed. Many of the latter hastily repaired to the Fauxbourg St. Antoine, exciting the populace to rescue the prisoners. Lafayette, being told that it would be dangerous to march through that quarter of Paris, as the people were in insurrection, placed the prisoners in the middle, some field-pieces in front, and marched his troops, (with some municipal officers at the head of the column,) directly through the Fauxbourg St. Antoine to the Hotel-de-Ville; and, while the mob insulted his troops with their exclamations, and even wounded one of his aids-de-camp, and some of the soldiers, by throwing stones, he lodged the prisoners in the *Conciergerie*, without farther bloodshed.*

Lafayette having thus decisively quelled the insurrection of the populace, found, on his return to Paris, that it was a necessary duty to oppose himself to the indiscreet friends of the king, who had created a great disturbance at the Tuilleries during his absence. He found that the apartments were filled with several hundred armed men, who had been admitted at a private door, by the first gentleman of the king's bed-chamber, and unknown to the national guards on duty at the palace. They declared that, fearing for the royal safety, they had assembled for the defence of the king; but the latter rebuked their indiscreet zeal; and, to satisfy the national guard, who were peculiarly irritated at their interference, he ordered that the intruders should be disarmed and dismissed. If this ceremony was performed a little roughly by the national guards, to the great displeasure of many who thought such treatment an ungrateful return for the zeal they had manifested, it must be ascribed to the jealous feelings which they had created. Lafayette himself did not arrive at the palace until after the order for disarming the intruders was issued; but he was exposed to the angry personal attacks directed against him by the suffering party. A part of the day had been employed in quelling the designs

* Moore's View, ii. 125, 6, 7.—Hist. Jacob. i. 270, 3.—Hist. French Rev. i. 215.

of the king's enemies, and it was now as necessary to oppose the king's friends. He found himself engaged in a quarrel with those of his own rank; and, before the eyes of his national guard, it was necessary to show, and even to affect, a rigour and severity which might attach no doubt to his conduct and opinions. This assemblage in the king's apartments, was variously stated to have been connected with external plans, of which Lafayette alone was ignorant, or, more probably, to have derived its source from the anxiety of some individuals for the king's safety.*

The singular occurrences of the twenty-eighth of February created general distrust, and when the king signified his intention of passing the Easter holidays at St. Cloud, the populace considered it as foreboding the flight of the king, and a counter-revolution. The king, however, persisted in his design, and on the eighteenth of April went into his coach, accompanied by the queen, the dauphin, and the princess Elizabeth. The populace immediately surrounded the carriage, and clamorously insisted on their majesties' return; but as they were surrounded by numerous detachments of the national guards, the king ordered the postillions to drive on: instead of keeping off the crowd, the guards closed before the horses, threatened the postillions if they should dare to proceed, and swore they would not permit the royal family to leave Paris. The king's domestic servants, and other officers of his household, were mal-treated, and the most insulting and abusive expressions were directed against the queen. Bailly, the mayor, hastened to the Tuilleries to suppress the disorder;—but he was not listened to. Lafayette ordered the national guards to open to the right and left, to clear away the multitude, and allow the king's coach to pass. He was not obeyed. In vain did they oppose this frenzy A set of orators, better adapted to the ears of the common people, exclaimed, "If the king escapes, there

* Moore's View, ii. 128–9, 130.—Toulong. Hist. i, 268–9.

will be a civil war, and the streets of Paris will be deluged with the blood of the citizens." The national guard refused to act: "We know," said the grenadiers, "that we are violating the law; but the safety of the country is the first of laws."—In short, the king and royal family, after having been nearly two hours in the coach, exposed to the insults and derision of the multitude and of the mutinous soldiery, were under the necessity of getting out of the carriage and walking to the palace, amidst the groans, hootings, and hisses of the multitude. Lafayette had arrived, at the first suggestion of danger. "If," said he to the king, "this be a matter of conscience with your majesty, we will, if it be necessary die to maintain it;" and he offered immediately to open a passage by force; but the king declined a resort to arms.*

The writers of all parties have done justice to the spirit and propriety which distinguished the conduct of Lafayette on this occasion. Disgusted at the shameful scene on the eighteenth, he sent in his resignation, observing, that since the national guards would no longer obey, he must cease to retain a command which was merely nominal. This event was no sooner known than all Paris was seized with a general consternation; nor could all the machinations of Lafayette's enemies prevent their soliciting, in a body, and under circumstances the most respectful to him, that he would reassume the command. It then appeared how much he was beloved by the troops which he commanded. All the battalions assembled, and appointed deputations to the general, expressing sorrow for their past conduct, and promising implicit obedience to his orders in future. They also sent deputations to the municipality and to the department entreating them to join in soliciting the general to resume the command.—The hotel of Lafayette was filled with these different deputations, from the time that he had given in his resignation, until the following morning at five o'clock. The

* Toulong. Hist. i. 270—2.—Hist. French Rev. i. 223-4.—North Am. Rev. No. xlvi, 161.

street in which his house stood, was crowded with the troops, all waiting with impatience for the news of his having yielded to their entreaties; but, finding that he still refused, they went in crowds to the Hotel-de-Ville, and begged of the municipality to use their influence with the general. The municipality, perceiving that citizens of all the sections joined in this request of the national guards, declared that they would become responsible for the future obedience of the battalions, and entreated the general to yield to the wishes of his fellow-citizens.—Lafayette expressed a proper sense of the honour conferred on him; adding, that he would not presume to give an immediate answer, but would, the following day, attend the municipality at the Hotel-de-Ville, and then deliver to them his sentiments. Accordingly, he appeared in the common hall at ten o'clock, where he found all the representatives of the common council, with deputies from all the battalions of national guards, assembled, and pronounced a discourse equally distinguished for modesty and good sense. He placed in a strong point of view, the horror which every enlightened citizen must have felt, at beholding those whose duty it was to support the laws, oppose their execution. He added, that if the capital, which was the cradle of the revolution, instead of respecting and obeying the executive powers, should besiege them with tumults, and fatigue them with insults, it would, from being the honoured *example*, become the *terror*, of the French nation; and that, in the marks of regard with which his fellow-citizens had honoured him, too much attention had been paid to an individual, but not enough to the laws: "In the affecting marks of attachment," said he, "that I have received, too much regard is shown to me, and too little to the laws. I am feelingly convinced that my comrades love me; but I am still to learn, how far they are attached to those principles on which liberty is founded."—And he concluded by refusing to resume the command.

When the refusal, and the observations, of the general,

became known, it was resolved that each battalion should assemble the following day, and make a declaration of their sentiments on the subject pointed out in his discourse. This was accordingly done by all the different regiments; and, in their declarations, instead of expressing attachment to their general, and wishes that he should resume the command, they spoke solely of their submission to the law, their zeal for the constitution, and their resolution to obey the commander-in-chief, without once mentioning the name of Lafayette.—The municipality, having verified the declarations of the troops, decreed, that the mayor, at the head of a deputation of eight members of the common council, should wait on the general, and represent to him, that it would endanger the state if he persisted in his first resolution, and that the greatest proof of patriotism he could give, would be to resume the command.—It was impossible longer to resist. Lafayette returned thanks to the mayor and the deputation in becoming terms: and the day following, having resumed the command, he expressed his sense of the honour done him by the various corps; and, being then on the parade before the Hotel-de-Ville, he proposed, that they should go in a body to the king, taking with them all their comrades whom they might meet, and express their sorrow and repentance for what was past, and renew to his majesty, their declaration of allegiance. This proposal was directly adopted: Lafayette conducted them to the Tuilleries; addressed the king, in the name of all the national guards, in the terms which had been agreed on; received a gracious reception and answer from the monarch, and, as soon as this was known, the troops expressed their satisfaction by repeated exclamations of "Vive le Roi! Vive le Restaurateur de la Liberte Francaise! Vive le Petit-Fils de Henri IV!"*

This return of the national guards to a sense of their duty, was highly provoking to a set of men who, unhappily for France, were at this time concentrated in the capital, and

* Moore's View, ii. 167, 171.—Hist. French Rev. i. 224.

who were continually endeavouring to create discord and confusion. The instrumentality of Lafayette in effecting this object, increased the odium in which he was held by the fomenters of anarchy; and his agency in the dismission of fourteen soldiers of the national guard, who had been particularly active in promoting the mutiny of the eighteenth, gave a fresh and violent impulse to their enmity. The discarded soldiers were feasted, and treated as persecuted patriots; while Lafayette was accused as an enemy of liberty and of being bought by the court. Emissaries were also employed to blacken his character and misrepresent his conduct, among the groups of idlers in the places of public resort. Placards were posted up, and pamphlets published against him. At the Cordeliers, some men were heard to declare, that it would be meritorious to assassinate him: and, at the Fraternal Society, a woman, fired by the eloquence of these orators, and intoxicated with the spirit of patriotism, called him, among other bad names, a second *Sisera*, and swore that she would take the earliest opportunity of entering his house, and driving a nail into his temples while he was asleep.*

The capital was now kept in a continual state of agitation by the daring and unprincipled men, who had the direction of the numerous incendiary societies; until at length, the unhappy monarch, being in dread of the utmost violence from the increasing rancour of his enemies, resolved to endeavour to escape with his family, out of the kingdom, or, at least, to a garrisoned town on the frontiers. On the night of the twentieth of June, 1791, the royal family left the palace in disguise, by a private issue which communicated with the Carousel, crossed the Pont Royal, and, on the Quai des Theatins, found the carriages which were waiting for them. At Chalons, the king was recognised by the post-master, who, being a royalist, did not betray him; but at St. Menehould, the decisive blow was struck. He was there fully known by

* Moore's View, ii. 172, 3.

Drouet, a frantic revolutionist, who instantly determined to prevent his escape: he, however, allowed him to proceed to the next post, but despatched a courier, with the intelligence, to Varennes. Here the unhappy prince was arrested, and conducted, amid the most excessive insult and torments, back to his capital.

The greatest agitation followed the flight of the king, and when this unexpected news was communicated to the assembly, Lafayette was accused as the author of the plot; But he was defended by Barnave; and the assembly deputed six commissaries, with orders to rescue him from the hands of the mob, who threatened him with death. Lafayette was not a participator in that ill-judged event; nor, to such a man, were the powers of six commissaries at all necessary. But it cannot be denied that the general was placed in a most critical situation, and that it required all his popularity to preserve his life. The king not having entrusted any one with his secret, no one felt himself called upon to defend him, and the *cote-droit* of the assembly, doubly injured by not having been informed of the plan, and by being left exposed to danger, openly complained of the monarch: thus all parties endeavoured to excite the spirit of the people, who, not knowing whom to blame, naturally directed their violence against the mayor and commander-in-chief, as negligent or faithless guardians of the public peace. Lafayette was placed in imminent peril: the fury of the populace against him was extreme, and nothing but the long and solid confidence which they had reposed in him, could have averted the first transports of their rage.—The king left the palace about midnight; but Lafayette was ignorant of his departure until six o'clock in the morning. He immediately wrote to a few friends whom he requested to meet at the Hotel-de-la-Rochefoucalt, and then repaired to the Hotel-de-Ville. The fury of the people subsided, when they perceived the tranquillity and firmness with which he advanced alone, amid the shouts and roarings of a prodigious crowd. But uneasiness and indecision still prevailed, and some observations on the misfortune that had happened, which seemed to require an answer from Lafayette, furnished him with the opportunity of saying to those who complained, "*If you call this event a misfortune, what name would you give to a counter-revolution which would deprive you of liberty?*" This observation revived the boldness of the discontented; and several voices cried out, "*Let us make Lafayette our king;*" all within hearing clamorously repeated this observation Lafayette, regarding them with a mingled look of pity and indignation exclaimed, "*I thought that you possessed a better opinion of me. What have I done, that you do not believe me fit for something bett r?*" Thereupon, the air was filled with loud shouts of "*Long live the general!*" and confidence and tranquillity were re-established. At this moment, the six commissaries arrived to protect him; but they found him sufficiently fixed in the public opinion to refuse any measures for his personal safety.—In the same hour, Lafayette was also attacked in the assembly: a member (Rewbell) remarked, immediately after the six commissaries were despatched to rescue the general, "M. de Lafayette is about to appear, and I request that he may be asked, whether he did not give, a month since, to the officers on guard in the palace, the counter-sign not to permit any one to pass out after midnight: there must have been some motive for this precaution· and we ought to know if———." Here the speaker was interrupted by Barnave, who said, "I demand that the assembly shall no longer suffer this discourse to be continued, and that it be not permitted to raise injurious surmises respecting men who have continually afforded proofs of their patriotism. Circumstances may arise, in which it is easy to cast suspicions on the sentiments of the best citizens; but the conduct of the commander of the national guard, since the commencement of the revolution, is a sufficient pledge that he merits all our confidence. It is our duty to testify it toward him, in the most signal manner."—Never was a vindication more triumphant, nor more generous. Barnave was at this time, and had long been, on ill terms with Lafayette, and the rupture between them was notorious. It had excited considerable interest, and all correspondence had ceased between the parties. It was a truly republican motive which urged Barnave to undertake the defence of one who was absent, and inculpated in so grave an offence, when the defender might have exposed himself to the suspicions which it was attempted to cast on the commander-in-chief. This just and generous action overpowered the assembly, and arrested an accusation, which would doubtless have been repeated, if the first had been received.

Lafayette was also openly accused by Danton in the Jacobin club, of having assisted the flight of the king. He was defended by Lamith; but, for a long time, vague suspicions rested on the conduct of the general. At that period, one party accused him of holding intelligence with the court; and the opposite side accused him of duplicity, having, as they said, caused the king to be arrested, after having facilitated his departure. "It is possible and probable," says Toulongeon, "that he winked at the departure of the queen, and that he was ignorant of that of the king. A great number of the best men desired the removal of the queen, as the only means of saving the king, herself, and the monarchy." It is true that he despatched a messenger after the royal family; and he could not possibly do otherwise, circumstanced as he was at that period: had he not done it, Paris would again have been devoted to the most dreadful outrages. His aid-de-camp, however, did not reach Varennes until after the royal fugitives had been arrested. When they returned to Paris, it was principally owing to the zeal, the courage, and the magnanimity of Lafayette, that they were not immediately destroyed. It was owing to him, that Paris was not a scene of horrible confusion: he had the boldness to declare in a debate in the national assembly, "that if any violence was offered to the king, he would, at the head of the national guards, proclaim Louis the seventeenth, king;" and this once more silenced the fury of democracy in Paris, and restored order and submission to legislative authority. If the charge of having instigated the royal family to escape, for the purpose of afterwards arresting them, were founded in fact, no odium could be too great, no obloquy could attach a sufficiently just reprehension, for so cold-blooded a piece of duplicity But the proof of his innocence is so incontrovertible, so positive and direct, that the mention of it must stamp an indelible impression on the mind of every man, and clear him entirely from so foul a calumny. The test of his innocence was the unfortunate Marie Antoinette, who, being asked on her trial, whether Lafayette had connived at their escape, positively answered, that he was totally ignorant of it.*

The assembly was compelled, by the popular ferment, to declare that the king should be kept prisoner in the palace of the Tuilleries, until the constitution had been presented for his acceptance. Lafayette as commander of the national guards, had the misfortune of being doomed to carry this decree into effect. But if, on the one hand, he placed sentinels at the gates of the palace, he opposed, on the other, with conscientious energy, the party which endeavoured to pronounce the king fallen from his throne. He employed against those who pressed that measure, the armed force in the Champ-de-Mars; and he thus proved, at least, that it was not from views of ambition that he exposed himself to the displeasure of the king, as he drew on himself, at the same time, the hatred of the enemies of the throne.† On the motion of Lafayette in the assembly, a general amnesty was subsequently granted to all those who had participated in the king's journey, or committed what could be called po-

* Stael Consid. French Rev. i. 410–11.—Hist. French Rev. i. 227—233.—Wars French Rev. i. Introd. xcii.—Etienne Rev. 156—160.—Senator. ix. 645, 659.—Moore's View, ii. 206.—Quart. Rev. xxviii, 305—8.—Toulong. Hist. ii. b. 28, Ap. 59, 115.

† Stael Consid. i. 423.

litical offences: he also obtained a decree, enabling every individual to leave France, and return, without a passport.

The unanimity which generally prevailed throughout France, from the time of the king's return to his acceptance of the constitution, was interrupted by a short, but disgraceful, riot at Paris. Several efforts had been unsuccessfully made by ill-disposed people to disturb the public tranquillity; but on the morning of the seventeenth of July, 1791, the magistrates were alarmed by the report that a large body of seditious persons were about to assemble in the Champ-de-Mars, the professed object of whom was to petition against the re-establishment of the king, a measure which the Jacobin club had been very active to promote. A great crowd of people flocked to the altar of the federation, which had not yet been removed, there to sign the remonstrance, followed by a declaration that they never would submit to be governed by Louis the sixteenth. At ten o'clock, M. de Lafayette arrived on the spot, and caused the barricades which had been erected, to be destroyed—A wretch, named Fournier, had the audacity to fire at him, with a pistol, pointed almost at his breast: the man was instantly seized, but Lafayette, with a false generosity, permitted him to be released, and he afterwards boasted of the act at the bar of the convention. At length, the municipal officers who accompanied the general, obtained a promise from the mob that they would disperse; and a body of national guards was stationed to prevent their reassembling. Several hours after, the municipality, who had met at the Hotel-de-Ville, were informed that the ferment was increasing, and that menacing plans against the national assembly were in agitation. At the same time, it was stated that two unfortunate persons, who had secreted themselves under the altar on which the signatures were received, had been murdered by the mob. Martial law was now formally proclaimed; and a red flag was displayed from a window of the Hotel-de-Ville. Lafayette immediately collected the national guard, and accompanied by the municipal authorities, marched to the Champ-de-Mars. They found it crowded by a furious multitude, who, instead of dispersing, insulted the troops with loud cries of "*A bas le drapeau rouge! A bas les bayonettes!*" Stones were thrown at the troops and municipal officers, in volleys. M. Bailly, the mayor, desired the troops to halt, and, after the formalities which the law required, Lafayette ordered part of them to fire over the heads of the mob. When they perceived that none were wounded, it confirmed them in an opinion which they had formed, that neither the general nor the mayor had any inclination to hurt them, and that they durst not fire with ball. From this idea they became more outrageous; the soldiers and some of the officers of the guards, were wounded; and they now received orders to fire with ball. Ten or twelve of the mob were killed, and a considerable number wounded.—The energy displayed by Lafayette in quelling this commotion, was generally approved of, and heartily so by the national assembly: a greater degree of order and tranquillity than had been known for some time before in Paris, was the consequence of it.*

On the thirteenth of September, 1791, the constituent assembly closed, and was succeeded by the legislative assembly. Not only Lafayette, but the Lameths, Adrien Duport, Barnave, and other sincere friends of the constitution, which had now been accepted by the king, could not be members of the second assembly, by that most impolitic decree which excluded all who had been members of the first. Lafayette, particularly from the arrest and imprisonment of the king, was become more than ever the object of hatred to the loyalists; and as to the Jacobins, he had already provoked all their fury by his conduct toward the duke of Orleans, and from his causing the companies of the insurgent regiments at Nanci, who were coming to Paris to raise the

* Toulong. Hist. ii. 53—4.—Hist. French Rev. i. 236.—Moore's View, ii. 237.

populace, to be arrested. From that moment the Jacobins attacked him with increasing violence: then Corypheus Marat, author of the "Friend of the People," constantly denounced him as the *traitor Lafayette*. The affair of the Champ-de-Mars brought this rage to its height: the republican party which then began to manifest itself, already wished to bring the king to trial, and united with the Jacobins, in opposition to Lafayette and the friends of the constitution. After the open attempt to assassinate their general, the national guard, especially the old French guard, grew furious: they imprecated the Jacobins, wished to destroy by a cannonade the club, which they called a cavern, and disperse the people who frequented it. But Lafayette consistently opposed, and allayed, the ferment.

When the constitution of 1791, was accepted by the king in the spirit of Washington, he resigned all command, alleging that the emergency which required his services, was now over, and that, as he derived his powers from the revolution, those powers ought to cease with it. His situation in the national guards, which he had now completely organized according to his original project, was filled by temporary commanders. The municipality of Paris caused a medal of gold to be struck in his honour, and presented him with a sword, and a marble bust of Washington. He had sacrificed a large part of his fortune for the revolution, but magnanimously declined any remuneration for his losses. Lafayette now retired to his estate of Chavagnac in Auvergne, accompanied by the esteem which his generous and disinterested conduct so well deserved. He was followed, as he had been for many years, by crowds wherever he went, and attended on his way by every form of popular enthusiasm and admiration.*

Not long after this retirement, a circumstance occurred which served to put in motion the two parties which were

* Nat. Gaz. Feb. 3, Sep. 13, 1824.—Moore's View, ii. 248.—Toulong. Hist. ii. 94, Ap. 25.—Biog. Notice, p. 10.

shortly to divide the kingdom, the constitutionalists and the republicans; and the event might have shown in whose favour the balance was likely to preponderate. The mayoralty of the judicious and patriotic M. Bailly, terminated in the month of November, 1791; and the once popular Lafayette appeared as a candidate to succeed him. He was opposed by Petion, a violent Jacobin, and a declared republican, on the one side, and, the king and queen, being prejudiced against him, by the whole influence of the court, on the other. It is almost unnecessary to state the issue of this unequal contest, and to add that Petion was elected mayor of Paris by a great majority. The small number of votes that Lafayette obtained was the source of great surprise to many people, when they considered his ardour in pursuit of the revolution, and his services to the people of Paris, which ought to have entitled him to their peculiar countenance and protection. But melancholy experience had evinced the increasing credit and power of the Jacobins, and it was evident that that pernicious society had not only gained the ascendancy over the minds of the populace, but was enabled to control even the assembly itself. The government in fact, was in their hands, if that may be called a government where the people are without control, and called to account for none of their actions;—a government from which it was time for all honest men to retire.*

> Quid est Catulle quod moraris emori?
> Sella in curuli struma Nonius sedet,
> Per consulatum pejerat Vatinius;
> Quid est Catulle quod moraris emori?

From the happy tranquillity to which he now gladly turned, Lafayette was soon called by the war with Austria declared April twentieth, 1792, in which he was, at once, appointed one of the three major-generals to command the French armies: he soon after obtained the rank of lieuten-

* Bertrand's Mem. i. 259.—Letters from Paris, ii. 205.—Hist. French Rev. i. 263–4.—Touloпgeon, ii. 94.

ant-general, and finally that of marshal of France, with a red ribband. Having received from the king the command of the army of the centre, destined to cover the frontier of Ardennes, he took the field in the beginning of May, 1792. Lafayette, together with Rochambeau and Luckner, had been previously summoned to Paris, to consult with the council; and Lafayette had greatly interested himself in bringing about a reconciliation among the ministers, whose dissensions had an evil effect on the public mind, and were likely to produce fatal consequences to the king. Notwithstanding the infamous combination of tyrants, at the treaty of Pilnitz, and the provocation which had been given to the French nation, Lafayette was one of those who thought it would have been more politic to have been less precipitate, and to have compelled Austria to appear, in every view, in the character of an aggressor. Such was the opinion of a man, whose judgment was in general sound, and whose patriotism none but a violent and desperate faction has ever presumed to question. But, placed by the unanimous voice of his country at the head of the arms of France, he prepared to repel the invaders.

Three separate bodies of troops were formed along the frontiers, from Switzerland to Dunkirk, under the direction of three commanders, enjoying not only the reputation of great military talents, but also the confidence of the nation: these were Lafayette, Rochambeau, and Luckner. Lafayette, who commanded the army of the centre, fixed his head quarters at Metz, and occupied Nancy, Thionville, and Luneville: he had upwards of twenty thousand men at his disposal, and was so posted as to continue the line of defence from the Meuse to the Moselle. The general officers under his command were De Wittgeinstein, De Bellemont, Crillon, Parquet, and Defranc. It was a part of the plan concerted in the French cabinet, that all the troops should be in motion about the same time, and form, if possible, a general rendezvous in the centre of the Austrian Netherlands.—Agreeably to this plan, Lafayette was to be at Givet by the thirtieth of April; and, although the orders only reached him on the twenty-fourth, and though he was in most respects very ill-appointed, he was, by great exertions, enabled to provide seventy-eight pieces of cannon by the twenty-sixth, and, on the same day, despatched a large body with the convoy of artillery, to penetrate by forced marches to Givet. On the first of May, Lafayette's advance took post at Bouvines, half way to Namur, and every thing appeared to promise success to the expedition. But the failure of the other parts of the grand army rendered it utterly fruitless, though Fayette continued to retain his post, and even slowly to advance upon the enemy. On the twenty-third of May, his advanced guard, under M. Gouvion, was attacked at Hamphine, near Florennes, by a force, as it afterwards appeared, superior to his own, which only amounted to three thousand men. The Austrian advanced guard was twice repulsed; but M. Gouvion, observing the great superiority of the enemy, effected a retreat with the greatest regularity. The next action in which this army was engaged took place on the eleventh of June, when the Austrians attacked the advanced guard of Lafayette, at Griselle, near Maubeuge; but M. Gouvion, aware of their design, began a retreating fight, in which his infantry was constantly covered by the hedges, and the enemy's columns suffered considerably from his cannon. As soon as the news arrived at the camp, Lafayette sent M. Narbonne with a considerable reinforcement on the flank of the enemy, while he himself advanced with the main army. The Austrians abandoned the field, and a part of their killed and wounded, to the French, who pursued them more than a league beyond the ground of their advanced guard, which again took possession of its former post. Though this action was crowned with victory, it was yet unfortunate for France, as it deprived the nation of one of its ablest generals and firmest patriots; Gouvion, the bosom-friend of Fayette both in America and Europe, was killed by the oblique stroke of a reflected ball.*

* Hist. French Rev. ii. 6. 12.—14.—Bert. Mem. ii. 59, 81.—Wars Rev i. 7, 9, 10.—Toulong. Hist. ii. 120.

At this period, the voice of Lafayette was again heard crying out in the cause of justice and humanity. He had commenced a reorganization of the army, improved the discipline, introduced simplicity in the military administration, formed bodies of light artillery, established military councils, and courts-martial; and in a word, he had exerted all his abilities in disciplining his troops, and supplying their necessities. But the treatment of prisoners had been such as to call forth his loudest censure, until prisoners of war were placed, by an express law, under the safe-guard of the nation. "The infamous conduct," said Lafayette in his despatches to the minister of war, "which has been exercised toward prisoners of war, demands, sir, exemplary vengeance. It is not the enemy, but the French army, that demands it. The universal indignation which reigns among us, authorizes me to declare, that brave soldiers are unwilling to fight, if their vanquished enemies are to be cast into the fangs of cowardly cannibals."*

At this period, the thread of court intrigue was so ravelled, that history can hardly follow it: the unhappy king was successively, the object, the tool, and the victim, of it. Too suspicious to abandon himself to any party, and too feeble to master them all,—the Girondists offered him their services—the *Mountain* threatened him—the Jacobins openly insulted him—the Feuillans obeyed him with fear and without confidence—the secret council of the queen promised to baffle them all—and foreign agents, watching all parties, having spies in all, knowing every thing, and opposing each other, were alone successful in their aim,—to create disorder and destruction. Open war was declared between the legislative and the executive powers; and was pushed to such an extremity, that Lafayette, who had now become the butt of every faction, believed it his duty to make a powerful effort, and prove the strength of his former popularity. Violences, of almost every degree of atrocity, were become

* Toulong. Hist ii. 125, Ap. 71.

common, and that public order, of which he had never ceased to speak on all suitable occasions, no longer existed.—He felt that, under these circumstances, his silence would be an abandonment of the principles to the support of which he had devoted his life: and, with a courage which few men in any age have been able to show, and with a temperance, which has always kept his conduct on one even line, he wrote the far-famed letter to the convention, dated from the entrenched camp of Maubeuge, sixteenth June, 1792, in which he drew a very formidable picture of the dangerous situation in which the nation was placed by the attempts of its enemies, both foreign and domestic, and plainly and without reserve, denounced the growing faction of the Jacobins, and called on the constituted authorities to put a stop to the atrocities which they were openly promoting: "Can you dissemble even to yourselves," said he, "that a faction, (and to avoid all vague denunciations,) the *Jacobin faction*, have caused all these disorders? It is that society which I boldly denounce: organized like a separate empire in the metropolis, and in its affiliated societies, and blindly governed by some ambitious leaders, this society forms a totally distinct corporation in the midst of the French nation, whose powers it usurps, by tyrannising over its representatives, and constituted authorities." In the course of this letter, he dared to say, "Let the royal authority be untouched for it is guaranteed by the constitution; let it be independent, for its independence is one of the springs of our liberty; let the king be revered, for he is invested with the majesty of the nation; let him choose a ministry which wears the chains of no faction; and if traitors exist, let them perish under the sword of the law." He, at the same time, addressed a letter to the king, expressive of similar sentiments.*

There was not another man in France who would have dared to take such a step, at such a time; and it required

* Toulong. Hist. ii. 148—159, Ap. 121.—Hist. French Rev. ii. 22 North Am. Rev. January, 1825, p. 162—3.

all Lafayette's vast influence to warrant him in expressing such opinions and feelings, or to protect him afterwards.—The agitation produced by this letter was extreme, and the proceedings of the disaffected of gloomy portent. At first the Jacobins seemed to shrink from a contest with Lafayette; they had heretofore spared, because they feared, and even hoped to gain, him: hoping no more to be able to triumph over his principles, they vowed his destruction; and their oaths of that description had never been taken in vain. The meeting of the Jacobins on the eighteenth of June, was tumultuous and outrageous in the highest degree. They proposed that Lafayette should be sent to Orleans as a traitor, and the most acceptable motion that was made was, that a price should be set on his head, and that *chaque citoyen put courir sus*;—that is to say, that any body that pleased might murder him. While such were the debates within doors, at the hall of the Jacobins, their emissaries without were busily employed in exciting the people to insurrection, and the occurrences of the twentieth of June too plainly evinced the success of their endeavours.—When Lafayette's letter was read, Vergniaux represented that the remonstrances of a general at the head of an army to the assembly, had the appearance of an attempt to overawe the legislature.—Gaüdet ironically remarked, that the letter was so much in the style of Cromwell, that it could not possibly be written by Lafayette. They began, therefore, by denying its authenticity; they declared it, in short a forgery.*

On the twentieth of June, the excitement produced by the machinations of the Jacobins, broke out in the most disgraceful manner. Twenty thousand men of the lowest rank, armed with pikes and lances, marched to the Tuilleries without knowing why;—they were ready to commit every crime, or could be persuaded to the noblest actions, according to the impulse of events, and of their leaders. These twenty

* North Am. Rev. January, 1825, p. 163.—Toulong. Hist. ii. 150—1. Hist. French Rev. ii. 23.—Moore's Journal, p. 115.—Moore's View, ii. 280—1.

thousand men made their way into the palace; and their savage oaths mingled with cries, their threatening gestures and deadly implements, exhibited a frightful spectacle.—Louis XVI. on this day showed all the virtues of a saint, and a degree of courage which had been supposed wholly incompatible with his character. The time was past for saving himself like a hero; but neither the threats nor howlings of this insolent mob could humble nor intimidate him; but he was under the necessity of wearing the red cap, the symbol of the Jacobins and the dreadful signal of massacre, which was placed on his head by the hands of a man inebriated with liquor, and ejaculating the most terrible oaths.—The assembly, ashamed of its auxiliaries, sent several of the deputies to save the royal family; and, at length, in consequence of a long and animated speech, delivered by Vergniaud, the populace was persuaded to retire.*

General Lafayette, indignant at what was passing at Paris left his army to appear at the bar of the assembly, and demand justice for the terrible day of twentieth June, 1792. He was a constitutional general, and whatever prospect of success appeared, it was his duty to take that dangerous, but patriotic step. He passed two days in securing the position of his army during his absence, and set out for Paris. In passing through Soissons, he saw the administrative body who praised his devotion to the country, predicted its inutility, and advised him of his danger. On the twenty-eighth of June, he arrived alone, and alighted at the hotel of La Rochefoucalt, where he was immediately waited on by several battalions of the national guards. A tree of liberty, ornamented with ensigns and cockades was planted before his door, and every circumstance evinced the return of affection in the people to their former friend and benefactor. The news of his arrival gave satisfaction to all the lovers of order and of the constitution, and struck the Jacobins with alarm. It was believed either that his army was in

* De Stael Consid. vol. ii. 47–8.—Wars French Rev. i. 20, 21.—Hist. French Rev. ii. 25.

full march after him, or that he was assured of such support in the capital itself, as would enable him to accomplish the object of his visit. When the king heard of the demand that he was about to make to the convention, he formed very high expectations relative to the success of that measure: but they were not of long duration.—Lafayette appeared at the bar unattended, with that confidence and dignity which integrity alone can give. Had the Girondists at this time joined him and his friends, they might perhaps still have prevented the entrance of foreign troops, and restored to the king that constitutional authority which was his due. The discourse, pronounced by the general, was replete with energy and patriotism, and as strong as the circumstances exacted. He avowed his letter of the sixteenth, and assigned as a reason for his appearance among them, the shame and indignation of the army at the outrage of the twentieth, which, he said, must have increased to an alarming degree, had he not thought it his duty to moderate their resentment against the factions of Paris, by assuring them that he would appear alone before the representatives of the nation, and demand, in their name, that order, obedience, and respect for the laws, should be restored. In the name, therefore, of that army, as well as of all good citizens, he demanded "the punishment of the instigators and executors of the violence of the twentieth, the suppression of the Jacobin societies, and that the assembly would take measures for preventing all attempts against the constitution from internal enemies, while the army was repelling foreign foes from the frontiers.' He closed his speech by words which well became him; "Such are the representations submitted to the assembly by a citizen, whose love for liberty at least, will not be disputed."—His discourse was received with applause, and the president invited him to the honour of a sitting. The consternation which prevailed for a short time, was dispelled by Gaudet, who stepped quickly to the tribune, and in a dexterous discourse, inveighed against the general for leaving the army, described the distrust which his counsels ought to excite in the legislative assembly, and desired that the minister of war might be questioned whether general Lafayette had, or had not, obtained permission to leave his post. This produced a debate ; and several severe speeches were made by those who would have remained over-awed, had not Gaudet began in the bold manner he did. The noise and cry of question now became pretty general ;—when the appeal nominal threw out Gaudet's motion by three hundred and thirty-nine against two hundred and thirty-four.*

This bold step of Lafayette's was attended with no success : on the contrary, it served to accelerate his downfall. The Jacobins redoubled their activity in rendering him odious to the populace. The name of Cromwell was echoed from every press ; but when Gaudet revived the recollection of the same man, dictating in the name of his army laws to the representatives of his country, the assembly were perfectly aware that they had neither tyrant nor soldier before them, but a virtuous citizen, who could not tolerate crime, under whatever banner it might pretend to range itself. The efforts of the Jacobins with the mob were effectual, and Lafayette, finding, after fruitless efforts to assemble the national guards, that no good was to be effected in Paris, left that city on the thirtieth of June, and returned immediately to his army. Before his departure, he waited on the king, who thanked him for the step he had taken, but did not profit by his further offers of service. His effigy was burnt the same evening at the Palais-Royal ; his conduct was represented in the journals as high treason ; he was called a liberticide and a second Cromwell, with this difference, that he acted in concert with the king against the liberty of the people ; and he was accused of having proposed to march with his army to Paris.

When Lafayette reached the army, he found that it, also, was now infected : he endeavoured to assure himself of its

* De Stael Consid. ii. 48, 9.—Toul. Hist. ii. 179.—Moore's View, ii. 228.—Bertrand's Mem. ii. 331.—Hist. French Rev. ii. 27.—Lett. from Paris, ii. 58.

fidelity, and proposed to the soldiers to swear anew to the constitution. A very large proportion refused, and it immediately became apparent, from the movements, both at Paris and in the army, that he was no longer safe. His adversaries, who were determined and interested to ruin him, were his judges; and they belonged to a party, which was never known to devote a victim without consummating the sacrifice. It was not long before Brissot prepared to denounce him to the assembly, and demand against him a decree of accusation; "I am grieved," he remarked, "at this affair, for no one esteems him more than I do; but why has he declared himself hostile to the Jacobins?" The resentment of this party appeared, for the present, to be principally directed against Lafayette. His consistency had mortally offended these factious spirits; they had tempted him with the highest bribes, and the most splendid promises,—but he proved inflexibly attached to the constitutional party, and determined to fall with the constitution. The spirit which he evinced in his late fruitless journey to Paris, determined them to exert themselves to procure his immediate dismission; their clubs had been employed for weeks in debates on his treason, and innumerable inflammatory addresses were presented to the assembly against him. The decision upon the charges against Lafayette was deferred to the eighth of August, when a long and tumultuous debate took place. The report of the committee concluded by proposing a decree of accusation, and was highly applauded by the mob in the galleries. At length the motion for the decree was rejected by four hundred and six voices against two hundred and twenty-four. It was evident, from this decision, that the assembly, weak and incompetent as it was, still preserved some share of decency in its character and proceedings: but the Jacobins had made their party certain; the mob were completely devoted to them, and they hoped to carry, by their force, the boldest measures.* The

* North American Review, January, 1825,—Hist. French Rev. ii.39.

very day subsequent to the acquittal of Lafayette, (the ninth of August,) the assembly, in consequence of the proceedings of the Jacobins, declared its sessions "*no longer free.*"

Meanwhile the general was using his utmost efforts in support of constitutional authority. Early in the month of August, he despatched one of his aids-de-camp to Paris, proposing to the king and royal family to take refuge at Compeigne, with he army. This was the best and safest course; but the persons who possessed the confidence of the king and queen hated M. de Lafayette as much as if he had been an outrageous Jacobin. The aristocrats of that time preferred running every risk to obtain the re-establishment of the old government, to the acceptance of efficient aid under the condition of adopting with sincerity the principles of the revolution; that is, a representative government. The offer of Lafayette was then refused, and the king submitted to the dreadful risk of awaiting the German troops at Paris.*

The tenth of August, 1792, soon arrived, a day replete with horror; a revolution then overthrew the monarchy, and gave a final blow to the power of the constitutional party. The palace was stormed by a furious mob, the most atrocious murders committed, the king and the royal family pursued to the national assembly, to which they had fled for safety, where the legislative body was compelled to supersede the king in order to save his life. For many days the phrenzy of the populace raged with unbounded violence, savage and dreadful in its effects. This absurd rage was not confined to living objects of resentment. They barbarously demolished every vestige of art which had the remotest relation to monarchy or aristocracy; among others, the bust of Lafayette was sought for, with a ridiculous assiduity, and demolished.†

* De Stael's Consid. ii. 56-7—Toulong. Hist. ii. 200.—Bertr. Mem. ii, 333—5.

† Hist. French Rev. ii. 60, &c.

The suspension and imprisonment of the king produced great astonishment in the armies; particularly in that commanded by Lafayette, who, by the sudden change of his position, appears to have meditated some important project, now rendered abortive by the new revolution. He was posted, at this critical moment, at Sedan, at the head of twenty-eight thousand men. As strenuously opposed to the tyranny of the Jacobins, as he was adverse to the despotism of the court, the general determined to support, with all his energies, the cause of the captive monarch, whose power had been rendered legitimate by the sanction of the constitution, and the oaths of the people. He called a council of war, to which he summoned every officer commanding a battalion, and finding among them a ready assent to the measures proposed by him, he immediately published a proclamation, in which he declared not only his own dissent, but that of the troops under his command, to the recent events that had occurred in the capital. But the national assembly had already anticipated the defection of Lafayette's army, and recurred to measures calculated either to gain the commander, or induce the troops to desert him. On the night of the twelfth of August, they accordingly despatched three commissioners to the army, to counteract the movements of the general Lafayette was accidentally apprized of these proceedings; and after stating the facts to the magistrates of Sedan, he advised them, in duty to the king and constitution, to arrest the commissioners, who, on their arrival there, were accordingly imprisoned.—In the mean time Lafayette returned to camp, and immediately distributed among the battalions an energetic and decisive letter, declaring the destruction of the constitution by a banditti, and the deposition of the king. "Citizens," he concluded, "you are no longer represented; the national assembly are in a state of slavery; your armies are without leaders; Petion reigns; the savage Danton and his satellites are masters. Thus, soldiers, it is your province to examine whether you will restore the hereditary representative to the throne, or submit to the disgrace of having a Petion for your king."—When this communication was first made to the soldiery, they announced, by their rage and exclamations, that they were actuated by that indignation which their leader was so desirous to excite. Lafayette had every reason to suppose that all the armies participated in this feeling; but he was mistaken. No sooner were the assembly informed of his defection, and of the arrest of their commissioners, than they immediately deprived him of the command, and nominated Dumourier the commander-in-chief, who received orders to march against the constitutional general. But this measure was soon rendered unnecessary: three new deputies had been despatched to procure the liberation of their predecessors, while a great number of emissaries received secret orders to repair to Lafayette's camp, and debauch the fidelity of his soldiers; in which they were too successful.*

Lafayette laboured in vain, for some time, to dissemble the critical situation in which he was placed. To have marched directly to Paris, would have exposed the king and his family to certain destruction; and, in erecting the standard of revolt in the provinces, he would have been opposed by the other armies, and a civil war must inevitably have followed. In addition to these considerations, France was, at this moment, pressed on all sides by the enemy, and the idea of a capitulation with the presumptuous invaders of his country, struck him with horror. He was resolved, therefore, whatever might occur, neither to leave the frontiers destitute of defence, nor to lose his reputation by means of a disgraceful compact. But the oath which he had taken to support the constitutional king, marked out a line of conduct from which he could not honourably swerve. He formed a plan to rally around him the neighbouring departments, and to form, with some of the members of the constituted authorities, a kind of congress, to which he expect-

* Wars French Rev. i. 45.51.—Hist. Rev. ii. 63.—Toul[illegible]

ed that many opposition members of the legislative body would unite themselves. Supported by the civil power, and seconded by the armies of the Moselle and the Rhine, he might have organized a powerful opposition, and re-established the constitution. But every circumstance necessary to the success of his project, failed together: the enemy, on the threshold of the empire, concentrated all his power; the versatile conduct of the king and court destroyed all confidence, and rendered all his measures ineffectual; and the habits of the soldiery, had taught them to know no other power but the decrees of the assembly: every thing concurred in crushing an enterprise which the rapidity of events had not afforded him time to mature, whose success, if only partial, might have opened the gates of the frontiers to the enemy, and which it was impossible after the events of the tenth of August, completely to effect. His own army now divined the predicament in which he was placed, and a general consternation began to prevail in his camp. Those regiments which had been loudest in their accclamations, announced by their conduct that their fidelity was beginning to waver; others murmured at their lot, and lamented their situation. It was also propagated with equal art and success, that a decree of accusation had been promulged against their commander; that disobedience to his orders had now become a duty; and that to recognise him any longer, was to violate the laws.*

* Toulong. Hist. France. ii. 269, 70—Hist. Wars Fr. Rev. i, 51, 2, 3.

"*National Assembly, August* 17, 1792.

"Decree of accusation against M. Lafayette.

"I. It appears to this assembly, that there is a just ground for accusation against M. Lafayette, heretofore commander of the army of the north.

"II. The executive power shall, in the most expeditious manner possible, carry the present decree into execution; and all constituted authorities, all citizens, and all soldiers, are hereby enjoined, by every means in their power, to secure his person.

"III. The assembly forbids the army of the north, any longer to acknowledge him as a general, or to obey his orders; and strictly enjoins that no person whatsoever shall furnish any thing to the troops, or pay any money for their use, but by the orders of M. Dumourier."

Notwithstanding the prevalence of these sentiments, a generous feeling seemed still to actuate the hearts of an army that had already resolved to abandon its general, and both time and opportunity were afforded him to provide for his safety. In a consultation with his friends, it was on all sides, allowed that it had become impossible to support the vigorous measures which they had determined to pursue, as they were abandoned by the whole nation, and even by their own troops. Immediate flight now became necessary to those who had but so lately hoped to decide the fate of an empire. However inevitable the measure, it was with reluctance that Lafayette consented to embrace it: he was not ignorant of the dangers which accompanied it, but he hoped, at all events, to be able to ensure the safety of his companions, and to appear rather unfortunate than culpable in the eyes of mankind. He accordingly resolved on the night of the 19th August, 1792, to set out, before the dawn of day should exhibit once more the discontent of an army formerly so much attached to him, and which still respected his misfortunes. He mounted his horse, accompanied by Latour-Maubourg, the friend of his youth;—Alexandre Lameth, formerly his enemy, but now determined to participate in his fate; and Bureau de Puzy, three times president of the constituent assembly. When he arrived at Bouillon, he sent back his escort, wrote from thence orders for the different posts occupied by his army, so as to secure its safety. None of the refugees attempted to seduce a single battalion to desert, and by such base and inglorious means, ensure the favour of the enemy; on the contrary, it was their sole wish to retire to some distant country, and hope for better days.*

The prime and immediate motive of Lafayette, in retreating from his army, was to avoid the decree of accusation which had converted his adversaries into his judges. He hoped to pass the posts of the enemy without being disco-

* Toulong. Hist. ii. 271.—Wars, Rev. i. 54

vered, and thus gain the territory of the republic of Holland. He was not driven, by the enemies of liberty, from the land on which he had been one of the first to endeavour to confer that blessing; it was in the name of that very liberty, that a party, rather opposed to him in principles than opinions, and still more in measures than in principles, accused and proscribed for having endeavoured to save and defend the party from whom he had conquered that liberty. His situation was without example in history. Marius fled from the procriptions of Sylla, his rival and personal enemy; the whigs and the tories, the Guelphs and the Gibelins upheld opposite and fixed parties and opinions;—they hated each other, because their efforts were directed to opposite ends; they were rather adversaries than enemies. In the present case, the question was only a choice of measures, to arrive at the same admitted point,—public liberty; but, as, in matters of religion, the intolerance of scism is more active and cruel than that of sect, so the rivalry between sections of the same party, was more bitter than between different parties.—The fate of the brave, disinterested, and patriotic Lafayette, is little calculated to exalt our opinions of human nature: on the one hand, we behold him abandoned by the people for whom he had made so many sacrifices; on the other, opposed by a combination of kings, while his attachment to the cause of constitutional monarchy was the source of his calamity. If he had erred, his error was the error of a young and ingenuous mind, which, in its ardent zeal for the liberty and happiness of his fellow-creatures, did not permit him to distinguish what was practicable, from what was merely speculative and visionary.

If, as it has been said, a more temperate and mature judgment would, probably, have led him to oppose that fatal degradation of the executive power, which finally proved the ruin of authority, of government, and of order, in France, still he was no more to blame than the rest of the constituent assembly; and though in his judgment, he may have erred, it must be admitted that he was always consistent in his principles. Faithful to his oath, to his king, and to his engagements, he was among the first to oppose all seditious designs, and among the most distinguished of those who contended for the maintenance of order and civil obedience. To have received with cordiality, the illustrious supporter of regulated liberty, would have been noble and magnanimous; —to imprison and persecute virtue and valour in distress, was mean and dastardly: but, from Tiberius to the present times, cowardice has been the uniform character of tyranny.*

When Lafayette diminished his escort, he set out with seven companions,† and arrived, after a rapid journey, in the neighbourhood of an advanced guard of Austrians. It was extremely dark, and their horses being greatly fatigued by the march, as well as a heavy rain, they found it impossible to proceed further; nor could they, from the same cause, retrace their steps, laying aside the risk of pursuit from the French. It was, therefore, necessary to carry a bold front, and endeavour to obtain permission to pass, without discovering their ranks and names. Colonel de Puzy advanced, and requested to speak with the officer commanding at Rochefort. Lieutenant-colonel count D'Harnoncourt, who held the command, wishing to send Puzy, as all emigrants had heretofore been, to the duke de Bourbon, commander of the neighbouring posts, the colonel replied that his companions and himself ought not to be confounded with the emigrants who bore arms against their country; that they were patriotic officers, attached to the constitutional laws, who had, in fact, left the army, and who demanded permission to seek an asylum in a country which was not at war with France. D'Harnoncourt, detaining Puzy, sent orders

* Toulong. Hist. ii. 272, 3.—Hist. Rev. France, ii. 67.

† These were Louis and Victor Latour Maubourg, Bureau-de-Puzy, Alexandre Lameth, Auguste Masson, Rene Pillet, and Cardignan.

to the rest to advance; which measure was unavoidable They were conducted to an inn, where Lafayette was immediately recognised. The commandant then told them that it would be impossible to depart before the next day: Puzy, at once, entrusted him with their names, which, however, he already knew, and which, produced nothing but some empty expressions of respect. In the mean time, a number of Austrian hussars arrived, and the commandant informed *his prisoners*, that, before they could proceed, it was requisite to obtain permission from the commandant at Namur. Puzy accompanied the officer who was despatched to that place. When the commandant heard that Lafayette was taken, he burst forth into the most extravagant expressions of joy, and refused to grant the passports which Puzy demanded.

On the twenty-first of August, the prisoners were conducted to Namur, where the commandant, the marquis de Chasteler, informed Lafayette that prince Charles had been commissioned by their royal highnesses to converse with him respecting the situation of France; and insinuated that, considering the just cause of complaint he had against his country, it was expected that he would exhibit some marks of it. "I know not," replied the general, "whether such a commission has been given; but I do not think that any one will dare to deliver it to me." At that moment, prince Charles entered. His obliging conversation was scarcely replied to by the prisoners; and when it was requested that the general officers should remain alone together, they became entirely dumb. "I think," said M. de Chasteler, "that the situation in which we are placed is painful to all parties; and that this visit had better be closed." And after the usual salutations, the commissioner departed.

At Nivelle, they were visited by an Austrian major, commissioned to receive the treasure which, it was supposed, Lafayette had secured, and which, he remarked, would be sequestered in behalf of his Chistian majesty: "All that I understand of this strange commission," said Lafayette to the major, "is, that, had he been in my place, M. the duke of Saxe Teschen would have stolen the military chest of the army." Their portmanteaus, however, were searched, and not more than the amount of two months' pay, for each officer, found in them.

Thus were these distinguished men exposed to the greatest indignities, because they had been the friends of the constitution, instead of being treated as prisoners of war, which was the only quality in which they could have been justly arrested and detained. A correspondence had taken place with regard to them, between the courts of Berlin and Vienna; and it was determined that they should be given up to the Prussians, as their fortresses were nearer, and were supposed to be able to receive and guard them more conveniently. They were accordingly conducted like criminals, in a common cart, to Wesel on the Rhine, where they were insulted in the most savage manner by the populace. Here they were put in irons, and confined in separate cells of the castle: they were attended by non-commissioned officers, who received strict orders never to permit them to remain for a single moment out of sight, nor to answer any questions that were put to them.

Lafayette, Puzy, and Laubourg, experienced a long series of sufferings, and the most barbarous usage. Transferred successively to Magdeburg, Glatz, Neisse, and Olmutz; deprived of the first necessaries of life; debarred from all communication with each other;—the hatred of their persecutors, in the refinement of its revenge, lost sight of policy altogether. It cried aloud, that this excess of barbarity was a warning to all those who maintained similar opinions, that safety depended solely on the power of their arms, and that the implacable passions of kings left no room for negotiation.

During his confinement at Wesel, it was intimated to Lafayette, by order of the king of Prussia, that his situation would be meliorated, provided he would draw up plans against France; but Lafayette exhibited, in an energetic answer, his scorn of such a proposition. Hence, the rigour of his confinement was increased; and he, and his companions, were soon after thrown into a wagon, and conveyed to the dungeons of Magdeburg. The most brutal care was taken that they should learn nothing respecting their families, concerning whose fate they experienced the most anxious solicitude, in consequence of the proscriptions that prevailed in France. They remained during a whole year at Magdeburg, in a dark and humid vault, surrounded by high pallisades, shut up by means of four successive doors, fortified by iron bars, and fastened with padlocks. Their fate, however, now appeared to be milder, as they were permitted to see each other, and allowed to walk for an hour each day, on one of the bastions.

After having been transported to Glatz, the prisoners were at length trasferred to Neisse, for the purpose of being delivered up again to Austria: their dungeon was still more dismal and unhealthy than any of those they had previously inhabited. Alexandre Lameth, who was dangerously ill, could not be removed with his companions. His mother obtained permission from Frederick William, for him to remain a prisoner in his states; and finally obtained his liberty.

The Prussians, at last, became unwilling to bear the odium of such unlawful and disgraceful treatment of prisoners of war, entitled to every degree of respect from their rank and character; but especially from the manner in which they had been taken. They, therefore, gave them up to the Austrians, who finally transferred them to dark and damp dungeons in the citadel of Olmutz. The sufferings to which Lafayette was here exposed, in the mere spirit of a barbarous revenge, are almost incredible. He was warned that he would never again see any thing but the four walls of his dungeon; that he would never receive news of events or persons; that his name would be unknown in the citadel and that in all accounts of him sent to court, he would be designated only by a number; that he would never receive any notice of his family, or of the existence of his fellow-prisoners. At the same time, knives and forks were removed from him, as he was officially informed, that his situation was one which would naturally lead him to suicide.*

Thus was the patriotism of Lafayette punished by privations and hardships which exceeded the rigours of inquisitorial severity. But he was sustained by a firm mind and quiet conscience; and bore his misfortunes with manly resignation. His sufferings were of no ordinary magnitude. The walls of his dungeon were twelve feet thick; and air was admitted through an opening two feet square, secured at each end by transverse massive iron bars. A broad ditch was situated directly before these loop-holes, which was covered with water only when it rained; at other times, it was a stagnant marsh, constantly emitting a poisonous, effluvium: beyond this, were the outer walls of the castle, so that the slightest breeze could never refresh the miserable captives, although the heat was almost insupportable. Sentinels, with loaded muskets, were stationed on these walls, who were prohibited to speak a word with them, and ordered to shoot them dead, if they attempted an escape. A strong guard was also posted before the door of the prisoners, who were forbidden, while on duty, either to sing, speak, or whistle.

Each cell had two doors, one of iron, the other of wood, nearly two feet thick; and both were covered with bolts, bars, and double padlocks. When the jailer, twice a day, brought their wretched pittance, it was scrupulously examined, to discover if there was any note or communication whatever contained in it. A miserable bed of rotten straw, filled with vermin, together with a broken chair, and an old

* North American Review, January, 1825, p. 164. —Wars Fr. Rev. ii. 57-8. Mem.—Lafayette, 126.-7.

worm-eaten table, formed the whole furniture of each apartment. The cells were eight or ten paces deep, and six or eight wide; and when it rained, the water flowed through the loop-holes, and off the walls, in such quantities, that they would sometimes awake in the morning, wet to the skin. When the sun did not shine, which happened very frequently in this wet country, the prisoners remained almost in total darkness during the whole day.*

After three different attestations on the part of physicians, pointing out the indispensable necessity of fresh air for Lafayette, he was permitted to walk in the fortress.

His sufferings, indeed, proved almost beyond his strength. The want of air and decent food, and the loathsome dampness and filth of his dungeon, brought him more than once to the borders of the grave. His frame was wasted by diseases, of which, for a long period, not the slightest notice was taken; and, on one occasion, he was reduced so low, that his hair fell from him entirely by the excess of his sufferings. At the same time, his estates in France were confiscated, his wife cast into prison, and *Fayetteisme*, as adherence to the constitution was called, was punished with death.†

But his friends were not inactive. In June, 1794, they prevailed on Dr. Erick Bollman, whose adventurous and philanthropic spirit easily led him to engage in the affairs of Lafayette, to proceed to Germany, ascertain what had been the fate of the unfortunate patriot, and, if he were still alive, to endeavour to procure his escape. By great address and courage, he affected the escape of count Narbonne from France, after the horrible massacres of the tenth of August, 1792, and succeeded in conveying him safely to England. In 1793, he had made an unsuccessful attempt to procure the liberation of Lafayette, by presenting a memorial to the king of Prussia, which was rejected.

* Mem. of Lafayette, pp. 127--8, 9.

† North American Review, No. 46, p. 165.

Traversing Germany in the character of a traveller in pursuit of instruction and knowledge, he ascertained that Lafayette had been surrendered to the Austrian government, and taken the route toward Olmutz.* Having reconnoitred the country along the frontier, he selected Tarnowitz, as a place of temporary retreat, in case an opportunity should occur of rescuing the prisoner from captivity. This point determined in his mind, he proceeded toward Olmutz, a strong Austrian fortress in Moravia, on the high road to Vienna, from which it is distant about one hundred and fifty miles.

At this period, the Austrian police, more rigorous than that of any country in Europe, France, probably excepted, was even more watchful than usual, because the events in France, and those in Poland, where a revolution had just been crushed by the united efforts of the surrounding powers, rendered all governments uneasy. Under such circumstances, the utmost caution was indispensable to success, and information became the more difficult to obtain, as all direct inquiry would inevitably have led to suspicion. At Olmutz, however, Dr. Bollman ascertained that several state prisoners were kept in the citadel, with a degree of caution and mystery, which must have been not unlike that used toward the half fabulous personage in the iron mask. It seemed highly probable that Lafayette was one of them, and acting upon this supposition, the doctor visited the hospital, and endeavoured to form an acquaintance with the first surgeon: he knew that the health of the prisoner was delicate; that he would not omit seeking medical aid; and that, of all the medical men in Olmutz, this military surgeon was the most likely to perform that office.

* The narrative of the unsuccessful attempt to rescue Lafayette, is in substance, extracted from an account of that noble affair, published in the Port Folio, vol. xxii. p. 93, and written by Dr. Bollman himself: hence its authenticity is indubitable, although it varies from other narratives lately published in the country.

The surgeon proved to be a man of intelligence, probity, and feeling. After several interviews, when the conversation turned on the effect of moral impressions on the constitution, Dr. Bollmann, drawing a pamphlet from his pocket, abruptly said, " Since we are on the subject, you attend the state-prisoners here. Lafayette is among them: his health is much impaired. Show him this pamphlet. Tell him a traveller left it with you, who lately saw in London all the persons named in it, his particular friends: that they are well, and continue attached to him as much as ever. This intelligence will do him more good than all your drugs."—At the same moment, he laid the pamphlet on the table, and perceiving that the surgeon knew not rightly what to reply, changed the conversation, and shortly after left him.

The manner of the surgeon convinced him that Lafayette was at Olmutz; and he knew the latter would devise means to improve the opportunity, should he receive the pamphlet. In a few days, the surgeon mentioned, of his own accord, that Lafayette wished to learn some further particulars respecting the situation of one or two of them, whom he named. On hearing this the doctor, appearing to have accidentally about him some white paper, but which, in fact, had been prepared for the emergency, sat immediately down, and wrote a few lines in French, which language the surgeon understood, in reply to the inquiries made, and finished with the sentence, " I am glad of the opportunity of addressing you these words, which, when read *with your usual warmth*, will afford to a heart like yours some consolation." The paper had been previously written over with sympathetic ink, a writing invisible unless brought out by the application of heat. The slight hint conveyed in the last sentence sufficed; Lafayette became acquainted with his projects; and his readiness to serve him in any practicable way. But the mode could be pointed out only by the prisoner, as he alone, from within, could judge what might be attempted, with any chance of success, from without.

To guard against suspicion, the doctor, on the day following, proceeded to Vienna, where he remained a considerable time, but confided his design to no person whatever. He had a carriage constructed there, in which were contrived convenient places for conveying secretly a variety of articles, such as rope-ladders, cords, a number of tools for cutting iron bars, and for similar purposes. These general preparations being made, he visited several gentlemen on their estates in Moravia, and took an opportunity of again touching at Olmutz, where he called on the surgeon, who returned him the pamphlet, formerly left for Lafayette. On examining it, he found that the margin had been written over with sympathetic ink, (lime-juice,) and, on applying heat, learned that the captive, on account of his enfeebled state of health, after repeated applications, had at last obtained permission to take an airing, in a carriage, at stated days in the week, accompanied by a military guard; and that by fathe easiest mode to restore him to liberty, would be to attack the guard on one of these excursions and then to take him off.

Having ascertained for his guidance, that Lafayette, in taking his ride, sat in an open carriage, with an officer by his side, a driver on the box, and two armed soldiers standing behind, Dr. Bollman returned to Vienna. As it was indispensable to have, at least, one coadjutor, he communicated his project to a young American gentleman, by the name of Francis Kinlock Huger, who had often mentioned to him, in conversation, that Lafayette, on arriving in America, first landed at his father's house, and there used often to have him on his keees, when a boy. He was a young man of uncommon talent, decision, and enthusiasm; possessed of a warm heart and a resolute mind; and he at once entered into the whole design, and devoted himself to its execution with the most romantic earnestness.

Having agreed on a plan, they publicly announced their intention of returning to England together; two saddle horses were purchased, and a steady groom was engaged to attend them. Thus, sometimes sending the groom a station or two forward, with the carriage; at others, leaving him to bring up the horses slowly, while they pushed onward in the carriage, they arrived at Olmutz.

These were the only two persons on the continent, except Lafayette himself, who had the slightest suspicion of any arrangements for his rescue, and neither of these persons knew him by sight. When they reached Olmutz, the doctor immediately visited the surgeon, and, knowing the day when the marquis was to take his ride, mentioned to him the same day as the one on which he intended to continue his journey. On that day, (eighth November, 1794,) the groom was despatched, at an early hour, to Hoff, a post-town about twenty-five miles distant, with orders to have fresh horses in readiness at four o'clock. It had been concerted between the parties, that, to avoid all mistakes when the rescue should be attempted, each should take off his hat and wipe his forehead, in token of recognition.

Their saddle horses were now ready at the inn, and Mr. Huger feigned some business near the town-gate, in order to watch the moment when the carriage should pass. As soon as he saw it, he hastened back to the inn. Our adventurers mounted, and followed it at some distance, armed only with a pair of pistols, and those not loaded with ball. Their success was calculated on surprise, and, under all the circumstances of the case, to take any person's life would have been unjustifiable, useless, and imprudent.

They rode by the carriage, and then slackening their pace and allowing it again to go ahead, exchanged signals with the prisoner. At two or three miles from the gate, the carriage left the high road, and passed into a less frequented tract in the midst of an open country: the plain was covered with labouring people. Presently the carriage stopped. Lafayette and the officer stepped out, and walked arm in arm, probably to give the former more opportunity for exercise. The carriage, with the guard, drove slowly on, but remained in sight. This was evidently the moment for their attempt. The two companions galloped up; and the doctor, dismounting, left his horse with Huger. At the same instant, Lafayette laid hold of the officer's sword, but could only half draw it from the scabbard, as the officer, a stout man, had seized it also. The doctor joining, he was presently disarmed; but he then grasped Lafayette, held him with all his might, and set up a tremendous roaring, not unlike that of Mars in the Iliad. The guard, on hearing it, instead of coming to his assistance, fled to alarm the citadel. The people in the field stood aghast. A scuffle ensued.—Huger passed the bridles of the two horses over one arm, and with the other hand, thrust his handkerchief into the officer's mouth, to stop the noise. The officer, the prisoner, and the doctor came to the ground. The doctor, kneeling on the officer, kept him down while the general rose.

All would now have been well, but one of the horses, taking fright at the scene and noise, had reared, slipped his bridle, and ran off. A countryman caught him, and was holding him at a considerable distance. The doctor, still keeping down the officer, handing a purse to the general, requested him to mount the horse left; and Mr. Huger told him, in English, to go to *Hoff*. He mistook what was said to him for a more general direction to go *off*—delayed a moment to see if he could not assist them—then went on—then rode back again, and asked once more if he could be of no service—and finally, urged anew, galloped away, and was out of sight in a minute.

The officer, recovering from his panic, fled toward Olmutz. The doctor and Mr. Huger recovered the horse that had escaped, and both mounted him, intending to follow and assist Lafayette. But the animal, less docile and tractable than the other, which had been trained to carry two persons, refused to perform this task, reared, and bounded, and presently threw both. Mr. Huger immediately exclaimed "This will not do! The marquis wants you. Push on; I'll take my chance on foot across the country." The doctor pushed forward, and Mr. Huger, who now had little chance of escape, was soon seized by the peasants, who had witnessed the scene, and conducted to Olmutz. These accidents defeated their romantic enterprise. Dr. Bollmann easily arrived at Hoff; but not finding Lafayette there, and being anxious to receive some intelligence of him, although he might readily have secured himself by proceeding to Tarnowitz, he lingered about the frontiers, 'till the next night, when he too was arrested, by order of the Prussian authority, at the requisition of Austria.

Lafayette remained unpursued: he had taken a wrong road, which led to Jagersdoff, a place on the Prussian frontier, and followed it as long as his horse could proceed. He was within a few miles of the boundary of Austrian rule and perceiving that his horse could go no farther, he accosted a man, whom he overtook on the road, not far from a village, and, under some pretext, endeavoured to prevail on him to procure him another horse, and to attend him to the frontier. The man apparently agreed, and went to the village for the horse. But the general had awakened suspicion by his accent, his appearance, his request, and his money. The man promptly returned from the village, but he came with a force to arrest the marquis, and conducted him before a magistrate. During three days, the period of his detention there, his name was at last recognized by an officer from Olmutz, to which fortress he was re-conducted.

All three of the prisoners were separately confined, without being permitted to know any thing of each other's fate. Mr. Huger was chained to the floor, in a small arched dungeon, about six feet by eight, without light, and with only bread and water for food; and once in six hours, by day and by night, the guard entered, and with a lamp, examined each brick, and each link of his chains. To his earnest request to know something of Dr. Bollmann, and to learn whether Lafayette had escaped, he received no answer at all. To his still more earnest solicitation to be permitted to send to his mother in America, merely the words "*I am alive*," signed with his name, he received a rude refusal.—Dr. Bollman was also put in chains, and conducted to a dismal dungeon, half under ground. Only a faint light broke into it, through a narrow, oblique aperture, made in a wall upwards of five feet thick. When he laid down at night, chained to the walls, he was attacked by myriads of famished vermin. Neither candle light, nor books, were allowed him, and his food was limited to what could be procured for four cents per day. In this dreadful situation he remained more than two months, without any communication with any person whatever except the jailer, nor did he ever from him learn the fate of Mr. Huger. In fact, at first, every degree of brutal severity was practised against both of them; but, afterwards, this severity was relaxed. They were placed nearer together, where they could communicate with each other; and their trial, which was protracted during the whole winter, was begun with all the tedious formalities, that could be prescribed by Austrian fear and caution; for they had dreamed, in Vienna, of a deep-rooted plot, and wide-extended conspiracy, and could not believe that such an attempt would be made merely by two individuals, and without any other design than simply that of restoring a man to freedom and to his friends.—By the powerful, but unknown intercessions of many of the personal friends of Dr. Bollman, in Vienna, but particularly through the influence of count Metrowsky, a nobleman living near the prison, the rigour of their treatment was not only greatly mitigated, but, on the conclusion of their trial, they were merely sentenced to two weeks additional confinement, after having been already imprisoned during eight months.—The doctor and Mr. Huger received many flattering marks of kindness and good will, even at Olmutz, before their departure, and their progress through Germany was a kind of triumph, though embittered by the recollection of the continued captivity of Lafayette. A few hours after they had left Olmutz, an order came from Vienna, directing a new trial, which, under the management of the ministers, would of course, have ended very differently from the one managed by Count Metrowsky; but the prisoners were already beyond the limits of the Austrian dominions.*

Lafayette, in the meanwhile, was thrown back into his obscure and ignominious sufferings, with hardly a hope that they could be terminated, except by death. The irons were so closely fastened around his ankles, that for three months he endured the most excruciating torture. During the winter of 1794–5, which was extremely severe, he was reduced almost to the last extremity by a violent fever; and yet was deprived of proper attendance, of air, of suitable food, and of decent clothes. In this state he was allowed nothing for his bed but a little damp and mouldy straw; round his waist was a chain, which was fastened to the wall, and barely permitted him to turn from one side to the other. No light was admitted into his cell, and he was even refused the smallest allowance of linen. Worn down by disease and the rigour of the season, he became miserably emaciated. To increase his miseries, almost insupportable mental anxieties were added to his physical distresses. He was made to believe that he was only reserved for a public execution, and that his chivalrous deliverers had already perished on the scaffold; while, at the same time, he was not permitted to know whether his family were still alive, or had fallen under the revolutionary axe, of which, during the few days he was out of his dungeon, he had heard such appalling accounts.†

Madame de Lafayette, however was nearer to him than he could imagine to be possible. She, together with her two daughters, Anastasia and Virginia, had been confined in the

* North American Review, January, 1825.

† Mem. of Lafayette, p. 190—192.—North American Review, January, 1825.

prisons of Paris. The twenty-seventh of July, 1794, (ninth Thermidor,) put an end to the reign of terror, and the greater part of the victims who had been doomed to the scaffold, were released from prison; but madame de Lafayette was not liberated for several months after, having been more than a year and a half in confinement. Notwithstanding the bad state of her health, and the earnest solicitations of her friends that she would remain a few months in the country, in order to re-establish it, she remained deaf to all their prayers, and inexorable in her determination to carry immediate consolation to the dungeon of her persecuted husband. Sending her eldest son (George Washington) for safety, to the care of general Washington in America, she set out, accompanied by her two daughters, in disguise, and with American passports. Anastasia, the eldest, was then sixteen, and Virginia, the youngest, thirteen years of age.

Passing under the name of Mrs. Motier she landed at Altona, on the ninth of September, 1795, and proceeding immediately to Vienna, obtained an audience of the emperor, who gave them permission, as it now seems probable, against the intentions of his ministers, to join Lafayette in prison, but absolutely refused to liberate him; observing, "*J'ai les mains liees.*" (My hands are tied.) They went instantly to Olmutz: but before they could enter, they were deprived of whatever they had brought with them to alleviate the miseries of a dungeon, and required, if they should pass its threshold, never again to leave it. They were treated with the greatest inhumanity, and refused liberty to hear mass on Sundays, or to have a servant to attend them. Madame de Lafayette's health soon sunk under the complicated horrors and sufferings of her loathsome imprisonment, and she wrote to Vienna for permission to pass a week in the capital, to breathe purer air, and obtain medical assistance. Two months after this, the commandant made his appearance for the first time, and after giving orders that the two young ladies should be confined to a particular chamber, informed madame de Lafayette that no objection would be made to her leaving her husband, but that, if she should do so, she must never return to him. There was a degree of refinement in this ingenious mode of heaping afflictions upon the head of the unfortunate, which almost outrivalled in iniquity all that had ever been written to depict the oppression of tyranny. The heroic woman seized a pen, and immediately and formally signed her consent and determination "to share his captivity in all its details," being "fully determined never again to expose herself to the horrors of another separation." Never afterwards did she make an effort to leave him. After this period, no complaints whatever were heard from the unhappy sufferers, who inhaled in their dungeons, an air thoroughly impregnated with the most noxious effluvium. The situation of the two lovely daughters was horrible.—Not allowed to be confined with their parents, they were guarded in separate dungeons; and, by a confinement of sixteen hours, they purchased the melancholy satisfaction of being with their father and mother during the remaining eight hours, of the day. But, with all those soft endearments which fall so sweetly from the lips of young and artless women, they helped to assuage, by their touching sympathy, those keener sorrows which refused to yield to the voice of philosophy.*

"The history of female virtue and female heroism," says M. de Stael, "presents nothing more rare in excellence, than the life and character of madame de Lafayette." Her name will be revered so long as virtue commands respect and admiration. She has, in our days, revived the name of Arria, who devested herself of the weakness of her sex, to bear all the oppression which a Claudius or a Nero could inflict. She composed herself for death in the arms and in the dungeon of her husband; but his deliverance produced a reprieve to a life so precious. He bore her to her native

Parl. Chron. xvi, 378–9, 380, 394.—Wars Rev. i, Note, 59, 60.—Port F[illegible]o, xix, 509.—North American Review, January, 1825.

France, to her own patrimonial woods of La Grange. Revived, not rescued, she lived to behold the return of her brave son, the reunion of her family, and then sunk into the tomb.

Another attempt was made to effect the liberation of Lafayette. When the emperor of Austria, in refusing the liberty of her husband to Madam de Lafayette, told her that "his hands were tied," he could, of course, allude to no law or constitution of his empire, and, therefore, his hands could only be tied by engagements with his allies in the war against France. England was one of those allies; and, therefore, general Fitzpatrick, in the house of commons, on the seventeenth March, 1794, and again on the sixteenth December, 1796, after a feeling and eloquent introduction, moved, "That an humble address be presented to his majesty, representing to his majesty, that it appeared to that house that the detention of general Lafayette, Alexandre Lameth, Bureau de Puzy, and Latour Maubourg, in prison, by order of his majesty's ally, the king of Prussia, was injurious to his majesty, and the cause of his allies; and humbly to beseech his majesty most graciously to intercede in such a manner as to his royal wisdom shall seem most proper, for the deliverance of these unhappy persons." He was supported by colonel Tarleton, who had fought against Lafayette in Virginia, by Wilberforce, by Fox, Sheridan, and Grey; and opposed by Pitt, the chancellor of the exchequer, Burke, Windham, the secretary at war, and Mr. secretary Dundas. Mr. Fox pleaded the cause of Lafayette with the most impassioned eloquence. The British parliament heard that sublime speech, and yet the representatives of a free country did not rise in a body to accede to the proposition of the orator, who, on this occasion, should have been only their interpreter. The ministers opposed the motions of general Fitzpatrick by saying, as usual, that the captivity of general Lafayette concerned the powers of the continent, and that England, in meddling with it, would violate the general principle which forbade her to interfere in the internal administration of foreign countries. Mr. Fox admirably combatted this wily and evasive answer; but, both motions were finally lost.* One good effect, however, followed from them. A solemn and vehement discussion, in which the emperor of Austria found no apologist, had been held in the face of all Europe; and all Europe was, of course, informed of the sufferings of Lafayette, in the most solemn and authentic way.

The illustrious individual who presided over the government of the United States, did not forget, in the dungeons of despots, the gallant soldier, with whom he had fought, side by side, on the plains of America. During the first year of Lafayette's imprisonment, in 1793, two letters were addressed to the American ministers at London and Paris, respectively, at the sole instance of the president, stating the interest taken by the president, and people of the United States in the fate of the Marquis de Lafayette, and requiring them to avail themselves of every opportunity of sounding the way toward his liberation, which they were to endeavour to obtain by informal solicitations; but if formal ones should be necessary, they were to watch the moment when they might be urged with the best prospect of success. In fact, the attachment of these illustrious personages to each other, yielded neither to time, nor to the remarkable vicissitudes of fortune with which the destinies of one of them had been chequered. The extreme jealousy, however, with which the persons who administered the government of France, as well as a large party in America, watched the deportment of Washington toward all those whom the ferocious despotism of the Jacobins had exiled from their country, imposed upon him the painful necessity of observing great circumspection in his official conduct on this delicate subject. A formal interposition in favour of the virtuous

* The motion on seventeenth March, 1794, was lost, 46 to 153.—Parl. Chron. ix, 642.—The motion on sixteenth December, 1796, was lost, 32 to 132.—Ibid. xvi. 375.

and unfortunate victim of their furious passions, would have been unavailing. Without benefitting the person whom it was designed to aid, it might have produced serious political mischief. But, in the year 1796, the American ministers employed at foreign courts, were instructed to seize every fair occasion to express unofficially the interest taken by the president in the fate of Lafayette; and to employ the most eligible means in their power to obtain his liberty, or to meliorate his condition. A confidential person had been sent to Berlin to solicit his discharge; but before this messenger had reached his destination, the king of Prussia had delivered over his prisoner to the emperor of Germany. Mr. Pinckney had been instructed, not only to indicate the wishes of the president to the Austrian minister at London, but to endeavour unofficially to obtain the powerful mediation of Britain, and had at one time, flattered himself that the cabinet of St. James would have taken an interest in the affair; but this hope was soon dissipated.*

After being disappointed in obtaining the mediation of the British cabinet, the president addressed the following letter to the emperor of Germany:—"It will readily occur to your majesty, that occasions may sometimes exist, on which official considerations would constrain the chief of a nation to be silent and passive in relation even to objects which affect his sensibility, and claim his interposition as a man. Finding myself precisely in this situation at present, I take the liberty of writing this private letter to your majesty, being persuaded that my motives will also be my apology for it.

"In common with the people of this country, I retain a strong and cordial sense of the services rendered to them by the Marquis de Lafayette, and my friendship for him has been constant and sincere. It is natural, therefore, that I should sympathise with him and his family in their misfortunes, and endeavour to mitigate the calamities they expe-

* Marsh. Washington, v. 339, note, 668-9.

rience, among which his present confinement is not the least distressing.

"I forbear to enlarge on this delicate subject. Permit me only to submit to your majesty's consideration, whether his long imprisonment, and the confiscation of his estate, and the indigence and dispersion of his family, and the painful anxieties incident to all these circumstances, do not form an assemblage of sufferings which recommend him to the mediation of humanity? Allow me, sir, on this occasion to be its organ; and to entreat that he may be permitted to come to this country on such conditions, and under such instructions, as your majesty may think it expedient to prescribe.

"As it is a maxim with me not to ask what, under similar circumstances, I would not grant, your majesty will do me the justice to believe that this request appears to me to correspond with those great principles of magnanimity and wisdom, which form the basis of sound policy and durable glory."

This letter, reflecting honour on the feelings and character of Washington, and expressing sentiments not more deeply cherished by him, than by a whole nation, was transmitted to Mr. Pinckney, to be conveyed to the emperor through his minister at London. How far it operated in mitigating immediately the rigour of Lafayette's confinement, or in obtaining his liberty, remains unascertained.

But the Journal of Congress of third March, 1797, contains a record, which will stand for ever as a blemish on the character of our country, although the principles which it exhibits, were, at that time, as odious to almost all the citizens of the republic, as they must be to the present generation. But, fiat justitia, ruat cœlum. On that day, the lamented orator and statesman, Robert Goodloe Harper, moved, for consideration, a resolution in the following words: "This house, strongly impressed with a just sense of the important and disinterested services rendered to their country, during the late war, by their fellow-citizen major-general

Lafayette, and deeply regretting the sufferings to which he is now subjected from a long and rigorous imprisonment, and which have equally excited their sympathy, and the ardent wish of their constituents for his deliverance, do *Resolve*, that the president of the United States be informed, that this house will see with the highest satisfaction, any measures which he may deem expedient to adopt toward effecting the restoration of their said fellow citizen to liberty."—Notwithstanding the eloquence of a Harper, this motion was lost by a majority of fifty-two to thirty-two: this result may be attributed to the cold-blooded fear of multiplying foreign negotiations, the calculating timidity which looked forward to a long train of political disputes, and to the circumstance of the resolution having been brought forward at a late hour on the last day of the session.*

The period at which Lafayette and his afflicted family, were again to taste the enjoyments of liberty was now rapidly approaching. They owed their liberation, in a great measure, to Napoleon Bonaparte, at that time general-in-chief of the army of Italy; but the American government, as we shall presently show, participated honourably in the act. At the treaty of Campo-Formio, which was preceded by the negotiation of Leoben and Udine, the young and victorious French general insisted, on his own responsibility that the prisoners at Olmutz should be immediately released from confinement. The Austrian ministers were unwillingly compelled to relinquish their prey; but attempted to compel Lafayette to receive his freedom on conditions prescribed to him: but this he distinctly and decidedly refused; and declared, with a firmness which it is hardly to be believed could have survived such sufferings, that he would never accept his liberation in any way that should compromise his rights and duties, either as a Frenchman, or *as an American citizen.*

John Parish, esquire, the American consul at Hamburg, had been indefatigable in his exertions, as the agent of the

* American Senator, iii. 77

United States, to procure the liberation, or at least improve the situation, of the illustrious sufferer. He had already solicited, and obtained, permission to supply him with small sums of money. At length, the emperor affected to listen with a friendly ear to the solicitations of the American government, and consented to his enlargement, upon condition that Mr. Parish would engage that he should leave Germany in ten days. On the twenty-fifth August, 1797, the consul addressed a letter to the baron de Thurgut, minister of state, containing the following passage: "Mr. Rameuf will have the honour of acquainting your excellency with the dispositions that have been made toward procuring a vessel for the prisoners, on their arrival in this city, (Hamburg,) to facilitate their passage to America. I beg permission for Mr. Rameuf to offer to the prisoners, as well in my own name as in that of the United States, whatever assistance and care they may stand in need of, at the moment of their enlargement."

To this letter the baron de Thurgut replied as follows: "The merchant Hirsch has been permitted to furnish, agreeably to your desire, the money necessary to defray the expenses that the family of Lafayette would be at for matters of convenience and pleasure. The baron de Buol, his majesty's minister plenipotentiary to the princes and state of Lower Saxony, will inform you of the particular deference of his majesty to the interest which the United States appear to take in the liberation of this prisoner." The same minister of state, in a letter of the thirteenth of September, 1797, to the baron de Buol, speaks in this language: "You will take care, M. Baron, to inform the American consul on this occasion, that his majesty, *having made no positive engagement with the French respecting the enlargement of this prisoner*, the motive of the particular interest that the United States of America, appear to attach to it, has contributed not a little to engage his majesty in this beneficent action; that, for the rest, his majesty will be always happ in furnishing the United States of America, on all occasions, real marks of his friendship and benevolence."*

It may be, that the Austrians were compelled to release Lafayette by the sword of the conqueror of Italy, but were willing to make a merit of it in the eyes of our government. It is not a little remarkable, that his release should have been effected by the co-operation of the two most conspicuous men of their age, one the founder of a republic, the other, of a despotism,—George Washington and Napoleon Bonaparte.

On the nineteenth of September, 1797, the precious light of heaven once more gladdened the heart of the much injured marquis; Madam de Lafayette and her daughters, having been confined twenty two months, and Lafayette himself, more than five years, in a disgraceful spirit of vulgar cruelty and revenge, of which modern history can afford very few examples. On that day, his fetters were knocked off, and accompanied by his wife and daughters, he left his prison under the escort of an officer, who was to deliver him into the hands of our worthy consul. Mr. Parish relates the manner in which he was received at Hamburg, in a very interesting manner:

" The marquis's departure from Olmutz," says that gentleman, " was notified to M. de Buol and myself, and I concerted measures for his being delivered over to me in my own house. Every thing was so arranged as to have the ceremony performed as quickly and secretly as possible; and the fourth of October was fixed for their being conveyed to my house. Mr. Morris and I dined that day with the minister, the Baron de Buol. I left them at four o'clock in order to be at home when they arrived. An immense crowd of people announced their arrival. The streets were lined, and my house was soon filled with them. A lane was formed to let the prisoners pass to my room. Lafayette led the way, and was followed by his infirm lady and two daughters. He flew into my arms; his wife and daughters clung to me.

* Port Folio, xix, 509-10, 11.

A silence, an expressive silence, took place, It was broken by an exclamation of, "my friend! my dearest friend! *my deliverer!* See the work of your generosity! My poor, poor wife, hardly able to support herself." And, indeed, she was not standing, but hanging on my arm, imbrued with tears, while her two lovely girls had hold of the other. The scene was extremely affecting, and I was very much agitated. The room was full, and I am sure there was not a dry eye in it. I placed the marchioness on a sofa: she sobbed and wept much, and could utter but few words. Again the marquis came to my arms, his heart overflowing with gratitude. I never saw a man in such complete ecstacy of body and mind.—He is a very handsome man, in the prime of life, and seemed to have suffered but little from his confinement. It required a good quarter of an hour to compose him.

"In the midst of this scene, the minister joined us: I introduced the marquis and his family to him, and then requested that the ceremony about to be performed, might be in a private room, and desired that the rest of the company might remain where they were.

"The minister, and his secretary, with the officer of the escort, Mr. Morris, and the prisoner, retired with me to an inner apartment, where M. de Boul, after a very handsome address to the prisoner, stated the particular satisfaction he had in delivering him over to a friend who loved and respected him so much: he then addressed me, and after some flattering compliments, reminded me of my engagement to the emperor, to have the marquis removed out of Germany in ten days, which I again promised to fulfil, when he told Lafayette that he was now completely restored to liberty.'*

After causing their rights, both as French and American citizens, to be formally recognised at Hamburg, Lafayette and his family went to Welmoldt, a little town in the territories of Holstein, where, during two years, they lived in retirement and tranquillity. About this period the joys of the happy

* Port Folio, xix. 511, 512.

circle were increased by the arrival of George Washington Lafayette from Mount Vernon, and by the marriage of Anastasia, the eldest daughter of Lafayette with M. Charles de Latour Maugourg, brother of the person who had shared her father's captivity.

Here Lafayette continued to reside, contented and happy, but anxiously observing the progress of events in France, until the revolution of the eighteenth Brumair, tenth November, 1799, promised for a time, to settle the government of his country on a safe foundation. He immediately returned to France, and established himself at La Grange, a fine old castle, surrounded by a moderate estate, about forty miles from Paris, which has ever since been his customary residence.

Returned to his country, Lafayette remained steady to those principles which had guided him through life,—which had led him to the wilds of America,—which had inspired him in the conflicts of revolutionary France,—had shielded him from the corruption of courts, and consoled him in the dungeons of captivity. When he discovered that his opinons of the character and views of Bonaparte were ill-founded, that he who had generously assisted to unlock his own chains, was already engaged in weaving shackles for his country, he broke off all intercourse with him, refused the share offered to him in public affairs, declined the senatorial dignity anxiously pressed on his acceptance, and by his bold restrictive vote, in 1802, against the consulship for life, snapped for ever the tie, which, under the paramount influence of gratitude, had for a moment bound him to a man, whose views differed so widely from his own. Bonaparte even went so far as to refuse to promote his eldest son, and his son-in-law Lasteyrie, though they distinguished themselves repeatedly in the army; and once, when a report of the services of the former in a bulletin was offered him, he erased it with impatience, saying, "These Lafayettes cross my path everywhere." Discouraged, therefore, in every way in which they could be of service to their country, the whole family was at last collected at La Grange, and lived there in the happiest retirement, so long as the despotism of Bonaparte lasted. Refusing inflexibly to bow before the sun of imperial power, the noble head of the family gave himself up exclusively to the endearments of domestic life, the pursuits of literature and science, and the interests and improvements of agriculture.*

For many years he continued to repose tranquilly in the bosom of his family. The restoration of the Bourbons, in 1814, made no change in Lafayette's relations: he remained an inactive spectator of the political changes which took place. He was too honest and too candid, too much an enemy to the anarchy of the Jacobin factions, and to the despotism of the emperor, to support either, or to be received into their confidence. The restoration of a Bourbon to the throne might have met his silent approbation, if the throne had been founded in a constitution, fairly admitting the representatives of the people to a share in legislation, and properly defining the extent and the measure of the executive authority; but the views of Louis' friends and allies were too arbitrary to lead them to expect his approbation and aid. He, however, presented himself once at court, where he was very kindly received; but the government they established was so different from the representative government which he had assisted to form, that he did not again appear at the palace.

But great and extraordinary events, once more forced for the moment, this modern Cincinnatus from his plough, to assist in councils which had for their object the fate of an empire, and which brought him before the world, in all the original splendour of his long-tried virtue. Napoleon landed from Elba on the first of March, 1815, and reached Paris on the twentieth. His appearance in the capital was like a

* Lady Morgan's France, p. 319.—North American Review, January, 1825.

theatrical illusion, and his policy seemed to be to play all men, of all parties, like the characters of a great drama around him. Wishing to obtain the powerful countenance and co-operation of Lafayette, he deputed Joseph Bonaparte, to whom Lafayette had been personally known, to consult and conciliate him; but the consistent patriot would hold no communion with the new order of things. He even refused, though pressingly solicited, to have an interview with the emperor; and when the ex-king of Spain observed that his name was placed first upon the list of peers, and urged his acceptance of the peerage, this was his answer; "Should I ever again appear on the scene of public life, it can only be as a representative of the people." To the *Acte Additionel* of the twenty-second April, 1815, confirming the principles of Napoleon's former despotism, but establishing, among other things, a hereditary chamber of peers, and an elective chamber of representatives, Lafayette entered his solemn protest, in the same spirit with which he had protested against the consulship for life. The very college of electors, however, who received his protest, unanimously chose him, first to be their president, and afterwards to be their representative to the *Corps Legislatif*.*

After a long and chequered interval, Lafayette appeared before his country, with the same immutability of principle, the same energy of spirit and force of eloquence, as was possessed by him to whom America raised statues, ere manhood had shed its down upon his cheek;—to whom the military spirit of France devoted a sword of victory, formed out of the dungeon-bars of the Bastile, which he had broken. As a member of the chamber of deputies, he exhibited to his country, a bright, untarnished, model of the true, pure, incorruptible constitutionalists of 1789, whose views for the liberty and happiness of their country had been successively and effectually frustrated, by the sordid selfishness of an-

* Lady Morgan's France, 315, 320.—Biog. Not. Fay. 13.—Mem Fayette, 106.—North Am. Rev. January, 1825.

tiquated privilege, by the factious intrigues of sanguinary democracy, and by the aspiring views of bold, boundless and despotic ambition.*

It was as a representative of the people that he saw Bonaparte, for the first time, at the opening of the chambers on the seventh of June, 1815. "It is about twelve years since we have met, general;" said Napoleon, with great kindness of manner: but Lafayette received the emperor with marked distrust; and all his efforts were directed, as he then happily said they should be, "to make the chamber of which he was a member, a representation of the French people, and not a Napoleon club."—Notwithstanding all Bonaparte's efforts to procure the nomination of the president of the chamber, the votes were divided between Lanjuinais, Lafayette, and Flangergues. On the first ballot, the two former had the highest number of votes; but, finding that the emperor had declared he would not accept Lanjuinais, if he should be chosen, Lafayette used great exertions and obtained a majority for him, over himself. Bonaparte was compelled, by circumstances to submit, as well as to recognise Lafayette as vice president of the chamber. From this moment until after the battle of Waterloo, which happened in twelve days, Lafayette did not make himself prominent in the chamber. He voted for all judicious supplies, on the ground that France was invaded, and that it was the duty of all Frenchmen to defend their country; but he in no way implicated himself in Bonaparte's projects, or fortunes, with whom it was impossible he could have any thing in common.†

At last, at nine o'clock on the evening of the twentieth June, 1815, Bonaparte arrived from Waterloo, a defeated and desperate man. During his absence from Paris, the different parties in the chambers had not been idle. All agreed that if Napoleon was victorious at the outset of the

* Morgan's France, p. 320.
† North American Review, January, 1825.—Mem. Fayette, 286.

campaign, any resistance to his government would be vain. Should disgrace and defeat attend his first enterprise, many had determined to cast off his yoke, and to cause him to abdicate the throne which he had usurped. Some, with Fouche at their head, hoped to prevent the desolation of France, by making peace with, and recalling the Bourbons. Others, believing that the allies, according to their declarations, would permit them to choose their government and their chief, proposed to offer the crown to the duke of Orleans, who seemed the only one of the Bourbon family, who had imbibed the proper principles of moderation. Another party, whose leader was the virtuous Lafayette, hoped that France might at length be permitted to enjoy some splendid and sublime constitution, approaching to the boasted models of the ancient republics. These three parties formed the decided majority of the deputies, and would all cordially and zealously unite in accomplishing the abdication of Napoleon.*

The dissolution of the representative body, and the assumption of the whole dictatorship of the country, now occupied the deliberations of Napoleon and his ministers.—Lucien vehemently urged the dictatorship as the only means of averting from his brother, the disgrace which his enemies were preparing, and the only means of saving the country. Regnault warmly supported him, and Decres and Davoust were inclined to the same opinion; but they were opposed by Fouche, Carnot, and Cambaceres. Napoleon said little. He attentively listened to the arguments of each party, and at length, expressed his firm determination to throw himself on the loyalty of the chambers, and concert with them the measures which the present critical situation of France required.—While the council was deliberating on the form of the message to be delivered to the chambers, the deputies met. Napoleon had ordered a bulletin of their proceedings to be sent to him, by a confidential agent, every quarter of

* Boyce's France, vol. ii. 116, 117.

an hour. The first bulletin filled the court party with alarm. *Lafayette had appeared in the tribune.* Bonaparte, in great agitation, reiterated the disastrous intelligence, "*Lafayette in the tribune!*" while a spoon, with which he was trifling fell from his hand, and his altered countenance betrayed his conviction that "all was over." The council was advised that he had moved that the sittings of the chamber should be declared permanent, and that every attempt to dissolve them should be resisted and punished, as high treason. All question respecting the dictatorship was now at an end, unless the emperor was resolved to add the horrors of civil war to the calamities which were devastating the frontiers, and threatened to penetrate to the very heart of France.—The council was, for awhile, lost in astonishment and fear, but the next intelligence recalled them to their recollection, and showed them all the danger which threatened Napoleon and his party. The ministers were ordered to appear in the chamber of deputies, and there answer to any questions which might be put to them. At first they hesitated whether they would obey this unexpected, and peremptory, and unconstitutional summons. Napoleon was indignant at the insult, and even spoke of putting himself at the head of the few troops in Paris, on whose fidelity he was assured he might depend, and marching to the hall, to dissolve the chambers by force. No one but Lucien was found sufficiently bold, or faithful, or unprincipled, to second this rash proposal. At this moment, a second and more peremptory summons arrived, requiring the immediate attendance of the ministers in the hall of the deputies. The council broke up in dismay, and nothing was determined, except that an extraordinary meeting should be summoned in the evening.*

It has been stated that the deputies assembled while the council of the ministers continued their deliberations. Lafayette had obtained intelligence of the subject which en-

* Boyce's France, ii. 134–5, 6.—Morgan's France, 321.

gaged their attention, and which had been so often discussed in the private assemblies at the palace. Two of the council, Thibaudeau, and Regnault de St. Jean d' Angely, who were opposed to the violent measure of the dictatorship, had even informed him that it would be taken instantly, and that in two hours, the chamber of representatives would cease to exist. There was, of course, not a moment left for consultation, or advice: the emperor, or the chamber, must fall that morning. He was sufficiently experienced in the manœuvres of revolutionary times, to know that not a moment was to be lost, and that all depended on striking the first blow. He therefore managed that the chamber should meet at an earlier hour than usual, and the president had no sooner taken the chair, than he presented himself at the tribune. For the first time for twenty years, he ascended the tribune on the twenty-first of June, 1815, with the same clear courage, and in the same spirit of self-devotion, with which he had stood at the bar of the national assembly in 1792, and uttered words which would assuredly have been his death-warrant had he not been supported in them by the assembly which he addressed. He had hitherto taken no share in their discussions. He had kept himself aloof, as if he were conscious of disgrace in belonging to the government which Napoleon had instituted. His appearance, therefore, excited the greatest surprise and the most lively expectation, and a profound silence reigned throughout the whole assembly. "Gentlemen," said he, "for the first time during many years, you hear a voice which the old friends of liberty may yet recognise. The country is in danger, and you alone can save it. The sinister reports, which have been circulated during the last two days, are unhappily confirmed. This is the moment to rally round the national colours,—the tri-coloured standard of 1789, the standard of liberty, equality, and public order. It is you alone, who can now protect the country from foreign attacks, and internal dissensions. It is you alone who can secure the independence and the honour of

France.--Allow a veteran in the sacred cause of freedom, and a stranger to the spirit of faction, to submit to you some resolutions, which the dangers of the present crisis demand. I am assured that you will feel the necessity of adopting them :—

"Art. I. The chamber declares that the independence of the nation is menaced.

"II. The chamber declares its sittings permanent. All attemps to dissolve it, shall be considered high treason. Whosoever shall render himself culpable of such an attempt, shall be considered a traitor to his country, and condemned as such.

"III. The army of the line, and the national guards, who have fought, and still fight, for the liberty, the independence, and the territory of France, have merited well of the country.

"IV. The minister of the interior is invited to assemble the principal officers of the Parisian national guard, in order to consult on the means of providing it with arms, and of completing this corps of citizens, whose tried patriotism and zeal offer a sure guarantee for the liberty, prosperity, and tranquillity of the capital, and for the inviolability of the national representatives.

"V. The minister of war, of foreign affairs, of police, and of the interior, are invited to repair to the hall of assembly."

No opposition was made to these resolutions, so alarming and so bold. The court party was taken by surprise, and absolutely thunder-struck. Well founded, indeed, were the fears of the emperor, when he heard that Lafayette was in the tribune, for these motions, which were at once adopted, with the exception of the fourth article, both by the representatives and the peers, substantially divested him of his power, and left him merely a factious and dangerous individual in the midst of a distracted state. The fourth article was suspended, as conveying an invidious distinction between the troops of the line, and the national guards ; but the latter availed themselves of the hint. They immediately assembled at their respective rendezvous, and a piquet was sent from every arrondissement, to do duty at the hall of the deputies, and to charge themselves with the protection of the national representation.*

The resolutions offered by Lafayette decided the fate of Napoleon. All, except himself, predicted the speedy termination of his reign. The day passed over without any event of consequence. The emperor hesitated as to the course he should pursue. The chambers exacted from the ministers the most positive and reiterated assurances that no designs were harboured against them. The citizens of Paris anxiously awaited the result of the impending struggle. Toward the beginning of the evening, Napoleon, hoping that the eloquence of Lucien, which had saved him on the eighteenth Brumaire, might be found no less effectual now, sent him, with the three other ministers to the chamber, having first obtained a vote that all should pass in secret session. It was certainly a most perilous crisis: it was a contest for existence, and no man could feel his life safe. Lucien rose, and made a partial exposition of the state of affairs, and the projects and hopes he still entertained. A deep and painful silence followed. At length M. Jay, well known about twenty years ago in Boston, under the assumed name of Renaud, as a teacher of the French language, ascended the tribune, and after a long, vehement, and eloquent speech, proposed to send a deputation to the emperor, demanding his abdication. Lucien immediately followed. He never showed more power, or a more impassioned eloquence: "It is not Napoleon," he exclaimed, "that is attacked; it is the French people. And a proposition is now made to this people to abandon their emperor; to expose the French nation, before the tribunal of the world, to a severe judgment on its levity and inconstancy. No, sir, the honour of this nation

* Boyce's France, ii. 137---140.--North American Review, January, 1825.

shall never be so compromised!" On hearing these words, Lafayette rose. He did not go to the tribune; but spoke, contrary to rule and custom, from his place. His manner was perfectly calm, but marked with the very spirit of rebuke; and he addressed himself, not to the president, but directly to Lucien. "The assertion which has just been uttered is a calumny. Who shall dare to accuse the French nation of inconstancy to the emperor Napoleon? That nation has followed his bloody footsteps through the sands of Egypt, and through the wastes of Russia; over fifty fields of battle, in disaster as faithfully as in victory; and it is for having thus devotedly followed him, that we now mourn the blood of three millions of Frenchmen."—These few words made an impression on the assembly, which could neither be resisted nor mistaken; and, as Lafayette ended, Lucien himself bowed respectfully to him, and, without resuming his speech, sat down.—It is stated that Lafayette, during this debate, said to Lucien, "Go tell your brother that we will *trust him no longer;* we will ourselves undertake the salvation of our country."*

It was determined to appoint a deputation of five members from each chamber, to meet the grand council of the ministers, and deliberate, in committee, on the measures to be taken. At night, this imperial committee assembled, under the presidency of Cambaceres, arch chancellor of the empire. It was composed of the ministers holding departments, the ministers of state, the president and four members of the chamber of peers, the president and four vice-presidents (one of whom was Lafayette,) of the representatives, the heads of the civil and military authorities of Paris, and some state-counsellors, peers, representatives, and citizens, who were invited by the emperor. The friends of Napoleon were the most numerous party.—A secretary announced the approach of the emperor, who was preceded by his three brothers. All the assembly rose. He saluted

* North American Review, January, 1825.—Morgan's France, 326

them respectfully, but with some embarrassment. They then reseated themselves, without waiting for any previous command, and a profound silence succeeded. Count Regnault who faithfully adhered to the fortunes of his master during all his vicissitudes opened the debate. He insisted that the glorious vacancies which unheard of sacrifices had made in the ranks of the army, ought to be filled up." If victory has ceased," said he, "to crown our standards, are there not other palms besides those which are sprinkled with blood? The olive of peace may still flourish on our menaced frontiers; but that it may bear permanent fruit, it must be planted by heroic hands." "The only conquest for which we fight is that of peace." I conclude with moving that the chambers make an appeal to French valour, while the emperor is treating of peace in the most steady and dignified manner."*

Lafayette next rose. Every eye was fixed upon him, and a profound silence reigned around. Napoleon was agitated almost to suffocation; but he speedily recovered himself, and assumed the appearance of indifference and unconcern.

"In love for my country," said he, "and ardent wishes to save it from the dangers which threaten to overwhelm it, I will not yield to the last speaker. The sincerity of his patriotism I am not disposed to doubt; but it is with pain that I am compelled to say, that the measures which he proposes would hasten and aggravate the calamities that we all deprecate. The fine army with which our northern frontiers were covered, is no more. It can oppose no effectual resistance to the hordes of foreigners, who have already passed our borders, and whose course is marked with devastation and blood. It is under the walls of Paris alone, that our scattered troops will be able to unite, and dispute with the enemy, the possession of the capital of the empire.

"Of the issue of the contest, I should not be doubtful. At the voice of their government, and to defend the liberty,

Boyce's France, ii. chap. iv. *et seq.*

the integrity, and the independence of his country, every Frenchman would fly to arms, and the invaders would be chased from our soil with sad discomfiture. But though the triumph would be certain, the contest would be long and dreadful. Our fruitful fields would be laid waste, and our rivers run with blood. Is it necessary to expose our country to these calamities? Is it necessary to fill it with widows and orphans? Are there no means by which peace may be obtained without compromising our honour?

"The last speaker has proposed that pacific overtures should be made to the allies; that while an appeal is made to French valour, the emperor should treat for peace in the most dignified manner. But with what prospect of success will he, or can he treat? Have not our enemies pledged themselves to a line of conduct which, adopted when the issue of the contest was uncertain, and while all France appeared to have rallied round the emperor of their choice, will not be readily abandoned, now that victory has crowned their efforts?

"Mingled sentiments of affection and respect prevent me from being more explicit. *There is but one measure which can save the country*, and if the ministers of the emperor will not advise him to adopt it, *his great soul will reveal it to him.*"

This speech, firmly and fearlessly delivered in the presence of Napoleon, excited many murmurs from the court party, and much applause from others. At the close of it, the emperor cast his eyes down, but immediately raised them again with a smile of disdain. The duke of Bassano (Maret) could not contain his indignation. He proposed that all who for twelve years had made parts of different factions, whose common object was the dethronementof Napoleon, should be placed under the surveillance of a more severe police: "had this measure been adopted," he continued, "a person who now hears me, (Lafayette,) and who well understands me, would not smile at the misfortunes of the country, and Wellington would not be marching to Paris. A burst of disapprobation, which even the presence of the emperor could not check, followed this insinuation. The duke attempted to proceed, and to explain what he had said; but the indignation of the assembly was extreme. Hisses, and the most violent expressions of censure, drowned the voice of the speaker.*

The deliberation continued during several hours; and the sentiments of Lafayette were supported in no equivocal terms, by Lanjuinais and Constant. The emperor, fearing that some resolution might be proposed fatal to his power, conversed a few minutes with Carnot and Lucien, in a low voice, when the former addressed the meeting, earnestly deprecating violent measures, and concluded by moving that the chambers should be invited to treat with the allied sovereigns, through an embassy of their own choosing. The impossibility of this measure being attended with success, was apparent to every one. It could not be supposed, when they had declared that they would never treat with Napoleon or his family, that the allies would be deluded by a mere quibble, and treat with any deputation from the chambers, while he still held the reins of power.—By adopting this measure, however, the object of both parties was answered. They equally wished to gain time to strike some decisive blow, for which neither was yet fully prepared. The assembly broke up. No one appeared satisfied, and it was easy to see that some great event was at hand. Before they separated, one of the members who had taken no part in the debate, exclaimed, with a voice purposely meant to reach the emperor's ear, "M. de la Fayette has struck at the root of the evil. I admire Napoleon; but in order that all France, and that posterity may think as I do, one great act is still wanting. Is there no one so much a friend to our happiness and glory, as to point out to him how he may still add to it?"

The deputies met early on the following morning, and after a most stormy and tumultuous debate, caused by the de-

* Boyce's France, vol. ii, chap. iv. *et seq.*

lay in receiving a message from the emperor, they passed a resolution that a deputation of five members should proceed to the emperor, and express to his majesty the urgency of his decision. At the suggestion of general Solignac, than whom no man stood higher in the estimation of every party, the chamber unwillingly agreed to wait for one hour to receive the message, and adjourned for that purpose. Solignac hastened immediately to the palace to endeavour to save the honour of that chief whom he still respected, although during five years, the emperor had eagerly seized every opportunity to mortify, insult, and disgrace him.—In vain had many of his ministers urged his voluntary abdication. The preceding night was passed in discussion, and it was not until the chambers had actually assembled in the morning, that the conditional promise was extorted from him, that if the negotiations of the chambers failed, he would make the sacrifice which was required. Lucien and Bertrand alone opposed his abdication, and persisted in urging him to dissolve the chambers, and crush his enemies by one decisive blow. Lucien had heard of the tumultuous opening of the sittings in the morning, and was well assured that a motion would soon be made that Napoleon had forfeited the crown. He hastened to his brother, to make one last effort ere it was too late. The idea of the declaration of a forfeiture irritated Napoleon to madness. He sent in great haste for Davoust, the minister of war, and abruptly inquired what force he could lead against the assembly if he were compelled to proceed to extremities. Davoust hesitated; and his reply proved that he would not involve himself in a violent and unconstitutional measure. "I understand you," said the emperor, "my sun is set:" and he abrubtly quitted the apartment.

When general Solignac was introduced, he explained with much feeling the purport of his mission. He stated the disposition of the chambers, and the method by which he had succeeded in averting, for one short hour, the fatal decision, and entreated the emperor to prevent the disgrace of forfeiture, by a speedy abdication. Napoleon had also learned, that if his abdication was not sent to the chamber within one hour, Lafayette had resolved to *move for his expulsion.* All Solignac's arguments were urged in vain. Napoleon was resolved to brave his fate. At length, the general, as his last resource, proposed a measure that he would fain have otherwise avoided, that he should abdicate in favour of his son. Napoleon consented. A secretary was summoned; the declaration was immediately drawn up; and Solignac hastened to the assemblywith this important paper, which was received with every mark of respect. Lafayette proposed that the person and interests of Napoleon should be placed under the protection of the national honour; and the resolution was carried by acclamation.—The president, Lanjuinais, Lafayette, the other vice-presidents, and the secretaries, proceeded to the Tuilleries, to thank him, in behalf of the nation, for the sacrifice he had made. "We found him," said general Lafayette to Lady Morgan, "upon this occasion, as upon many others, acting out of the ordinary rules of calculation; neither affecting the pathetic dignity of fallen greatness, nor evincing the uncontrollable dejection of disappointed ambition, of hopes crushed, never to revive, and of splendour quenched, never to rekindle. We found him calm and serene: he received us with a faint, but gracious, smile, and spoke with firmness and pre cision."

The nation being left without a government by the abdication of Napoleon, the first care of the chambers was to appoint a committee who should provisionally assume the chief command. This crude government lasted only a few days. Its prncipal measure was sending a deputation to the allied powers to treat for peace, at the head of which was Lafayette. The five commissioners repaired to the head-quarters of Blucher, whose army had advanced one day's march before that of the duke of Wellington, and requested a suspension of arms while they proceeded to the head quarters of the allies with pacific overtures. To this the Prussian general gave a peremptory refusal: he would not agree to an armistice for a single hour. Within the walls of Paris alone would he listen to overtures of peace. He would explain nothing; he would listen to nothing short of unconditional submission and the possession of Paris. Their passports he could not refuse, and after much unpleasant altercation, they proceeded to Haguenau, were the allied sovereigns had now arrived. They were received with much apparent deference, and the conferences immediately commenced. When the French plenipotentiaries declared that Napoleon had abdicated his throne, they were interrupted by the demand of the British minister, that he should be delivered unconditionally into the power of the allies. This proposition excited the utmost astonishment and indignation; and Lafayette immediately replied, that Napoleon having voluntarily abdicated, that he might be no obstacle to the welfare of France, his person was under the protection of the national gratitude and honour, and that when it was proposed to the French people to commit an act of unexampled treachery, he did not expect that a prisoner of Olmutz would be selected as the fittest medium for its execution. The demand was immediately waived.

The allied monarchs did not intend to enter into any negotiations, nor explain their real intentions, which were to restore the Bourbons. They therefore, delayed the conferences on the most absurd and frivolous pretexts. After three conferences, the commissioners departed, perfectly unacquainted with the demands of the allies, but having received an assurance, as false as it was positive, that "the foreign courts made no pretentions to interfere with the form of the French government." When they arrived at Paris, Lafayette found, to his great regret, that the city had capitulated, and that Wellington and Blucher were about to enter the capital. Paris surrendered on the third of July, 1815; and what remained of the representative government which Bonaparte had created for his own purposes, but which Lafayette had turned against him, was soon afterwards dissolved On the sixth of July, he spoke to the assembly of the conferences of Haguenau, and of the patriotic sentiments of the departments through which he had passed. On the morning of the eighth of July, the doors of the assembly were found guarded and closed. Although the deputies had neither the power nor inclination to resist this arbitrary act, they had too much spirit and patriotism to separate without solemnly protesting against its injustice. Lafayette received a great number at his own house, and proceeded with them to the president's, when, more than a hundred members having signed the procès-verbal, they retired quietly to their homes.*

Lafayette went immediately to La Grange, from which, in fact, he had been only a month absent, and resumed his agricultural employments. There, in the midst of a family of above twenty children and grandchildren, who all looked up to him as their patriarchal chief, he lived in simple and sincere happiness, and in complete retirement, until the year 1817, when he was elected a deputy from La Sarthe, although opposed by the whole influence of the government. He was a conspicuous member of the chamber, and in all his votes has shown himself constant to his ancient principles. When the ministry proposed to establish a censorship of the press, he resisted them in an able speech; but Lafayette was never a factious man, and, therefore, he has never made any further opposition to the present order of things in France, than his conscience and his official place required. That he does not approve the present constitution of the monarchy, his votes as a deputy, and his whole life, plainly show; and that his steady and temperate opposition is matter of serious anxiety to the family now on the throne, is apparent, from their conduct towards him during the last ten years, and their management of the public press since he has been in this country. In fact, the course which he has pursued, not only since the restoration of the Bourbons, but during the reign of Napoleon, ought to be viewed by the citizens of this republic, as a motive for fresh esteem and gratitude. He

* Boyce's France, ii, chap. v, *passim*, p. 262—267, 343.

has uniformly acted, in regard to the arbitrary maxims and measures of the imperial and royal administrations, like one who deemed the voluntary allegiance which he had paid in his youth to the principles of freedom, as perpetually obligatory, and paramount to all considerations of personal interest and security, at any period or in any situation. In the chamber of deputies, under the existing government of France, he always stood forth the champion of constitutional and natural rights, and the adversary of despotic doctrine and rule, with a firmness, serenity, and dignity, which must have finally extorted the admiration even of the *ultras*, who so often sought to force him down by clamour and menaces. He came to this country a *liberal* by generous instinct and enlightened reason;—he has remained so through all vicissitudes and dangers. He has never deserted the banners under which he first contended; he has done honour to the political school in which he was formed, by proving that the true disciple can never be an apostate nor a prevaricator. It is enough to say, that he is eminently obnoxious to the governments of France, Austria, and Prussia; —he is odious to them and to the Russians, as the veteran and inflexible apostle of that creed which they most dread, and are most anxious to suppress;—he is the worst of liberals in their eyes; a patrician by birth, the subject of a monarchy, who deserted to republicanism at the first opportunity; who would never afterwards bend the knee to absolute power, and whom they have been unable to crush, although he has raised his voice to all the globe against their doctrines and designs, and become the model and patriarch of constitutionalists.*

M. de Lafayette now withdrew himself entirely from political affairs, encircled by those he best loved, and conscious that he had done every thing for his country that his powers and opportunities had allowed. Let us follow this "last of the Romans," for a moment, to his peaceful retreat, and contemplate the man who had rode upon ruder storms, and dared greater

* North American Review, January, 1825.—National Gazette, February 4, 1824.

dangers, than almost any other of the age, calmly and contentedly enjoying the substantial luxuries of domestic life.

The chateau of La Grange lies in the fertile district of La Brie; so remote from any high road, so lonely, so wood-embosomed, that a spot more sequestered, more apparently distant from the bustling world, and all its scenes of conflict and activity, can scarcely be imagined.* It is situated about forty miles from Paris, amid prolific orchards and antiquated woods. The chateau is of singular construction, quadrangular, and ornamented by Moorish towers at each angle, which have no unpleasing effect. This estate, belonging to the fortune of his wife, and a small farm in Auvergne, were all that remained of his wealth: he had lost every thing besides, in the madness of revolutionary confiscation. The building is ancient, (having been founded by Louis Le Gros,) and simply furnished: the wood which adjoins it, is beautiful, divided in the old style, by long green alleys, intersecting one another, and admirably adapted for a studious walk, or for reading, remote from noise.

It was here that, in 1802, he received with tearful eyes, and joyful smiles, the celebrated British statesman who had so eloquently and pathetically pleaded his cause in the British parliament. Lafayette had become acquainted with Mr. Fox at an early age, during a visit to London. There was too much congeniality in their souls not to produce an early and strong sentiment of friendship. While the hero was promoting the cause of liberty in America, the statesman laboured, with equal zeal, in the British house of commons, to inspire an obstinate and unenlightened ministry with respect for the rights of humanity, and mercy for the suffering Americans.

Lafayette resides on his estate in rural simplicity, and unostentatious hospitality; and there are few Americans who do not offer their respects to the benefactor of their country. No silly affectation—no studied welcome—no idle airs of ceremony,—are seen there. The benevolent countenances, and warm

*The account of La Grange and its inhabitants is compiled from Lady Morgan's France, Trotter's life of Fox, Memoirs of Lafayette, &c. &c.

welcome, of a good and amiable family, are delightful to the hearts of those, who go to La Grange with the same feelings as the steps of the weary pilgrim approach the shrine of sainted excellence.

Modest, plain, and unassuming in his general deportment, Lafayette has ever been averse to parade and ostentation. Habited in his gray coat and round hat, with a cane in his hand, and accompanied by his grandson, he would ramble over his farms, visiting his sheep-folds, his cow-stalls, and his dairies, and enjoying, with much relish, the avocations of agriculture. His manner to the peasantry, and to the workmen engaged in the various rustic offices of his domains, was extremely gracious, and he freely engaged in lively and familiar conversation with them. And this condescending kindness was repaid by boundless affection, and respect amounting almost to veneration. In a plain, but spacious, room of the chateau, the peasantry of the neighbourhood, assemble, (1816,) every Sunday evening, in winter, to dance to the merry sound of the violin, and are regaled with cakes, and *eau-sucrée*. The general is usually, and his family are always, present at these rustic balls; the younger members occasionally dancing among the tenantry. In the summer, this patriarchal re-union takes place in the park, where a space is cleared for the purpose, shaded by the lofty trees which encircle it.

Living in this simple manner, in the bosom of a tender and affectionate family, the general exhibits the bright example of a public man, content with little, free from envious and angry feelings, and willing to live in dignified silence, when he had not the power to do good. His benevolent features; his frank and warm manners, which make him almost adored in his family; and a placid contentedness, amounting to cheerfulness, altogether have an irresistible effect in gaining the affections and esteem of those admitted to his more intimate society. Not only true to his principles, and faithful to his country, but affectionate to his family, and kind to his friends, he is eminently worthy of being pronounced a good father, a good husband, a good citizen, a good patriot, and a good man.—As simple in their dress, as in their manner of living, it would be in vain to seek for splendid dresses, jewels, or any of the trappings of worldly vanity, at La Grange. "The jewels of the Lafayette family are those of the mother of the Gracchi."

The benevolence, humanity, and generosity of Lafayette, might be illustrated by a multitude of examples, a selection from which will prove, that whether amid the turmoils of war, the perplexities of politics, or the pleasures of retirement, he never forgot the duties of a man, or ceased to feel the impulse of a noble heart. We have already recorded his benefaction to the sufferers from fire in Boston, in 1787; his supplies of clothing and absolute necessaries, to the American soldiers, at different periods; his humanity to the sick and the wounded; his kindness to indigent or distressed Americans, in France, &c. &c. A few anecdotes of the same nature, will serve to exalt his character.—Towards the close of the year 1777, or beginning of 1778, Lafayette arrived at the camp near Albany, at the very moment when one Butler, a captain in the British army, was about to be executed, by the command of Arnold. He instantly arrested the punishment, in order to examine into the case. The man was undoubtedly guilty, but the young general took advantage of some informality in the proceedings, and the deliverance of Butler was the first act of his command. —At a time when his liberality had so reduced his funds, that he was obliged to write to France to procure supplies, he, one day, while inspecting the camp, perceived a man miserably dressed, seated at the foot of a tree, his face covered with his hands, and elbows resting on his knees, so profoundly immersed in melancholy, that he did not perceive the approach of the general: Lafayette stopped some minutes to observe him, and hearing him sigh, inquired the cause of his grief, with a tone of voice and sweetness peculiar to himself. The man informed him that he had recently joined the army, and had left a young wife, and two little children, who depended entirely on his industry for their support, and that the forlorn condition of his family did not allow him a moment's peace. The general inquired his address, and told him not to distress himself, as he would provide for his family. It is hardly necessary to add, that this promise was faithfully kept.*—Early in the year 1780, a young native of Ireland† was compelled to leave Ireland, in consequence of his patriotic zeal in favour of the freedom and independence of his country; and he retired to Paris, where he met with general de Lafayette. At that time, an invasion of Ireland from France, was the topic of conversation in the military and political circles of the French capital. Lafayette made many inquiries of the young Irishman, concerning the state of Ireland; and they separated for the time. The patriotic exile of Erin subsequently returned to his country, established a newspaper, was dragged before the Irish house of commons, for his ardour in the cause of oppressed Ireland, and ultimately felt himself compelled to emigrate to the United States, after undergoing a most vexatious and expensive prosecution.—He arrived at Philadelphia, in the year 1784, in company with a gentleman who had a letter of introduction to general Washington. This gentleman proceeded to Mount Vernon, where he found Lafayette. In the course of conversation, the latter inquired about his young Irish acquaintance, whose examination before the house of commons had been published in the American papers. He was then informed that the persecuted Irishman had arrived in Philadelphia. A few days afterwards, Lafayette visited that city, and sent for the gentleman for whom he had evinced so much solicitude. An interview took place. The general asked many questions, and, among others, what his young friend intended to do in this country? He replied that, as soon as he received funds from Ireland, it was his intention to establish a newspaper. The next morning, the Irish gentleman received a polite note from Lafayette, enclosing *four hundred dollars*, in notes of the

* Mem. of Lafayette, p. 24, 25.

† Mathew Carey, Esq. now living in Philadelphia.

bank of North America, without any explanation of its object. The grateful stranger hastened to the lodgings of the general, to express his feelings on the occasion; but the benevolent hero had taken his departure from the city, on his way to New-York, to embark for Europe.—With the money thus received, a paper was forthwith established; and, after years of laborious, honourable, and patriotic exertions, the Irish gentleman, who, from adverse events in Ireland, never received the expected remittances from that country, has attained a degree of respectability, wealth, and eminence, no less useful to the public, than creditable to himself.—Comment on an act so opportunely beneficent, proceeding from motives so purely philanthropic, so evincive of his ardent attachment to liberty and to its friends throughout the world, and so productive of valuable private and public advantages, would be entirely superfluous: the facts will touch the heart of every man of sensibility, and shed additional lustre on the pure and exalted character of the "friend of Washington, of America, and mankind."*—At Green Spring, Virginia, Lafayette dashed into the fire of Cornwallis' infantry, and met with captain Doyle, of the third Pennsylvania regiment, wounded in the leg, and leaning against a tree. The general ordered his servant to dismount, and dismounting himself, placed Doyle on his attendant's horse. While he was assisting him to mount, the wounded officer received a musket ball in his left shoulder. But the gallant Lafayette did not leave him until he saw him in a place of safety, and thus saved the life of one of the bravest captains of the Pennsylvania line.†—During the French revolution, when the commune of Paris insisted on his acceptance of his emoluments as commander-in-chief of the national guard, which he refused to accept, he used to them the following language: "If I required pecuniary assistance, I

* It is a remarkable circumstance, that after a separation of nearly half a century, the actors in this scene again met on the spot where it was first opened by the well-timed munificence of Lafayette; and that, with singular *keeping*, it was closed by the voluntary and honourable repayment of the gift.

† Allen M'Lane's Journal.

would have demanded it: but, at this time, when the sufferings of our citizens, and the necessary expenditures, are so great, I cannot consent to increase them. My fortune is sufficient for the station which I hold."*—In the beginning of 1822, soon after the revolution in Piedmont, many distinguished Italians, threatened with the vengeance of the Sardinian government, fled into France. Louis XVIII, being cousin to the king of Sardinia, formed the dastardly project of apprehending, and punishing these poor refugees. One of them applied to Lafayette for protection, who requested an American gentleman to take the Italian out of France with him, as a servant. The exile was soon included in the passport under a feigned name, and they were on the point of setting out for Havre, when information was received that the Bourbon government had altered their intentions, and would no longer molest the refugees from Piedmont.—When Lafayette embarked for America, in 1777, he possessed an income of one hundred and forty-six thousand francs, or about twenty-eight thousand seven hundred dollars. During the six years, from 1777, to 1783, he expended in the American service, of his private fortune, seven hundred thousand francs, equal to one hundred and forty thousand dollars!†—We conclude these anecdotes, with an incident which presents his character in the most delightful point of view:—In March, 1803, congress made a grant of eleven thousand five hundred and twenty acres of land to general Lafayette. In the year following, he was authorized to locate his warrant on any vacant land in the territory of Orleans; and, on the seventh April, 1806, his agent in this country did locate a tract of one thousand acres vacant land, adjoining the city of New-Orleans. On the third March, 1807, congress, without adverting to this location in behalf of the general, and indeed, wholly unconscious of the fact that it had been made, granted to the corporation of the city of New-Orleans, a space of six hundred yards around the fortifications of the city, including a valuable portion of the very

*Mém. Hist. 183.

†Colonel Hayne's Speech in Congress, December 20, 1824.

land which had been previously entered by Lafayette. He was immediately informed of the fact. It was stated to him that his right to this land was unquestionable, and the legal opinion of an eminent lawyer and jurist was forwarded to him, with the assurance that, in a contest with the city of New-Orleans, he must succeed. The value of the land had been discovered, and fifty thousand dollars could, even then, have been obtained for the general's title to it. But what was the conduct of Lafayette, on being informed of these facts? He, promptly and without hesitation, communicated to his agent, "that he would not consent even to inquire into the validity of his title; that he could not think of entering into litigation with any public body in the United States; that the property had been gratuitously bestowed upon him by the United States, and it was with them to say what had been given;" and he accompanied these declarations with a positive direction to his agent to relinquish his entry, and to make a location elsewhere. This was done, and the land substituted for that which was lost, is of very inconsiderable value; while on a portion of that which was so generously relinquished, now stands a valuable part of the city of New-Orleans, valued, according to correct estimates, at from *four to five hundred thousand dollars.**

On the twenty-fourth of December, 1807, Lafayette experienced a blow which it required all his religion and philosophy to support. His wife,—his best friend, his faithful and heroic companion; adorned with every virtue; pious, modest, generous, and faithful; affectionate, yet firm, and gentle, yet resolved,—the long-tried wife of his bosom, at length sunk under her misfortunes, and was torn from the arms of her husband at an age when she might have expected many years of happiness in store. But the dastardly ferocity of tyrants brought to an untimely grave, in the forty-seventh year of her age, a woman who was once the soul of her numerous family, the support of the poor, the ornament of her country, and the honour of her sex.—She was, indeed, a superior and admirable woman, possessing

* Colonel Hayne's (of S. Carolina,) Speech in Congress, Dec. 20, 1824.

the high polish of the ancient nobility, eloquent, and animated. In the society of a cherished husband, and affectionate children, she regretted nothing of past splendour, and was happy in retirement.—In *her* charming daughters, was found none of that insipid languor, or wretched affectation, which, in young women of fashion, so much destroys originality of character, and shows us, in one fashionable young lady, the prototype of ten thousand.*

Their only son, George Washington Lafayette, served from the commencement of the war, in 1800, as one of the *guides d'honneur* to the guards of the first consul, and armed and equipped himself at his own expense, and never consented to receive any pay. General Grouchy appointed him his aid-de-camp, as he was extremely intelligent, brave, active, and an officer of great merit. Bonaparte extended the resentment he bore the father to all attached to the family of Lafayette. But this unworthy treatment did not prevent George Washington from continuing his services, with great and distinguished activity, even when the emperor caused it to be insinuated to him that he ought to tender his resignation. At the battle of Eylau, he twice saved the life of general Grouchy. The latter made a brilliant report of his conduct, and requested a promotion for him and the legion of honour: the great and magnanimous Napoleon petulantly erased his name from the report, not even permitting it to appear in the bulletin! The young officer, nevertheless, continued in service, and did not retire to La Grange, until after the ratification of peace at Tilsit.—In 1803, he married mademoiselle de Tracy, daughter of the count and senator of that name, a very engaging and interesting lady. They have five children, the eldest of which is a young woman of twenty years of age, the favourite of her grandfather.—In 1795, he was sent with his tutor to America, to avoid the horrors of French democracy. As soon as he was informed of his arrival in Boston, general Washington wrote to a friend, the honourable George Cabot, requesting him to visit the young gentleman, and make him acquainted with the relations between

* Mem. Lafayette, p. 303-4.—Trotter's Life of Fox, p. 202.

this country and France, which would prevent the president of the United States from publicly espousing his interest; but "assure him," to use Washington's words, "of my standing in the place of, and becoming to him, a *father, friend, protector, and supporter*."*

Mademoiselle Anastasie Lafayette, married Charles Latour Maubourg, the brother of her father's companion in misfortune. He united to a cold, yet agreeable exterior, great sensibility and courage, with very little ambition. His family consists of four children, of whom two are married, and one of them has two children.—Mademoiselle Virginia Lafayette married M. de Lasteyrie, nephew of the celebrated agriculturist of that name. He served with his brother-in-law, George Washington, in the campaigns of Jena, Eylau, Friedland, &c. where he greatly distinguished himself. The emperor, who knew that he was the son-in-law of Lafayette, gave him neither the cross of honour, nor any military advancement; and always erased his name from the list of officers recommended for promotion.—This amiable and most interesting family seem united by one bond of affection, and to desire nothing beyond the circle of their tranquil mansion: they constantly present for contemplation, the most perfect unity of family interests, habits, taste, and affections.†

Blessed with the *mens sana in corpore sano*,—in the full possession of every faculty and talent he ever possessed, the memory of Lafayette has all the tenacity of unworn youthful recollection. His conversation is brilliantly enriched with anecdotes of all that is celebrated, in character and event, for the last fifty years. He speaks and writes English with the same fluency and ease as he does his native tongue; and has made himself master of all that is best worth knowing in English literature and philosophy. He converses upon almost every subject worthy to engage the mind of a great and good man; sometimes in French, sometimes in English; always with eloquence,

* Mem. Lafayette, 280–1, 293. —Biog. Dic. 591.—Trotter's Life Fox, 202

† Mem. Lafayette, 271, 293, 294.—Lady Morgan's France, 322.

fluency, and spirit. In his epistolary correspondence, he is every where bold and patriotic; and his letters are marked by the frankness and penetration of a noble and vigorous mind. His elegant, and well-chosen collection of books, occupies the highest apartment in one of the towers of the chateau. It is a circular room, adorned with the busts of Washington, Franklin, and other distinguished American patriots. Here, seated at his desk, he can see, on his left, his whole farm, and his stables, and on his right, the park, and a very large and elegant lawn, covered with luxuriant grass. Like the study of Montaigne, it hangs over the farm-yard of the philosophical agriculturist. "It frequently happens," said he to Lady Morgan, "that my merinos, and my hay-carts, dispute my attention with your Hume, or our own Voltaire."*

The unbent and noble figure of Lafayette is still as upright, bold, and vigorous, as the mind that informs it. Grace, strength, and dignity, distinguish the fine person of this extraordinary man; who, though fifty years before the world, engaged in scenes of strange and eventful conflict, does not yet appear to have passed his climacteric. Bustling and active in business, graceful and elegant in society, it is difficult to trace in one of the most successful agriculturists, and one of the most perfect fine gentlemen, a warrior, and a legislator.—But the patriot is always discernible. His manners are plain and unostentatious; his address kind and conciliating. During the American revolution, his sedateness and gravity, and the simplicity of his manners, could not fail to attract attention. Conversing about him one day at the table of general Washington, Mrs. Washington remarked that all his dress was singularly plain,—that he never wore ruffles—and that he had nothing like show about him, except in the caparison of his horse.—He is now nearly sixty-eight years of age; his portly form, about five feet eleven inches high; his eyes, and eye-brows, prominent; but his fine forehead, partially concealed by a wig. His graceful and dignified manners soon put his company perfectly at their ease. Great

*Morgan's France, 323—Fox's Life, 204.—Mem. Lafayette, 299.

mildness beams in his countenance, which, in conversation, is brightened by a smile which carries with it evidence that it proceeds from the heart. He is lame, from a fracture of the thigh bone in the year 1803, but not so much as materially to impede his progress. His dress is that of the plainest citizen.

Such is Lafayette. His name has long been consecrated to fame; and his existence has been so intimately woven into the history of his country, that her records and her chronicles must have mouldered into nothing, ere his renown shall be forgotten, or the memory of his deeds have faded into oblivion. His illustrious name will be venerated by posterity; for his virtues and his deeds have distinguished it in an age, "when extensive celebrity is no trifling possession; when the world appears to have conspired for the destruction of mediocrity; and is agreed to repulse, with contempt, the ambitious pretenders that besiege, on all sides, the temple of renown."

Lafayette, desirous of again beholding the scenes of his youthful glory, having expressed his intention of re-visiting this country, congress, on the fourth of February, 1824, "*Resolved*, that whenever the president shall be informed of the time when the marquis may be ready to embark, a national ship, with suitable accommodations, be employed to bring him to the United States." The modest, unassuming, and consistent patriot, declined the honour of going in a national vessel, preferring a passage in a private ship. On the twelfth of July, 1824, he embarked on board the packet ship Cadmus, and on the sixteenth of August, landed at New-York, when first arose the sound of that universal acclamation, which has since been echoed from the Cordilleras and the Andes.

Republics have been charged with ingratitude, and Europeans, ignorant of the whole structure of our government, and the course of our policy, have supposed that the charge is justified by our own example. But when it shall become fully known abroad how the United States have, on all occasions, acted towards general de Lafayette; when it shall be understood that, in addition to other proofs of our gratitude,* we approach him in his old age with the expressions of our affectionate attachment, it may perhaps be acknowledged that there can be no better inheritance than the gratitude of a free people.

To conclude in the language of a celebrated writer,† it may, indeed, be said, that Lafayette, himself, enjoys a singular distinction: for it is a strange thing in the providence of God, one that never happened before, and will, probably, never happen again, that an individual from a remote quarter of the world, having assisted to lay the foundation of a great nation, should be permitted thus to visit the posterity of those he served, and witness, on a scale so vast, the work of his own sacrifices; the result of grand principles in government, for which he contended before their practical effect had been tried; the growth and maturity of institutions which he assisted to establish, when their operation could be calculated only by the widest and most clear sighted circumspection. We rejoice in it, for it is, we doubt not, the most gratifying and appropriate reward that could be offered to a spirit like his. In the beautiful phrase which Tacitus has applied to Germanicus, *fruitur fama;* for he must be aware, that the ocean which rolls between us and Europe, operates like the grave on all feelings of passion and party, and that the voice of gratitude and admiration, which now rises to greet him from every city, every village, and every heart, of this wide land, is as pure and sincere as the voice of posterity.

* On the twenty-eighth of December, 1824, an act was passed by congress, directing the secretary of the treasury to pay to general Lafayette, in consideration of his services and sacrifices in the war of the revolution, the sum of two hundred thousand dollars; and also granting to him and his heirs, one township of land, to be laid out and located under the authority of the president, in any of the unappropriated lands of the United States.—By this act, the respresentatives of the American people have conferred a lasting benefit on their country; they have performed a great moral duty; they have substantially proved to the world that republics are not always ungrateful.

† North American Review, January, 1825.

THE TOUR

OF

GENERAL LAFAYETTE

Through the United States.

CHAPTER I.

LANDING OF THE NATION'S GUEST AT NEW-YORK, AND HIS VISIT TO THE EASTERN STATES IN 1824.

As soon as it was known in the United States that the Marquis Lafayette had once more embarked for the shores of his adopted country, a general joy pervaded the nation, and all classes of citizens were prepared to take a lively interest in his arrival. The cities of New-York and Boston particularly, anticipated the event with some degree of impatience, and entered into such general arrangements for his reception, as were best calculated to do honour to themselves and their illustrious guest.

General Lafayette, accompanied by his son, George Washington Lafayette, Mr. Auguste Le Vasseur, and one servant, arrived in the harbour of New-York on the morning of the 15th of August, in the ship Cadmus, captain Allyn, after a pleasant passage of 31 days from Havre. His arrival was made known by the Telegraph at an early hour, and spread through the city with electrical rapidity. Broadway was soon thronged, and the Battery crowded with people, who sallied forth with the expectation that the hero and veteran of two revolutions, would come directly to the city. The arrangements of the city authorities, however, for his reception, having been seasonably communicated to him, he landed at Staten Island, and was conducted to the seat of the Vice President, where he remained through the day, and passed the night. Fort Lafayette fired a salute as the ship passed, and a salute was fired as the General landed.

In the city the national flag was immediately hoisted and displayed at all the public places during the day.

Proceedings, upon reception of the Marquis Lafayette into the city of New-York, on Monday, the 16th of August.

Arrangements of the Corporation.

The committee of arrangements of the Corporation have the pleasure to announce to their fellow citizens the arrival of the distinguished guest of their country, the Marquis de Lafayette.

The following are the arrangements made for his reception in the city:

The Committee of Arrangements of the Corporation, the Generals and other officers of the United States Army, the officers of the Navy, the Major Generals and the Brigadier Generals of the Militia, the President of the Chamber of Commerce, the Committee from the Society of Cincinnati, will proceed at 9 o'clock this day, to Staten Island, where the Marquis is lodged, and escort him to the city. They will be accompanied by the steam-boats, all with decorations, except that in which the Marquis is embarked, which will only have the flag of the United States, and the flag of New-York; bands of music being in each.

The Marquis' embarkation will be announced by a salute from Fort Lafayette, and the steam-ship Robert Fulton.

The forts in the harbour will also salute as the vessels pass.

The masters of vessels are requested to hoist their flags at mast-head, and where convenient, to dress their vessels.

The bells of the city will be rung from 12 to 1 o'clock.

The portrait room of the City Hall is appropriated to the Marquis, where, during his stay, he will after this day, between the hours of 12 and 2 o'clock, receive the visits of such of the citizens as are desirous of paying their respects to him.

The Committee of Arrangements of the Corporation having accepted the proffered services of the steam-ship Robert Fulton, and the steam-boats Chancellor Livingston, Oliver Ellsworth, Henry Eckford, Connecticut, Bellona, Olive Branch, Nautilus, &c.; they were all superbly dressed with flags and streamers of every nation, and directed to meet and form an aquatic escort between the south part of the Battery and Governor's Island, and thence proceed in order to Staten Island. The spectacle, as the boats were assembling, was truly interesting and beautiful. The Battery was crowded with respectable people of both sexes; Castle Garden was filled, and every boat that arrived to take its station, was completely crowded with elegant dressed ladies and gentlemen. The appearance of the Robert Fulton, as she came down the East River, from the Navy Yard, escorted by the Connecticut and Oliver Ellsworth, all superbly decorated, was rich beyond description. Her yards were manned to the round-tops, with about 200 seamen from the Constitution, who made an elegant appearance, and a battalion of marines, under the command of Major Smith, was on board, with a band of music, and many of the Naval Officers upon this station, together with several ladies and private gentlemen.

Arrived at the place of redezvous, the several vessels comprising the fleet took their station, and proceeded in regular order to the quarantine, as follows:—First, the Chancellor Livingston, on board of which were the committee of the Corporation, Major General Morton and suite, a number of the members of the Cincinnati, including Colonels Willet, Varick, Trumbull, Platt, and others, together with a few ladies, several officers and professors from West Point, accompanied by the excellent military band attached to that institution. On the right of the Chancellor, and about a length in rear, was the Connecticut, and on the left, to correspond, was the Oliver Ellsworth. Directly in the rear of the Chancellor, was the Robert Fulton, whose lofty masts and wide-spread arms, which literally swarmed with men, towered proudly above her less pretending, but not less gay and beautiful consorts. On the right of the Robert Fulton, about a length in the rear, was the Bellona, and on the left, the Henry Eckford, in a station to correspond; and the squadron was closed by the Olive Branch and Nautilus. The signals exchanged, and the steam-boats having attained their stations, as above stated, the squadron got under weigh, amidst the cheers of thousands of delighted spectators, The view of this fleet will perhaps never be forgotten. It was not only unique, but beyond a doubt, one of the most splendid spectacles ever witnessed on this part of the globe. The squadron, bearing six thousand of our fellow citizens, majestically took its course towards Staten Island, there to take on board our long expected and honoured guest. At 1 o'clock the fleet arrived at Staten Island, and in a few minutes, a landau was seen approaching the Hotel, near the ferry. The Marquis, the Vice-President, and the Ex-Governor Ogden, of New-Jersey, having alighted, a procession was formed, and the venerable stranger, supported by these gentlemen, followed by all the officers of the Island, and a crowd of citizens, passing through a triumphal arch, round which was tastefully entwined the French and American colours. As soon as the Marquis and suite entered on the broad stairs, connected with, and leading to the steam-boat which was to convey him to the city, he was received by the committee of the Common Council, who conducted him on board the Chancellor Livingston. On entering this splendid vessel, the marines paid him military honours. He was now introduced to the committees from most of our honoured Associations, and the General Officers, representing the Infantry. The West Point band all this time was playing "See the Conquering Hero Comes," "*Ou peut on etre mieux,*" "Hail Columbia," and the "Marseilles Hymn." The steam-ship now fired a salute, and the whole squadron got under weigh for the city, in the same order as before, except that the Bellona and Olive Branch, fastened each side of the Cadmus, (the ship which brought the General from France,) decorated with colours, and filled with passengers, majestically moved up the Bay. The sea was smooth and placid, and the breeze cool and agreeable. The most interesting sight, was the reception of the General by his old companions in arms: Colonel Marinus Willet, now in his eighty-fifth year, General Van Courtland, General Clarkson, and the other worthies, whom we have mentioned. Colonel Fish, General Lewis, and several of his comrades were absent. He embraced them all affectionately, and Colonel Willet again and again. He knew and remembered them all. It was a re-union of a long separated family.

After the ceremony of embracing and congratulations were over, he sat down along-side of Colonel Willet, who grew young again, and fought all his battles o'er. "Do you remember," said he, "at the battle of Monmouth, I was volunteer aid to General Scott? I saw you in the heat of battle. You were but a boy, but you were a serious and sedate lad. Aye, aye; I remember well. And on the Mohawk, I sent you fifty Indians, and you wrote me, that they set up such a yell, that they frightened the British horse, and they ran one way and the Indians another."

No person who witnessed this interview, will ever forget it; many an honest tear was shed on the occasion. The young men retired to a little distance, while the venerable soldiers were indulging recollections, and embracing each other again and again; and the surrounding youth silently dropt the tear they could no longer restrain. Such sincere, such honest feelings, were never more plainly or truly expressed. The sudden changes of the countenance of the Marquis, plainly evinced the emotions he endeavoured to suppress. He manfully supported this truly trying situation for some time, when a revolutionary story from the venerable Willet, recalled circumstances long passed: the incident, the friend alluded to, made the Marquis sigh; and his swelling heart was relieved, when he burst into tears. The sympathetic feelings extended to all present; and even the hardy tar rubbed away the tear he could no longer restrain. The scene was too affecting to be continued, and one of the Cincinnati, anxious to divert the attention of the Marquis, his eyes flowing with tears, announced the near approach of the steam-ship. The Marquis advanced to the quarter railing, where he was no sooner perceived by the multitude, than an instantaneous cheer most loudly expressed the delight they experienced. The other steam-boats in succession, presented themselves, and passed, each giving three enthusiastic cheers. The Marquis was delighted, and especially with the activity and quickness, with which 200 of our gallant seamen manned the yards of the steam-frigate, previous to the salute. About 2 o'clock, P. M. the fleet arrived off the Battery. What an impressive scene—3000 men, making a splendid appearance, formed in line with a battering train. The ramparts and parapets of the Castle, were lined with ladies and gentlemen. The flag-staff, the windows, and even the roofs of the houses facing the Bay, were literally crowded with spectators. Hundreds of boats and wherries surrounded the Battery. The Marquis left the Chancellor Livingston in a barge, commanded by Lieutenant Mix, of the Navy, accompanied by the committee of the Corporation, and the Cincinnati, the Generals of Infantry, &c.; and landed amidst the cheers and acclamations of 30,000 people, who filled the Castle, Battery, and surrounding grounds within sight. The Marquis now entered the Castle, which was tastefully carpeted from the landing place to the receiving rooms. He then partook of some refreshment, and was introduced to some distinguished citizens. Perceiving the restless anxiety of nearly 3000 persons in the Castle, to see the General, the Marquis advanced to the centre of the rear of the

Castle, and was greeted with loud cheers. From Gastle Garden, he proceeded with the appointed committee, and the military and naval officers, to review the line of troops under the command of Brigadier General Benedict. The muster was, on this occasion, unusually numerous and splendid, each corps vieing with the others in paying a tribute of respect to the soldier of the revolution, the friend and companion of Washington. After the review, the General, accompanied by general Morton, entered a barouche, drawn by four horses.

The committee of the Corporation, accompanied by the General's son, George Washington Lafayette, and his secretary, Mr. La Vasseur, followed the carriages. The General was escorted by a corps of cavalry, and at the head of the column of troops, proceeded up Broadway to the City Hall. The crowds which had assembled to pay honour to the respected visitor, and to be gratified with a view of his person, were such as almost to prevent the passage of the carriages and the troops. The scene could not but have afforded to the General the most delightful gratifications.—The houses to the very roofs were filled with spectators, and to the incessant cheers of the multitude, graceful females signified their welcome by the silent, but not less grateful and affecting testimony of the waving of handkerchiefs.

Arrived at the City Hall, the Marquis was conducted by the committee to the Common Council chamber, where the corporation were assembled. The members of the Common Council rose on his entrance, and upon being presented by the Chairman, Alderman Zabriskie, to the Mayor, his honour addressed him in the following speech:—

Address of the Mayor.

General—In the name of the municipal authority of the city, I bid you a sincere welcome to the shores of a country, of whose freedom and happiness you will ever be considered one of the most honoured and beloved founders.

Your only contemporaries in arms, of whom indeed but few remain, have not forgot, and their posterity will never forget, the *young and gallant Frenchman* who consecrated his youth, his talents, his fortune and his exertions, to their cause—who exposed his life—who shed his blood, that they might become free and happy. They will recollect with profound emotion, so long as they remain worthy of the liberties they enjoy, and of the exertions you made to obtain them, that you came to them in the darkest period of their struggle—that you linked your fortune with theirs, when it seemed almost hopeless—that you shared in the dangers, privations and sufferings of that bitter struggle, nor quitted them for a moment, till it was consummated on the glorious field of Yorktown. Half a century has passed since that great event, and in that time your name has become as dear to the friends, and as inseparably connected with the cause of freedom, in the old, as in the new world.

The people of the United States look up to you as to one of their most honoured parents—the country cherishes you as one of the most beloved of her sons. I hope and trust, sir, that not only the present, but future conduct of my countrymen, to the latest period of time, will, among other slanders, refute the unjust imputation, that republics are always ungrateful to their benefactors.

In behalf of my fellow citizens of New-York, and speaking the warm and universal sentiments of the whole people of the United States, I repeat their welcome to our common country.

Permit me to add, that the moment of my life, to which I shall look back with the greatest pleasure and pride, will be that, in which it fell to my lot, to be an organ, for expressing, however feeble, a nation's gratitude.

General Lafayette's answer.

Sir—While I am so affectionately received by the citizens of New-York and their worthy representatives, I feel myself overwhelmed with inexpressible emotions. The sight of the American shore, after so long an absence, the recollection of the many respected friends and dear companions, no more to be found on this land, the pleasure to recognise those who have survived, this immense concourse of a free republican population, who so kindly welcome me, the admirable appearance of the troops, the presence of a corps of the National Navy, have excited sentiments, to which no human language can be adequate. You have been pleased, sir, to allude to the happiest times, the unalloyed enjoyments of my public life ; it is the pride of my heart to have been one of the earliest adopted sons of America : I am proud also to add, that upwards of forty years ago I have been particularly honoured with the freedom of this city. I beg you, Mr. Mayor, I beg you, gentlemen, to accept yourselves, and to transmit to the citizens of New-York, the homage of my profound, and everlasting gratitude, devotion, and respect

The General and his son were then introduced to the members of the common council individually.

After the adjournment of the Common Council, the Marquis received the marching salute in front of the City Hall, and again entered the Hall, accompanied by his son and suite, and in the Governor's room received the Society of the Cincinnati, composed of his surviving brothers and companions in the field, a small number of whom still remain to meet and congratulate their long absent, but highly respected friend and fellow soldier. Here also he was met by the officers of the army and navy, and many citizens and strangers. From the Hall he was accompanied by the Common Council, and many distinguished persons, to the City Hotel to dine, escorted by the troops.

The whole exhibition, from the landing at the Battery, to the time of the dispersion of the people at the Park, was in a high degree interesting and gratifying. The numbers collected were perhaps unequalled on any former festive occasion. The houses through Broadway were filled with spectators of the first respectability, and the street was crowded with people. Every expression of good feeling was manifested from the windows, doors, and side-walks; the stranger was welcomed with unfeigned cordiality; and we think it must have afforded to the Marquis an unusual degree of delight to find that his services were remembered and acknowledged, and his name cherished by a free and grateful people.

The day was singularly fine—the water scene exceeded in splendour and effect, any thing of the kind that has ever been exhibited here. The appearance of the military was highly creditable in equipments, movements, and discipline; and we have not a doubt their appearance, when contrasted by his recollection with the suffering troops of the war of Independence, must have made a deep impression upon his mind.

On Wednesday morning, the 18th, in compliance with an invitation from Captain Rodgers, commandant of the Navy Yard, General Lafayette, attended by the Committee of Arrangements, and a select circle of ladies and gentlemen, proceeded in the elegant steam-boat Chancellor Kent, to visit the Navy Yard at Brooklyn.

As the James Kent passed the Grampus, lying in the North River, a salute of 21 guns was fired.

The Kent then proceeded round the battery and up the East River, until she came to anchor at the dock, where the steam-frigate is moored, when the Marquis and the ladies and gentlemen of the party disembarked—the United States frigate Constellation firing at the same time a salute of 21 guns. On landing, he was received by three cheers from 200 sailors drawn up for the occasion.

The General then went on board of the steam-frigate, and was much pleased with the construction of this formidable and unique naval battlement.

On returning, the jolly tars gave three more hearty cheers, and the General proceeded in a barge to the Navy Yard; when another salute of 21 guns was fired on his landing, and he was received by a battalion of marines.

The General was then conducted on board the Washington 74, where refreshments were provided for the whole party. After refreshing himself, the General took a rapid survey of the ships, and those now building, and returned on board the Kent, when another salute was fired by the Constitution.

Upon the return of the Marquis Lafayette from the Navy Yard on Wednesday, he was introduced, with his son, to the Historical Society, at their room in the Institution, at 2 o'clock P. M. According to a resolution, passed the day before, they were made members of the Society. The President, Dr. Hosack, in his speech to the Marquis, said:

"General Lafayette—In compliance with the unanimous resolutions of the New-York Historical Society, I have the gratification to announce to you your election as an honorary member of this institution, and to present to you a copy of their transactions.

"In announcing to you the resolution of this society, permit me to observe, that it was the exclusive object in the formation of this institution, to collect, preserve, and record the materials appertaining to the history of our state and country. Among these, none have been so precious as those relating to the Revolution, in which you bore a memorable and distinguished part, and to whom, under providence, our country is signally indebted for its independence, and the prosperity and success that have followed in its train.

"In the name of this institution, I also tender to you their congratulations upon your safe arrival, which affords you the opportunity to witness the happy condition of that country in whose behalf, the sword of your youth was drawn, and personally to bear your testimony to the blessings which have followed the achievements that have been accomplished by the united efforts of a Washington, and his illustrious companions in arms. General, my bosom glows at the associations which these events bring to our recollection, and every heart in this assembly throbs with inexpressible emotions at the sight of the hero who this day enters their Hall, and confers a lasting honour upon the sittings of this Society.

"Long, long, Sir, may you live to enjoy the homage so justly due, and spontaneously offered from the hearts of a free and grateful people, for the services you have rendered to this nation, to the world, to liberty, and to the ever memorable establishment of the only example on earth—a pure unmixed republican form of government.

"The same heroic page that records these events, will also inscribe in golden capitals, the immortal names of WASHINGTON and LAFAYETTE."

General Lafayette thereupon rose and replied as follows:—

"Sir—With the most lively gratitude, I receive the honour which the Historical Society of New-York have conferred by electing me one of their members.

"Permit me also thankfully to acknowledge the flattering manner in which you are pleased to announce this mark of their benevolence.

"The United States, Sir, are the first nation, on the records of history, who have founded their constitutions upon an honest investigation, and clear definition of their natural and social rights.

"Nor can we doubt, but that, notwithstanding the combinations made elsewhere by despotism and aristocracy, against those sacred rights of mankind, immense majorities in other countries, shall not in vain observe the happiness and prosperity of a free, virtuous, and enlightened people."

The President of the Society next addressed M. George Washington Lafayette as follows:—

"George Washington Lafayette—In accordance with the resolution of the New-York Historical Society, I have also the honour to present you a similar evidence of membership, with that conferred upon your illustrious Sire.

"May you, Sir, emulate his talents and his virtues; and may the same undaunted spirit which led him to offer his life at the altar of freedom, animate the bosom of the son in the same glorious cause."

To which the following reply was made :—

Sir—I cannot find words adequate to the feelings which I experience at this moment.

"Permit me to beg of you to present to the members of this Society, the homage of my profound respect and gratitude, for the unexpected honour, at this time conferred upon me."

The Marquis and his son were then conducted into the Gallery of Fine Arts and the Lyceum, and afterwards returned to the City Hotel, accompanied by Dr. Hosack, General Van Courtlandt, and Aldermen Hone and Wyckoff.

In the evening the General gave a dinner to Captain Rodgers and the Naval Officers on this station—after which he rode out and made several calls.

At a meeting of the Common Council for the despatch of business in the evening, (Wednesday,) Alderman Zabriskie made the following remarks :—

"Mr. Mayor—At the request of the committee, appointed by the Common Council, for the reception of General Lafayette, I rise with no ordinary emotions, to propose for the adoption of the Common Council, the two resolutions, now before me; resolutions which I feel justified in asserting, will pass with the unanimous approbation of this Board. The first, sir, is a resolution, that a committee be appointed to wait upon General Lafayette, and request that he will be pleased to sit for his Portrait, to be placed either in this room, or in the Gallery of Portraits in the City Hall. This room in which we meet, to transact the municipal concerns of this city, is graced with the full length portraits of a Washington, a Clinton, a Jay, and a Hamilton—individuals who have established a name which will be transmitted to future generations, and which will remain as imperishable as the principles upon which are founded the government, under which we have the happiness to live, and in the formation of which, they took a distinguished part. The Portrait Room in your Hall is embellished with the portraits of many of our most distinguished citizens, civil, military, and naval, and who have contributed in no small degree, to establish a national character throughout the world—and permit me, sir, to add, that there is no individual now living, whose portrait will be received with greater admiration and interest, than that of our illustrious visitor, General de Lafayette. His name is identified with liberty and the rights of man in this, and the trans-atlantic world. With these few unpremeditated remarks, I now beg leave to submit the Resolutions.

Whereas the Common Council are desirous of perpetuating the memory of a man, who will be distinguished in the annals of our country, for his love of freedom and military glory--whose name will be associated by posterity with that of Washington, the illustrious founder of our Republic—and as the portrait of one so venerated, will be always favourable to virtue and patriotism:

Resolved, Therefore, that the honourable, the Major General the Marquis de Lafayette, be requested to favour this Common Council, with sitting for his portrait, to be placed in the Gallery of Portraits of the Common Council, among those great and good men, who have done honour and service to our country.

Resolved, That the committee of arrangements be requested to wait upon the Marquis, with a copy of this resolution, and on his acceding to the request, that they carry the same into effect.

Resolved, In testimony of the high respect which this Common Council entertain for George Washington Lafayette, the son of the Marquis de Lafayette, whose virtues we trust he bears with the honoured name of his father, be made a Freeman of this city, and that the certificate of freedom, handsomely engrossed, be presented to him in a Golden Box.

Resolved, That the committee of arrangements have the above resolution carried into effect.

Alderman Doughty rose and offered the following resolution:—

"Resolved, That the proceedings of this Board, in relation to General de Lafayette, together with the address of the Mayor to him, and his answer thereto, with his signature in his own proper hand writing, and the signatures of the Mayor, Recorder, and the members of the Common Council, be handsomely engraved on vellum; one copy thereof to be presented to the General, and one copy to be placed among the Archives of the Common Council.

The committee of arrangements were appointed to carry this resolution into effect.

The above resolutions were unanimously adopted by the Board.

The Mayor read a letter from Captain Francis Allyn, of the ship Cadmus, presenting a portrait of General Lafayette to the Corporation, with a request that it might be placed in the City Hall. The Board accepted the same, and passed a vote of thanks to Captain Allyn, the donor.

To an address of the Gentlemen of the Bar of New-York, assembled at the City Hall on Thursday morning, to pay the Marquis their respects, he made the following reply :—

"Testimonies of esteem from so respectable a body as the Bar of New-York, are highly flattering. I most deeply sympathize with you, gentlemen, in your regret for our friend Hamilton, whose prodigious talents made him as eminent in your profession, as he had been in our military, when he deserved Washington's most intimate confidence. The truly republican forms of the American institutions, cannot but endear them to every citizen of the United States. Yet, to any one, who, with an American heart, has had opportunities of a comparison with those of other countries, the blessings of those institutions must appear still more conspicuous."

The same attention was also paid the Marquis by the French gentlemen of the city, both residents and citizens. The number of his countrymen present on this occasion, including the respectable and wealthy individuals of that nation, amounted to more than two hundred and fifty: and an address was delivered in their behalf by Mr. Chegary, in the French language. Among the party collected, we understand he recognised an old fellow soldier, who had fought under him in this country during the revolutionary war, and had served in the French army twenty-five years.

To the affectionate address of the French gentleman the Marquis Lafayette replied as follows :—

"It is a great happiness for me, on my arrival in this land of liberty, to receive the address of my countrymen.

"At the moment of my departure, the testimonials of affectionate attachment of many of my fellow citizens, the parting accents from the shores of France, left in my heart the most grateful emotions. I delight to participate with you, the feelings which I experienced in this happy American land, to which I am bound by so many ties. We also, patriots of 1789, sought to establish the national dignity, the security of property, and the happiness of our beautiful France, upon the sacred foundations of liberty and equality. Notwithstanding our misfortunes, the cotemporaries of that epoch will inform you, that the revolution of '89, has greatly ameliorated the condition of an immense majority of the people. Do not let us despair of the cause of liberty: it is still dear to the hearts of Frenchmen, and we shall one day have the felicity of seeing it established in our beloved country."

At 12 o'clock, the Nautical Society, chiefly composed of our most respectable masters of vessels, assembled on board the ship Cadmus, Captain Allyn, and proceeded to the City Hall. Here they were severally introduced to the General, who received them in his usual frank and cordial manner.

The packet ship Cadmus, was dressed with the flags of all nations: and in compliance with a public invitation, thousands of our citizens repaired on board in the course of the day, and partook of a cold collation, liberally prepared by Captain Allyn and her owners.

After the Marquis' arrival at New-York, he early announced his intention to visit Boston, where he had been particularly invited by distinguished individuals, and by the city authority; especially as the commencement at the University in Cambridge, the literary jubilee of the State, was to be celebrated in a few days. While in New-York, he received invitations from Philadelphia, Albany, New-Haven, Hartford, and some other cities, to make a visit to those places; but his desire was first to visit Boston, if possible.

The interesting visit at New-York being closed—at an early hour on Friday morning, a scene of general bustle and activity commenced, preparatory to the departure of the General for Boston. The city corporation had provided an elegant carriage to accommodate him on his journey to Boston, and deputed four of their number to attend him on his route. At 7 o'clock, the Horse Artillery, commanded by Colonel Arcularius, paraded in Broadway, in front of Washington Hall; and at 8 o'clock, they took up their line of march to Harlem, where they superseded the escort which accompanied him to that place. This escort consisted of a squadron of cavalry, the Corporation in carriages, the Fayette Guards, the General, Field, and Staff officers of the Artillery and Infantry of the city, and a number of citizens mounted.

The General was met at Harlem, on Friday morning, by a deputation from the town of New-Rochelle, who presented him with the following address:—

"The inhabitants of the town of New-Rochelle, have deputed Gideon Coggeshall and Laird M. H. Butler, to wait on Major General Lafayette, to express to him their happiness, on his safe arrival, in the bosom of that country, for whose liberty he so nobly fought and bled, and to request him to allow them the pleasure of expressing personally to him their feelings of gratitude for his important services, in that arduous struggle, from which emanated that glorious independence, now their proudest boast."

He stopped at New-Rochelle, and took refreshment. "Do you remember, General," said one, "who began the attack at Brandywine?" "Aha! Yes—it was Maxwell, with the Jersey troops!" "So it was! so it was!" replied the delighted interrogator. "Well, I was with his brigade!" A warm grasp of the hand was all the utterance to feelings, which were meet reward for a life spent in the cause of liberty. The utmost joy, and the most affectionate welcome was expressed in all the towns and villages through which he passed to the line between New-York and Connecticut.

At Byram Bridge he was received by a troop of Connecticut Horse Artillery. The first troop of New-York Horse, and the Connecticut squadron, escorted him to Putnam's Hill, where a salute was fired; after which Colonel Arcularius' troop gave the General nine cheers, as their duties here closed. The General returned them his warmest thanks.

The following extract of a letter from a young Lady at Greenwich, bearing date Friday evening, August 20th, will further illustrate the reception of the Marquis on his route:—

"The news that the Marquis de Lafayette was to pass through this town to-day, was received yesterday afternoon. Nothing however was done, and I began to fear that old Connecticut would disgrace itself; but this morning, the spirit of '76 appeared to animate all ranks and descriptions. Orders were given for the troops to proceed to Byram, and escort the General to Norwalk, where, it was understood, the New-Haven troop would be in waiting. Fortunately, it entered into the heads of a few, that an arch, erected over Putnam's Hill, would have a fine effect. A number of ladies volunteered their services in erecting and adorning it; and the Reverend Doctor Lewis, who was himself a chaplain in the revolutionary army, was requested to write a short inscription. The inscription which was hung in the centre, surrounded by a wreath of sweetbriar and roses, was as follows :—" This arch, on the hill rendered memorable by the brave General Putnam, is erected in honour of the illustrious, the Marquis de Lafayette—the early and distinguished champion of American liberty, and the tried friend of Washington." The arch was very tastefully enwreathed, and from its top waved the flag which the regiment of this place carried in the battle of Whiteplains.

" After waiting till nearly 5 o'clock, our ears were gladdened with the sound of their approach. The cannon which had been previously sent on, fired, the church bell rang a merry peal, and hundreds of spectators, of both sexes, stationed on and about the hill, welcomed the General with loud huzzas, and waving of hats and handkerchiefs. When the Marquis arrived at Tracy's Hotel, (within 40 rods of the arch,) he dismounted, and was there introduced to the venerable Doctor Lewis, who took him by the hand, and (as near as I can recollect,) addressed him as follows :—

" ' Sir,—With the millions of America, I welcome you to this land of freedom, and rejoice that God has spared my life to see that veteran General, who so eminently distinguished himself in procuring her liberties.'

" The Marquis then advanced to the arch, supported by the Reverend Doctor Lewis, and his son, the present minister of the parish. The inscription was read to him by the latter. He appeared much pleased and affected, advanced a few steps, bowed to the gentlemen who were stationed on one side of the hill, turned to the ladies on the other side, and said,—'My friends, I am very much obliged to you for the attention you have paid to me, and feel happy to find myself among you.'

" He then walked down the hill, took his carriage, and proceeded on his journey, expecting to lodge at Norwalk, or Bridgeport at night. On parting with him, Doctor Lewis said, ' Sir, America loves you'—' And, Sir,' said the Marquis, '*I truly love America.*' "

The cavalcade arrived at Stamford about half past five, and the private Mansion of the honourable John Davenport was thrown open for his reception. The General remained at this house for half an hour, and received the visits of many hundred persons of both sexes. A salute was fired, the bells rung, and this beautiful town with its gay inhabitants, particularly distinguished for many handsome women, exhibited all the life and gayety of a city. Hundreds of ladies and gentlemen, for ten miles round, visited this town, to see and pay their respects to Lafayette. He left Stamford at six, intending if possible to reach New-Haven that night.

The Connecticut troop which met the General at the line, accompanied him through Stamford, and proceeded until they met the escort provided further east.

All business was suspended during the day on the whole route;—all persons were arrayed in their best attire, and many remained for hours upon the road, waiting for the cavalcade.

Many old revolutionary soldiers met him on the route, and held hasty discourse on scenes and subjects which they never can forget.

He arrived at Norwalk, at 8 o'clock P. M. where his arrival was announced by a salute from the heights, and discharges of musketry. Two companies of uniform militia were in waiting to salute him. An arch was formed across the bridge, with the following inscription:—"Welcome Lafayette," in large letters, on a white ground. On one side of the arch, the American flag was displayed, and on the other a French flag. As the General had been expected from about 11, A. M. Norwalk was filled with people from the surrounding country, at an early hour in the day, who remained anxiously waiting until the time of his arrival. All business in the town was suspended. Among those assembled, were several revolutionary heroes, with bosoms beating high, at the thought of shaking by the hand their old and beloved comrade, whose memory was associated with periods of trial and endurance, which few who experienced them, now remain to relate. Gaptain Gibbs, an old revolutionary officer, about the same age with the Marquis, and who was with him in the revolution, joyfully seized his old friend by the hand, and introduced him into the village hotel. The General easily recognised him, although so great a length of time has elapsed since they have seen each other. Mr. Betts, who was also in the revolutionary service, had the honour of an introduction. The ladies and gentlemen of Norwalk, immediately repaired to Cook's Hotel, to bid the Marquis welcome. The Marquis departed about 9 o'clock at night, leaving the open barouche, and taking the close carriage.

At Saugatuck the militia were prepared throughout the day, to fire a salute; but owing to the lateness of the hour when the cavalcade approached, it being 10 at night, the villagers could do no more than give their loud huzzas, as the General passed.

Mill River Bridge was handsomely decorated with colours, by the captains of the coasting vessels at anchor in the harbour.

The General arrived at Fairfield about half past ten at night. In this beautiful town, great preparations were made to receive him; but as he had not made his appearance at a late hour, it was supposed he would not arrive until the following day. It was calculated that between 1000 and 1200 persons were collected here, including the inhabitants. They all remained until late in the evening, still hoping that he might be on his way; but they were at length reluctantly compelled to give up the hope, and all retired, except a few of the most distinguished inhabitants of the town, who remained at the Washington Hotel, until the General arrived. But before we mention the manner in which he was received, we must, in justice to Fairfield, state that the villagers had arranged themselves in beautiful order in the day, and so continued until night. The ladies formed themselves on one side of the green, and the gentlemen on the other. The female children of the various schools were placed in a row immediately in front of the ladies, with their instructers at their head—the male children being similarly arranged in front of the gentlemen.

An elegant table was spread at Mr. Knapp's Hotel—the young ladies of Fairfield having done themselves the highest honour by the taste, as well as patriotism they exhibited on the occasion. The decorations of the table were planned on a style of the greatest elegance; the dishes were quite enveloped with evergreens and scattering flowers; and the due proportions were observed in the succession of viands, as well as in the harmony and contrast of colours, which maintained a kind of silent correspondence, from the opposite sides of a splendid cone, that occupied the centre. On taking their seats at the table, the guests might have supposed themselves invited to a feast of wreaths and flowers, studded with the "crimson hail" of winter-greens, cran-berries, and amare-dulcis. The table was like the bed of some fairy's enchanted garden, so entirely did the decorations overshadow and conceal the rich collation beneath. When this verdant veil was removed, the scene was changed as suddenly as at the dissolving of a spell, and the company could not repress their surprise. The General expressed his gratification at this specimen of female taste, and regretted that it should be so quickly destroyed, to gratify that of the gentlemen.

At the table, in conversation, he said he remembered well the disasters of 1779—he remarked that he had passed through this village in 1778, the year previous to its being burnt. He also declared the high gratification he felt with the parade on Putnam's Hill, and that it gave him great happiness to recollect that the Flag displayed above the arch across the road, cut through the rock, was taken from the enemy at White Plains, in the revolutionary struggle.

The General remained nearly an hour, and then proceeded to Bridgeport to lodge, accompanied by many of the inhabitants.

He arrived between 11 and 12 at night. Here also preparations had been made to receive him, equal to those in any other place. The military and citizens remained throughout the day and evening, expecting him. The original plan was, that the General should dine at Washington Hotel. Late as it was when he arrived, several of the inhabitants heard of it, and repaired to the Hotel to welcome him; but all honours were necessarily dispensed with until morning. At an early hour a salute was fired, the bells were rung, and bands of music added life to the general scene of festivity. The General received the attentions of the citizens on the porch, where he had taken his station, shaking hands with them all, and joyfully recognising among them, some of his old companions in arms. He recollected Captain Brewster, formerly of the Revenue cutter, of New-York; also, Salmon Hubbell; and a number who were privates in the revolutionary army knew their old General, and had the honour of shaking him by the hand. Nearly all business was suspended in the town on Friday, and the troops remained under arms from 11 in the morning until late at night.

The Marquis left Bridgeport about 7 on Saturday morning, escorted by the citizens on horseback, and departed amidst the discharge of artillery, the ringing of bells, and the cheers of the people.

He arrived at Stratford between 8 and 9, where he remained about half an hour—a salute was fired, the flags were hoisted, and the citizens formed along the Main-street, cheered him as he passed. He stopped at Mr. Marshall's Hotel a short time, and then departed with the blessings of the inhabitants.

In the following note to the Mayor of New-Haven, the Marquis had announced his intention to visit that city :—

Sir,—With profound gratitude I have received the flattering invitation contained in your letter of the 17th, which your honourable committee were pleased to deliver to me. It could not but add to my former intention to visit your respected metropolis. I much regret that a previous engagement at Boston, does not permit my stay at New-Haven to be this time as long as I could wish. But I anticipate the honour and pleasure to express to you the morning after to-morrow, my high and grateful respects.—I have the honour to be, Sir, your most obedient servant, LA FAYETTE.

Notwithstanding the above annunciation, the citizens of New-Haven expected he would enter the city on the night of the 20th, and their preparations to welcome him were made on the most extensive scale—but owing to the assemblages of citizens which occupied the roads, all eager to welcome and salute him, he could only reach Bridgeport at midnight. His near approach to New-Haven was nevertheless announced by a spontaneous illumination of the city, and at "the noon of night" its entire population was in the streets.

The Governor's Horse Guards had been sent out to meet General Lafayette at the town of Orange, where they remained through the night, and on the arrival of the General in the morning, relieved the escort from Bridgeport; and, accompanied by that from Milford, and a great number of citizens who had joined them on horseback and in carriages, set out for New-Haven. They entered the city on Saturday morning, under a handsome military escort, which conducted the General and suite to Morse's Hotel, where the General, with his suite, was received by the Mayor and other public authorities, Governor Wolcott, and other distinguished gentlemen, amidst loud and unceasing acclamations. Here he was met by the veterans of the revolution, the friends and associates of other days, several of whom he recognised and embraced as his companions in arms, and all were received with a brotherly and fond regard. After receiving the respects and congratulations of the citizens, together with a large number of ladies, and many gentlemen from various parts of the country, some of whom came a distance of forty miles to see him, he was saluted by the various military corps drawn up in front of the hotel, who passed him in review, attended by a division of the students of Yale College, in procession; after which he took breakfast with the Mayor, Aldermen, &c. with about one hundred invited guests, which was handsomely served up by Mr. Morse, at the expense of the city.

From the Hotel the General was conducted to the Green in the centre of the town, where several companies of fine troops were paraded; and it is difficult for a stranger to conceive any thing equal to the scene here presented to the spectator; that fine, level, and verdant piece of ground, surrounded by rows of shady elms, and just beyond, by the neat and often elegant mansions of the citizens, overtopped by three new and beautiful churches, and crowned with such cheerful and enthusiastic throngs; enlivened also by the bells, and military instruments, and the gayety of female dresses and faces, from a region proverbial for excelling in beauty; at a distance also bounded by the venerable walls of Yale College, for a kind of classic horizon; all this when actually before the eyes had not a little the effect of pure magic. The Address to him was presented by the Honourable Mr. Edwards.—To the following paragraph of it, were appended notes—that "In 1778 the General was encamped in that town, with a body of troops; and that in 1785, he was presented with the freedom of the city."—"A generation has passed away since our fathers saw you encamped on yonder fields; they beheld your merits, and hastened to enrol your name as a fellow citizen." Governor Wolcott made him welcome to the State in a short and affectionate address. The reply was equally affectionate.—The introductions to him were very numerous, and his recognition of many of his old companions in arms, was wonderful. The venerable Colonel Tallmadge, of the old army, had rode all night to meet him; and, without introduction, was recognised and embraced by him; so also was Major Munson. Other revolutionary officers were introduced, and numerous events of times "which tried souls," were recalled. The scene was truly affecting, not a dry eye could be seen. The beautiful and accomplished Madame G. whom he had known in the Parisian circles, was recognised; the presentation of Mr. Wadsworth, of Hartford, recalled to the General's feelings the merits of his worthy father, who was Commissary General of the French army, when in America; and the son of old Roger Sherman, recalled to mind the patriotic services of that venerable and truly honourable statesman and signer of the Declaration of Independence. An old soldier, on being introduced, exclaimed:—"*I saw you, General, descend from your horse, and at the head of your division, ford the Schuylkill, then four feet deep, on two cold nights of November, in succession.*" Then turning to the spectators, with brimful eyes, he added, "*Yes, he never shunned any fatigue or danger, and always led the way.*" Those who have seen Lafayette when meeting the old soldiers, can only estimate the impressions of the scene. In one of his movements he was accompanied by between 200 and 300 students of Yale.—Among them was Stephanus Gallaty, the Greek youth from Scio, aged 14.

The military parade was brilliant;—the roar of artillery loud, and the acclamations and shouts of the people incessant. More than three hundred ladies, with their children, were introduced. His pleasure in seeing this array of grace and beauty was visible. At the house of the Honourable Mr. Daggett, he was introduced to the widow of Colonel Barber, slain in the revolution; and to Miss Ogden, grand-daughter of General Wooster, killed at Danbury. He then visited the seat of Mr. Deforest, and partook of the hospitality of his amiable lady. He then was conducted to the University, and appeared struck with the immense improvements which every where presented themselves. Here he received the congratulations of the President and Faculty of the College, and visited the Library and Mineralogical Cabinet. He afterwards visited the widow of the late Governor Trumbull, who was in the family of Washington most of the revolutionary war. As he passed the *unique* burying-ground of this city, he was pointed to the grave of Humpreys, whom he had long known and respected. He also passed and noticed the graves of Whalley, Dixwell, and Goffe, the English Commonwealthmen, who sought and found an asylum in America. Returning by the Green, he passed the troops, who fired a *feu de joie*, and returned to the Hotel.

About 3 o'clock the General took his departure, on the lower road, by East-Haven, Guilford, Saybrook, and Lyme, to New-London, on his way to Boston, escorted by the troops and civil authorities as far as East-Haven, there he pointed out the residence of the late Reverend Mr. Street, where he had been hospitably entertained forty-five years ago, and expressing a desire to see his descendants, was received by his children and grand-children, and other ladies and gentlemen of the town. Here he took leave of the escort from the city, and proceeded on his journey, attended by a detachment of cavalry from Branford.

At Branford his reception was very gratifying; two companies of foot awaited him; and a vast concourse of people assembled from all quarters to receive him, joined in acclamations at his approach.

At Old Guilford, a town no less interesting for its primitive republican New England manners, than for the early date of its settlement, he was received with a cordial welcome. Three companies of militia were paraded on the Green, and saluted him with artillery and small arms. Crowds pressed around the General; and there were some of the older ones, who found they had not quite forgotten to feel again as they felt in the Revolution. In short, "Guilford souls" will not speedily forget the day that brought the companion of Washington among them, to offer them his hand, and to remind them of the cause in which it once wielded the sword.

In these towns he stopped but a short time, but long enough o receive and return the gratulations of many of the inhabitants.

At Killingsworth he remained an hour, received similar attentions from the military and the citizens; and then passed on to Saybrook, where he lodged.

Here the inhabitants, partaking of the same feeling which prevailed throughout this part of the country, had made preparations for receiving the General in the handsomest manner; and as he was expected several hours earlier than he arrived, the table was spread and decorated, and a feast provided suitable to the occasion.

In the morning he was waited on by the inhabitants, and shown every mark of respect, till half past 6 o'clock, when he crossed Connecticut river, and pursued his way towards New-London. He travelled with such great expedition, that he went from New-Haven to Saybrook in six hours, a distance of thirty-six miles, including all his stops upon the road.

It would have been impossible to have travelled through the towns of Connecticut without feeling a part of the enthusiasm which pervaded all classes. Even the poor lads who drove the carriages entered fully into the common feeling, and seemed proud of their honours. They wore silk ribands fastened to the button holes of their waistcoats, by way of distinction; and while waiting to receive their illustrious passenger, usually became persons of no inconsiderable interest and attention with the hundreds who stood around. "Behave pretty now, Charley," said the driver of Lafayette's coach, to one of his horses, "behave pretty, Charley—you are going to carry the greatest man in the world."

On Sunday morning, the General left Saybrook, and proceeded on his way to New-London, and being met by the Committee and a few citizens, in Waterford, he was escorted to the mansion of Judge Perkins, where, with the spontaneous acclamations of a great body of citizens, and with heartfelt gratulations, he was received under a national salute of 24 guns from Fort Trumbull. The General, with great dignity and composure, gracefully saluted the citizens; when he was met and conducted in a respectful and affectionate manner by his old friend and companion in arms, General William North, to the Hall assigned him. He was there introduced to a committee from Norwich, and another from Stonington, who had repaired to New-London, to solicit him to visit those places on his tour.

The citizens who wished it, were then introduced to the General, and from the cordial and polite manner in which they were received, were satisfied that the man whom they delighted to honour, was richly deserving of the respect shown him. Public service having now commenced, out of reverence for the day, and the feelings of the people with whom he dwelt, the General repaired to the Presbyterian meeting-house, where the Reverend Mr. M'Ewen officiated, and thence to St. James' Church, where service was performed by the Reverend Mr. Judd. Afterwards he called to pay his respects to Madam Huntington, the widow of the late General Jedediah Huntington, and Madam Perry, the mother of the late Commodore; when he returned to his quarters, and for about an hour devoted his time to receive the salutations of ladies and gentlemen, who called on him. At three, dinner was announced, and he was seated in a small circle of friends, among whom were General William North, General Ebenezer Huntington, General Burbeck, and Doctor John R. Watrous, who were his companions when his noble and generous mind first put forth its energies in the cause of our country. After a short sitting, in sweet and patriotic sympathy and friendly intercourse, he arose and departed with his suite, escorted by the committees of New-London and Norwich, for that city.

On General Lafayette's arrival in the city of Norwich, a national salute was fired. On his alighting at the Hotel, a pertinent address from the Mayor was delivered, to which he returned an appropriate and feeling reply.

After this ceremony many eagerly pressed forward to be presented, congratulating themselves on the pleasure they had in seeing their Country's Liberator, in this free and happy nation.

In the evening, the General and suite, together with the city officers, and the Committee of Arrangements, sat down to supper. During the repast, reiterated cheers were frequently ascending from the people in the street; to each of these bursts of enthusiasm the General arose and presented himself at the window, where the admiring multitude as often echoed it. After supper the General and suite left this for Plainfield, accompanied by the Deputation and an escort of citizens. The deputation continued with him to Rhode-Island line, where he was met by the Committee from Providence.

As the procession left the city of Norwich, a National Salute was fired amid continued peals of the bells.—On his arrival at Jewett City the whole village was illuminated, as were all the houses between there and Plainfield, and also in the latter village, although they had, like the citizens of Norwich, but a short notice of the General's approach.

A delegation from the Town Council and those associates of the Cincinnati composing the General Committee of the town of Providence, was despatched towards Hartford on Friday, with a view of meeting the General, and tendering him the earnest wishes of the inhabitants, that he would honour them with a visit. On Sunday morning, it was feared by the General Committee, that from a change in the General's expected route, their delegation might not be able to see him until he should have arrived in the State, and two gentlemen were despatched on the other two different roads to Connecticut, with similar instructions to those of the first Committee, the return of which gave information that the General, in company with the first Committee, was at Eaton's, in Plainfield, and would proceed into town in the course of the forenoon of Monday. Early on that morning, the troops and citizens were in readiness to meet him, and the western road was lined with citizens, crowding towards the point where the reception was to take place.

The Town Council and their associates received the General about 2 o'clock, at the line of the town, where he alighted. He was then received with military honours, and conducted to the barouche prepared for his reception, and being seated, was greeted with a spontaneous burst of feeling, from the immense concourse of spectators. The procession was then put in motion, agreeably to the order of arrangements; and when formed, extended more than a mile. The General, uncovered, rode alone in the barouche, drawn by four white horses, bestowing through the whole march, the most complaisant smiles and greetings on all around; shaking, most cordially, the hands of those who crowded around the carriage and took advantage of every pause in the procession, to obtain the honour of a grasp of the hand of Lafayette—a circumstance which every citizen will be proud hereafter to tell his children. As the General proceeded up the hill leading from Olneysville, he was again greeted with the shouts of a large collection of citizens, assembled on the high bank directly over the road.

The Marine Artillery, stationed on the Dexter Training Ground, pealed their welcome as he passed, and the General soon entered the populous part of the town. In passing through High and Westminster-streets, and until he arrived at the court-house, he was welcomed by that most expressive token of affectionate interest, the waving of white handkerchiefs by the fair hands of the ladies, who crowded every building from which they could obtain a view of this distinguished personage. Many females, we observed, in the excess of their feelings, suspended this token of welcome, to gaze more intently at the object whom they appeared alone to see in the whole procession, and many a fine eye was wet with the gush of a tear, which the rush of so many sublime and sympathetic emotions sent warm from the heart.

On arriving in front of the State-House, the General alighted, and was received in a peculiarly interesting manner. The poplar avenue, leading to the building, was lined on each side with nearly two hundred misses, arrayed in white, and holding in their hands bunches of flowers, which (as the General proceeded up the avenue, supported by the Governor's Aids) they strewed in his path, at the same time waving their white handkerchiefs. The General was afterwards pleased to express the peculiar and high satisfaction he took in this simple and touching arrangement.

On reaching the landing of the stairs, the General turned towards the multitude, and at the same moment, the veteran Captain Stephen Olney, who served under the General repeatedly, and was the first to force the enemy's works at Yorktown, in which he was seconded, at another point, almost simultaneously, by Lafayette, approached the General, who instantly recognised his old companion in arms, and embraced him in the most earnest and affectionate manner. A thrill went through the whole assembly, and scarcely a dry eye was to be found among the spectators, while the shouts of the multitude, at first suppressed, and then uttered in a manner tempered by the scene, evinced the deep feeling and proud associations it had excited.

The General was then conducted to the Senate Chamber, where he was appropriately introduced to his Excellency, the members of the Committee, Town Council, &c.

After this ceremony, he came below, and there, in the most familiar manner, shook hands with a number of ladies and gentlemen.—Among the rest, the venerable William Russell, now in his 85th year, was introduced to him. The General shook both the veteran's hands in a most affectionate manner, and in an annunciation, that slightly marked a foreign accent, said he was extremely happy to take his old friend by the hand once more, as it recalled to his memory the delightful associations of his youth. Mr. Russell appeared at first scarcely to comprehend the scene, but in a moment, as if the whole had rushed upon his recollection, he exclaimed in a voice broken by age and still more subdued by feeling, 'Oh, my dear Marquis, how happy am I to see you once more! I remember well the time I served under you as a volunteer on Rhode-Island!' The General was evidently touched, and on this, as on several other occasions, the tear started to his eye.

The Town Council and Committee, with their illustrious guest and his suite, his Excellency the Governor of the State of Rhode-Island and his suite, the Honourable Jonathan Russell, the Committee of Aldermen of the city of New-York, and the Committee attending from the city of Boston, and from the government of Massachusetts, with a few other guests, repaired to the dining-hall, where an elegant entertainment was provided.

At about half past four, the troops (at the particular request of General Lafayette, who expressed his admiration of their discipline and fine military appearance,) were drawn up for review, in a line extending on Benefit-street, toward Pawtucket. The General then proceeded on foot, and was greeted, on entering the street, with the same joyous acclamations. Supported by the arm of the Governor, he walked in front of the line of troops, stopping to shake hands with all the principal officers.

On arriving at the extreme wing he halted, and his carriage was drawn up for his reception; which he entered, accompanied by his Excellency, Colonel Bowen and Zachariah Allen, Esq and amid the cheers of the people, left the town. He was escorted into Massachusetts by the Town Council, Cincinnati, &c. and a numerous company of citizens on horseback and in carriages.

The General, on being asked if he was not fatigued with his exertions, promptly replied, that he experienced too much *pleasure*, to find any time for fatigue.

At Pawtucket, he was met by the aids of Governor Eustis, who had been despatched the day before to receive him at the line of the Commonwealth, and to escort him on his way to the capital. Although it was now evening, at several places on the road large bodies of militia were collected to salute him; and assemblies of ladies and gentlemen were occasionally met, who offered this illustrious stranger, but respected friend of their country, their tribute of applause and affection. He was too sensible of the sincerity and warmth of their felicitations, not to delay his journey at several villages, and to reciprocate their kind and cordial salutations. It was nearly midnight when he reached the town of Dedham, about ten miles from Boston. Most of the houses in this pleasant village were handsomely illuminated; and a great number of the inhabitants of both sexes were assembled to greet him. During the short stay he was able to make here, he was introduced to many of the principal citizens of the town and vicinity, who had been anticipating his arrival for some hours. When he passed through Roxbury, at 1 o'clock, he was accompanied by a large cavalcade of citizens of that place and from Boston; and a salute was fired by the Roxbury corps of artillery. His arrival here was also announced by the ascent of rockets from an eminence in the centre of the town; and the note of preparation was thus given for the parade and pleasure of the succeeding day, which had been anticipated with uncommon interest and delight. Lafayette and suite proceeded to the mansion of his Excellency the Governor, to which they had been invited; and the meeting between them was truly affectionate and cordial.

On Tuesday the 24th, the inhabitants of Boston hailed the morning light with peculiar emotions, and were abroad at an early hour, preparing for the general testimonies of gratitude and respect to be presented to the "nation's guest." Many of the older citizens recollected him in his youthful days, when he visited the town, *forty-six* years ago, at the request of Congress and Washington, to prevail on the French admiral to co-operate with his fleet in a contemplated attack upon the British forces at Rhode-Island. They had not forgotten his zeal and ardour in the cause of America. They knew his great attachment to and respect for the *immortal* chief of the American army, and the confidence which Washington cherished for Lafayette. Here too were many revolutionary officers and soldiers, who had often witnessed his unwearied activity and personal courage in seasons of difficulty and danger. The Society of Cincinnati in this State contained many of his personal friends, who shared with him in the toils and honours of the war of Independence; they had assembled, also, to offer the hand of friendship and affection to their distinguished brother in arms; and to tell him of the happiness which he had been instrumental, with others, in securing to *ten millions* of freemen. The curiosity of the young was awakened to hear of the generous deeds and meritorious services of this celebrated visitor from the old world. They were eager to learn his worth and his virtues. For they knew their grave and sober sires would not be so greatly moved by the approach of any ordinary character, whatever might be his title or his fame. The sensibility of the female breast was excited to a lively glow, in reflecting upon the character of this eminent foreigner, who had not only given proofs of great devotion to the cause of America, and to the interests of civil liberty, but whose moral and social virtues claimed for him the respect and admiration of all those who loved innocence or commiserated distress. And all classes, without intending to lessen the pre-eminent services and virtues of Washington, who under providence, was the great and chief agent in achieving our Independence, and in preserving it, after it had been once established—or to undervalue the important efforts and courage of many other revered heroes and patriots, too numerous to be here named. All, all, were eager to join in the spontaneous offering of gratitude and affection, to one so justly celebrated and so *greatly beloved*.

He entered the city, the capital of the state, about 11 o'clock; and his reception was a triumph and a jubilee. The day was as bright as his laurels, and as mild as his virtues.—The various bodies designated to compose the procession, and perform the honours of the day, assembled at an early hour. The cavalcade was formed in Common-street, at 9 o'clock. It was very numerous, and consisted of the citizens of Boston, of all ranks and classes, on horseback. Proceeding to the extreme southern part of the city, near the line of Roxbury, they were joined by the Mayor and Aldermen, and members of the Common Council, the Society of Cincinnati, a great number of public civil characters, and strangers of distinction, all in carriages; by the General and Field Officers of the first division of militia, and officers of the army and navy of the United States. An innumerable concourse of people on foot lined the side-walks of the spacious street, where the procession was to be formed, the entrance to the city from Roxbury, and fortunately named WASHINGTON-STREET. The cavalcade then proceeded to the mansion of Governor Eustis, which is a short distance within the town of Roxbury, and escorted General Lafayette and suite to the line, where the city authorities and others, who were to compose the procession, were in waiting to receive him. Here he was greeted by the immense assemblage of citizens, with repeated and enthusiastic acclamations, for several minutes, when the Mayor welcomed him with much feeling, in the following speech:—

"Sir—The citizens of Boston welcome you on your return to the United States; mindful of your early zeal in the cause of American Independence, grateful for your distinguished share in the perils and glories of its achievements.—When urged by a generous sympathy, you first landed on these shores, you found a people engaged in an arduous and eventful struggle for liberty, with apparently inadequate means, and amidst dubious omens. After a lapse of nearly half a century, you find the same people prosperous beyond all hope and all precedent; their liberty secure; sitting in its strength; without fear and without reproach.

"In your youth you joined the standard of three millions of people, raised in an unequal and uncertain conflict. In your advanced age you return and are met by ten millions of people, their descendants, whose hearts throng hither to greet your approach and rejoice in it.

"This is not the movement of a turbulent populace, excited by the fresh laurels of some recent conqueror; it is a grave, moral, intellectual impulse.

"A whole people in the enjoyment of freedom, as perfect as the condition of our nature permits, recur with gratitude, increasing with the daily increasing sense of their blessings, to the memory of those, who, by their labours and in their blood, laid the foundation of our liberties.

"Your name, Sir,—the name of LAFAYETTE, is associated with the most perilous, and most glorious periods of our Revolution;—with the imperishable names of Washington, and of that numerous host of heroes which adorn the proudest archives of American history, and are engraven in indelible traces on the hearts of the whole American people.

"Accept then, Sir, in the sincere spirit in which it is offered, this simple tribute to your virtues.

"Again, Sir, the citizens of Boston bid you welcome to the cradle of American Independence, and to scenes consecrated with the blood, shed by the earliest martyrs in its cause."

General Lafayette then rose in his carriage, and in a most interesting manner, replied as follows:—

"The emotions of love and gratitude, which I have been accustomed to feel on my entering this city, have ever mingled with a sense of religious reverence for the cradle of *American*, and let me hope it will hereafter be said of *Universal* liberty.

"What must be, Sir, my feelings, at the blessed moment, when, after so long an absence, I find myself again surrounded by the good citizens of Boston—where I am so affectionately, so honourably welcomed, not only by old friends, but by several successive generations; where I can witness the prosperity, the immense improvements, that have been the just reward of a noble struggle, virtuous morals, and truly republican institutions.

"I beg you, Mr. Mayor, Gentlemen of the City Council, and all of you, beloved citizens of Boston, to accept the respectful and warm thanks of a heart, which has for nearly half a century, been particularly devoted to your illustrious city."

The reply of the General was received with new plaudits of the assembled people; and "welcome, welcome Lafayette! friend of Washington! friend of America! friend of Liberty!" was repeated again and again; and the heights of Dorchester and Roxbury echoed with the joyful acclamation.

The procession was then formed, and passed through Washington, Milk, Broad, State, Court, and Common-streets, to Boylston-street, adjoining the south part of the Common, in the following order:—"Three marshals, the Boston corps of Light Dragoons, a battalion of Light Infantry, composed of the Fusiliers, Boston Light Infantry, Winslow Blues, Washington Light Infantry, New-England Guards, Rangers, and City Guards; and a full band of music. Then followed the Chief Marshal, attended by aids; members of the City Council, Committee of Arrangements, the President of the Common Council, and senior Alderman, all in carriages. Here was placed another Marshal, immediately preceding the elegant barouche, drawn by four beautiful white horses, in which rode the distinguished guest of the city and of the nation, accompanied by the Mayor, with Marshals also on either side. The son and friend of Lafayette, and gentlemen Aldermen from New-York, next followed in carriages; and these were succeeded by the Society of the Cincinnati, public characters, Judges and Legislators, and distinguished strangers, in carriages also. Immediately after two Marshals; Field and Staff officers of the militia, mounted on horseback, and followed also by two Marshals. The cavalcade of citizens, of all ranks and in great numbers, with Marshals attending, closed the voluntary but triumphant procession.

The dwelling-houses and stores on the streets through which the procession was conducted, were crowded with inhabitants in every part. The ladies thus situated, caught the enthusiasm of the occasion, waved their white handkerchiefs, and, with smiles and gladness, greeted the veteran hero, who appeared affected and delighted by these demonstrations of a joyful welcome.

Excepting the cavalcade, the procession passed through the Common from Boylston to Park-street, on the eastern margin, and between two lines of children, of both sexes, belonging to the several schools in the city. Their ages were from about eight to twelve, and nearly three thousand in number. Their dress was neat and uniform; the misses in white, and the masters in white pantaloons and blue spencers. They also wore ribands on their breasts, stamped with a miniature likeness of Lafayette. As the carriage in which the General rode was passing, one of the misses darted from the line where she was standing, and requested to speak with him. She was handed into the carriage, and by the Mayor presented to Lafayette, who pressed an affectionate kiss on her blooming, yet blushing cheek. She had confidence, however, to address him, and place a wreath of flowers which she held, on his head. He made her a short but affectionate reply, and placed the wreath on the seat of the carriage. Attached to the wreath of flowers was a small piece of paper, carefully folded, which contained these lines: said to be composed by the mother of the child.

> "An infant hand presents these blushing flowers,
> Glowing and pure as childhood's artless hours,
> Where roses bloom, and buds of *promise* smile,
> Repaying with their charms the culturer's toil.
>
> Oh! *take them* FATHER, they were cull'd *for you!*
> (Still bright with warm *affection's* sacred dew—)
> O let them live in thy benignant smile,
> And o'er thy *brow of glory* bloom awhile!
>
> 'Twined with the *laurel* Fame on thee bestow'd,
> When thy *young heart* with patriot ardour glow'd;
> *Self exiled* from the charms of *wealth* and *love*,
> And *home*, and *friends*, thou didst *our champion prove*,
> And, by the side of Glorious WASHINGTON,
> Didst make our grateful country *all thine own!*
>
> Go, fragile offering, speak the ardent joy
> Our bosoms feel, which *Time* can ne'er destroy!"

Arches were thrown across several of the principal streets, through which Lafayette was conducted, covered with evergreens and flowers, and containing appropriate mottos. There were two in Washington-street.—On one of these was very legibly written—"1776—WASHINGTON and LAFAYETTE. *Welcome Lafayette—A Republic not ungrateful.*" On the other

> "WELCOME LAFAYETTE."
> "The Fathers in glory shall sleep,
> Who gather'd with thee to the fight;
> But the sons will eternally keep
> The tablet of gratitude bright.
> We bow not the neck
> And we bend not the knee,
> But our hearts, LAFAYETTE,
> We surrender to thee."

When the procession arrived at the steps of the State House, near the head of Park-street, salutes were fired by a battalion of artillery, on the eminence on the western part of the Common, and at the Navy Yard at Charlestown. Salutes were also fired by a batallion of artillery, placed on the heights of Dorchester, (now South Boston,) when General Lafayette reached the line of the city, at 11 o'clock.

The Governor and Executive Council of the Commonwealth were assembled in the spacious Senate Chamber to receive Lafayette in the name of the Representatives of the people, and in pursuance of their resolve of June preceding, as well as in accordance with their own personal feelings and wishes. His Excellency the Governor, here addressed him with great feeling,* in the following concise and pertinent speech:—

"SIR, OUR FRIEND,—In the name of the government, and in behalf of the citizens of Massachusetts, I have the honour to greet you with a cordial, and affectionate welcome.

"We thank God, that he has been pleased to preserve you through the scenes of peril and of suffering, which have distinguished your patriotic and eventful life, and that we are indulged with this occasion of renewing to you our grateful acknowledgments for the important services which you have rendered to our common country.

"In the last surviving Major General of the American revolutionary army, we recognise a benefactor and friend, from a distant and gallant nation; who, inspired by a love of liberty, subjected himself in his youth to the toils and hazards of a military life, in support of our rights. Under our illustrious Washington, you were instrumental in establishing the liberties of our country, while your gallantry in the field secured to yourself an imperishable renown.

"With the enjoyment of the blessings of independence, we shall never cease to associate the name of Lafayette, and our prayer to heaven will be for his health and prosperity."

To which the General, with much animation, replied:—

"SIR,—When, in the name of the people and government of this State, your Excellency is pleased so kindly to welcome an American veteran, I am proud to share the enjoyments of such a reception with my revolutionary companions and brother soldiers. Sir, I am delighted with what I see, I am oppressed with what I feel; but I depend upon you, as an old friend, to do justice to my sentiments."

Afterwards, a great number of gentlemen were introduced to Lafayette, in the Senate Chamber; of whom were the Judges, and other public officers of the United States, of the State and of the City; members of the society of Cincinnati, with their venerable and distinguished President, Honourable John Brooks, late Governor of the Commonwealth. Lafayette recognised his old military and personal friend at the first sight, and embraced him with great cordiality and affection

* Governor Eustis was so affected, that he had to call on one of his aids to read a greater part of the address.

Some other veterans of the revolutionary army, who were present, he also recollected; and discovered strong emotions as they approached him and took his hand. Indeed, he was so eager to meet them, that he very generally first seized them, and clung to them with all the affection of a brother. The scene was inexpressibly affecting. There was not a heart untouched—not a cheek unmoistened by the falling tear. To weep then was not weakness; it was proof of gratitude and of a generous feeling, which is an honour to human nature.

By particular request, and to gratify the wishes of the people collected in front of the State House, General Lafayette appeared in the colonade of this superb edifice, where he was greeted with loud and continued cheers. He was then conducted by the committee of arrangements to the residence provided for him at the head of Park-street. A public dinner was given by the city authorities, in honour of their noble guest; and the invitation was extended to Senators and Members of Congress, the Governor and Ex-Governor of the Commonwealth, judicial, and other public characters.

A committee of the society of Cincinnati called upon General Lafayette at the residence of the Governor, in Roxbury, and before his entrance into Boston. They were anxious to offer him their congratulations at the earliest moment; and to bid him welcome to the land they had unitedly struggled to defend. And a few days after his arrival, the whole Society waited on him, when their President made the following address:—

"Sir,—The Society of Cincinnati of the State of Massachusetts seize the earliest moment after your arrival in this city, of extending to you the hand of friendship and affection. We offer you our most cordial congratulations on your safe arrival again, after the lapse of forty years, on the shores of our favoured country, once the theatre of our united toils, privations, and combats, with a powerful foe, but now the peaceful domain of a great, a free and independent people. We hail you, sir, in unison with the millions of our fellow citizens; most respectfully hail you as a Statesman, as a Philanthropist, and as the early, inflexible, and devoted friend, not only of our beloved country, but of the sacred principles of civil liberty and human rights. But we greet you under more tender and hallowed associations; in the endearing relation of a brother soldier, who, in the ardour of youth commenced in the field with us your career of glory, in the holy cause of Liberty and American Independence.

"But here recollections crowd upon our minds too powerful for utterance. Words would but mock the deep emotions of our hearts should we attempt to express them, in contemplating the character, attributes, and services of the paternal Chief, under whose auspices we trod together the field of honour. To the profound veneration and love for his memory that penetrates your bosom, we refer you as to a transcript of our own. It would be vain to imagine the joy that would swell the great mind of Washington, were he still living to recognise with our nation, the generous disinterestedness, the glowing ardour, the personal sacrifices, and the gallant achievements of his much loved Fayette. But it is equally vain to endeavour, on this occasion, to exclude such interesting reflections from the mind, or to deny it the melancholy pleasure of lingering on the solemn reality, that not a single individual of the General Staff of the army of the American Revolution now survives to participate in the joy that your presence in the United States has awakened.

"To us it is peculiarly grateful that you are permitted after a lapse of so long a period, to witness the consummation of the principles of our revolution. You will perceive, sir, that the hopes and predictions of the wise and good men who were your particular associates in the arduous struggle, have been fulfilled and surpassed. You will behold a great people united in their principles of jurisprudence, cemented together by the strong ties of mutual interests, and happy under the fostering influence of a free and energetic government.

"You will, therefore, allow us to reiterate our felicitations on your safe arrival among us, and to welcome you once more to the good land which your youthful valour contributed to elevate and distinguish.

"May your future life be as tranquil and happy as your past has been useful, uniform, and glorious."

To which the General returned the following answer :—

"Amidst the inexpressible enjoyments which press upon my heart, I could not but feel particularly eager and happy to meet my beloved brothers in arms. Many, many, I call in vain ; and at the head of them, our matchless paternal Chief, whose love to an adopted son, I am proud to say, you have long witnessed—But while we mourn together, for those we have lost, while I find a consolation in the sight of their relations and friends, it is to me a delightful gratification to recognise my surviving companions of our revolutionary army—that army so brave, so virtuous, so united by mutual confidence and affection. That we have been the faithful soldiers of independence, freedom, and equality, those three essential requisites of national and personal dignity and happiness; that we have lived to see those sacred principles secured to this vast Republic, and cherished elsewhere by all generous minds, shall be the pride of our life, the boast of our children, the comfort of our last moments.—Receive, my dear brother soldiers, the grateful thanks, and constant love of your old companion and friend."

On Wednesday was the anniversary of commencement in Harvard University, at Cambridge. The corporation had requested the president, to send a particular invitation to General Lafayette, to be present on the occasion. He had expressed a wish, soon after his arrival at New-York, to attend that literary anniversary. The corporation heard of his intention with great satisfaction. They were sensible of his love of literature, and of his attachment to this ancient seminary. And they remembered, that the governors of the college appreciated his merits *forty years* before, by conferring upon him the highest honours they could bestow. At a meeting of the corporation on the 21st of August, it was voted—

"That the corporation learn with peculiar satisfaction, the intention of General Lafayette to visit this part of our country, at the period of the approaching commencement, and regard the event as auspicious to that joyous and interesting anniversary, and respectfully request, that he will favour the university with his company on that occasion; and thereby afford to the members of the university, and to those who are candidates for its honours, the opportunity of seeing and honouring the distinguished patriot and soldier, whose willing sacrifices were devoted to the cause which has secured to the successive races of American youth, the blessings of education in a land of freedom; and whose virtuous and glorious career holds forth to the rising generation, a bright example of the qualities which ought to adorn those, who aspire to aid in the councils, or maintain the rights and interests of a free people."

General Lafayette was escorted from Boston to Cambridge, on Wednesday morning, by a company of cavalry, and accompanied by the Governor and Supreme Executive Council of the Commonwealth. In passing through Cambridge Port, he was gratefully cheered by the assembled citizens, and eloquently addressed by Judge Fay, in the name of the whole, in the following interesting manner :—

"General Lafayette,—The citizens of Cambridge present themselves before you, to greet your arrival in their country with an affectionate welcome, and to offer the simple homage of grateful hearts to the early and constant friend of American liberty—the steady and uniform asserter of the rights of man. They desire to make known to you the profound sentiments of gratitude and admiration, with which their bosoms are inspired by the recollection of the generous and distinguished services rendered by you to the United States in their struggle for national existence. In that struggle, you made a voluntary offering of your life and fortune on the altar of civil liberty! In so doing, you sought no rewards, but in the conscious magnanimity of the act and in the lasting gratitude of a whole people. Those rewards you have, Sir, and long, long may you enjoy them.

"Permit us to remind you, Sir, that on this spot was assembled the first army of our revolution ;—that here Washington first assumed the command of that army, and entered upon the momentous contest, which terminated in our national independence, that independence, which your own disinterested and noble efforts contributed so essentially to achieve.

"To you, General, the friend and companion in arms of our beloved Washington—the benefactor of our country—the soldier of liberty—to you the citizens of Cambridge again tender their heartfelt welcome, and pray you to accept their fervent wishes, that all your future days may be full of happiness and honours."

The reply of Lafayette was characteristic and affectionate. He was met by the Corporation and Professors, on his arriving within the precincts of the college, and thus addressed by the learned President Kirkland :—

"We bid you welcome, General Lafayette, to the most ancient of the seminaries of our land. The Overseers and Fellows of the University, the Professors and other officers, the candidates for the academic honours of this day, and the students, tender you their respectful, their affectionate salutations. We greet you with peculiar pleasure, at this literary festival, gratified that you regard the occasion with interest, and espouse the attachment, which as members of a republic, we cannot fail to cherish to the cause of learning and education.

"As a nan, sustaining his part through various scenes, prosperous and adverse, of an eventful life, your character and course, marked by moral dignity, have challenged particular respect and sympathy. As the patron, the champion, and benefactor of America, you have a relation to us, by which we call you our own, and join gratitude and affection to exalted esteem. The early and costly pledges you gave of devotion to the principles and spirit of our institutions, your adoption of our perilous and uncertain contest for national existence, your friendship in the hour of our greatest need, have associated your name in the minds and hearts of Americans, with the dearest and most affecting recollections. The fathers teach their children, and the instructers their pupils, to hold you in love and honour; and the history of these States takes charge of your claims to the grateful remembrance of all future generations.

"It is a pleasing reflection attending the progress of these communities, that it justifies our friends and supporters; and that the predilections and hopes in our favour, which you indulged in the ardour of youth, have been followed by good auspices till your advanced age. We are, indeed, happy in presenting you the fruit of your toils and dangers, in the kindly operation of the causes, which you did so much to call into action, and we rejoice in every demonstration we are able to give, that your care for us has not been vain. Knowing how you feel yourself to have a property in our welfare, and sensible of the enjoyment accruing to your generous spirit from our prosperity, we find in these considerations, new motives to maintain liberty with ardour; and in the exercise of our functions, feel bound to endeavour to send out from our care, enlightened and virtuous men, employing their influence to secure to their country the advantages, and prevent and remedy the evils attending the wide diffusion among a people of political power.

"Accept our wishes and prayers for your health and happiness. May the Invisible Hand which has been your safeguard thus far, continue its protecting care. May the Supreme Disposer, the Witness and Judge of character and conduct, having appointed you a long and tranquil evening of days, receive you to the final and glorious reward of the faithful in a perfect state."

The following is the substance of the General's reply:—

"It is with real pleasure, Sir, that I find myself again at this University, which I visited for the first time, more than forty years ago. The great improvements which have been made here during the interval, are striking evidences of the tendency of liberal political institutions, to promote the progress of civilization and learning. I beg you to accept my warmest thanks for your kind expressions of personal civility to myself, and my best wishes for the continued prosperity of the valuable esta blishments over which you preside."

When he entered the place provided for the celebration of commencement, where a numerous company of ladies and gentlemen had assembled to attend the ceremonies and literary performances of the day, there was an instantaneous and universal acclamation; not stunning and boisterous; but the decorous and chastened greeting of an intelligent audience. When he reached the stage, he bowed repeatedly to the assembly, with great apparent sensibility. Several of the young gentlemen, alluded to him in their orations; and some dwelt particularly on his early devotion to the cause of America, in the struggle for independence, with great effect. These notices, though short and indirect, were calculated to excite the grateful recollections of the audience; who responded to the sentiments with enthusiastic acclamations.

On Thursday, by particular request of the literary society of "*Phi Beta Kappa*," so called, in the university, General Lafayette attended the celebration of their anniversary at Cambridge. It was never known before, that any one, however distinguished, either for literature or virtue, was invited to dine with the society, unless a member of some other branch of the association. The departure in this case, from the invariable usages and rules of the society, is proof of the very high estimation in which Lafayette is held, and of the disposition, in all classes of citizens, to manifest their respect for his character. He proceeded to the university, about 1 o'clock, when he was again greeted with the hearty cheers of the citizens, as he passed the high-way, and when he arrived. The public performances on this occasion, were an oration and a poem. The latter was prepared at very short notice, and had particular reference to the visit of the illustrious hero and philanthropist. It purported to be the vision of the *Genius of Liberty*. It was a felicitous effort of the poetic muse. The gradual but certain dissolution of ancient despotic systems was predicted, as by the spirit of inspiration ; and the blessings and joys of well-regulated freedom were described with a masterly pencil, as extending and spreading in all parts of the civilized world. It was the electrifying voice of genius, speaking to hearts full of gratitude and swelling with joyous emotions.

The orator was not less happy in his subject, nor less ingenious and eloquent in its illustration. Lafayette was very sensibly affected by this unexpected expression of gratitude for his early services, and by the strong emotions manifested by the assembly, at the name of Washington. The hours passed in the dining hall were consecrated to reminiscences of the interesting events which occurred in the revolutionary contest, to grateful recollections of the statesmen and heroes, who advocated and defended the cause of freedom, and thus led the way in the glorious march of human improvement and happiness, which the present generation is so rapidly pursuing. Here were assembled the judges of the land, the ministers of religion, the legislators of the state and nation, several of the heroes of the revolution, and numerous eminent literary characters from various parts of the United States, to unite with the younger sons of Harvard, in offerings of affectionate gratitude to a man, who had no gifts of power or titles of honour to bestow ; but whose useful services and uniform course of honourable and benevolent purpose, in their estimation, claimed a higher tribute than was due to sceptered princes, or the most renowned conquerors of ancient or modern times.

Thursday and Saturday mornings, for several hours, he received the personal compliments and congratulations of a great number of the inhabitants of Boston and its vicinity, of both sexes. They were presented to him, on the spacious area of the ground floor of the State House. The house provided for his residence while in the city, though unusually large, was not well adapted for such crowds of visitors as pressed to behold him. Many aged people were presented, who had served with him in the revolutionary war, or recollected events of that period, which they were desirous to relate. Some were on crutches, and others bared their arms to show the honourable scars occasioned by the bayonet or ball of the enemy, in the "glorious fight" for freedom. Some could boast of having fought under his command, or by his side, at Brandywine and Monmouth ; and others, that followed in his path of peril and glory in Virginia, in 1781, and assisted in successfully storming the redoubt at Yorktown, on the memorable evening of the 15th of October, which decided the fate of Cornwallis.

He seized the hands of these his old companions in arms, with great eagerness and emotion; and while they, in the honest pride of their souls related their "hair-breadth escapes," which led the spectators almost to envy their claims to such honourable boasting, the veteran hero exclaimed, "O my brave Light Infantry! My gallant troops!" Several aged citizens who were personally engaged in opposing the British forces, who marched to Lexington and Concord, for the purpose of destroying the Provincial stores collected at the latter place, were present at this interview. A gun was also shown to General Lafayette, from which was fired the ball, which killed the first of the regular troops slain on that memorable occasion. These meetings revived recollections important to be preserved, and served to remind the rising generations of the principles and deeds of their fathers. We trust they did not awaken any angry or hostile feeling towards an ancient enemy; but served only to kindle our gratitude to Almighty God, for his gracious interpositions in our behalf, and to perpetuate our respect for the remains of those who offered up their lives for our freedom and welfare.

On Friday morning, committees from Portsmouth, Newport, Haverhill, Newburyport, and from Bowdoin College, waited on General Lafayette inviting him to visit those respective places; where the people were desirous to see him, and to offer personally their welcome salutations.

To a kind and affectionate invitation of the citizens of Portland to Lafayette to visit Maine, the General returned the following respectful answer :—

"Sir—When I had the heartfelt gratification to embark on this happy visit to the United States, I anticipated the pleasure to pay my respects to the citizens of the State of Maine, and the town of Portland. That intention could not but be confirmed by the flattering invitation you have been pleased to transmit. I much regret that previous engagements, and the propriety not to defer for a long time my journey towards the seat of government at Washington City, make it impossible for me, at this moment, to indulge my eager desire to visit the town of Portland. But on my return to this part of the Union, and most certainly before I leave the American shore. I shall have the honour, personally to offer to the citizens of Portland, the tribute of my respect and gratitude.

Be pleased, Sir, to accept my respectful acknowledgments and regard. LAFAYETTE."

The Selectmen of the ancient town of Plymouth were prompt in offering an invitation to General Lafayette to visit that place before leaving the United States. A letter from the Chairman, in behalf of that body and their fellow citizens, was delivered to him on the morning after his arrival in Boston, by the venerable Dr. Thacher; to which he gave the following reply:—

"Sir—Nothing could afford me a greater satisfaction than to have the honour to pay my respects to the citizens of Plymouth; nor will I leave the shores of America before I have enjoyed this heartfelt gratification. But my present, first visit to this part of the Union, is shortened by previous engagements, and the obligation to go towards the seat of government at Washington City. I anticipate the time when it will be in my power personally to present the citizens of Plymouth with my grateful and affectionate acknowledgments for their kindness to me. Be pleased to accept the tribute of these sentiments, and to believe me with much personal regard, Yours, &c.

LAFAYETTE."

The Marquis Lafayette left his place of residence in Boston at 10 o'clock, accompanied by Governor Eustis and suite, Governor Brooks, the deputation from New-York, the Mayor and committee of arrangements of Boston, and proceeded to Charlestown, which he previously engaged to visit, at this time. As he passed through the streets in the north part of the city, the people pressed around him, testifying their regard, and cheering him on his way with repeated acclamations. Raised arches, wreaths of ever-green, and variegated colours, added to the brilliancy of the scene. He was met at the centre of the bridge, which is the dividing line between Boston and Charlestown, by the Chief Marshal and his aids, and conducted to the square, where a committee of the citizens of that town was in waiting to receive him. A procession was then formed, headed by two Marshals, and escorted by a regiment of Light Infantry, and a battalion of artillery, with martial music, consisting of the committee of arrangements, General Lafayette, his son, and friend, who accompanied him from France; the Governor and suite, Governor Brooks, and General Dearborn, Judges of the Courts, and members of the Supreme Executive

Council of the State; deputation from New-York, Mayor and committee of Boston, officers of the army and navy of the United States, and of the militia of the State; strangers of distinction, and civil officers of the town of Charlestown. It proceeded to Bunker Hill, where the chairman of the committee of the town, addressed Lafayette as follows:—

"Sir—In behalf of the inhabitants of Charlestown, the committee of arrangements present their respectful salutations to General Lafayette, and bid him a cordial welcome to this town. This joyful occasion revives high national feelings and recollections, and touches the springs of gratitude, by reminding us of that interesting period of our history, which gave to our country a gallant hero, and to the rights of mankind a steadfast champion. While we participate in the thrill of delight which every where hails the visit of our illustrious friend, we cannot suppress the peculiar emotion of our hearts on receiving you, Sir, on the memorable heights of *Bunker*. On this holy ground, immortalized by the dead, and sacred to the names of revolutionary heroes. Over these heights, liberty once moved in blood and tears;—her chariot on wheels of fire. Now she comes in her car of peace and glory; drawn by the affections of a happy people, to crown on these same heights, with civic honours, a favourite son, whose early strength was given to her sacred struggles, and whose riper years are now permitted to behold the splendour of her triumphs. In the fulness of our hearts we give thanks to Almighty God, who has guided and guarded your high career of peril and renown.

"Permit us, beloved General, again to welcome you to our borders;—to express our ardent hopes, that your valuable life may be prolonged to the utmost limits of earthly happiness;—that the land which has been enriched with the dew of your youth, may be honoured as the asylum of your old age;—that the country which now blends your fame with the mild lustre of Washington, may henceforth hail you as a citizen of Washington's country;—and that, during the residue of your years, you may live amidst the attentions, as you will for ever live in the hearts of a grateful and admiring people."

To this address the General replied:—

"With profound reverence, Sir, I tread this holy ground, where the blood of American patriots—the blood of Warren and his companions, early and gloriously spilled, aroused the energy of three millions, and secured the happiness of ten millions, and of many other millions of men in times to come. That blood has called both American continents to republican independence, and has awakened the nations of Europe to a sense, and in future, I hope, to the practice of their rights. Such have been the effects of a resistance to oppression, which was, by many pretended wise men of the times, called rashness; while it was duty, virtue;—and has been a signal for the emancipation of mankind.

"I beg you, sir, and the magistrates, and the citizens of Charlestown, to accept the homage of my gratitude for your kind welcome, and of those sentiments of affection and respect, which, for so many years, I have cherished towards their town."

While on this memorable eminence, he was informed by Governor Brooks, of the recent association for erecting a monumental pillar on that hallowed spot, to perpetuate the remembrance of the justly celebrated battle of the 17th of June, 1775; when a few regiments of undisciplined militia, made a brave stand against a large regular British force, commanded by Generals of great experience and courage. This great event, so important in the annals of our country, as it convinced the English government of the resolution of the colonies to maintain the liberty which they claimed, and of the daring courage of the American people. This event is to be commemorated in June, 1825, when fifty years will be completed, by an oration, and other public appropriate services and ceremonies. General Lafayette expressed great satisfaction at the proposal. He requested that he might be considered a subscriber for the monument; and assured the gentlemen present, that it would be his wish and endeavour to attend the celebration.

On his visit to the encampment of the *New-England Guards*, the General tried his skill in gunnery, and directed one of the field pieces with such good aim, as to pierce the target. A large assemblage of the visitors of the encampment announced his success with reiterated cheerings.

He then dined with Governor Eustis, in Roxbury, in company with nearly two hundred of the most distinguished strangers now on visits here and citizens—of whom were many of the surviving worthies of the Revolution.—The front of his Excellency's seat was beautifully decorated, and fire-works were exhibited on the lawn. He returned to town at 8 o'clock, and in the evening attended a ball given by Mrs. *Sears*, in Bacon-street.

On Saturday August 28th, numerous deputations, and revolutionary characters, called on the General at his quarters One of the latter exhibited the *Firearm*, by a discharge of which the first British *regular* killed in the war of the revolution was shot at Concord bridge, on the memorable 19th April, 1775. The event is recorded in the annals of that day. Satisfactory evidence was given, that the ball which did the first execution on the British advanced guard, was fired from this gun. The General appeared much pleased at seeing this relic, and suggested the expediency of perpetuating its identity, by inserting a plate on the stock, with an inscription, containing the particulars of the event. It belonged to Capt. Buttrick, and was presented, it is understood, by one of his descendants, who promised to execute the suggestion of the General, and remarked, that the gun should be transmitted to the latest posterity of the original owner. A number of revolutionary reminiscences occurred in this interview, which we have not room to particularize.

The General then repaired to the State-house, and received the congratulations of the citizens of both sexes, who, during two hours, presented themselves in continued succession. One of the revolutionary worthies, (Jonathan Leonard of Canton, in Norfolk,) holding in his hand a number of old *Continental* bills, thus addressed the Guest:—"*Here, General, are some of our Old Friends, who helped us to carry on the war.*" Among the presentations was an interesting Greek youth from Scio, named *Pandies Ralli*, whose father was one of the first martyrs in the present eventful struggle of the Greek Patriots, being one of the hostages executed at Constantinople. This lad, we are informed, with his mother, and family, fled from the sack of Scio, and is now receiving an education, under the care of our Foreign Missionary Society. He was noticed with much affection by the General. In the afternoon he proceeded to Medford, to dine with Governor Brooks, accompanied by the Mayor.

On his way to Medford he passed through Charlestown and West Cambridge, and arrived at Medford about 3 o'clock. It was at a very late hour that the citizens of *Medford* ascertained that the town would be honoured with his presence; but their preparations to welcome him were appropriate and elegant.

Under an arch the Selectmen of the town were assembled:

and Turell Tufts, Esq. their Chairman, delivered to him the following address :—

"General Lafayette—The Selectmen of Medford, as the Representatives of the town, deem it a grateful and honourable part of their duty to bid you welcome.

"They are proud, Sir, that Medford is the birth-place of one of your companions in arms—A man, who, by his bravery in the field, his patriotism and civic virtues, contributed to acquire as much glory to our country, as honour to himself.

"We rejoice, Sir, that you both live to meet again, and to enjoy together the consolations fairly derived from your virtuous and heroic deeds.

"The minds of our countrymen traced your course with anxious solicitude, through the French Revolution, from your first success in the cause of Liberty, until the spirit of oppression confined you to a dungeon; and their hearts were gladdened, when, by the influence of our Great and Good WASHINGTON, their Friend was at last set free.—In the rich harvest you are now gathering of the expressions of esteem and gratitude of this numerous people, whose freedom and happiness your exertions so essentially contributed to establish, we hope you will find some compensation for all your trials, sacrifices, and sufferings—and we feel much complacency that, in this respect you have gained so complete a triumph over the Monarchs of the world.

"Again, Sir, we bid you a cordial welcome! and hope the testimonials of approbation you are receiving from every heart and every tongue, will for ever remain an instructive lesson to mankind, that Patriots who endure faithfully to the end, shall not lose their reward."

The following is the substance of the General's reply:—

"Sir—I am most happy, in visiting the town of my old brother Soldier and Friend, General Brooks, to be received with so kind a welcome. You speak of some compensation! Compensation, Sir,—the smallest part of the delight which I have experienced, would more than repay me for all sufferings, past, or to come.

"I beg you, to accept my grateful acknowledgments for this cheering welcome."

This welcome was repeated by the acclamations of the assembled citizens, which were renewed on his arriving at the Governor's residence. The civic arches and decorations were honourable to the zeal and good feelings of the citizens, and to the taste of the ladies of Medford, who took a lively interest in this spontaneous tribute of gratitude.

The General, in proceeding to Medford, passed through Salem-street, and the taste and patriotism of the citizens of the northern section, were displayed in numerous and elegant decorations of the street, incessant cheers, and waving of handkerchiefs. His carriage proceeded slowly, and he appeared to notice all the arches (fifteen in number) under which he passed, and particularly one, (the production of the daughter of a Member of the City Government) which bore an inscription, formed on a white ground, with green buds, "*Fayette—We will never forget thee.*"

On Monday the orders of the Commander-in-chief, for a review of a portion of the militia, in honour of the visit of the surviving Major-General of the revolutionary army, our distinguished Guest, were executed with promptness and uncommon effect. The day was fine. At an early hour, a superb Brigade, (composed of five full regiments of infantry, a regiment of artillery, and the Salem Independent Cadets) commanded by Brigadier-General James Appleton, paraded on the Common, on which tents and marquees had been pitched for their accommodation, and which with the commissary's tent, and the tents of the Suffolk Brigade, and the marquees attached to the Head-Quarters (where the Independent Cadets, commanded by Lieut. Colonel Amory, did guard duty) exhibited an extensive encampment. At the same time the Boston Brigade, commanded by Brigadier-General Lyman, and composed of three full regiments of infantry, four companies of artillery, and a troop of dragoons, also paraded and formed the order of battle at 8 o'clock. The whole field was commanded by Major-General Crane, of the first division.

The line nearly filled up the borders of the spacious training-field, and exhibited a martial spectacle unequalled in extent, brilliancy, and efficiency by any former military review. The corps of cavalry, artillery, and flank companies, were in complete and superb uniforms; and in the whole line of infantry, the troops, with scarcely an exception, were in blue coats and white under clothes, with knapsacks, &c. complete. It was estimated that the number on the field exceeded 6500.

General Lafayette, on foot, was escorted by the Cadets from his residence to the State-house, where he was received by his excellency the Commander-in-chief, and suite They were then escorted to the Common. He was received by loud shouts from the troops along the whole line. The General was then saluted by the Brigades, under Generals Appleton and Lyman, in succession. He then took a position in front of Head-Quarters, and received the marching salute of the whole division. Experienced judges, foreign and native, did justice to the discipline and steadiness of the movements.

A spacious and well ornamented marquee had been erected by order of the Governor on the rising ground of the Common, for a collation for the Officers and invited Guests. It much exceeded any other arrangement of the kind ever seen here. In this edifice,* His Excellency, and the distinguished Guest, the Officers of the Field, the Executive Council, Cincinnati, Civil and Judicial Officers, Foreign Consuls, Officers of the Army and Navy, Governor Miller, the Clergy, the City authorities, Strangers of distinction, and General and Field Officers of the Militia not on duty, partook of a sumptuous and well-attended entertainment. A few toasts were given, which were received with acclamations, particularly that of the Commander-in-chief, complimentary of the Guest; that of General Lafayette in praise of the fine appearance and excellent conduct of the troops, and that of General Brooks, who gave "*The Commander-in-chief of these troops.*"

The order of battle having been re-formed, the Brigade under General Appleton performed numerous evolutions, with the utmost precision and fine effect.

The Boston Brigade, under General Lyman, then occupied an hour in similar evolutions,—particularly those against cavalry, by the formation of squares of regiments, and by the retreat within them, when hard pressed, of the skirmishers and artillerymen, each retiring with their colours and an allotted portable article essential to their utility; then rushing out, remounting and firing their deserted guns, after the assailing cavalry is repulsed. This mode of defence was practised with effect by the British army at Waterloo.

The exercises being completed, and the usual ceremonies of the field performed, the troops were dismissed. The Ge-

* The marquee was 176 feet by 60; containing six tables 170 feet long, on which there were 1300 plates set,—which were afterwards increased to 1600. The collation was prepared by Mr. Dudley Bradstreet

neral was then re-escorted to his quarters, amidst continued cheers.

In the evening the General held a levee, at which many hundred ladies were introduced to him. He then attended a ball given by Mrs. Elliot, in Bacon-street.

"Should it be supposed by the sober citizens of other countries, or by those in our own, who did not join in these offerings of grateful admiration to Lafayette, and who therefore could have felt nothing of the enthusiasm which such scenes are calculated to produce; that there was too much parade, or an undue measure of sensibility manifested on this occasion; it may be proper to observe, that no conclusion is to be drawn from this great rejoicing, that the people of Boston, or in fact of the United States, are disposed to pay higher regard to eminent men of the military, than in the civil department; or that they have so little discrimination, as to bestow applause upon merely splendid achievements. It is believed to be a fact, that the most intelligent and sober part of the community were as ready to engage in these processions and ceremonies, as those of the more common and uninformed class of citizens. How could it be otherwise? These are convincing proofs of the zeal, disinterestedness, and devotion of General Lafayette to the cause of American liberty and independence—of his bravery, activity, judgment, constancy, and fidelity—of his attachment to Washington and other patriots, and of their regard for him; and of his uniform support of regulated liberty in his own country. In his early days he had risked every thing, and had done every thing which an individual could possibly endure or attempt, in our behalf. He had *now*, in advanced life, left his own beloved retirement in a distant hemisphere, to visit this land of liberty, and of his affections, to behold the prosperity, order, enjoyment, and felicity of a great people. His character too, is unstained by bloodshed and crime; it is consecrated, on the contrary, by the prayers, and tears, and benedictions, of all good men in America and Europe. Who will then censure or wonder, that he should be received by the moral and sober people of America, with all that cordiality and enthusiasm, which were discovered on his arrival amongst us? We do not forget Washington; our beloved and almost adored Washington—nor are we insensible to the merits and virtues of other statesmen and heroes of our own country. But, surely we may be allowed to greet this old distinguished benefactor with a cordial welcome, without subjecting ourselves to the charge of extravagance, or caprice.

"The character of the militia in Boston, and generally through the state, has been much improved within the last fifteen years. They have recently adopted a cheap uniform; and great improvements have been made in adopting the modern system of tactics. The independent companies need not decline a comparison with regular troops; and, what is very important to the respectability of the militia, their officers are intelligent and ambitious, and actuated by a patriotic spirit, which is a pledge of fidelity, and a stimulus to honourable exertion. The high praise bestowed upon the militia at this review, was justly merited."

General Lafayette left Boston on Tuesday morning for Portsmouth, in the state of New-Hampshire, intending to pass through Marblehead, Salem, and Newburyport, on his way to the former place. A number of distinguished citizens, and a Committee of the City Council accompanied him to the northern line of the city; and the Governor's aids attended him to the extreme part of the state, adjoining New-Hampshire. On his route he was greeted by the inhabitants of Chelsea, Lynn, and Marblehead, with great feeling and respect, alike honourable to themselves, and gratifying to the friend and guest of the nation. Addresses were also made to him, in these several towns, expressive of their gratitude for his services, and of the lively sense they had of his present visit to the country.

In passing through Lynn, General Lafayette was received by the citizens with distinguished marks of respect.

At about half past 8 o'clock, he arrived at the bridge, (over the draw of which was thrown a handsome arch,) under the escort of the Boston company of cavalry, which immediately joined the other battalion; when the whole moved towards the Hotel.

On the arrival of the procession at the Hotel, which was very handsomely decorated with flags and ever-greens, the following address was delivered to the General by John White, Esq. the Chairman of the Committee of Arrangements:—

"General—The inhabitants of this town have chosen me their organ, to greet you with a sincere and hearty welcome, on this joyful occasion. A duty on which I enter with mingled emotions of profound veneration, gratitude, and affection, towards you, Sir, our nation's early, disinterested, and unvarying friend and benefactor.

"The deep, intense, and indelible feelings of this free and happy republic towards you, General, who so eminently and successfully contributed to raise her to her present proud and powerful attitude among the nations of the earth, can be no more forcibly illustrated, than in that spontaneous homage of the heart, which you see displayed around you, on your arrival upon our favoured shores; and which, like a halo of glory, encircles you in your progress through our country. This, General, is a language not to be misunderstood, compared with which the most laboured declamation must be faint and powerless.

"Although your present appearance among us, like the transit of a brilliant and beneficent planet, commissioned to proclaim good will to man, in its rapid career among innumerable worlds, is short and fleeting, the emanations of the bright and joyous light which it sheds around you, will continue with us to guide our steps, and cheer our hearts to the latest moment of our existence.

"Permit me now, General, to express my individual joy at the happy consummation of those ardent wishes, which I had the honour to express to you twelve years since, in your native country—for you have re-visited us, and you see that "all hearts and arms are open to receive you."

To this the General made a very affectionate reply.

The General was then conducted to the Hall, where he was introduced by the chairman to the ladies, committee of arrangements, municipal officers, revolutionary soldiers, clergy, and many citizens, but being engaged to breakfast at Marblehead, his stay was restricted to thirty minutes. On leaving the Hotel, the General ascended the barouche, with the chairman of the committee, and the procession proceeded through the town. At the western end of the common was erected a beautiful civic arch, most elegantly decorated with ever-greens, surmounted by a wreath enclosing the following inscription:—

"Welcome Lafayette! Conqueror of hearts."

On the top of which was perched a beautiful gilt Eagle. Suspended under the arch by festoons of ever-greens was a wreath, surrounding this inscription:—

"Washington and Lafayette."

After passing this arch, the procession entered between two lines of children of the town, neatly and prettily dressed, who threw boquets of flowers before the General, and into his carriage. Next in order were two long lines of the citizens, reaching to another very handsome arch of ever-green, under which was suspended a wreath surrounding these words:—"October 19th, 1781." The procession continued over the common towards Market-street, through which he passed, and at its entrance passed under a beautiful canopy, formed on one side by a majestic elm, and on the other by large trees planted for the occasion, united at the top, and tastefully hung with wreaths and garlands of flowers. At this place was the following inscription:—

"Welcome Lafayette, to thee we owe the sweets of Liberty."

On the entrance of the procession to Front-street, another beautiful arch was presented, to which was suspended, under thirteen sun flowers, representing stars, this inscription:—

"Thou gavest to us thirteen talents. Lo! we have gained eleven more.—Receive our gratitude."

Under this inscription were eleven other sun flowers. In Broad-street was another handsome arch, made entirely of trees, wreaths, and garlands, on which was the following inscription:—

"The voice of ten millions welcome."

The procession then passed into Chesnut-street, and through part of Fayette-street, into Essex-street, where another magnificent arch was erected, most beautifully decorated, on the centre of which was inscribed "1776," and below this, was inscribed these words:—

"The man whom the people delight to honour.—Welcome Lafayette.—Yorktown.—Monmouth."

On the reverse, being the last arch, was this inscription:—

"Tho' lost to sight, to memory dear."

The procession moved in fine style through this arch, and proceeded to the eastern boundary line of the town, where the Lynn escort delivered their illustrious guest to the authorities of Marblehead. A salute of 13 guns was fired by the Lynn and Danvers Artillery, on the entrance of the General upon the lines of the town, and another of 24 guns when he passed over the Common.

On his entrance into Marblehead, he was saluted by 13

guns from a battery erected on the heights at the entrance of the town, and greeted by shouts of applause and welcome from the whole population, who, with the troops of the town were assembled for his reception; and was conducted to the house provided to receive him under a national salute of 24 guns from Major Greene's battalion of Artillery. Here he was introduced to the Authorities of the town, and was addressed in behalf of the town by the Hon. John Prince, chairman of the committee; after which, our illustrious guest with his suite, and several strangers of distinction, partook of a breakfast in the public hall, arranged in a style of superior elegance.

After breakfast the General was conducted to another apartment, where all the citizens, the officers of the brigade, and many strangers were most cordially received by him; among whom were several revolutionary soldiers, and the Pilot who landed him in Marblehead on his second arrival in this country, whom he recognised, and saluted with marks of the highest satisfaction.

He also expressed a wish to have a particular interview with some of the descendants of the late General Glover, with whom he was formerly in habits of intimacy; and was accordingly, with his suite, conducted to the house of Robert Hooper, Esq. On being introduced to Mrs. Hooper, daughter of the late General, he was much affected, and expressed the highest interest at meeting a child of his old and particular friend.

After being escorted through the principal streets of the town, he was accompanied by the Committee of Arrangements to the Salem line, under another salute of 24 guns, and the loud and gratulatory shouts of the warm-hearted inhabitants.

His reception at Salem was very distinguished and splendid. At the entrance of the town, he was met by the Selectmen and committee, a numerous cavalcade, and a large body of citizens in carriages, and received a salute of artillery; on advancing a short distance within the bounds of the town, the bells commenced ringing, and the escort was joined by a battalion of light infantry, and a body of seamen, of about two hundred, in blue jackets and white trowsers, with ribands on their hats, stamped with the name of Lafayette.

With the hearty cheers of these hardy sons of Neptune, the General appeared to be peculiarly impressed. Over South Salem bridge were two tastefully decorated arches—one bearing the inscription "WELCOME ILLUSTRIOUS CHIEF! *Receive the pledges of thy Children to sustain with fidelity the principles that first associated* LAFAYETTE *with the destinies of America.*" These arches were surrounded by an immense number of citizens, who made the air ring with their huzzas and welcomes. The figure of an Indian Chief characteristically dressed, bore labels inscribed "*Lafayette and Liberty. Welcome generous Lafayette.*"

Civic arches, historical and patriotic inscriptions, memorable eras, wreaths of flowers and ever-greens, banners and flags, were displayed in many of the streets, enlivening the scene, animating the cheers, and affording grateful recollections.

Central-street was gayly dressed in colours, and on an elegant arch were inscribed the names of distinguished patriots of the revolution, crowned with those of WASHINGTON and LAFAYETTE. In North-street a similar arch bore the inscription:—"*Honour to him who fought and bled for the happiness and peace we now enjoy.*" On an arch at Buffum's corner, was inscribed, "LAFAYETTE, *the friend of Liberty, we welcome to the land of liberty. He did not forget us in our adversity—In our prosperity we remember his services with gratitude.*" Near the above, another arch bore a likeness of Lafayette, surmounted by an eagle.

Near the avenue leading to the bridge, at which, in February, 1775, Colonel Leslie, with a detachment of the British 64th regiment, met with a repulse in an attempt to carry off some cannon deposited in the vicinity, were banners, with the following inscription:—

"*Leslie's Repulse*, 1775.
Lafayette's Renown, 1824.

Washington-square was decorated with two arches, tastefully ornamented, one bearing the name of the General, in oaken characters, and the second a bust of Washington.

On Washington-square the General passed between two lines of boys, about one thousand in number, arrayed under their respective instructers, all bearing Lafayette badges. One of the gates of the square bore this inscription:—"*The children welcome with joy, the illustrious benefactor of their fathers.*" And as the General passed, they shouted "*Welcome Lafayette.*"

Notwithstanding the heavy rain, this youthful band could not be prevailed upon to leave the ground, but remained bravely at their post, until they had shared with their parents in the honour and happiness of greeting the nation's guest.

From Washington Square the procession passed to the Lafayette Coffee House, in Essex-street, where, upon a stage erected in front of the house, the General and his suite, the invited guests, and other gentlemen of distinction, were received by the Committee of Arrangements. Judge Story, the President of the day, in presence of the committee and company upon the stage, and of an immense concourse of people, then delivered in the most interesting and elegant manner to General Lafayette the following Address:—

"General Lafayette—

Sir—Forty years have elapsed since the inhabitants of this town had the pleasure to welcome you within its limits. Many who then hailed your arrival with pride and exultation, have descended to the grave, and cannot greet you on your long desired return. But, thanks to a good Providence, many are yet alive who recollect with grateful sensibility the universal joy of that occasion. Your disinterested zeal in embarking in a cause, deemed almost hopeless—your personal sacrifices in quitting a home endeared by all the blessings with which affection and virtue can adorn life—your toils and perils in the conflicts of war and the vicissitudes of a discouraging service—your modest dignity and enthusiasm on receiving the homage of a free people—these were all fresh in their memories, and gave an interest to the scene, which cannot be described, but which Time has hallowed with his most touching grace. I stand now in the presence of some, venerable in age and character, who were the delighted witnesses of that interview, and whose hearts again glow with the feelings of that happy day.

"To us of a younger generation—the descendants of your early friends and companions in arms—a different, but not less interesting privilege belongs. We are allowed the enviable distinction of meeting, in his riper years, one, whom our Fathers loved in their youth. We welcome you to our country—to our homes—to our hearts. We have read the history of your achievements—your honours—and your sufferings. They are associated with all that is dear to us—with the battle grounds consecrated by the blood of our heroes—with the tender recollections of our departed statesmen—with the affectionate reverence of our surviving patriots. Can we forget that we were poor and struggling alone in the doubtful contest for Independence, and you crossed the Atlantic at the hazard of fortune and fame to cheer us in our resistance? That you re-crossed it to solicit naval and military succours from the throne of France, and returned with triumphant success? That your gallantry in the southern campaigns checked the inroads of a brave and confident enemy? That your military labours closed but with the surrender at Yorktown, and thus indissolubly united your name with the proud events of that glorious day. We cannot forget these things if we would.—We would not forget them if we could. They will not be forgotten, until America ceases to be a Nation.

"But we have yet higher sources of gratification on the present occasion. You have been the friend not merely of America, but of France, and of the cause of Liberty throughout the World. During a long life, and in the most trying scenes, you have done no act for which virtue need blush, or humanity weep. Your private character has not cast a shade on your public honours. In the palaces of Paris and the dungeons of Olmutz, in the splendor of power, and the gloom of banishment, you have been the friend of justice, and the asserter of the rights of man.—Under every misfortune you have never deserted your principles. What earthly prize can afford consolations like this? The favour of Princes and the applause of Senates sink into absolute nothingness in comparison with the approving conscience of a life devoted to the good of mankind. At this very moment you are realizing the brightest visions of your youth, in the spectacle of ten millions of people, prosperous and happy under a free government, whose moral strength consists in the courage and intelligence of its citizens. These millions welcome you to the shores of the West with spontaneous unanimity; and the voice which now addresses you, feeble as it is, repeats but the thoughts that are ready to burst from the lips of every American."

To which the General made the following very appropriate and affecting reply:—

"On my happy return to this shore of liberty, I had anticipated the pleasure to revisit the town of Salem, to witness her so much increased prosperity, to recall with surviving old friends, our revolutionary recollections. But in the affectionate welcome of the new generations, I find additional causes for delightful gratification.

"You have been pleased, Sir, to allude to several circumstances of my life. The first of them I have shared in common with my dear companions during our American glorious struggle. In the transactions of another hemisphere, I have made it a constant object not to be unworthy of the American education it had been my happy lot to receive.

"I request you, Sir, the gentlemen of the committee, and all the citizens of Salem, to accept of the respectful thanks of a grateful and very anciently affectionate heart."

A very impressive circumstance occurred in the delivery of the Honourable President's address, which produced an electric effect upon all present; after enumerating the distinguished benefits conferred upon our country by Lafayette, he said, "we could not forget them if we would—we would not forget them if we could."—A spontaneous ascent was immediately returned by the crowd, No, never! and was repeated by thousands of voices accompanied by deafening shouts of applause. The General was then introduced to the citizens of the town, and other gentlemen, among whom were several revolutionary officers and soldiers, who had come from various parts of the country to welcome their old General, who recalled to his memory many striking incidents which occurred in the revolutionary war, in different parts of the country while they were serving under his command. At 3 o'clock the General was escorted to Hamilton Hall by the battalion of Light Infantry.

A company of about three hundred gentlemen, with their invited guests, partook of a very sumptuous dinner at the Hall, at which the Honourable Judge Story presided.

This spacious and elegant Hall (which bears the name of the lamented friend of Lafayette,) was decorated with great taste and elegance by the ladies of Salem, who contributed their share to the preparations for this welcome visit. The whole effect was beyond our power of description. The Orchestra was ornamented with wreaths and festoons of flowers and ever-greens, encircling the inscriptions—

Welcome, welcome, be the brave
To the homes he fought to save.

LAFAYETTE, our friend in times which tried men's souls.

La Grange.

LAFAYETTE IN AMERICA;
Ou peut on etre mieux
Qu' au sein de sa famille.

Under the Orchestra was suspended a golden harp, beautifully ornamented. In a recess above the chair of our distinguished guest was a bust of Washington, crowned with an olive wreath, the American Eagle holding a crown over the head of Lafayette, and an elegant arch supported by columns containing the names of the Presidents of the United States.

On each side of this were triumphal arches, and all were decorated with wreaths of flowers and ever-greens.

Inscriptions were displayed in other parts of the hall; among them the following:—

Hail, gallant chief, our country's early friend,
Long life be thine, and brightening to the end.
Though France claim thy birth, HERE AT HOME shalt thou be,
For thine is the love of the brave and the free.

The columns were ornamented with wreaths of oak-leaves, and the room was hung with festoons of flowers, ever-greens, and flags. The elegant chandelier and lamps, mirrors and window-curtains, were beautifully encircled with wreaths and festoons. Flowers, plants, and rich and beautiful paintings, were distributed in various places. The whole arrangement discovered great taste and elegance.

Among the invited guests, were the son and suite of our illustrious guest, General Dearborn, his Excellency the Colombian Minister, Colonel Pickering and Colonel Lee, of the revolutionary army, Colonel Harris and Everett, aids of his excellency the Governor, General H. A. S. Dearborn, General Wingate, of Portland, and the ordained clergy of the town.

About half past 5 o'clock General Lafayette took leave of the company at the Hall, attended by a deputation from the Committee of Arrangements, who were instructed to accompany him to Ipswich, but the General entreated the committee to dispense with this attention, on account of the inclemency of the weather, and he was escorted out of town by the battalion of cavalry.

At Beverly and Ipswich he received from the assembled inhabitants, the same cordial welcome with which he had been greeted in other towns, through which he passed. The selectmen of these places waited on him, and offered him the congratulations of their fellow citizens; the people greeted him with repeated cheers of "*welcome, welcome, Lafayette*;" and arches were erected at several public places, containing appropriate mottos. The houses of the villages through which he passed, after the evening set in, were brilliantly illuminated.

The following address was delivered at Beverly, by the Honourable Robert Rantoul:—

"General—The inhabitants of Beverly bid you welcome. We welcome you to our country—that country which owes so much to your aid in the acquisition of her independence. We receive you not merely as the friend of our beloved country, but as the friend of man. Your labours, your sacrifices, your sufferings in the cause of liberty, demand our gratitude. Tyrants receive the commanded adulation of their slaves, but to the benefactors of our race belong the spontaneous effusions of our hearts. Accept our sincere congratulations that you live to witness the order, the prosperity, the happiness that results from our free institutions; and may the evening of your days be solaced with the reflection that those principles of government, to the support of which your life has been devoted, and which alone can secure the enjoyment of rational liberty, are fast spreading their influence through the whole family of man. Wishing you long life and uninterrupted happiness, we bid you farewell."

It was evening when he arrived at Ipswich, and the weather was very inclement. The inhabitants had, therefore, assembled in the meeting-house to receive him. Thither he was conducted by a committee of the town; and on his entrance, he was greeted with great exultation and joy. One of the committee addressed him as follows:—

"General Lafayette—Accept from the people of Ipswich, their cordial congratulations on your arrival in their country, and within their own borders. To this ancient town, Sir, we bid you a joyful welcome.

"Having devoted to our beloved country, in her weak and critical situation, the vigour of your youth and the resources of a mind intent on the cause of freedom and humanity, and committed to a common lot with her, your own destinies, that country can never forget the services you rendered, and the sacrifices you incurred, for her defence and protection, when assailed by overbearing power.

"We rejoice in having an opportunity of presenting ourselves in this house, consecrated to the worship of the God of our fathers, who has kindly raised up friends and patrons of the cause of our country and of liberty, to pay to you our grateful respect for your eminent labours.

"Most of those who acted in, or witnessed the great scenes

in which you bore so conspicuous a part, have now descended to the tombs of their fathers. The present generation can rehearse only what they have heard with their ears, and their fathers have told them. But the name of Lafayette is not confined to any generation. While the liberties of America shall endure, it will descend from father to son, associated with those of the immortal Washington, and other heroes and sages of our revolution, as the friend of our country, of liberty, and of man.

"Illustrious benefactor—may the blessings of heaven ever attend you, and may your remaining days be as happy, as your past have been perilous, useful, and honourable."

To which the General made the following reply :—

"Sir—The attentions paid me by my American friends, I receive with inexpressible gratitude. I regret that so many of my friends here, should be exposed on my account to this storm. I have ever considered it my pride and my honour; that I embarked in the cause of Independence in this country; and I rejoiced when I found myself again landed on the American shores. You, kind Sir, the people of this town, and all who are assembled in this solemn place, will please to accept my thanks for this expression of your attachment, and receive my best wishes for your individual prosperity and happiness."

He reached Newburyport a little past 10 o'clock, where he passed the night. His lodgings were the same which Washington occupied, when he made his tour through the northern states, in 1789, the first year of his presidency. The following address was made to him, by the chairman of a committee of that town :—

"General Lafayette—The citizens of Newburyport are happy in this opportunity of greeting, with the warmest welcome, a distinguished benefactor of their country.

"The important services which you rendered this people in the day of their distress; the devotedness which you manifested in their perilous cause, and the dangers which you *sought* for their relief, are incorporated in our history, and firmly engraven upon our hearts.

"We would lead you to our institutions of learning, charity, and religion; we would point you to our hills and valleys covered with flocks, and smiling in abundance, that you may behold the happy effects of those principles of liberty, which you was so instrumental in establishing.

"Our children cluster about you to receive a patriot's blessing. Our citizens press forward to show their gratitude. Our nation pays you a tribute, which must remove the reproach that republics are ungrateful.

"As the zealous advocate for civil liberty, we bid you welcome; as the brave defender of an oppressed people, we make you welcome; as the friend and associate of our immortal Washington, we bid you welcome."

General Lafayette replied in his usually courteous and animated manner, and evinced his great sensibility to the kind and friendly greetings with which he had been received. He here also met several veterans of the revolutionary army; a gratification which he enjoyed in almost every place he visited. Though the number is rapidly lessening, a few remain in most of the populous towns of the Commonwealth.

One of those presented to General Lafayette at this place, was Mr. Daniel Foster, one of the non-commissioned officers of the Light Infantry corps, commanded by "the Marquis" in 1780, and who brought with him the *cutlass* which he then gave to the non-commissioned officers of the select corps. [*He also made a present of a handsome cut-and-thrust sword to each Officer of the Light Infantry, his favourite corps.*"] The General greeted the old soldier with cordiality, and on seeing his own mark on the blade, assured him he looked upon him as "one of his own family."

He left Newburyport Wednesday morning for the capital of New-Hampshire. The escort contemplated to have attended him on his way to the bounds of the state, was prevented by the heavy rain. It was at his urgent request that it was dispensed with. The committee of the town, however, accompanied him to Hampton, where he was met by a deputation from Portsmouth, and conducted on his intended route. When passing through Greenland, a procession of the citizens was formed, by which he was attended through the village. Here he was welcomed also by salutes from an artillery company, by civic arches, and repeated acclamations of the assembled people. One of the arches was supported by two young ladies, representing Liberty and Peace. One presented him with a wreath, adorned with flowers, and said, "*Venerable sire, condescend to receive this emblem of the hero's glory, as the token of a nation's gratitude and love.*" The other presented him the olive branch, saying, "*Good and peaceful servant, peace and happi-*

ness await you." He received these with complacency, took each young lady by the hand, and made an affectionate reply.

He then proceeded to Portsmouth, where he arrived about noon. He was conducted into this town by an escort on horseback, and a procession of carriages, composed of the civil, judicial, and legislative authorities; officers of the United States, and of New-Hampshire, &c. &c. The margin of the avenue leading to the centre of the town, was lined with children, with the inhabitants of both sexes in the rear; who greeted him with their cordial welcomes and repeated acclamations. Salutes were fired, and the streets through which the procession passed, were crowned with arches, decorated with wreaths of ever-green and garlands of flowers. The procession moved through several streets to Franklin Hall: and here when General Lafayette alighted, the chairman of the Selectmen addressed him thus:—

"Sir—The Selectmen of Portsmouth, in behalf of their fellow citizens, most respectfully and heartily bid you welcome.

"Enjoying, as we do, the happiness of a free government, we cannot but feel grateful to all, by whose exertions it was obtained. Those intrepid men among ourselves, who in the hour of danger stood forth in defence of their country's rights, have a lasting claim upon our regard. But in contending for the liberty of their country, they were striving to secure their own happiness, and the prosperity of their children. *They* found a motive for exertion in their own interest; which, while it derogates nothing from the value of their services, places in light, the pure zeal and contempt of private advantage, which led *you* to our aid, from the shores of a foreign land. *Their* love of liberty was necessarily the sentiment of patriotism; *yours* was an ardent desire for the general welfare of mankind.

"After an absence of forty years from our country, most of which have been passed in scenes of unexampled excitement and perplexity, it gives us peculiar pleasure to find you still the firm and consistent friend of liberal principles. We have watched the progress of your eventful life with unaffected sympathy; whether at the head of the National Guards, in the dungeons of Magdeburg and Olmutz, in the Chamber of Deputies, we have found nothing to lessen our esteem for *the early friend of America.*

"Permit us then to receive you as our guest; and to pay you such honours as are in our power to bestow. They are the voluntary tribute of warm and grateful hearts. We wish our children to learn, that eminent virtue affords the highest claim to honourable distinction; and that among a free people, merit will not fail of its appropriate reward.

"We beg you to accept our sincere wishes for your health and happiness, and our prayers will be offered, that your example may animate the wise and good in every nation, to contend manfully and perseveringly for the freedom and happiness of the world."

To which the General made the following reply:—

"Gentlemen—It would have been to me an inexpressible gratification on this first visit to the eastern parts of the Union, after so long an absence, to have been able to present the several towns of New-Hampshire with my personal respect, and to have witnessed the great improvement of a State, to which I am bound by early sentiments of attachment and gratitude.

"Obliged, as I find myself, to take a southern course towards the seat of government, at Washington, I am happy to revisit, at least, the town of Portsmouth, where the remembrance of past favours mingles with most grateful feelings for your present affectionate and flattering reception.

"I thank you, gentlemen, for your constant concern in my behalf, during the vicissitudes to which you are pleased to allude. The approbation of a free, virtuous, and enlightened people, would be the highest reward for any one who knows how to value true glory; still more so, when it is bestowed on an adopted son.

"To the citizens of Portsmouth and their worthy Selectmen, I offer my most respectful and affectionate acknowledgments."

Governor Morril gave him the hearty welcome of the State, in the following address:—

"General—Forty years have rolled away since you left this asylum of liberty, for your country. During this eventful period our cities have advanced, and villages have been reared; but our Langdon, our Chilley, our Poor, our Sullivan, and our Washington, have passed from the stage of human action, and are gone to the land of their fathers. Although they are gone, their sons survive, and the patriotism and love of liberty which animated their breasts, and excited them to those glorious acts, during our revolution, in which you, Sir, shone so conspicuously, are now cherished in the bosoms of their posterity;—and we rejoice to be numbered among them;—and in the name of the patriotic citizens of New-Hampshire generally, allow me to say, that it is with no ordinary emotions we receive and welcome you to our State.

"We receive you, Sir, as the friend of our nation, of liberty, and the rights of man.

"We welcome you as the magnanimous hero, who in early life, from the most pure and disinterested motives, quitted your native country, and repaired to these Colonies, then the seat of war, (contending for independence,) to embark in the struggle for the preservation of those rights, and the achievement of those privileges, which are more precious to the patriot than life itself. And, Sir, it is our ardent desire, that the gratitude of republics, but more especially of the Republic of the United States, and the smiles of Heaven, may rest upon you to the last period of your life."

The General, in his characteristic reply, alluded very affectionately to his departed associates; and the interesting changes which had taken place since he left the country. It is not necessary to add, that he expressed with emotion his acknowledgments for the cordiality of his welcome.

Numerous presentations took place;—of which were at least thirty old soldiers. These scenes are always in the highest degree interesting and affecting. They are all *heart.* He recognised General Smith, of Portland, who served as Captain in his favourite Light Infantry for three years. On clasping the hands of these associates in perils and adversity, he continually repeats, "*I am very happy.*" The dinner was sumptuous.—The Hon. Mr. Parrott presided, assisted by N. A. Haven, E. Cutts, jun. E. G. Parrott, L. Boardman, B. Penhallaw, E. Roberts, W. M. Shackford, and S. Larkin, Esq'rs.

The President associated "General Lafayette and the Rights of Man."

General Lafayette responded—"the town of Portsmouth—May the blessings of the republican institutions ever give the lie to the narrow, selfish sophistry of European Aristocracy and Despotism."

There was a very splendid ball in the evening, in honour of Lafayette, which he attended and where a great number of ladies were presented to him. He left Portsmouth, 11 o'clock at night, to return to Boston, having engaged to be there on Thursday morning. While at Portsmouth he received pressing invitations to visit Exeter and Dover, but was obliged to decline them.

He reached Boston about 7 o'clock, Thursday morning, and after taking some necessary repose, he received a number of revolutionary officers and soldiers; and deputations from several towns in the interior, lying on his route to Connecticut. He then repaired to the Council Chamber, and took leave of the Governor and other members of the Supreme Executive: and afterwards set off for Lexington and Concord, and thence to Bolton, on his way to Worcester. He left Boston at about two o'clock, in a carriage provided by the State for his accommodation, and attended by the Committee of Arrangements of the city, and by the Governor's aids, who waited on him to the bounds of Connecticut. When he left the city, he expressed the gratification and delight he had experienced from the interesting recollections which had occurred to his mind, and from the great cordiality and affection with which he had been received. The Mayor assured him, that he and others were happy in the opportunity they had to manifest their attachment and respect to the early and faithful friend of the nation, and the firm and uniform friend of civil liberty.

When he passed through West Cambridge, the whole population of the town were assembled to honour the friend and guest of the nation, and to gratify their patriotic feelings by beholding this justly celebrated personage.

The civic arch which extended across the road near the meeting-house, in West Cambridge, bore this inscription:—

"Welcome! Friend of Washington!
Fayette! Fair Freedom's champion!"

Artillery corps stationed on the eminences adjoining the public road saluted him as he passed; and the country rung with loud huzzas and joyful acclamations. At the line of Lexington, he was received by a troop of horse, and cavalcade of citizens, who conducted him into that ancient town On his way, he passed under an arch, bearing this inscription:—"*Welcome, friend of America, to the birth-place of American liberty.*" Salutes were again fired, and he was then conducted to the monument erected in memory of the attack of the

British troops upon the militia of that place, April 19th, 1775. He was here welcomed and addressed by E. Phinney, Esq. in behalf of the town, as follows :—

"General—In behalf of the Committee of Arrangements, and the inhabitants of Lexington, allow me, Sir, to tender you the assurance of their most respectful and cordial welcome to this town. Impressed with a sense of the important services you have rendered to this country, they meet you on this occasion, and upon this memorable spot, with hearts swelling with every emotion which a generous love for your exalted character, and a grateful remembrance of the distinguished lustre of your deeds, can inspire.

"On this hallowed ground, consecrated by the blood of the first martyrs to liberty, was kindled that flame which roused a nation to arms, and conducted them through peril and blood, to a glorious independence. Here a small band of patriots, hurled the first signal of defiance to a host in arms, and taught the enemies of their country, the appaling truth, that Americans dared to die in defence of their rights.

"These hardy and virtuous yeomanry of our country, offer you the sincere tribute of their warmest affections. Among them, your presence has awakened emotions too powerful for utterance. With the name of Lafayette, is associated every comfort which sweetens the fruit of their toil, every charm which crowns the altar of domestic happiness. Under the shadow of that glorious fabric, which your hand assisted in rearing, they repose in peace and security.

"Permit us, Sir, in common with grateful millions, to express our earnest solicitations, that a life which has, for so many years, been steadily devoted to the cause of rational liberty; which has so long encountered without dismay the frowns of arbitrary power, may be preserved for many years to come, a blessing and an honour to mankind; and when you, Sir, and your brave associates in the war of the revolution, shall have ceased from your earthly labours, instead of the Fathers, may their children rise up to bless your memory, and emulate your virtues."

The General in his reply, alluded with sensibility to the pleasure he felt in being able so early to visit scenes so memorable.

Near the monument, he was introduced to *fourteen* of the militia company, which had assembled at that time, and on whom the regular troops fired, when eight of the number were slain.

After this very interesting scene, General Lafayette proceeded to Concord, and was met at the line, between that place and Lexington, by a committee of the town, and a respectable cavalcade of the intelligent yeomanry of the vicinity; there was also an escort composed of several companies of the militia. The procession thus formed, moved towards the village, and the disinterested visiter was conducted to a spacious bower, prepared for his reception, and tastefully decorated with ever-greens and flowers, by the ladies of Concord. As he entered the village, he received a salute from the artillery corps, and the vocal salutations of the inhabitants of both sexes, who had assembled to present him their grateful offerings. The peals of the village bell prolonged the acclamations of the admiring throng. The following inscription was to be seen in a conspicuous place in the arbour—"*In* 1775, *the people of Concord met the enemies of liberty; In* 1824, *they welcome the bold asserter of the rights of man,* LAFAYETTE." A sumptuous repast was provided for the occasion; and the tables were covered with all the delicacies the season and country could afford.

When General Lafayette had entered the arbour, one of the citizens addressed him in the following speech:—

"The inhabitants of Concord, by this delegation, welcome you, General, to their village. We thank you for affording us an opportunity here to offer our humble tribute of gratitude, for services long since rendered, but still held in lively recollection. You, Sir, now behold the *spot on which the first forcible resistance* was made to a system of measures calculated to deprive the whole people of these States of the privileges of freemen. You approved this resistance. A just estimate of the value of rational liberty led you disinterestedly, to participate with strangers in the toils, the privations, and the dangers of an arduous contest. From the 19th day of April, 1775, here noted in blood, to the memorable day in Yorktown, your heart and your sword were with us. Ten millions of grateful people now enjoy the fruits of this struggle. We can but repeat to you, Sir, the cordial, affectionate, respectful welcome offered you at your first arrival on our shores, and which we are assured will be reiterated wherever you move on American ground."

The General was, as usual, extremely happy in his reply, and alluded with sensibility to the memorable scenes of April 19th, 1775.

The ladies of Concord and vicinity, were present at this civic and patriotic repast; and it added much to the interest and splendour of the scene. Coffee was served up, as a counter-part of the entertainment; and Lafayette appeared to be highly pleased with the hearty reception which he met in this hospitable town. Some revolutionary characters called upon him here, who had not before seen him since he arrived, and were received with great cordiality. He spoke of the gun which had been shown him in Boston, by an inhabitant of Concord or vicinity, and which was first fired against the ministerial troops of Britain. He said "it was the alarm gun to all Europe and to the world; for it was the signal, which summoned the civilized world to assert their rights, and to become free."

The visit at Concord was necessarily short, as he had engaged to pass the night at Bolton, about twenty miles distant. He left Concord at sun-set; and was escorted on his route to Bolton, by a company of cavalry, and several gentlemen of distinction belonging to that place and vicinity. He was every where greeted by the people, who collected in companies at various places, to offer him their hearty welcome. The houses on the road were illuminated, and bonfires were kindled on the adjoining hills. The militia of Bolton were assembled to receive him, though it was late in the evening when he arrived. The Selectmen offered him their salutations and welcome, in the name of the town. He passed the night at the hospitable mansion of Mr. Wilder, where taste, variety, and elegance, contributed to render his reception very distinguished. Mr. Wilder had resided much in France, and was particularly acquainted with Lafayette and family. Committees from Lancaster and Worcester waited on him at Bolton, to learn his plans, and the probable hours of his being in those places, and to communicate the desires of the people, to present him their tribute of affection and regard.

He visited Lancaster early on Friday morning, where all classes of the inhabitants were assembled to bid him welcome, and to express the affectionate sentiments by which their glowing bosoms were animated. A corps of cavalry still escorted him—a national salute was fired—and the turnpike gate, at the entrance of the village, was ornamented with garlands of flowers and ever-greens, and displayed this inscription:—" *The* FREE *welcome the* BRAVE." He was conducted through lines, formed by the citizens of both sexes, to an elevated platform, prepared in the centre of the village, and near the church; where he was addressed by the Reverend Pastor—

"General Lafayette—In behalf of the inhabitants of Lancaster, I offer you their cordial congratulations on your arrival in a country, whose wrongs you felt and resented; whose liberties you so valiantly defended; and whose interests and prospects have always been dear to your soul.

"We all unite with the few surviving veterans, who were with, loved, and respected you on the high places of the field, in giving you a welcome to this village, once the chosen residence of savages, and the scene of their most boasted triumph; and rejoice that you visit it under the improvements of civilized life, in prosperity and peace.

"It gladdens us, that we and our children may behold the man, whom we have believed, and whom we have taught them to believe, was second only to his and our friend, the immortal Washington. We participate in your joy, on beholding our institutions in vigour, our population extended, so that, since you left us, from a little one we have become millions, and from a small band a strong nation; that you see our glory rising, our republic placed on an immoveable basis, all of which are in part, under Providence, to be ascribed to your sacrifices, dangers, and toils.

"We wish you health and prosperity. We assure you that wherever you shall go, you will be greeted by our fellow countrymen, as one of the chief deliverers of America, and the friend of rational liberty, and of man. It is especially our prayer, that on that day in which the acclamations and applauses of dying men shall cease to reach or affect you, you may receive from the Judge of character and Dispenser of imperishable honours, as the reward of philanthropy and incorruptible integrity, a crown of glory which shall never fade."

It is unnecessary to add, that this eloquent and pious greeting excited strong emotions in the General, and had an impressive effect on the assemblage who heard it.

The following is a report of General Lafayette's reply:—

"Accept my thanks, Sir, for the kind welcome you have offered me in the name of the inhabitants of Lancaster. In returning to this country after so long an absence; in receiving such proofs of gratitude and affection wherever I go; in witnessing the prosperity of this land—a prosperity you are pleased to say, I have been instrumental in promoting;—I feel emotions for which no language is adequate. In meeting again my former friends, in seeing the children and grand children of those who were my companions in the war of the revolution, I feel a gratification which no words can express. I beg you to accept, Sir, and to offer to these people, my grateful, my affectionate acknowledgments."

The surviving soldiers of the revolution were then introduced to him, and were received with those cordial and touching feelings, which cannot be described. He noticed with affability the interest which the ladies discovered in pressing forward to greet him. After receiving attentions, and reciprocating heart-felt delight, for about fifteen minutes, he remounted his carriage, and pursued his journey, amidst cordial huzzas and a salute of artillery.

His approach to the flourishing village of Sterling was announced by a salute of artillery, and he was introduced by two beautiful companies of Light Infantry, under Captain Dana, of Sterling, and Captain Merriam, of Princeton. Under a spacious arch of ever-greens and flowers, bearing a label in gold capitals,

"WELCOME LAFAYETTE;
America's adopted Son,
Brother and friend of WASHINGTON.
Our land in trouble found a friend in thee,
We'll not forget thee in prosperity."

He was met by the Selectmen, who, by their Chairman, Mr. Isaac Goodwin, addressed him as follows:—

"General Lafayette—The Selectmen in behalf of the citizens of Sterling, welcome your arrival at their village. The name of this town associates with it the recollection of another transatlantic hero, who like yourself, Sir, felt a sympathy for our father's wrongs, and whose sword was unsheathed for their redress. Lord Sterling, the gallant and the generous, now sleeps in the dust, but the memory of America's benefactors will survive the decay of time. The multitudes that hail your march through this part of our country are not the assemblages of idle crowds, seeking to gratify a morbid curiosity, but, Sir, the men around you are the independent possessors of their fields, and the defenders of their homes. From hoary age to lisping childhood, our whole population are eager of contributing deserved honours to the companion of WASHINGTON, the benefactor of our country, and the friend of mankind."

To which, in substance, the General replied :—

"I feel grateful for my kind reception here. I rejoice in your prosperity, and am happy to be among you. The name of your town recalls the recollection of Lord Sterling. He was my intimate friend as well as companion in arms. I venerate his memory, and when in New-York I had the pleasure of calling upon his family."

After reviewing the troops composed of Artillery, commanded by Captain Maynard, Light Infantry, and Infantry, the latter commanded by Captain Holcomb, he continued his journey.

At West Boylston his welcome was cordial and gratifying; although his stop was necessarily very short. Another corps of cavalry, under Captain Estabrook, joined the splendid military escort. He was accompanied the whole distance from Boylston to Worcester by many citizens from the neighbouring towns.

The General entered the limits of Worcester about half past 10 o'clock, and was welcomed by a general burst of joy from a large body of citizens. Here, a barouche drawn by four beautiful grays was in readiness to receive him. He was accompanied in the barouche by the Honourable John Lincoln, Chairman of the Committee of Arrangements.

On the road the escort was joined by a regiment of volunteer Infantry, under Lieutenant Colonel Ward. The road was thronged with people, all eager to greet the welcome Visiter. When the Guest arrived at an arch of colours, near Doctor Paine's residence, he was welcomed by a salute, the ringing of the bells, and increased cheerings of the accumulated population. The gray-headed Veterans of the Revolution, regardless of ceremony, pressed up to the barouche to shake hands as he passed along. Upon Court hill he passed under a triumphal arch, so tastefully decorated by the Ladies as to attract the admiration of all who saw it. The children of the Schools, ranged in interesting order, and ornamented with LAFAYETTE badges, threw laurels in his path, as he passed. These scenes are always peculiarly impressive on the heart. On a string of colours, extended across the street near the Bank, was the historical motto :—*Hitherto I have only cherished your cause,* NOW *I go to serve it.*" Alluding to his reply to the American Commissioners in France, in 1776. Underneath were inscribed :—

"BRANDYWINE, JAMESTOWN, VALLEY-FORGE, YORKTOWN."

At these spots the cheering was increased and prolonged.

He took breakfast, by previous invitation given at Bolton, with Judge Lincoln's Lady, whose spacious mansion, elegantly decorated, had been thrown open, and was filled to overflowing with Ladies, who greeted their Country's Benefactor with smiles and tears, while their handkerchiefs were waved in token of welcome. Before breakfasting, Judge Lincoln delivered in an animated and impressive manner, the following address :—

"General Lafayette—

"The citizens whom you see assembled around you, have spontaneously thronged together, to offer you the tribute of their affection, their respect, their gratitude.

"In the name of the inhabitants of Worcester, the *shire* of an extensive county of more than 75,000 population, in behalf of all who are present, and in anticipation of the commands of those, whom distance and want of opportunity occasion to be absent from this joyous scene, I repeat to you the salutations, which elsewhere have been so impressively offered, upon your arrival in this country, and your visit to this Commonwealth. Welcome, most cordially welcome, to the presence of those who now greet you!

"Your name, Sir, is not only associated with the memorable events of the American Revolution, with the Battle of Brandywine, the retreat from Valley-Forge, the affair near Jamestown, and the triumph at Yorktown, but the memorials of *your* services and *our* obligations exist, in the Independence of the nation which was accomplished, in the Government of the people which is established, in the Institutions and Laws, the arts, improvements, liberty, and happiness, which are enjoyed. The *Sword* was beaten into the *Plough-share* to cultivate the soil which its temper had previously defended, and the hill-tops shall now echo to the sea-shore the gratulations of the independent proprietors of the land, to the common Benefactor of all ranks and classes of the people.

"Wherever you go, General, the acclamations of Freemen await you—their blessings and prayers will follow you. May you live many years to enjoy the fruits of the services and sacrifices, the gallantry and valour of your earlier days, devoted to the cause of freedom and the rights of man; and may the bright examples of individual glory and of National happiness, which the history of America exhibits, illustrate to the world, the moral force of *personal* virtue, and the rich blessings of civil liberty in Republican Governments."

The General, in reply, said, in substance :—

"That he received with much sensibility the expressions of kind attention with which he was received by the Inhabitants of the town and county of Worcester—that he was delighted with the fine country which he had seen, and the excellent improvement and cultivation which he witnessed—that he saw the best proofs of a great, prosperous, and happy people, in the rapid advancement of the polite and useful arts, and in the stability of our free institutions—that he was especially much gratified in the great improvements of the face of the country, because he was himself a farmer—that he felt happy to observe such decided proofs of industry, sobriety, and prosperity.—He begged the citizens to be assured of his affectionate and grateful recollection of their reception of him—he thanked them for all they had manifested towards him, for the kind expressions which had been offered him by the committee, and, in a feeling, impressive manner, reciprocated their good wishes."

After the introduction of numerous Ladies, the troops paid him their honours, and received evidence of his satisfaction at their soldier-like appearance and conduct. He resumed his journey between 2 and 3 o'clock, and was accompanied by the Committee of Arrangements some miles on his way. On this occasion, speaking of the attentions he received, he remarked, "It is the homage you pay to the *principles* of your government, and not to *me*."

A company of Cavalry was sent from Sturbridge to escort the General from Charlton, and a company of Artillery was paraded to give him the usual salute. As soon as he came within sight of the village, which was about two miles distant, the marshals of the day arranged the Ladies and Citizens in columns two deep, and ten or twelve feet distant, extending from Porter's Stage-house across the Common, and continuing some distance down the turnpike. Where the road meets the Common, two pillars had been erected about thirty feet in height, which supported a line tastefully ornamented with ever-greens, festoons, flowers, and flags. Rows of ever-greens were planted, forming a beautiful walk, within which the spectators were arranged. As the Marquis and his suite came up to the head of the procession, he was received from his coach by a committee, and introduced to a few citizens, when he proceeded up the procession, attended by a band of music, his suite, the delegation from Worcester, the Clergy, and Committee of Arrangements; the columns of spectators remaining on their posts. At a signal, cheers were given with all the ardour of enthusiastic patriotism. During the intervals there was a profound silence, and the most perfect order, except the reiterated echo of "Welcome LAFAYETTE, Friend of America," &c. announced by single voices.

Near the middle of the procession, and within the lines, were arranged a large company of revolutionary officers and soldiers, some of whom had served under Lafayette. To each one the General was introduced. The scene was touching. As they grasped the hand of the venerable Hero, in a number of instances the tear was seen to roll down the furrowed cheek of the veteran soldier. Many seemed unable to reply to the kind expressions of their beloved Marquis, who himself was deeply affected. A thrill of feeling indescribably tender pervaded the numerous spectators. A number of ladies there had the opportunity of taking him by the hand, who were in numerous instances melted to tears at the expressions of his kind regards, together with the interesting associations which his presence awakened. A company of small misses dressed in white, and decorated with garlands and flowers, attracted his attention, and reached out their little hands to be received in his. He then passed into the house amidst the most animated cheers and a thousand benedictions.—The whole was a scene of feeling, in which all the people seemed to be wrought up to the extreme of exquisite emotion. Never did we witness any thing that wore so much the aspect of the moral sublime. Gratitude, veneration, sympathy, and affection, all combining in vigorous exercise, created a state of mind, such as very rarely exists, and which can be better conceived than described.

General Lafayette was to have been received on the northern line of Connecticut by a troop of horse from Tolland county, but it being uncertain what time he would be detained on the road, the troops after waiting a suitable time returned to their homes. Fourteen miles from Hartford he was met by the first company of Governor's Horse Guards, commanded by Major Hart. The General was expected in town on Friday evening, and preparations were made to illuminate Morgan-street, Main-street, and State House Square, the commencement of which was to have been announced to the citizens by two discharges of artillery. The evening was dark and rainy; but notwithstanding the unfavourable circumstance, our streets were crowded with anxious and inquisitive spectators, consisting not only of our citizens, but visiters from a distance and the surrounding country. About 12 o'clock a discharge of guns from the out skirts of the town, or from East-Hartford, (for we could not say which,) announced, as was supposed by many, the approach of the General. "He is coming," was shouted by thousands—instantly the houses and stores of many of our citizens, particularly about State House Square, presented the most grand and beautiful display of the light that can be imagined. The Hartford Bank, from the taste with which it was decorated, and the brilliant light which broke through from the windows attracted numerous spectators; the elegant columns of free stone in front of the building were entwined with wreaths of ever-green, interspersed with flowers of various colours, and the doors arched and festooned with similar materials. A superb arch was erected on the west side of the State House, adorned with ever-greens; upon a transparent ground was inscribed "*Welcome Lafayette*"—within the scroll, at one end of the arch, was the inscription "*York-Town*"—upon the other "*Monmouth.*" This transparent painting was brilliantly illuminated. The State House and Phenix Bank, with many elegant mansions in different parts of the city, where preparations were made for a brilliant display of fire works, were disappointed in this expression of joy, by the arrival of a messenger, about one o'clock, with the intelligence that the General would sleep at Stafford, about twenty-six miles from the town—the lights were suddenly extinguished, and the citizens retired to rest for the night. The sound of cannon again aroused us from sleep at dawn of day, and though the weather continued inclement, people poured into the city through every street. About 10 o'clock, A. M. a discharge of artillery, and the ringing of all the bells, put it beyond a doubt that the General had indeed arrived. A carriage was furnished by Dame. Wadsworth, Esq. who, with Henry L. Ellsworth, Esq one of the city committee, had attended him from Stafford. He passed the bridge across Connecticut river attended by his son George Washington Lafayette, Mr. Vasseur, his secretary, and Mr. Colden, under the escort of the First Company of Horse Guards. At the entrance of Morgan-street was erected an elegant arch, extending across the road, composed of evergreens, with an inscription, "*Our Illustrious Citizen, Lafayette,*" upon canvass—this again was surmounted with American colours. The procession moved up Morgan-street, to its intersection with Main-street; here the crowded assemblage of citizens commenced the acclamations of "*Welcome Lafayette.*" As the General with his escort moved leisurely down Main street, towards the State-House, shouts of loud huzzas greeted him at every step. The General answered this tribute of joy with bows and smiles, and a waving of the hand—he alighted at Bennet's Hotel, where he was received by the Mayor of the City, and His Excellency Governor Wolcott. The following address was presented by the Mayor in behalf of the city corporation :—

"General Lafayette—In behalf of my fellow-citizens, I bid you a cordial *Welcome*, to the city of Hartford : a place many years since honoured by your presence ; and though most of those individuals, whose exertions were then united with yours to effect the freedom and independence of this favoured country have been removed ; still I trust you will discover in their descendants the same spirit of hospitality and patriotism, for which they were distinguished.

"This occasion, Sir, is peculiarly calculated to recall to mind, those great and interesting events, which have taken place since your first efforts in favour of an infant country, with *feeble means* contending against superior and lawless powers.

"Your marshal deeds, your counsels, and personal sacrifices, have always been felt and acknowledged, by the people of the United States, and esteemed as signally instrumental, in effecting their independence, and securing those blessings which they now enjoy.

"The best reward, for all this, I doubt not, you will find, in beholding the country filled with flourishing towns and villages, inhabited by freemen, possessed of the knowlede of their native rights, and in a condition to protect and defend them ; exhibiting universal and unequivocal proofs of sincere affection and gratitude, to the *illustrious Benefactor* of their country.

"The names of Washington and Lafayette, with the present, and all future generations, will be associated, with liberty, freedom, and happiness.

"While expressing these sentiments, permit me to add my sincere personal wishes for your prosperity; that your stay in our country may be long and happy, and that the best of Heaven's blessings may ever attend you."

At the Hotel the General partook of a repast ordered by the Corporation, at which the Governor, Mayor, and Common Council, with several other distinguished citizens and strangers were invited guests. After resting about an hour, a barouche drawn by four elegant white horses, emblematical of the joyous occasion, received the General, accompanied by the Governor, from whence they proceeded to review the troops. As the carriage commenced its movements up Main-street, we were struck with a reflection upon the interesting coincidence, that on this very spot where stood his carriage, General Washington first met General Rochambeau, at the head of the French army, after their arrival from France to aid in the cause of the revolution. Here Washington and Hamilton, and several other American officers first shook hands in the presence of Lafayette, with the officers of the French army. This place too, was in front of the mansion where those officers convened from day to day to project and mature the siege of York-Town, which ended in securing our independence—the parent of those joys which this day lighted up the countenances of so many thousands. This surely was hallowed ground. The General's carriage was attended by others, in which were his son George Washington Lafayette, and the General's Secretary, Mr. Vasseur, Mr. Colden, General Terry, and others of the Committee of Arrangements. As he began to move, the immense multitude gave nine cheers. The military was supposed to exceed one thousand, under the command of General Johnson. We cannot detail the order of the military procession, nor could we do justice to their merits. It was difficult for the military to make its way through the immense crowd; every window was crowded with ladies, waving their white handkerchiefs to the General. As he passed the north line of the State-House, the procession wheeled towards State-street, and having reached the front of the State-House, the General with his escort alighted and was conducted within the railing, where was an assemblage of children of about eight hundred; the misses all dressed in white, wearing badges with the motto, "*Nous vous aimons* LAFAYETTE." A gold medal was presented him by one of the children, which was enclosed in a paper containing these lines:—

Welcome thou to freedom's clime,
Glorious Hero! Chief sublime!
Garlands bright for thee are wreath'd,
Vows of filial ardour breath'd,
Veteran's cheeks with tears are wet,
"*Nous vous aimons* LAFAYETTE."

Monmouth's field is rich with bloom,
Where thy warriors found their tomb,
York-Town's heights resound no more,
Victor's shout our cannon roar,
Yet our hearts record their debt,
"*We do love you* LAFAYETTE."

Brandywine, whose current roll'd
Proud with blood of heroes bold.
That our country's debt shall tell,
That our gratitude shall swell,
Infant breasts thy wounds regret,
"*We do love you* LAFAYETTE."

Sires, who sleep in glory's bed,
Sires, whose blood for us was shed,
Taught us, when our knee we bend,
With the prayer thy name to blend;
Shall we e'er such charge forget?
No!—"*Nous vous aimons* LAFAYETTE."

When our blooming cheeks shall fade,
Pale with time, or sorrow's shade,
When our clustering tresses fair,
Frosts of wintry age shall wear,
E'en till memory's sun be set,
"*We shall love you* LAFAYETTE."

The General was then conducted into the Senate Chamber, which was tastefully decorated with various ever-greens, where the Governor addressed the General, as follows:—

"Dear General—I rejoice in this opportunity of renewing to you my salutations in this ancient capital of Connecticut, where a virtuous and enlightened people, have, during nearly two centuries, enjoyed republican institutions, which were devised by themselves, and which have been administered by agents, annually designated by their voluntary suffrages. The principles which you have advocated in council and defended in the field, have been here triumphantly established, and by the favour of Heaven, we hope to transmit them, unimpaired, to our latest posterity.

"These principles are now diffused on every side, from the ocean to the high plains of the Missouri; and from the lakes to the gulf of Mexico. Over this great region, our sons and our daughters, parents of future millions, are rapidly extending science, religion, industry, and all those arts which perpetuate and embellish powerful communities.—Literature and commerce augment our strength and resources. We are united with elevated spirits from every country, who have come here to enjoy all that freedom of opinion and of action, with which our own minds are imbued. You can proceed to no spot where you will not be met by Patriots, who have aided your exertions in both hemispheres, or by their admiring relations, and in every class you will find an interesting proportion of Frenchmen, including numbers of the descendants of those early emigrants, who imbibed the liberal and gallant spirit of your Fourth Henry. Every class of citizens will instantly recognise in you an illustrious benefactor of the United States, and of mankind, and they will unite in spontaneous benedictions, with ardent invocations to the Supreme Being, that your life may be prosperous, with a happy transition to a glorious immortality."

The following is in substance the verbal reply of General Lafayette:—

"Sir—I feel very happy in viewing such resources of strength in New-England; which resources should be cherished with union, as there is such a powerful opposition abroad to your free principles. I am delighted with the manifestations of feeling shown towards me;—Pleased with the moral habits and character of the people of the State, exhibiting in action a *pure* Republic. I am also highly gratified with the fine appearance of your Military."

The ladies were introduced to the General, and taken by the hand in the most affectionate manner; but the want of time would not permit the introduction of a large concourse who crowded at the doors for admission. From this interesting ceremony, the General proceeded to review the troops, taking his station upon a platform under the elegant arch, erected at the west front of the State-House. The General surveyed the troops, apparently with the attentive eye of an officer long accustomed to command. He discovered much satisfaction at their elegant appearance, and was heard to say, particularly of the Governor's Foot Guards, commanded by Major Olmsted that it was equal in discipline and appearance to any company he had ever seen. A company of old revolutionary officers and soldiers consisting of about eighty, and commanded by Judge Hillyer, passed in review near the platform, and each of them shook hands with the General. It is impossible to refuse these veterans a share in the honours of the day. There was a rush from every quarter to witness this scene—many of these had been wounded—some with one eye—and the health of all, more or less impaired in the services of their country. No! Soldiers of the revolution, your country will never forget that to you, under the guidance of Providence, and led on by Washington and Lafayette, they owe the blessings of liberty and independence. Several old men were introduced to the General in the course of the day, whom he seemed, from their respectable deportment, to recognise as fellow-soldiers. One instance was noticed in particular, where the General observed, "I think, Sir, you belonged to the revolutionary corps."—"Yes, Sir," was the answer. From the review of the troops, the General was conducted to his barouche, and again passed down Main-street to the Hotel, and from thence was escorted on foot, to the mansion of Daniel Wadsworth, Esq. Here a committee of gentlemen presented him with the sash worn by him at the battle of Brandywine, which was used to bind up the wound he received, and afterwards presented by him to General Swift, of Cornwall. He thanked the gentlemen who presented it for their attention. After spreading and observing it critically, with a cheerful smile, he returned it to the committee. The General expected to have gone through Wethersfield, (where preparations had been made to receive him in a handsome manner, and under an elegant arch,) on his way to Middletown; but his engagements to be in New-York, and his extreme fatigue, would not allow of his complying with this arrangement. The steam-boat had now been waiting for three hours beyond its stated time. It became necessary to hurry his departure. Having taken leave of the gentlemen and ladies present, he was attended by some of the Committee of Arrangements to the steam-boat, which left here about 4 o'clock, P. M. amidst the salutes of cannon, and the shouts of thousands of gratified and grateful spectators.

The General and his suite arrived at Middletown, Upper Houses, about 6 o'clock.—When the Boat first appeared, a salute of 13 guns was fired.—At the landing place, he was received by a deputation, consisting of thirteen distinguished citizens of Middletown, with the first Marshal; and escorted by a squadron of cavalry, commanded by Colonel R. Wilcox, proceeded to the bridge which crosses the northern line of the city.—He was here received by the corps of Artillery, Riflemen, and Light Infantry, under the command of Colonel Walter Boothe, of the 10th Regiment of Infantry, who joined in escorting him to the large and elegant building occupied by Mr. Charles Francis, where preparations had been made for giving him an elegant dinner. The windows and tops of houses were thronged with females, who were constantly waving their handkerchiefs, as expressive of their feelings at seeing him. On his arrival at the house, he was addressed by the Mayor, to which he made an appropriate reply. After which the Mayor presented him to the several members of the Common Council, gentlemen of the Clergy, and the veterans of the Revolution. He was then persuaded to take a seat in the Barouche, and was escorted through the principal streets in the city; the houses were brilliantly illuminated, and added much to the magnificence of the scene. On his arrival at the Boat, he was cheered by the multitude who had followed him. At 7 o'clock he again embarked on the beautiful Connecticut, and though the evening was lowering, all the villages on the river were illuminated, bands of music were playing, and cannon firing. Mr. Ellsworth, one of the liberal proprietors of the Boat, had also provided a band which answered the salutes from the shore. Before reaching Saybrook, the weather cleared, the moon burst forth in its calm and serene splendour, to witness the enthusiasm of the ladies of that and the neighbouring towns, who, though it was late at night, were drawn up, dressed in white, on a platform, and music, cannon, and brilliant illuminations, were prepared to honour the Guest of the Nation. He then tranquilly and safely descended the Sound.

CHAPTER II.

PROCEEDINGS IN NEW-YORK ON THE GENERAL'S RETURN FROM HIS EASTERN VISIT—HIS JOURNEY UP THE HUDSON RIVER.

General Lafayette returned from his Eastern tour, and landed in New-York, from on board of the Steam-Boat Oliver Ellsworth, September 5, about 1 o'clock, P. M. A national salute was fired from the Franklin 74, at the Navy Yard, as he passed. The citizens along the shores and wharves of East River, for two miles, kept up a continued acclamation for the whole distance. The Oliver Ellsworth was decorated with flags, and had on board a fine band of music. He was received at the Fulton-street wharf by the Committee of the Corporation, and conducted to his lodgings at the City Hotel. The streets were filled with people, whose anxiety to see him was unabated.

The anniversary of the birth-day of Lafayette, the 6th September, when he attained his 67th year, having been selected by the Cincinnati veterans, to give him a dinner, he was escorted, at the appointed hour, to Washington Hall, by the Lafayette Guards. The room was splendidly and tastefully decorated: over the head of the General was sprung a triumphal arch of laurels and ever-greens, in the centre of which appeared a large American eagle, with a scroll in its beak bearing the words "September 6th, 1757," (the day and year in which he was born.) On its right, a scroll bearing, "Brandywine, 11th September, 1777;" on its left, "York-Town, 19th October, 1781." In the rear of the General's chair was planted the grand standard of the Society, entwined with the national colour of thirteen stripes. On the right was a shield bearing a rising sun; on the left, a shield with the State Arms. In the centre of the room there was a splendid star, studded with others of less magnitude. From this star two broad pendants from the Franklin 74, were crossed and carried to the four corners of the room. At the lower end of the room was a most exquisite transparency, executed by Childs, representing the Goddess of Liberty, with an eagle holding a wreath of laurels. In her left hand was a scroll with the word "WELCOME." On its right was a column, on which was placed forty muskets, forty pistols, and forty swords; on its left a similar one; beneath it a shield with thirteen American stripes, and thirteen stars supported by two six-pounders, as likewise a coat of mail of steel, such as were worn by Napoleon's cuirassiers; and on the right and left ten field drums. Around the room were tastefully displayed 60 banners, bearing the names of distinguished officers of the revolution, who had fallen in battle, together with the regimental standards of the corps of artillery, and a number of trophies of our navy, which were handsomely tendered by Captain Rogers, and Lieutenant Goldsborough.

Colonel Varick, the President of the Society, presided at the table, assisted by General Clarkson, Colonel Fish, General S. Van Rensselaer, Colonel Troup, and several other distinguished officers.

On Tuesday, at 11 o'clock, General Lafayette, accompanied by the Mayor, the Committee, and several other members of the Corporation, visited Columbia College. He was introduced into the College by Colonel Fish, Chairman of the board of Trustees, and received in the library by the President and faculty. President Harris then delivered a very appropriate address; to which the General made a very pertinent reply.

On Wednesday, at 1 o'clock, the General embarked on board the Chancellor Livingston, to visit the fortifications of the harbour, and was received as he entered, by the West Point Band, sent down for the occasion, playing a fine military piece composed by their leader, Willis. Among the guests were the members of the Cincinnati, the Officers of the Navy, the Corporation, and the General Officers of the Militia. Owing to the rain, the party did not land at Governor's Island, but a salute was fired from the Castle, as the Chancellor passed. On nearing the fortress at the Narrows, that bears the name of our Guest, the sun burst forth for awhile, and as the boat approached, another pealing salute from the heavy cannon there mounted, awoke the echos of the neighbouring heights, and told that HE was come. The General was escorted on shore by Colonels Maccrea and Bankhead, and received at the portal by Major Gates, commanding the fortress, who conducted him to the square, where the garrison, consisting of only a company of United States artillerists, saluted him. The whole party were then conducted around the fort, and no little admiration was expressed, at its massive and almost impregnable walls, its firm and deep set arches, and apparent power, both for offensive and defensive war. A sumptuous table was spread, loaded with cold dishes, fruits, and every variety of delicacy, and tastefully ornamented. Over head and around it, was a continued drapery of flags, the standards of the United States and of France being intertwined, and forming an arch over the seat assigned to Lafayette. Between the colours shone forth the brightly burnished muskets of the soldiers, with their other accoutrements; and on the table itself were smaller silken flags, bearing the inscriptions of the memorable names and deeds of the revolution. One in particular, in front of

Lafayette, bore on it, "Brandywine," "Monmouth," and "York-Town."

The associations of this entertainment were most delightful. It seemed as if the men of two ages had met to do honour to one whose name shall live through all time. At the head of the table, where Colonel Maccrea presided, sat Lafayette, and his old associates of the Cincinnati. At the foot, Colonel Bankhead, with George W. Lafayette, and the officers of the army, most of them young men. The interval was occupied by the guests generally. The soldiers of other days, and the soldiers of this, together with those who owe to the one the possession, and to the other the preservation of their independence, all united in homage to the friend of Washington, the companion of Hamilton, the pure and virtuous Lafayette.

On Thursday the Fire Department mustered to the utmost of their strength, and paraded in the park, where the General, (after returning from the Oratorio given by the Choral Society in St. Paul's Church,) viewed their engines, and the other apparatus belonging to the dauntless guardians of the city.

All the Fire Engines in the city, amounting to 44, with hook and ladder companies, and two engines from Brooklyn, were arranged in a line around the park, and all the Firemen stood a little in advance, holding their drag ropes. After passing round the line, the General returned to the hall, and made his appearance on the piazza, where he remained in company with Thomas Franklin, Chief Engineer, and many ladies and gentlemen, to witness the exhibition.

In the centre of the Park, the ladders of the company were erected in the form of a Pyramid, on the top of which was placed a miniature house, filled with combustibles. The Engines having all approximated the centre, to within a suitable distance, and having been charged with water, at a signal the house was fired, and forty-six powerful water spouts were all directed at the object in an instant. The spectacle for the moment was beautiful beyond description. Such was the skill of the engineers that every spout seemed to strike the common centre, and a mighty fountain in the form of a colossal column, or cone, was thus, as if by enchantment, in the twinkling of an eye, beheld rushing up and descending like a shower of liquid silver. When the sun shone out the fountain sparkled all over like a palace of ice, or a magnificent dome of crystal; and the wind now and then blew upon the spray and carried off a cloud of vapour: the arch of a rainbow appeared above, with all its brilliant colours. The engines appeared to great advantage; they were all in the finest order.

On Friday, in pursuance of an invitation from the Trustees of the Free Schools of New-York, the General visited some of the Schools, and afterwards reviewed the whole collected for that purpose in the Park.

A large class of the scholars in the female school recited the following lines:—

Welcome HERO, to the West,
To the land thy sword hath blest!
To the country of the *Free*,
Welcome, *Friend of Liberty!*

Grateful millions guard thy fame,
Age and youth revere thy name,
Beauty twines the wreath for thee,
Glorious *Son of Liberty!*

Years shall speak a nation's love,
Wheresoe'er thy footsteps move,
By the choral pæan met—
Welcome, welcome, *Lafayette!*

At one o'clock, the General, by particular invitation, visited the African Free School, which embraces 7 or 800 scholars; about 450 were present on the occasion. Here it was announced to him that under the Presidency of the Honourable John Jay, in 1788, he was elected an Honorary member of this Society, which the Marquis well recollected.

The General then retired to his lodgings for a few moments, until the children of all the schools could be assembled in the Park; he then returned and reviewed the whole, to the number of about 5000, arranged by their teachers in regular order, and surrounded by at least 5000 spectators. The scene was truly interesting, and afforded a peculiar gratification to the General, who well knew that the schools of America were the nurseries of freedom, and the basis of American liberty.

The General again returned to his quarters, where he had scarcely arrived, before the 9th Regiment of New-York Artillery, under Colonel Alexander M. Muir, appeared before the Hotel, in fine order, and full panoply, to escort him to the seat of his old comrade, Colonel Nicholas Fish, who, forty years ago, mounted the breach with him at York-Town, and with whom he had engaged to dine. On descending to the steps, agreeably to previous arrangements, Colonel Muir dismounted and advanced, and in behalf of himself and the officers of his regiment, presented the General with an elegant sword, of great beauty, and of finished workmanship. In performing this very pleasing office, Colonel Muir delivered the following address:—

General—The officers of the 9th Reginent New-York State Artillery, anxious to manifest, in common with their fellow-citizens, their esteem for you, as the champion of their country—the associate and friend of Washington, have deputed me to present to you this sword; the belt and mounting of which, being exclusively of the manufacture of this city.

"It is unnecessary to repeat the many signal services which you have rendered to this country; it does not comport with the character of soldiers to multiply words or expressions —it is sufficient for them to know that you were always to be found in the front rank of those who shed their blood, and expended their treasure, in the glorious cause of liberty, during that eventful time which "tried men's souls." These services are not forgotten by a grateful posterity—they are engraven on the hearts of a free people, by whom you will ever be remembered as the illustrious benefactor of these United States.

"May your declining days be as happy as your youthful and maturer ones have been useful and glorious, and your name ever be associated with liberty, freedom, and benevolence.

"Permit me, General, to add my personal wishes for your health and happiness, and to assure you that I shall consider the circumstance of having been chosen as the organ of the officers whom I have the honour to command, to present this sword, as one of the most agreeable and interesting of my life."

The General kindly accepted the sword, and in doing so, made the following reply:—

"With the highest pleasure and gratitude, I receive this most valuable present, from a distinguished corps of citizen-soldiers, every one of whom knows that swords have been given to man to defend liberty where it exists, to conquer it when it has been invaded by crowned and privileged usurpers.

"Accept, dear Colonel, and let all the officers and soldiers of your corps accept, my most affectionate thanks."

The following is a copy of the inscription on the Sword:—

"Presented to Major-General Lafayette, by Colonel Alexander M. Muir, in behalf of the Officers of the Ninth Regiment New-York State Artillery, 10th September, 1824, as a small token of the esteem in which he is held by them for his private worth, and distinguished services during the war which gave independence to the United States."

The belt is of exquisite workmanship, richly embroidered with gold. On it are inscribed, in silver embroidery, the figures 76, and the letters L. F., thus—" L. '76. F." The plate of the belt is large, and sufficiently elegant to correspond.—The ground-work of the plate is occupied with appropriate military devices, and around these are the four following inscriptions:—

"The Marquis De Lafayette, Born in France, 6th September, 1757."

"Joined the American Army of the Revolution as a volunteer, and was wounded at the battle of Brandywine, 11th September, 1777."

"Commanded the army in Virginia during the campaign of 1781, and was at the attack at York-Town, 19th October, 1781."

"Revisits the United States of America on an invitation from Congress, and landed at New-York, August 16th, 1824."

After reviewing the Regiment, and receiving the marching salute, the General ascended his carriage, and was escorted to the seat of his old friend and associate, as before mentioned, where he dined in company with a select party.

General Lafayette, on Tuesday evening, very affectionately took leave of Captain Allyn, at his room, City Hotel, and at the same time presented him with a superb writing desk, (made by N. Smith Prentiss, of this city,) replete with every thing necessary for a gentleman's toilet, bearing this inscription, "General Lafayette to his excellent friend Captain Allyn, August 15th, 1824."—He also sent kind remembrances to such of the officers and crew of the Cadmus as remained on board, presenting to the chief mate, Mr. Daniel Chadwick, a beautiful case of mathematical instruments mounted in silver. The Cadmus sailed on Wednesday, for Havre.

After two postponements on account of bad weather, the arrangements and decorations for the Ball, in honour of Lafayette, at Castle Garden, were finally completed, and it took place on Tuesday evening. The weather during the day and the evening was very fine, and afforded the guests unexpected security and pleasure.

The company commenced entering the Garden about half past six, and closed about ten o'clock, consisting of about six thousand ladies and gentlemen. The arrangements without, were such as to secure perfect safety and order in entering the Castle, and to prevent detention.

Immediately in front of the gate which forms the first entrance to the Garden, was erected a pyramid of the height of seventy-five feet, brilliantly illuminated, and surmounted by a double triangle, likewise illuminated, presenting the appearance of a star encircling the letter F. The Bridge leading to the Castle, which stands off from the Battery, into the bay, 250 feet, was this evening an immense covered way, carpeted the entire distance, hung with numerous lamps, and decorated with ever-greens. Through this magnificent entrance, the company found their way into the interior of the Garden.

The Castle, which is a circle, and covers a surface of about 600 feet, was enclosed with an awning at an altitude of seventy-five feet, the dome of which was supported in the centre by a column dressed with pale blue and white, and inscribed with the names of men immortalized with that of Lafayette, in the cause of freedom. This column was encircled with an immense cut glass chandelier, composed of thirteen separate ones, representing the thirteen original states; while it formed at its summit, the centre, whence hung the flags, signals, and standards of various nations, looped and festooned with much good taste, making a covering for the company, and a splendid military and naval dress for the coarser canopy above.

This object, which was the first that met the eye, and formed at the base but a slight obstruction, had a very imposing appearance, and produced a fine effect. The whole seemed to operate like a charm upon the visiter, as he entered, who, with elevated and sparkling eyes, and with looks of enraptured admiration, came forward from the massy and low-browed entrance, with increased grace in his step, and airy lightness in his feelings. Every one seemed to feel at home, and to appropriate the scene and its pleasures to his individual enjoyment and use.

The roof was supported by thirteen transparent columns, capped with a circle of light, and based with the armoreal insigna of the several states, under a shield of the Union, to denote their dependence on the same, and richly flanked with a falling drapery. Between the columns were to be seen the names of the original states, in gilded letters, encircled by laurel wreaths, and suspended between American ensigns, and a profusion of 'striped bunting.'

The General made his appearance about 10 o'clock. Immediately the dance and the song was at an end. The military band struck up a military air, and Lafayette was conducted through a column of ladies and gentlemen, to a splendid pavilion, immediately opposite to the great entrance. Not a word was spoken of gratulation—so profound and respectful, and intellectual, was the interest which his presence excited; nothing but a subdued and universal clap broke the general silence, and that but for a moment.

The interior of the pavilion, which was composed of white cambric, festooned, and otherwise varied with sky blue, and surmounted with an American Eagle, over the letter F, was richly furnished. Among other interesting objects, we noticed a bust of Hamilton, placed upon a Corinthian pillar, and illuminated with a beautiful lamp.

But the most interesting of all the exhibitions were those presented in front of the pavilion, and seen from it, immediately over the entrance to the Garden. A triumphal arch of about ninety feet space, adorned with laurel, oak, and festoons of flags, &c. were seen, based upon pillars of cannon fifteen feet high. A bust of Washington, supported by a golden eagle, was placed over the arch, as the presiding deity. Within the arch was a painting, nearly 25 feet square, of a fine colossal figure, representing the Genius of our country, rising in her native majesty and strength, supported by the American Eagle, and exhibiting a scroll inscribed to Fayette, with the words—"Honoured be the faithful patriot."

Soon after the General entered, the painting just alluded to, was slowly raised, which exhibited to the audience a beautiful transparency, representing *La Grange*, the mansion of Lafayette. The effect was as complete as the view was unexpected and imposing. Another subdued clap of admiration followed this tasteful, and appropriate, and highly interesting display.

In pursuance of the arrangements made for that purpose, General Lafayette, his son, and suite, together with a select party of ladies and gentlemen, repaired on board of the steamboat James Kent, directly on retiring from the Grand Fete of Tuesday evening, and proceeded up the Hudson river, to visit Albany, and the intermediate towns upon the river. The party embarked a few minutes after 2 o'clock, Wednesday morning, among the guests were the members of the Cincinnati, with their President, Colonel Varick; His Honour the Recorder and several of the Corporation; Governor Johnson, of Louisiana; Mrs. Lewis of Virginia; Colonel Alexander Hamilton, and his mother, (widow of the late General Hamilton;) General Morton, Colonel Platt, and a number of others.

The boat made very good progress until she arrived off Tarry-Town, where a very dense fog came on; but such was the anxiety of General Lafayette to reach West Point at the appointed time, (10 o'clock,) that Commodore Wiswall determined to push slowly on. It was impossible for the pilot to see five rods ahead. The result was, that at about 7 o'clock the boat ran aground upon what is called the Oyster Bank. Here she was obliged to remain for several hours—to the great disappointment of those on board, and also of the thousands who had collected at West Point, to witness his reception, and the tens of thousands at the villages above, which he was expected to pass before dark. As soon as it cleared away, so that the shores were discernible, it was found that every height and cliff were covered with people, anxious to do their utmost in honouring the Guest of the nation. At Stony Point, in particular, there was a large collection of people, a flag was hoisted, and a salute fired from a field piece stationed there for that purpose. One man, more eager than the rest, clambered down the rocks with the agility of a mountain goat, armed with a large musket, which a loud explosion gave us to understand was heavily charged. The boat was near in shore, and as the smoke cleared away, he waved his hand and exclaimed, "There, General, I give you the best I can!"

The population at West Point, including the officers, professors, cadets, the artisans, and their families, &c. &c. ordinarily amount to about one thousand persons. But from day-light yesterday morning, until ten o'clock, the ladies and gentlemen from the country adjacent, continued to flock in sloops and other craft, in great numbers. The suspense from the hours of 9 till 12 was very anxious; but at about fifteen minutes after 12, the welcome signal of his approach was given; and there was instantly more bustle and confusion than there has been before witnessed on the Point since the army of the revolution; the clangour of arms, the thrilling notes of the bugle, and the spirit-stirring drum, imparted life and animation to this wild and magnificent region.—The lofty bank of the Hudson was lined with spectators; and the Cadets were in line, as if they had een summoned from their barracks by the wand of a magician.

The James Kent, gorgeously decorated with flags, came proudly on, cutting away the foaming current, as though she dared Neptune and all his host to strife; and came majestically along side of the dock at half past 12. The General was here received by Colonel Thayer, the commander of the post, accompanied by Major-Generals Brown and Scott, with their respective suites, together with the officers and professors upon the station, under a salute of twenty-one guns from a detachment of artillery, posted upon the bluff, directly north of the old barracks. A landeau was in readiness to receive the General as he stepped ashore, in which he ascended the hill to the plain, followed by a long procession, consisting of the Cincinnati, the officers of the station, gentlemen from New-York, and from the river towns above, delegates from the towns of Newburgh, Poughkeepsie, Clermont, Hudson, and Albany, &c. &c. He was received on the plain by the corps of Cadets, whom he reviewed; and afterwards received the marching salute in front of the marquee erected for him, and witnessed several evolutions, which evinced the perfection of discipline. From the parade ground the General repaired for a few moments to the quarters of Generals Brown and Scott, at Mr. Cozzen's, where the ladies assembled in a spacious room adjoining the library, and partook of refreshments prepared for the occasion. At half past two, the General was conducted by Colonel Thayer to the splendid library of the institution, where the corps of Cadets were individually presented to him by Major Worth; the gentlemen upon the Point who had not previously been introduced, were then presented; after which the ladies were severally introduced.

From the library, the General repaired to the Mess-room of the Cadets, elegantly fitted up for the occasion, and sat down to a dinner, which, whether we regard the quantity, quality, the variety, or the style in which it was served up, we may at once pronounce a sumptuous one.—Including the Officers, Cadets, the Cincinnati, Corporation from New-York, and guests, more than four hundred persons sat down at the table. Colonel Thayer presided, assisted by Major Worth. General Lafayette and General Scott were seated on the right of the President, and General Brown and Colonel Varick on his left. At a cross table at the head, were seated the members of the Cincinnati, and at another similar table, at the other end of the hall, were the members of the Corporation of New-York with Mr. George Washington Lafayette, on the right of the Vice-President. The room was tastefully and elegantly decorated. Festoons of ever-green were suspended from pillar to pillar, in every direction through the spacious hall. Back of the President's chair hung the star-spangled banner. Over the chair was a large spread, and elegantly wrought eagle, with the words "September, 1757," issuing from the streamer in his beak, and "York-Town" grasped in his claws. A crown of laurel, interwoven with roses, was suspended over the General's head. Over the window on his right, was the name of Washington, wrought in leaves of ever-green, and on the left that of Lafayette. At the other end of the hall hung a full-length portrait of "the Father of his Country;" and upon the right wall, in the centre, that of Jefferson, and on the left, President Adams.

At 6 o'clock, the company rose from the table, and the General and his friends re-embarked on board of the James Kent, and proceeded to Newburgh.

Through the whole distance of the Highlands, the hardy mountaineers who inhabit many of the glens manifested their respect by showing themselves ever and anon, and discharging their muskets from the crags and cliffs which in some places seem to frown over the heads of the passing traveller, as the steam-boat ploughs her way close at the base of the mountains. In passing Cold-Spring, a salute was fired from a piece of artillery stationed near the shore for that purpose. A salute was also fired from New-Windsor, (near the old Encampment of the Revolutionary Army.) Unfortunately, however, the delay occasioned by the morning accident, had detained the party so long that the shades of night began now to close in, and on the arrival of the steam-boat at Newburgh the twilight had so far advanced as to render objects indistinct at a very short distance. A corps of infantry were drawn up in handsome array upon the wharf, to receive the General, by whom he was escorted to the Orange Hotel, where he was received by the corporation of the village, by the President of which he was addressed.

The General made a brief and pertinent reply to this address; after which he entered an open carriage and was escorted through the principal streets of the village, which were thronged with people, who were delighted with a glimpse of the General's face, caught even by the aid of a flickering lamp: over the streets at short distances, arches had been erected which were tastefully festooned with ever-greens and flowers, and on several of them were suspended appropriate inscriptions. On one of these arches was the following inscription:—"Thrice welcome Lafayette Columbia's bright Occidental Star." Another arch was formed by the planting of two well grown forest trees, and bending their tops together. The inscription suspended from this lofty arch was too high for the rays of our feeble lamp. The inscription upon another arch was, "Lafayette and Liberty—Welcome Illustrious Chief." But the arch which was far the most beautiful, was erected by the ladies; it extended from the houses on each side of the street, and formed one grand and two smaller arches; these were so richly and beautifully ornamented with festoons and flowers, that they would have answered well for decorations to the portals of the temple of Flora herself; the inscription here was "Welcome our hero, Lafayette." Having returned to the Orange Hotel, an address was presented to the General by Johannis Miller, Esq. President of the Orange county Agricultural Society, in behalf of said Society.

The General was then ushered into the grand saloon of the Orange Hotel, attended by the Committee of Arrangements, consisting of Messrs. Rose, Ruggles, Smith, Fisk, and others, together with the Trustees of the village. The ladies and gentlemen of the village, and several hundreds from the adjoining towns, had then the honour of a presentation, and were received with the accustomed affability and kindness of our illustrious guest, until, completely exhausted with the fatigues of the day, and of the preceding night, he was compelled to seek a few hours repose. The hall of audience was ornamented with much taste, and it was in this room that the supper-table was bountifully spread, at 11 o'clock, when the General was sufficiently refreshed to take a seat at the table. On the right of the chair were the words—"Brandywine, 11th September, 1777," encircled by a wreath of ever-greens, and on the left, the words "York-Town, 19th October, 1781," formed in the same manner. At the other end of the hall was a portrait of Washington, and the whole apartment was splendidly decorated with festoons and flowers of every variety of the season, and brilliantly illuminated by the light of several chandeliers, reflected from a large number of elegant mirrors.

The arrangements at this place were extensive and unusually imposing, but the time of the General's arrival was so late, that much derangement was the consequence. His arrival having been expected the day before, the people had been assembling for nearly two days; and it was computed that, independently of the troops on duty, there were at least 10,000 persons in the village. The public houses were all illuminated; and a splendid ball was given at Crawford's Hotel.

At 12 o'clock, the steam-boat Chancellor Livingston which had also been detained on her passage up by the fog, made her appearance from Albany, when the most of the guests from New-York, both ladies and gentlemen, returned to the city. Among the former were the two Miss Wrights, who have lately arrived from France, and whose "View of the American Society and Manners," has acquired some considerable notoriety. The General and his suite came on board of the Kent at about the same hour, and retired to rest, when the boat made sail, and before day-light anchored off Poughkeepsie.

Our National Guest has no where received a more flattering reception, than at the beautiful, ancient, and patriotic village of Poughkeepsie; nor has more promptitude, vigour, and taste, been displayed in the arrangements at any other place. At sun-rise all hands were "piped" on deck, and a more imposing spectacle has rarely been presented. The high bluffs below the landing place, were covered with troops, and thousands of citizens were crowding the wharves, showing themselves in large groups from the neighbouring heights, and windows of the houses standing within view of the river. All ages and sexes seemed to press anxiously forward to show their gratitude to their welcome visiter. At half past 6 o'clock, the boat got under way, and took a turn upon the river, while a salute was fired by a corps of artillery stationed upon one of the heights. When the General appeared upon deck, the welkin rang with the cheers from the crowds upon the shore, which were returned from the boat. The boat was then drawn up to the wharf, where a company of horse, many of the officers of General Brush's division on horseback, all mounted on elegant horses, and in complete uniform, together with several uniform companies, were drawn up in great order under the direction of Major-General Brush, assisted by Colonel Cunningham. General Lafayette was then conducted by Thomas T. Oakley, General James Tallmadge, Judge Emott, and Philo Ruggles, Esq. to a barouche, with four beautiful white horses, in which the General took his seat, attended by Colonel Huger, of South Carolina, General Van Courtland, General Fish, and General Lewis. A barouche, also drawn by four white horses, was then drawn up, which was occupied by the son of General Lafayette, and gentlemen attending them. After being conducted to the pleasant and extensive piazza in front of Mr. Forbus' house, and after being introduced to the clergy and gentlemen attending, he was cordially addressed by Colonel Henry A. Livingston.

To this address, the General returned a neat and feeling reply.

A procession was then formed under the direction of the committee, to the Poughkeepsie hotel, at about 8 o'clock, where the General sat down to a sumptuous breakfast, handsomely served up by Mr. Myer. At the head of the table hung the well-known and venerated portrait of Washington, and at the opposite end, the Grand Banner of St. Tammany. On each side of the hall, at suitable distances, were suspended banners, with the arms, name, and motto, of each state in the union. Over the centre of the table, hung a canopy formed of festoons of flowers and ever-greens, of various kinds, belted by a riband, on which was inscribed the names of the thirteen original States. Over the folding doors, were the well-known words of "Welcome Lafayette" made with great accuracy, wholly of pink-coloured blossoms of china-astor, and on one of the walls, were inscribed the names of Washington and Lafayette, wrought in laurel leaves, and encircled in garlands of flowers. Directly in front of the General's seat, stood a representation of the temple of Fame; and the whole suite of apartments were decorated in a style to correspond with the above.

Immediately after breakfast, and with a praise-worthy promptness, the escort was formed, and the General was attended to the boat with every possible mark of respect; the troops again repaired to the heights; and on hauling into the stream, another salute was fired from the artillery, and afterwards several vollies of musketry were fired, with a precision which the General was pleased to say resembled very much the firing of regular troops. The shores were again lined with people, who cheered in all directions.

Passing rapidly up the river, preparations were made for landing with Governor Lewis, at the dock, near his elegant country seat. The boat arrived at about 12 o'clock, and on coming along side, carriages were found in readiness to convey the party to the mansion which stood at some distance from the road, which wound through a beautiful copse to the house. On alighting, the General and suite were introduced to the family, and were shortly after introduced into an apartment, where an elegant collation was provided: peaches, grapes, and melons, were mingled with more substantial fare, and every variety of wine sparkled on the table. After remaining an hour and a half, the General took leave of this hospitable family, and embarked, in order to continue his voyage to Albany.

Soon afterwards, in passing the seat of James Thompson, Esq. a boat came off with a large basket of peaches, of enormous size, and excellent flavour, and with several elegant bouquets of flowers.

In passing the landing at Kingston, (four miles from the village,) a large collection were found to have assembled; a salute was fired from the shore, and hearty cheers given and returned. At this place, Colonel Henry Livingston, who commanded a regiment under Lafayette in Rhode Island, and at Valley Forge, came on board. The General had just been inquiring of Colonel Fish, what had become of his old friend Henry Livingston, and received him most affectionately.

The steam-boat arrived at Clermont at about 4 o'clock in the afternoon, and came to anchor off the elegant mansion of Robert L. Livingston, Esq. formerly the seat of the late Chancellor Livingston. Before the boat arrived at the dock, it was discovered that the groves were literally alive with people, of all ages and sexes, equally anxious with the hospitable proprietor, to manifest their respect for their expected guest, and greet his landing. But while the rocks and glens, and even trees to their top-most branches, presented this animated spectacle, the General, his suite, and friends, were still more surprised by the appearance upon the lawn of this romantic and secluded place, of a regiment of well-disciplined troops, drawn up to receive him.—There were several vessels at anchor in the stream, one of which (a large sloop) was decorated with flags, and a streamer floated from her mast, with the motto of "Welcome Lafayette," in large letters. On landing, a salute was fired from this vessel, which was unexpectedly returned from a field piece planted in a thick copse of trees upon the shore. The General then ascended the shore, and was conducted by Generals Lewis and Fish, to the mansion of Mr. Livingston, where he was received by that gentleman with the utmost courtesy and cordiality.—After the friends of Mr. Livingston, assembled on the occasion, had been presented, the General reviewed the troops upon the lawn, by whom he was honoured with a *feu de joie*. At this moment, a long procession of the ancient and honourable fraternity of Freemasons, consisting of a Chapter of Royal Arch Masons, and the members of "Widow's Son Lodge," of Redhook, emerged from a grove, and on being presented to the General, an appropriate address was delivered by Palmer Cook, Esq. W. M. of the aforementioned lodge.

After a brief and pertinent reply, the General accepted of an invitation to visit the seat of Edward P. Livingston, Esq. which is situated but a short distance to the north, upon the same elevated and beautiful plain. His reception was equally cordial and flattering as before. An excellent cold collation, together with refreshments of every suitable kind, were served up. And while the company were partaking of these, the steam-boat Richmond, Captain William Wiswall, came gayly down, and anchored along side of the James Kent, having on board Major-General Jacob Rutsen Van Rensselaer, and suite, Brigadier-General Fleming, and suite, the Mayor of Hudson, (Rufus Reed, Esq.) Dr. Tallman, late Mayor, and Colonel Strong, as delegates from the city of Hudson, together with the Hudson Band, and two elegant uniform companies, under the command of Colonel Edwards. This addition to the company already on the ground, repaired immediately to the seat of Mr. E. P. Livingston, from whence, after refreshments were served out to them by Mr. L. and Commodore Wiswall in person, General Lafayette was escorted back to the seat of his liberal entertainer. As night came on, the troops and crowd from the country dispersed, and the Hudson troops were taken on board of the steam-boat James Kent, where refreshments were ordered, and the forward deck and cabin assigned to them for the night. In the evening the whole of Mr. L's. splendid suite of apartments were brilliantly lighted up, and an elegant ball was given in honour of the General's company. The assemblage was very numerous, and a brilliant circle of ladies, arrayed in all the charm of health, beauty, and rich and elegant dresses, were contributing to the festivity and joy of the occasion, by "tripping the light fantastic toe," or by conversation sparkled with wit, or adorned by the graces of polished manners and education. Among the guests this evening, in addition to those already named, were the Honourable Edward Livingston, of New-Orleans, the Honourable Walter Patterson, Captain Ridgeley, of the Navy, the Honourable Peter R. Livingston, A. Vanderpool, Esq. of Kinderhook, Mrs. Montgomery, (widow of the gallant General who fell at Quebec,) and many others whose names are not recollected. During the evening a sumptuous supper was served up in a style of magnificence rarely, if ever equalled in this country. The room selected for this part of the *fete*, was an extensive Greenhouse, or Orangery, and the effect was indescribably fine. The tables had been made and fitted for this occasion, and were spread beneath a large grove of Orange and Lemon trees, with bending branches of fruit, and many other species of exotic shrubs and plants. Flora also, had profusely scattered her blossoms; and the whole scene seemed to partake of enchantment. The beholder stood gazing, as if bound by the wizard spell of the Magician. The night was dark and rainy; but this contributed to the general effect of the *fete*, inasmuch as the darkness heightened the effect of the thousand lamps by which the surrounding groves were illuminated. There was also a fine exhibition of fireworks, which had been prepared and brought from New-York for the occasion. It having been found inconvenient to provide suppers for so many on board of the boat, the whole detachment of troops were invited by Mr. L. to supper in the Green house, which invitation was accepted. At 10 o'clock, General Lafayette retired from this scene of gayety and beauty, and at two the hall was closed, and the company separated, not only highly gratified with the entertainment, but with the manner in which it was got up and imparted to his guests, by Mr. L. whose style of living closely approximates that of the real English gentleman, and whose wealth is equalled by his kindness and liberality.

At 9 o'clock on Friday, the General again embarked, and proceeded on his way, and before 10 o'clock, was in sight of Catskill. The long wharf which projects half a mile into the river, was occupied by two battalions of troops.—The highlands which nearly exclude the whole village from a view of the river, were covered with people, and on the arrival of the James Kent at the dock, a salute of 13 guns was fired from the artillery on one of the heights. The arrangements of General Lafayette rendered it absolutely necessary that he should be at Albany on that day to dinner, and hence it was utterly impossible for him to make any stay at Catskill, although he was earnestly pressed to dine by a very respectable delegation. The General, to gratify the feelings of thousands who were assembled at the landing to hail his arrival and bid him welcome, consented to land and pass through the principal streets, in an elegant carriage, accompanied by the Committee of Arrangements, and escorted by the military, and a large assemblage of citizens in procession. In front of Crowell's Hotel the procession halted, and the General was received by the acclamations of a large concourse of people, eager to see, and embrace the Nation's Guest. Amongst the company was a body of the heroes of the revolution, whose furrowed features, silver locks, and tottering steps, bespoke age and hard service. But at the sight of their old General, they rushed forward to meet the quick-extended grasp of their old Commander. Among the number, was an old servant who was with Lafayette when he was wounded at the battle of Brandywine. This was a touching scene, few eyes were dry, either among the actors or spectators; but the General's time was so short, that he was constrained to leave the further honours that awaited him in this place, bid adieu to the citizens, and embark for Hudson.

The boat arrived at Hudson a few minutes before 2 o'clock, but the same reason that prevented a longer stay a Catskill, also rendered it impossible, consistent with his arrangements, to make any considerable stay here. On landing, the crowd was so great that it was almost impossible to proceed, notwithstanding the active exertions of Colonel Darling, the Marshal of the day, assisted by the military. The General was conducted to an elegant barouche, drawn by four beautiful black horses, attended by four grooms in a special livery. After the General, followed a number of other carriages, with his retinue, and the different delegates from the river towns. The procession passed up Ferry to Warren-street, where an arch was erected, which for its size and elegance of construction, exceeded any that had been previously seen on the tour. The whole street, which is more than a mile in length, was choked with the crowd. And the windows, as at Catskill, were filled with ladies, whose snow-white hands and handkerchiefs, were gracefully waved in the air, while the crowd in the streets were cheering, and the General, with his usual condescension, was bowing, or endeavouring to bow, to every individual in the multitude. About half-way up the street, stood another arch, elegantly adorned; and at the head of the town was a third, superior to all, on the top of which stood a colossal figure of the Genius of Liberty, well proportioned and painted, holding in her hand the American standard, which being of unusual size, floated in the air with an imposing effect. To each of the arches of which we have spoken, were suspended appropriate inscriptions. On arriving at the square, at the head of Warren-street, the procession wheeled and returned to the Court-house, when the troops and citizens opened to the right and left, and all that could, passed through, and up to the Court-room. All the seats without the bar were filled with the "Daughters of Columbia," forming a large and interesting group of well-dressed and beautiful females. The Court-room was superbly decorated—displaying more labour, taste, and skill, than any decorations of the kind that were seen on the route. At the entrance of the bar, on either side, stood a beautiful Corinthian pillar, with caps and cornices of the composite order of architecture, elegantly wrought and ornamented with leaves and gold. On the top of each of these pillars was placed a globe, and the whole were united at the top by a chain of flowers of every hue, festooned with laurel and roses. The General was conducted to this rich and beautiful portal, where His Honour the Mayor delivered an interesting address.

General Lafayette briefly replied to the address, after which the members of the Common Council were severally presented to him. A most interesting and affecting spectacle was then presented; sixty-eight veterans of the revolution, who had collected from the different parts of the country, formed a part of the procession, and were next presented; and it so happened that several of them were officers, and many of them soldiers who had served with Lafayette. Notwithstanding that they were admonished that the greatest haste was necessary, yet every one had something to say; and when they grasped his friendly hand, each seemed reluctant to release it. One of them came up with a sword in his hand, which, as he passed, he remarked was "given to him by the Marquis," at such a place, "in Rhode Island." Another, with a tear glistening in his eye, as he shook the hand of the General, observed—"You, Sir, gave me the first guinea I ever had in my life—I shall never forget that."

The officers of the militia were next presented, and after

them, the ladies. But time would not allow of delay; and many thousands who were eagerly pressing forward, were disappointed in not being introduced to the man whom they had assembled to honour. In passing down the street, however, on arriving opposite Allen's hotel, where arrangements had been made for the dinner, the solicitations were so warm and earnest, that the General was constrained to alight and take a glass of wine in the long room. And here, again, was presented a specimen of Hudson taste, which deserves every commendation. The hall was decorated in a style of elegance, that would compare only with the Court-house. The General stopped but for a moment, when he re-entered his carriage, and returned to the boat, followed by the shouts and blessings of thousands. On leaving the dock, three cheers were given by the multitude and returned from the boat—after which a salute was fired from the hill near the Observatory. In passing up the river, the docks at the villages of Coxsackie, New-Baltimore, and Coeymans, were crowded with people, who cheered the General repeatedly, and with as much enthusiasm as though they had had a nearer view. At Castleton, a large collection of people had assembled, and a salute was fired from a six pounder.

In consequence of the unavoidable delays on the way, a freshet in the river, the contrary winds and tide, the James Kent did not arrive at her moorings at the Overslaugh, until five o'clock (on Friday)—three hours later than was originally contemplated. The consequence was, that the arrangements of the committee for the city of Albany were deranged; the committee themselves, consisting of Alderman Townsend and Humphrey, Colonel Bacon, and others, (in addition to the New-York delegation, which had accompanied the General from New-York,) who had been waiting to receive their guest, were much fatigued; and the troops, who had been on duty since 7 o'clock in the morning, without refreshment, were nearly exhausted. On landing, the General was conducted to a superb landeau, drawn by four white horses, and carriages were in readiness for the gentlemen accompanying him. The procession was quickly formed, and moved rapidly on to Greenbush, escorted by a detachment of horse, commanded by Major General Solomon Van Rensselaer, Marshal of the day, assisted by Colonel Cooper. On arriving at the centre of the village, the General was conducted to a large marquee, erected beneath an arch, similar to those heretofore described, and bearing appropriate inscriptions, where he was received by the members of the Corporation, who welcomed him with an appropriate address; after which, refreshments were served, and the procession moved on. Night was now rapidly setting in, and the delay at the Ferry, for the want of a sufficient number of boats, rendered it quite dark when the General landed in Albany. It was, however, easy to discern, that the preparations for the event had been extensive, and that a prodigious assemblage of people were yet impatiently awaiting his approach. He was welcomed, in behalf of the citizens, by Stephen Lush, Esq. one of the oldest and most respectable of the inhabitants of Albany, who rode in the carriage with him. A large detachment of troops were on duty, and a salute was fired by a corps of artillery, stationed near the Ferry-stairs, which was answered by the old Clinton field-piece, which has long stood upon the hill back of Albany, to send its thunder forth, echoing among the distant hills, on all patriotic occasions. On entering the city, the procession passed under an arch, inscribed "The Hero is Welcome." At the junction of Church and South Market-streets, stood another arch, large and beautiful, inscribed, "We remember thy deeds—We revere thy worth—We love thy virtues." At the foot of Beaver-street, near the Museum, stood a third stupendous arch, displaying by its festoons and the disposition and variety of flowers interwoven with evergreens, much beauty in itself, and taste in the ladies, whose delicate fingers had formed and ornamented it.—On entering the foot of State-street, on the site of the Old Dutch Church, stood a temple, richly ornamented, around the pillars of which the ivy was gracefully entwined. On the top of the temple, stood a large living eagle, who proudly flapped his wings as the chieftain passed. Many of the houses were illuminated, among which were the capitol, and the whole block of Gregory's buildings, including the houses of Chancellor Sanford, Mr. Gregory, Isaac Hamilton, Esq. and the extensive establishment of Mr. Cruttenden. On the front of the latter was a transparency, executed by Inman, of this city, representing the reception of General Lafayette by the Genius of Liberty, who proffers him a scroll; and in the back ground was seen the ship Cadmus, in which he made his passage from France. The elevated situation of these lofty buildings, contributed to give the illumination a splendid and elegant appearance; and the effect was greatly heightened by the bright light cast upon the military, the cavalcade, and the immense concourse of people, who otherwise would only have been felt instead of seen. On alighting at the capitol, the General was conducted to the Senate Chamber, where he was received by the Honourable Ambrose Spencer, Mayor of the city, and the members of the Corporation. He was addressed by the Mayor in the following words:—

"Sir—Your visit to this country is received with universal and heartfelt joy. Your claims upon the gratitude and the friendship of this Nation, arise from your heroic devotion to its freedom, and your uniform assertion to the rights of man. The progress of time has attested the purity of your character, and the lustre of your heroism; and the whole course of your life has evinced those exalted virtues, which were first displayed in favour of the independence and liberty of America.

"In the hour of difficulty and peril, when America, without allies, without credit, with an enfeebled government, and with scanty means of resistance, confiding in the justice of her cause and the protection of Heaven, was combating for her liberties, against a nation, powerful in resources and all the materials for war, when our prospects of success were by many considered more than doubtful, if not desperate, you devoted all your energies and all your means to our defence; and after witnessing our triumphant success, your life has been consecrated to the vindication of the liberties of the old world.

"When Franklin, the wisest man of the age, pronounced you the most distinguished person he ever knew, when Washington, the illustrious hero of the new world, honoured you with friendship the most sincere, and with confidence the most unlimited, they evinced their just discernment of character, and foresaw the further display of faculties and virtues which would identify your name with liberty, and demonstrate your well founded claims to the gratitude, the love, and the admiration of mankind.

"The few surviving statesmen and soldiers of the Revolution have gathered around you as a friend and a brother—the generation that has risen up since your departure, cherish the same feelings, and those that will appear in the successive future ages, will hail you as the benefactor of America, and the hero of liberty. In every heart you have a friend, and your eulogium is pronounced by every tongue. In behalf of the inhabitants of this ancient city I welcome you most cordially and tender to you their civic honours. I salute you as an illustrious benefactor of our country; and I supplicate the blessings of Heaven on a life sanctified in the sublime cause of heroic virtue and disinterested benevolence."

To this address, which we beg leave to pronounce forcible and elegant, the General returned the following reply:—

"Sir—The enjoyments of my visit to the beautiful and happy shores of the North River, cannot but be highly enhanced by the affectionate reception, the civic testimonies of esteem, which are conferred upon me in this city, and by the manner in which you are pleased to express sentiments so gratifying to my heart. Not half a century has elapsed since this place, ancient, but small, was my head quarters, on the frontiers of an extensive wilderness, since as commander in the northern department, I had to receive the oath of renunciation to a royal distant government, of allegiance to the more legitimate sovereignty of the people of the United States. Now, Sir, Albany has become a considerable city; is the central seat of the authorities of the state of New-York. Those wildernesses rank among the most populous, the best cultivated parts of the union. This rising generation, has, in two glorious wars, and still more so in her admirable institutions, asserted an indisputable superiority over the proud pretenders to a control upon her.

"To these happy recollections, Sir, you have the goodness to add remembrances of my early admission among the sons and soldiers of America, of friendships the most honourable and dear to me. I will not attempt to express the feelings that crowd on my mind, and shall only beg you, Sir, and the gentlemen of the Corporation, to accept the tribute of my respectful and devoted gratitude, for the city of Albany and her worthy magistrates."

The members of the Common Council, and those friends who had been specially invited, having been introduced, the General was then conducted to the Governor's apartment, where he was received by his Excellency Governor Yates, who addressed him as follows:—

"General—A million and a half of freemen congratulate you on your arrival in this state; and as their chief magistrate, and in their behalf, I bid you welcome.

"On your appearance, the recollection of former days recur to us afresh, but it is impossible to give our ideas utterance.

"Those among us whose immediate ancestors or connexions

were actively engaged in that arduous and mighty effort for a nation's freedom—in which you so essentially contributed, experience emotions the most exquisite, on this happy and highly interesting occasion; and if this be so with regard to them, who can describe the sensations of the few surviving revolutionary soldiers and patriots, your companions in arms.

"It is impossible for language to depict the feelings of a grateful nation, emancipated from thraldom by your aid—happy in the full enjoyment of their rights and privileges, and flourishing in arts, on beholding their distinguished benefactor, (who is so justly ranked among the most prominent of their deliverers) again revisiting their shores, after an absence of two-score years.

"It is, General, one of the most pleasant circumstances of my life, that I am favoured with the honour of personally addressing you; and may the blessing of the Almighty always attend you, and may your course through life be as happy as it has been glorious."

This affectionate address was answered by General Lafayette, as follows :—

"Sir—The kind welcome you are pleased to express in behalf of the free and happy citizens of the State of New-York, is an additional claim to my gratitude towards them, and a particular obligation conferred upon me by their respected chief magistrate.

"The inexpressible feelings, which the presence of my revolutionary companions, and the affection and esteem of the succeeding generations could not fail to excite, mingle in my heart with the delight I enjoy from the sight of the wonderful improvements, superior to the most sanguine anticipations, which, in the space of forty years, have so clearly evinced the power of enlightened patriotism under republican institutions.

"I beg your Excellency to accept my affectionate and respectful acknowledgments."

The suite of the Governor having been presented to the General, together with his Excellency's particular friends, he was conducted from the capitol to the residence of Matthew Gregory, Esq. (who mounted the ramparts with Lafayette and Hamilton at York-Town,) where many of the most distinguished gentlemen of the city and state, were assembled to pay him their respects. Among them were Governor Clinton, the Chancellor, and Judges of the Supreme Court, the Lieut.

Governor, and principal officers of the state, &c. &c. After remaining here for the space of an hour, the General was attended to the lodgings prepared for him at Cruttenden's, and where a rich and bountiful supper was spread for the Corporation and its guests. The Mayor presided at this entertainment, assisted by Alderman Van Ingen; and a number of toasts were drank by way of concluding the banquet.

Over head, in front of the chair of the president, was the painted inscription—"Lafayette the Guest of the Nation," and on the reverse—"York-Town, October 19th, 1781." Among the festoons were the words wrought in flowers—"Flora's Tribute." On the right of the chair hung the portrait of Lafayette, painted in 1783; and on the left that of the late Robert Morris. Farther down the room stood a marble pedestal, surmounted with the bust of Washington, crowned with a wreath of laurel; and an American Bald Eagle hovered over the door. After remaining a short time in the drawing room, the General, accompanied by the distinguished gentlemen before mentioned, (excepting Governor Clinton, who did not attend, in consequence of the recent death of his son,) repaired to the Assembly Chamber of the Capitol, which was echoing to the music and the dance of a splendid ball, given in honour of the "Nation's Guest." The room was handsomely, though not profusely, decorated with wreaths and festoons, and the pillars entwined with ivy. The Speaker's Chair was entirely shrouded or enveloped in shrubbery of ever-greens and flowers, and in front, in the centre of a large and beautiful garland, was the following inscription:—"Welcome brave Lafayette; we hail thee as the Nation's Guest and early friend." From the staff projecting forward from the gallery, floated a broad streamer, bearing the hero's name. Over the Speaker's chair, the well known full length portrait of Washington preserved its place, encircled by a wreath of laurel; and the walls were hung round with banners, inscribed with the names of the following Generals of the Revolution, viz. Schuyler, Lincoln, Hamilton, Lingan, Wayne, Warren, Montgomery, Greene, Knox, Wooster, Heath, Gates, Clinton, M'Dougall, and Gansevoort. General Lafayette stayed but about an hour amidst this scene of pleasure and gayety, during which time the ladies and gentlemen moved in procession before him, and were severally honoured with an introduction. At 1 o'clock, he retired to obtain that repose which the incessant fatigues of the week must have rendered not only desirable, but highly necessary.

On Saturday morning, the General rose in excellent health and spirits, at an early hour; and as the arrangements of the day required that no time should be lost, the calls of gentlemen commenced at a most unfashionable time. Among other gentlemen, Mr. Clinton called, pursuant to a request from the New-York Literary and Philosophical Society, of which he is President, to present the General with a diploma of membership. And in performing this duty, he addressed the General in an appropriate manner.

In replying to this forcible and elegant address of our distinguished fellow-citizen, General Lafayette remarked in substance, "that the honour conferred on him was rendered the more gratifying to his feelings by the reflection, that the evidence of it was presented to him by the highly respected son and nephew of two of his departed brothers in arms, and warm and personal friends and companions."

At 8 o'clock the military were again under arms, and appeared before the General's lodgings, to escort him through a number of the principal streets, and thence to one of the elegant canal packet-boats, in which the Corporation had invited him to take a trip to Troy, and thence by land to Lansingburg, Waterford, and home by way of the Cohoose Falls, where the boat was in readiness to receive him. The procession moved down State, South, Pearl, and Lydius-streets, to South Market-street, and thence up the second lock, near the seat of the Patroon. The day was uncommonly fine, and the military appeared to excellent advantage.—The crowd was very great; the whole mass of citizens being in motion, and multitudes having flocked in from the surrounding country. It was 12 o'clock before the General, together with the Corporation and their guests, embarked on board of the "Schenectady Packet," which was gayly dressed for the occasion. The embarkation was announced by a salute from cannon stationed on the hill, near the seat of Elias Kane, Esq. The Albany Band occupied a boat which preceded the packet, and a boat which followed was occupied by the officers of the Albany Military Association and their friends. Next followed two or three large packet boats filled with spectators, and the banks, the whole distance, were lined with people. Among the guests of the Corporation were Governor Yates, Mr. Clinton, the Chancellor and Judges, General Lewis, Colonel Fish, Colonel Huger, the Hon. Peter R. Livingston, and many others. The boats were briskly propelled onward by six horses each, selected for the occasion. In passing the Half-way-House, a large basket of delicious grapes, in rich clusters, and adorned with flowers, was sent on board as a present to the General, from the Shakers at Neskayuna. At the United States garrison, at Gibbonsville, the General stopped, and was received within the walls of the arsenal by a salute of 21 guns. Having returned to the packet, the party moved on to the lateral canal, leading to the river, through which they descended and entered the Hudson by one of the "sprouts" which form the Delta of the Mohawk. At this place eight row-boats, all dressed with flags, the broadest of which bore the popular name of "Clinton," were in readiness to tow the packet across the river, which service was expeditiously performed.

The General landed at Troy on a platform, erected and carpeted for the occasion, and a salute was fired. He was received by a deputation of the citizens, consisting of Messrs. Tibbitts, Russell, Mallory, Dickinson, Cushman, Paine, and others, by the former of whom he was presented with a handsome address.

The crowd was here very great, but they were orderly; and the military parade was rendered more formidable by the addition of two companies of uniform troops from Albany. A procession was here formed, which was escorted through the principal streets; the General riding, as usual, in an open carriage, attended by Colonel Lane, to the "Troy House," kept by Mr. Titus. On arriving here, he was received by the Common Council of the city, and an address was delivered to him by Mr. Recorder Clowes.

The concourse of people was immensely great; and such was the anxiety to see the illustrious visiter, that he went out upon the piazza, and gratified the multitude as long as his time would allow. The piazza was handsomely adorned with festoons of ever-greens and roses, and in the centre was perched a large living eagle, with a miniature of Lafayette upon his neck. While standing here, a deputation from the Troy Royal Arch Chapter of Masons were introduced to him. They came with a request that he would favour the Chapter, then in session in the tabernacle above, with the honour of a visit. The request was immediately assented to; and he was received, together with his son, with masonic honours.

The officers and members having been severally presented, the General retired to the dining-hall below, where a cold collation was handsomely and bountifully provided. While partaking of a little refreshment, the following note was presented to him, and the invitation promptly and cheerfully accepted:—

"To General Lafayette.—The Ladies of Troy, having assembled at the Female Seminary, have selected from their number a committee to request of General Lafayette that he would grant them an opportunity of beholding in his person, their own, and their country's generous and beloved benefactor."

The General, prompt in his movements, together with those gentlemen of the party who chose, repaired to the Seminary; and here a scene of deep and delightful interest transpired. On arriving at the gate of the institution, an arbour of evergreens, which, like Jonah's gourd, sprang up in a night, was found to extend the whole distance to the building, which is about 200 feet. At the entrance of this arbour was the following inscription:—"America commands her Daughters to welcome their Deliverer, Lafayette." At this place the General was met by the Committee of Arrangements, and Mrs. Colonel Pawling pronounced a pleasing address—which, as usual, received a brief and pertinent reply.

On entering the institution, the General was presented to Mrs. Willard, the principal, and afterwards the pupils were presented by her, for which purpose they were arranged in two lines along the hall leading directly from the arbour.—Two of the pupils, daughters of the Governors of Vermont and Michigan, then advanced and presented the following lines, entitled "Lafayette's Welcome," and written for the occasion by the principal:—

And art thou, then, dear Hero, come?
And do our eyes behold the man,
Who nerved his arm and bared his breast
For us, ere yet our life began?
For us and for our native land,
Thy youthful valour dared the war;
And now, in winter of thine age,
Thou'st come, and left thy lov'd ones far.
Then deep and dear thy welcome be;
Nor think thy daughters far from thee:
Columbia's daughters, lo! we bend,
And claim to call thee Father, Friend!

But was't our country's rights alone
Impell'd Fayette to Freedom's van?
No! 'twas the love of human kind—
It was the sacred cause of man—
It was benevolence sublime,
Like that which sways the Eternal mind!
And, benefactor of the world,
He shed his blood for all mankind!
Then deep and dear thy welcome be;
Nor think thy daughters far from thee!
Daughters of human kind, we bend,
And claim to call thee Father, Friend!

These lines were afterwards, by particular request, sung with great sweetness and pathos, by Miss Eliza Smith, of Worcester, Massachusetts, in the choruses of which the young ladies generally joined, and the whole was executed with much effect. The General was much affected, and at the close of the singing, with eyes suffused in tears, he said—"I cannot express what I feel on this occasion; but will you, madam, present me with three copies of those lines, to be given by me, as from you, to my three daughters."—It is wholly unnecessary to add that the request was complied with. The General then retired, and was conducted by the Committee of Arrangements back, through the arbour, along the sides of which the pupils had formed themselves in close order, to the number of about 200. It was a most interesting spectacle, thrilling the soul with delightful anticipations. Female education was far too long neglected, even after the sombre clouds of the ignorance and prejudice of the dark ages had been dissipated. "The human mind," says Cicero, "without instruction, is like a field without culture." The visit of the General to Troy, short as it was, afforded him great satisfaction. He talked much about it, and frequently spoke of his visit to the Seminary, as one of the most interesting and delightful moments of his life.

By this time the day was so far advanced that the visit to Lansingburgh, Waterford, and the Falls, was necessarily relinquished, though with great reluctance, particularly on the part of General Lafayette, as he wished both to gratify the wishes of those villages, and to enjoy a farther opportunity of examining that great work, from a short section of which he had that morning derived so much pleasure. It was, however, necessary to embark and return to Albany, which was accordingly done—the whole party partaking of an excellent dinner on board of the boat.

On landing at the head of the Basin, he was escorted as before, but through different streets, back to his lodgings. In the evening he visited Governor Clinton, and afterwards his Excellency Governor Yates, whence he was escorted to the steam-boat, where he embarked on his return to New-York, at about 12 o'clock. General Muir was detached by the Governor, with Majors Henry and Webster, aids of Major General Stephen Van Rensselaer, to accompany General Lafayette to New-York as an escort.

On Sunday morning, the General stopped at Red-Hook and visited Mrs. Montgomery, widow of General Montgomery, who fell in storming the city of Quebec, December 1775, where he met a numerous collection of friends, and partook of a sumptuous dinner. About 2 o'clock, the General took an affectionate leave of Mrs. Montgomery and guests, and retired on board of the steam-boat, on his way to New-York. At 7 o'clock the boat came to at Fishkill landing, and the General called on Mrs. Dewitt, grand-daughter of the former President Adams, where he was courteously as well as splendidly received, amidst a numerous collection of friends assembled to greet their country's guest. To add to the enjoyments of this interview, the General had the pleasure of shaking cordially by the hand another of his brave Light Infantry, adding, "the Light Infantry were a brave corps, and under my immediate command." "Yes," returned the old soldier, "and you gave us our swords and plumes." The General made but a short stay, took leave of his friends, and returned to the boat under a salute of three hearty cheers.

The boat arrived at Courtlandt-street wharf, New-York, at 3 o'clock in the morning, and at 5 the General returned to his lodgings, after a most delightful excursion.

On Monday afternoon, in consequence of previous arrangements, General Lafayette partook of a dinner at Washington Hall, to which he had been invited by the Grand Lodge of this State. From 5 to 600 of the craft, decorated with their sacred symbols, were present. Language is inadequate to give a correct description of the scene.

After the General's return to New-York, he received the following address, enclosing 150 dollars, which had been raised by a liberal contribution amongst the children of Catskill, after he left that village.

"*The Children of the village of Catskill to General Lafayette.*"

"While the most distinguished civil honours of our country have justly been paid to the friend of Washington, and the champion of liberty, we ardently pray, that our moral and religious privileges may be continued, promoted, and appreciated; and as we are aware that the enlightening, civilizing, and ameliorating influences of the Bible, are the strongest and most efficient means of maintaining the glorious advantages we enjoy: we, the children of the village of Catskill, solicit General Lafayette to permit us to constitute him a life Director of the American Bible Society; presuming that you, Sir, will duly appreciate the motives which have induced us to adopt this expression of our gratitude for services too essential to American freedom ever to be forgotten."

The General was much pleased with the attention, and returned his kind acknowledgments for the honour done him.

Previous to the General's departure on Thursday morning, the Cincinnati Society, the Mayor, and the Honourable Corporation of the city and county, and a large collection of citizens, met, by appointment, in the audience chamber in the City Hotel, at 9 o'clock. Soon after they were assembled, the Nation's Guest entered the room, and after saluting round the semi-circle all his old companions in arms, and the Honourable Corporation, and the citizens, he was addressed by Gurdon S. Mumford, Esq. as follows:—

"General Lafayette—Sir, how inscrutible are the ways of Providence, and His works past finding out! I hold in my hand a relic, nothing less than the Cane of the immortal Franklin; this large gold-headed cane was bequeathed to our beloved Washington; and by whom can this relic, now exhibited to you, be better transmitted to posterity, than through the putative son of Benjamin Franklin, for such I may be permitted to call you, from the very affectionate manner in which he uniformly advocated your disinterestedness and devotedness to the prosperity of our beloved country.

"The hand that held this cane, when an American agent in London, at the time the Stamp Act was passed, wrote to his intimate friend, Charles Thompson, Esq. of blessed memory, but now no more on earth, that the Sun of Liberty was set, and that we must in America "light up the candles of industry and economy."

"The hand that held this cane was among the foremost in signing our Independence.

"The hand that held this cane met Lord Howe, sent out to conciliate America. His Lordship expressed "the extreme pain he would suffer in being obliged to distress those he so much regarded." "I feel thankful to your Lordship," replied Franklin, "for your regard. The Americans will show their gratitude, by endeavouring to lessen the pain you may feel on their account, in exerting their utmost abilities to take good care of themselves."

"The hand that held this cane signed the definitive Treaty of Peace, which consummated our Independence.

"You will recollect, Sir, that at threescore years and ten, Dr. Franklin embarked in a merchant vessel for France, disregarding the risks he run, provided he was in the way of his duty, serving his country, and, providentially for these United States, he arrived safe in France. Suppose, for a moment, that he should have been captured on his passage to France, with a rebel commission in his pocket, what would have been the inevitable consequences? Most assuredly the same line of conduct would have been dealt out to him as was so severely adhered to by the British government, in the case of another disinterested patriot, Henry Laurens, formerly President of Congress, taken on his passage to Europe, and immersed in the Tower of London during the remainder of the war.

"With these impressions, permit me to deliver this relic into your hands for safe keeping, to serve as a memorial to future generations.

"I wish you much health and happiness."

To which the General replied :—

"Sir—I receive this relic with infinite satisfaction, and shall transmit it as requested. You make a great sacrifice, and evince great disinterestedness."

Immediately on the conclusion of this ceremony, the General left the Hotel, and was escorted by the troop of horse of the second and third regiments, the battalion of the eleventh, the battalion of the third doing duty with muskets, and the battalion of infantry of the second regiment, to the steam-boat James Kent, at the foot of Courtlandt-street.—He was also accompanied by the Cincinnati Society, and a number of distinguished citizens. The boat left the wharf amidst the repeated cheers of an immense multitude, assembled on the surrounding wharves, to bid adieu to their much beloved guest. The General remained on deck (bowing with the utmost complacency,) until he could be no longer distinguished by the spectators from the shore.

CHAPTER III.

THE GENERAL'S TOUR THROUGH THE MIDDLE STATES TO THE CITY OF WASHINGTON—RECEPTION BY CONGRESS.

On the arrival of General Lafayette upon the shore of New-Jersey, he was waited upon by General Dayton, Colonel Kinney, and Major Kean, of the suite of Governor Williamson, and conducted to Lyon's Hotel, where he was received by the Governor himself, and introduced to a number of distinguished citizens of New-Jersey. While here, a full basket of large and delicious peaches were presented to the General, from the extensive fruitery of Mr. Taphagan. The General was accompanied to Jersey by the Mayor, Recorder, Members of the Common Council, the Society of Cincinnati, and several other gentlemen, all of whom were politely invited to visit and join in the festivities at Newark, and dine with the company at Elizabethtown. After remaining a few minutes, the General, with his Excellency Governor Williamson, entered a superb carriage, drawn by four beautiful bay horses, and a cavalcade was formed, which proceeded leisurely towards Newark, escorted by a squadron of New-Jersey cavalry, and two companies which had been invited from New-York. Arrived at Bergen, it was found that the inhabitants of that little town had assembled at the Inn, and were so anxious to pay their respects to the General, that he was constrained to alight for a moment. Here, unexpectedly, he was formally addressed by a delegation from the town, and presented with a superb cane made from an apple-tree under which Washington and Lafayette dined, when passing through that town, during the revolution, and which was blown down by the violent gale of the 3d of September, in 1821. The cane is richly mounted with gold, and bears the following inscription :—" Lafayette," on the top, and round the head the words—" Shaded the hero and his friend Washington, in 1779—Presented by the Corporation of Bergen, in 1824."

As General Lafayette re-ascended his carriage and left the ancient village, he was heartily cheered. On approaching the

Passaic bridge, in the vicinity of Newark, a salute was fired from the hill. Having ascended the hill and entered this charming town, it was found that if the military display, and the number of people on the way, had not been so great as was anticipated, both were now far more imposing than one could have supposed. On the green, near Dr. Griffin's Church, were one or two regiments of troops drawn up in a line, in front of a regular encampment of tents, and the broad streets and commons were literally crowded with people. But as the procession passed through the town, it was found that the troops at first seen, formed but a small proportion of the whole. Three thousand infantry and five hundred horse were under arms, and the windows of every house were as full of spectators as the streets. The General was conducted around the extensive lawn south of the Episcopal Church, to the seat of Major Boudinot, where he was introduced to the Judges of the United States District, and Superior State Courts, and to the principal officers of State, and the leading gentlemen of the village, and surrounding country. While here, a deputation from Morristown, his ancient head quarters, waited upon the General, and through their Chairman, presented an appropriate address, in pursuance of a resolution passed at a meeting of the citizens of that town.

The General replied that nothing would afford him greater satisfaction than to visit a town with which so many endearing associations were connected in his mind; but that his arrangements were such, that a visit to Morristown now, were impossible; on his return from the south, however, he should avail himself of some opportunity to pay the patriotic citizens a visit.

After partaking of refreshments, a procession was formed consisting of the principal officers present, the Corporation of Newark, the Members of New-York Corporation present, Colonel Varick, General Morton, and other members of the Cincinnati of New-York, together with delegates and distinguished citizens of New-Jersey, which proceeded to the south end of the green, now environed with troops, and entered between the two columns. At the entrance were ranged in two lines, twenty-four male singers, who sang the following lines:—

Hail! the gallant Chief, whose fame
Is pure as Heaven's ethereal flame!—
Who comes our peaceful fields to cheer,
A Father of ten millions dear!

Oh! strew the blooms of vale and grove—
Bright as our tear—warm as our love!
The present and the past are met
To bid us welcome Lafayette!

The General, followed by the procession, then passed up through the centre of the green until he came within a few yards of a magnificent bower, where he was received by twenty-four females, ranged in the order as before, who sang the following lines:—

We weave the wreath, we pour the wine,
Where smiles like sparkling sun-beams shine,
And hail the thousands fondly met
To greet the matchless Lafayette!

Unseen, around the flow'r-dress'd way,
Shades of the dead in glory play!
While hearts beat high and eyes are wet,
The winds of Heaven hail Lafayette!

He then passed between the lines, the path, as he approached, being strewed with roses and other flowers, and passed through the portico into the splendid rural temple, which had been erected for his reception, where a feeling address was pronounced by Theodore Frelinghuysen, Esq. Attorney-General of the State, in behalf of the town of Newark. The General made a very feeling reply. There were a great number of revolutionary soldiers present. One who was introduced to the General was more than 100 years old. An old lady also pressed forward, whose husband had served with Lafayette, and would not be restrained from shaking hands with the hero.

The bower prepared for the reception of the General was splendid beyond description. The base of the temple covered an area of about 35 feet diameter, and was formed of thirteen arches, representing the thirteen original states, surmounted by a dome, representing the western hemisphere. The pillars which sustained the dome, were fifteen feet in height, and of due proportion. On either side, extending directly back, were colonnades of twelve arches each, intended as arbours for the ladies. But the front was the most imposing. The portico was lofty, and formed four grand triumphal arches, supporting what might be called a tower. On the top of this stood a large and finely wrought golden Eagle, with a crown of laurel in his beak, and on one side a cornucopiæ, and the olive branch and cap of liberty in his talons. In the centre of this portico was erected a platform, on which were two large chairs, and over that intended for the General, hung a canopy in the form of a cone, wreathed with flowers of bright and various hues. In front of the portico, beneath the capital of the pillar, was the name of Lafayette, in large letters wrought of white blossoms Over the several arches forming the portico, were the following inscriptions:—*On the West:* "Now I am going to serve you." *On the South:* "For him whom a nation delights to honour." *On the North:* "We ne'er shall look upon his like again.' *On the East:* "His laurels shall never fade."

The cornices of the portico, within and without, were richly ornamented with flowers, wrought in the body of the work, so as to resemble festoons; and the arches of the interior of the temple were also adorned with flowers. On each side of the portico, extending to the distance of one hundred and fifty feet, and running forward in a moderate angle, were colonnades of twelve arches each, representing the twenty-four states; and, with the portico as a common centre, binding the whole, representing the union of the states. These colonnades formed extensive and beautiful bowers, and were filled with ladies, who advanced in columns after the General was seated, and were introduced. The workmanship of the temple and arbours, which we have attempted to describe, was as neat as the design was beautiful and classical. Every thing was interwoven with the greatest skill and compactness; and by the aid of the verdant box, the artist was enabled to form cornices, capitals, and fret-work, with almost as much exactness as could be preserved in sculpturing marble. It was indeed a fairy palace; and we can give no better idea of its appearance at a distance, than by referring to the foliage in Mr. Vandelyn's picture of the Palace and Garden of Versailles. For the design and execution of this work, the innabitants of Newark are indebted to William Halsey, Esq.

The General, in company with the Governor, and others, then proceeded to review the troops; after which, he received a marching salute, and returned to the house of Major Boudinot, where a sumptuous collation was spread, which was prepared by Mr. Morton, of the Newark Hotel. The repast was moistened with a choice glass of wine. Before rising from the table, Colonel Ward, Chairman of the Committee of Newark, proposed the following toast, which was drank with rapturous applause—"*Our distinguished Guest, General Lafayette.*— We thank France for her Son: May America not forget, and

Europe feel to good purpose the influence of his bright example."

This toast was responded by General Lafayette as follows·—*The town of Newark.*—And may her population, prosperity, and industry, increase in the same wonderful proportion I have been delighted to witness."

The hour of four having arrived, the General retired, and proceeded to Elizabethtown, accompanied by the Governor and suite, a long cavalcade of officers and private gentlemen, and preceded by an escort.

The General arrived at Elizabethtown on Thursday, a little past 5 o'clock, and was received with the utmost enthusiasm. Two large triumphal arches with suitable ornaments and inscriptions, were erected at conspicuous places and proper distances across the principal street, through which the procession passed. On arriving at Rivers' Hotel, the General was received in due form by the Corporation, and an appropriate address delivered by Caleb Halsted, jr. to which a brief but pertinent reply was returned.

At 6 o'clock the party sat down to an excellent dinner given by the Corporation. The room in which it was served was ornamented for the occasion, and no where has more good feeling been manifested than here. The Grand Lodge of New-Jersey had convened at Elizabethtown to pay the honours of the fraternity to their distinguished brother, and he accepted an invitation to visit them in the course of the evening, which invitation was complied with. From thence, at 10 o'clock, he was escorted to the residence of General Dayton, where he lodged. On Friday morning he breakfasted with Governor Ogden, after which he was introduced to the principal citizens of the place, and several surviving soldiers of the revolution.

At 10 o'clock, preparations for his departure having been made, the General entered a superb barouche, prepared by the Corporation for his use, and proceeded for Rahway, escorted as before, and attended by a numerous cavalcade of citizens in carriages and on horseback. On his arrival at Rahway, he was greeted by the assembled population of the village, and an address was presented by a committee, who invited him to partake of a collation, which invitation was accepted.—A splendid arch was thrown across the street, under which he passed. A committee from Woodbridge here met the General, with carriages for himself and suite, and at 12 o'clock the party moved off for that village, accompanied by Governor Williamson and his staff, &c. and arrived at 1 o'clock, where they halted on the green, and the General alighted. Here was a company of revolutionary veterans, formed in line to receive him, with labels "76" on their hats. Their wives, children, and grand-children, in regular procession continued the line, down which the General passed, giving and receiving the most affectionate salutations. At the end of the line, and at right angles with it, stood nine interesting girls, with each a large letter formed by flowers on their breasts, spelling the name Lafayette. The device was a happy one, and attracted the particular attention of the General, who was highly gratified by it. A very impressive address was delivered to him by Mr. Stryker, which received a suitable reply. Another collation was here spread for the company, which having been partaken, the General proceeded for New-Brunswick at 2 o'clock, and arrived at 4. Two beautiful arches of ever-greens and flowers were formed here, through which the procession passed, and was conducted to the City Hall, where he was received in due form by the Corporation, and an address delivered by Dr. Taylor, the Recorder. After receiving the congratulations of the citizens, who were introduced, he was conducted to Follett's Hotel, where a splendid dinner was provided, in a spacious dining-hall, which was beautifully ornamented with wreaths, festoons, inscriptions, &c. &c. While at this place, a committee from the citizens of Monmouth waited upon him with an address, inviting him to pay them a visit. This, however, he was not able to do, consistently with his other engagements. The General passed the night at New-Brunswick, and departed at 7 o'clock the next morning, for Princeton, escorted by a squadron of cavalry under the command of Major Vandyke.

At an early hour in the morning, strangers, and the inhabitants of the neighbouring country flocked into Princeton to catch a glimpse of the Hero; all was life and animation. A little past 10 it was announced that the General was coming. He passed through the town accompanied by a numerous escort of cavalry, until he arrived opposite the centre gate of the College Campus.—The gate was thrown open, and the company assembled formed, the ladies on the right and the gentlemen on the left, leaving an avenue for him to pass to a splendid temple, erected in the centre of the Campus. Having entered the gate and proceeded half way to the temple, under the conduct of Captain Stockton, and J. S. Green, Esq Marshals of the day, he was received by our committee, and addressed in an appropriate speech by Richard Stockton, Esq. in behalf of the citizens. This ceremony being gone through, he was led to a splendid temple. The front facing the street was tastefully decorated; and in a conspicuous situation over the entrance, in large letters, was placed the following motto:—

Literæ virtutem celebrant:
Salve
Dux clarissime,
nobis amicissime,
nobis carissime,
Lafayette.*

The interior was carpeted, contained two sofas, and was decorated with the paintings of Washington, and the battle of Princeton, the battle of York-Town, and the portraits of Drs. Witherspoone and Smith. The decorations, both of the temple and refectory, were the workmanship of the ladies, and did honour to their taste and skill.

On entering the temple the General was received by President Carnahan, and introduced to several gentlemen present, when the President proceeded to deliver to him a degree of L. L. D. which had been conferred on him during the Presidency of Dr. Witherspoone, and is signed by the Doctor and several members of the Corporation at that time. The degree was accompanied by the following neat, elegant, and highly interesting address by Doctor Carnahan:—

"General—Your arrival in the United States has been hailed with a joy as ardent as it is universal; and permit me to say, we are happy to mingle our congratulations with those of our fellow-citizens in bidding the gallant soldier, the friend of Liberty and of Man, welcome to these shores—welcome to Nassau Hall. In common with others, we enjoy the rich blessings of freedom and independence, which your generous aid, at a time of gloom and trial, contributed, under God, in an eminent degree to establish.

"Residing also on a spot renowned in the story of our glorious Revolution for one of the most brilliant exploits of our beloved and revered Washington, surrounded with objects that daily remind us of the arduous struggles of that eventful period,

* Translation—"Letters celebrate heroism: Welcome most renowned General, most friendly to us, and most dear to our hearts, Lafayette."

we cannot forget the generosity of that noble-minded youth who came, like an angel from Heaven, to aid the oppressed and to vindicate the rights of man. We stand on consecrated ground. These classic groves, these venerable walls, have witnessed other scenes than the peaceful contests of the Muses, and retired labours of virtuous youths, ambitious to ascend the hill of science. A mercenary and foreign foe possessed these walls—a ruthless soldiery polluted these academic shades. But the wrongs of Nassau Hall were amply revenged. The sword of Washington, your companion and friend, and the blood of the gallant Mercer, redeemed this seat of science.

"Fully restored to its original destiny by the peace that succeeded the siege and surrender of York-Town, (in which you, Sir, bore a distinguished part,) this College has annually sent forth Alumni, who have held no secondary place in maintaining the freedom and independence of the nation, so ably achieved.

"Here young men from different States have acquired not only the elements of science, but what is of more importance in a government like ours, the love of liberty, and the veneration of those brave men "who fought and bled in freedom's cause." Here, on each succeeding anniversary of our National Independence, our youth have vied with each other in recounting the sufferings, the labours, and the dangers, that attended our Revolution—in celebrating the wisdom and magnanimity of our statesmen—the valour and heroism of our warriors. And permit me to assure you, that on these occasions no name demanded and received a purer and more deserved tribute of praise, than that of Lafayette. Hence the love of liberty and of country that have ever distinguished the sons of Nassau Hall. And if the memory of virtues so sublime, and services so useful, has cherished in our youths a devotion to the principles of 1776, how deep and how salutary must be the impression made by the cheering countenance and living voice of one who exhibited these virtues and performed these services? Happy Youth! who have the felicity to see the man whose property and whose blood were freely given to purchase their inheritance, returning after a lapse of nearly half a century to behold the glorious results of his youthful enterprise, and to receive the thanks of a nation. Yes, generous Youth! Long will you remember this day, and the important lesson that it teaches.—You have before you a model of magnanimity and successful enterprise, equal to any of which you read in Roman or Grecian story.

To which the General made the following reply :—

"Gentlemen—While the name of this city recalls important military remembrance, it is also connected with that of the illustrious college, which, in diffusing knowledge and liberal sentiments, has greatly contributed to turn those successes to the advantage of public liberty. Your library has been destroyed; but your principles were printed in the hearts of American patriots. I feel much obliged, Sir, to your kind recollection of the diploma, which the signature of my respected friend Doctor Witherspoone, renders still more precious to me; and I beg you, gentlemen, and you, interesting grandsons of my contemporary friends, to accept my affectionate acknowledgments."

The General was surrounded by his Excellency the Governor of New-Jersey, the Professors of the College and Seminary, the Reverend Doctor Green, &c. The General's son and secretary were also in the group.

The company, (ladies, citizens, and students of College, and Seminary, and invited strangers,) having been introduced in turn to the General, repaired to the refectory, where a splendid entertainment was provided. After the repast, the General was conducted to the College Library, and thence again to the temple, to view the picture of Washington, which decorated it. He said he thought it an excellent likeness of Washington when he first knew him. The General appeared highly pleased with his reception. From the temple he was conducted to an elegant barouche, and left Princeton about half past 12 o'clock for Trenton.

A lady of Princeton, a grand-daughter of Doctor Franklin, presented Lafayette with an elegant breast-pin, enclosing a lock of the Doctor's hair.

The Infantry and other military, assembled at Trenton, consisting of Light Infantry and Cavalry, from the counties of Hunterdon, Somerset, Burlington, and Gloucester, under the command of General Vliet, were paraded near the boundary line of the Corporation, to receive the General upon his arrival, and were there reviewed by him. After which a procession was formed, and he was conducted to the head of Warren-

The procession then moved down Warren-street, across the lower bridge, and down Bloomsbury-street, until it came to Market-street, up Market-street to Mill Hill, over Mill Hill, and the Upper Bridge, into Greene-street, up Greene-street to Perry-street, down Perry-street to Warren-street, down Warren-street to Second-street, and up Second-street until it came to the State House Yard; the military then opened to the right and left, and General Lafayette and suite, preceded by the Committee of Arrangements, the Governor and suite passed through.

The Committee then opened to the right and left, and the General and Governor, and their suites, passed under the arch erected at the State House Gate, and was received by a choir of young ladies who greeted the General with an ode, composed for the occasion.

The General was then escorted into the Assembly Room by the Governor, followed by the Committee of Arrangements, the General's suite, the Governor's suite, and other military officers. The General was received by the Mayor and Common Council, convened for the occasion, when a cordial address was delivered by the Mayor. To which the General returned a feeling and appropriate answer.

The General was then conducted by the Mayor and Common Council, attended by the Committee of Arrangements, and escorted by the military to the Trenton House, where lodgings had been provided for him—and where a sumptuous dinner was served up—at which were the Governor and suite, Mayor and Common Council, and a large number of officers and citizens.

In the evening the General attended a handsome entertainment, ordered by the Society of Cincinnati, at the City Tavern, where he spent the evening with his brother officers of the Revolutionary Army.

The day was uncommonly fine. An immense number of spectators thronged the town from all parts of the adjacent country.

A spacious arch was thrown across the head of Warren-street, and one near the intersection of Second-street, handsomely decorated with laurel, and ever-greens and flowers, appended in festoons. Over the front gate of the State House Yard, where the General entered, the old arch was placed, which in 1789 was erected in honour of General Washington, by the citizens of Trenton, as he passed on to New-York to take upon himself the office of President of the United States, Congress being then convened in that place.

In the evening, the arches in Warren-street were handsomely illuminated.

On Sunday morning he went to the Presbyterian Church, and in the afternoon visited Joseph Bonaparte, with whom he spent two hours. It was an interesting meeting—both were deeply affected, and warmly embraced each other. Returning to Trenton, the General dined with Colonel Cadwallader, with Governor Williamson and suite, &c. The Philadelphia Committee, and Secretary of State, &c. of Pennsylvania, and the aids of Governor Shultze of Pennsylvania, were introduced to him in the course of the evening.

On Monday, September 28th, the General crossed the Delaware at Morrisville, thirty miles from Philadelphia, where he was met by Governor Shultze and suite, under an escort of 250 cavalry. A vast concourse of people were assembled to hail the Guest of the Nation, and bid him welcome. The Governor received him upon his landing with the following address:—

"General Lafayette—The citizens of Pennsylvania behold, with the most intense feeling and exalted regard, the illustrious friend and companion of Washington.

"With sentiments of the highest veneration and gratitude, we receive the early and great benefactor of the United States, the enlightened statesman, philanthropist, and patriot of both hemispheres.

"The sincere and universal joy which your arrival has diffused over the nation, is no where more deeply or enthusiastically felt, than in Pennsylvania; whose fields and streams are rendered memorable by your achievements; whose citizens were the followers of your standard, and the witnesses of your sacrifices and toils, in defence of American liberty. The eventful scenes of your useful life are engraven on our hearts. A nation has rejoiced at your successes, and sympathized with your sorrows.

"With ardent pleasure we have ever observed your strenuous exertions as the friend of man; and whilst your great services, rendered in the cause of humanity, have commanded our admiration, the purity of your motives has insured the love and affection of Americans.

"With the best feelings of the heart we now approach you,

with the assurance that, if any thing could add to our happiness on this interesting occasion, it would be the hope of enjoying the distinguished honour of your permanent residence among us, and that a long and splendid life of usefulness may be closed in this State, whose soil has been moistened with your blood, generously shed in the cause of virtue, liberty, and independence."

To which General Lafayette made the following reply :—

"Sir—On the happy moment, long and eagerly wished for, when I once more tread the soil of Pennsylvania, I find in her affectionate welcome, so kindly expressed by her first magistrate, a dear recollection of past favours, and a new source of delightful gratifications. The very names of this State and her Capitol, recall to the mind those philanthropic and liberal sentiments, which have marked every step of their progress.

"Pennsylvania has been the theatre of most important events; a partaker in the arduous toils and meritorious sacrifices, which insured the success of our glorious and fruitful revolution. I particularly thank you, Sir, for your gratifying mention of my personal obligation to the Pennsylvania line, nor will I ever forget, that on Pennsylvania ground, not far from this spot, I enjoyed, for the first time, the delight to find myself under American tents, and in the family of our beloved Commander in Chief. Now, Sir, Pennsylvania is in full possession, and reaps all the prosperities, and happy consequences, of that great national union, of those special institutions, which, by offering in a self-governed people the most perfect example of social order that ever existed, have reduced to absurdity and ridicule the anti-popular arguments of pretended statesmen in other countries. In whatever manner I may be disposed of, by the duties and feelings in which you have been pleased to sympathize, I shall ever rank this day among the most fortunate in my life; and while I beg your excellency personally to accept my cordial acknowledgments, I have the honour to offer to him, as Governor of the State, a tribute of profound gratitude, and respected devotion, to the citizens of Pennsylvania."

Having ascended his barouche and six, the General proceeded on his way; and did not reach Frankford until seven o'clock in the evening—such being the throngs which lined the roads, and the number of the welcomes offered, and which he could not refuse. He passed the night at Frankford.

A 9 o'clock on Tuesday morning, he left Frankford with a numerous escort of Dignitaries and citizens. The population of the city poured forth at an early hour to meet him. Carriages, horsemen, and pedestrians, filled every avenue from Frankford to Philadelphia, a distance of nearly five miles; and the windows and stages were thronged with females, all eager to welcome him. Loud and reiterated as were the acclamations, the voices could not give full utterance to the overflowing hearts.

In a field of forty or fifty acres, at the entrance of the city, a Division of Militia, composed of Cavalry, Artillery, and Infantry, were drawn up in hollow square to receive the Patriot Hero, whose approach was announced by a salute of one hundred rounds of artillery. This military spectacle is described as grand in the extreme. The General, uncovered, was seen standing in his barouche by the whole field. The car of Saladin, it is said, could not exceed, in accompaniments, that of Lafayette. The troops exceeded 5400. After the review, which the General made on foot, he received the saluting honours in his barouche.

The line of march into the city was then taken up. It extended nearly three miles, and passed through numerous streets. More than six hours were consumed in proceeding from Frankford to the State House, a distance of about four miles. A full description of this procession, and the decorated arches cannot be given—the following is an outline: —

A cavalcade of 100 citizens preceded; followed by 100 Field and Staff officers.—Then came a square of cavalry; a band of Music mounted, and a corps of 160 cavalry.—Next, a Brigade of Infantry, (2000 strong,) with flank companies.

Committee of Arrangements.

General Lafayette and Judge Peters in the splendid barouche.

Then followed four other barouches, drawn by four horses, with Governors Shultze and Williamson, and suites, the General's family, and distinguished individuals.

Then three cars of large dimensions, containing 120 revolutionary heroes and worthies, each characteristically decorated. The cars bearing on the front, "Washington," on the rear, "Lafayette," and on the sides, "Defenders of our country," "The survivors of 1776."

Then advanced 400 young men. Then the PROCESSION OF TRADES, led by a car, containing a body of Printers, at work at case and press—the latter striking off and distributing copies of an Ode on the occasion, followed by the Typographical Society, with a banner, with the inscription, "LAFAYETTE—*The Friend of Universal Liberty, and the Rights of the Press.*"

Then followed 200 Cordwainers, (with banners, badges, emblems, &c. The other trades were also decorated;)—300 Weavers;—150 Rope-makers;—150 Lads, uniformly dressed; —100 Ship-builders;—700 mechanics of different professions, not enumerated;—150 Coopers, with a car, containing a Cooper's shop, the workmen fitting the staves and driving hoops:—Then came 150 Butchers, well mounted, and neatly dressed in their frocks;—then 260 Cartmen, mounted, with aprons trimmed with blue; and a body of 150 Riflemen, in frocks, dressed with plaids, leopard skins, &c. A company of Artillery, with two pieces; a Brigade of Infantry, (1800 strong,) and the New-Jersey Cavalry. A body of 300 farmers closed the procession.

Besides the above, there were the Red Men of the State, the Lafayette Association, the True Republican Society, the Washington and Lafayette Society; and the German American Society.

The whole appearance of this truly *Grand Procession* was august and imposing. As it passed, Lafayette! Lafayette! sprang from the voices of a multitude that rolled on, and on, and on, like wave after wave of the ocean, in numbers we shall not presume to name, [but which were estimated at 200,000,] Lafayette beat in every heart—Lafayette hung on every tongue —Lafayette glowed in every cheek—Lafayette glistened in every swimming eye—Lafayette swelled on every gale. The whole city and country appeared to have arrayed themselves in all their glory, and beauty, and strength, at once to witness and adorn the majesty of the spectacle; and the fashionable part of the community seemed determined to exhibit the perfection of taste in the beauty of the decoration of their persons, and the richness of their attire. In Chesnut-street, wreaths were cast into the barouche, as it passed, and many of them were from the fair hands of the Quakeresses.

After the procession had passed through the principal streets, the front halted at the old State House, which contains the Hall in which the *Declaration of Independence* was signed in 1776.

Here the General alighted, passed under a most magnificent

triumphal arch, and was conducted to the Hall, which is forty feet square, and was decorated in a most splendid manner. Among the decorations was a Statue of Washington, and Portraits of William Penn, Franklin, Robert Morris, Francis Hopkinson, Greene, Wayne, Montgomery, Hamilton, Gates, Rochambeau, Charles Carrol, M'Kean, Jefferson, Hancock, Adams, Madison, Monroe, and Charles Thompson. The portrait of Washington by Peale, occupied the first place, and was most splendidly decorated. Here were assembled the City authorities, the Society of Cincinnati, the Judges, Officers of the Army and Navy, and the Committee of Arrangements, all seated on superb sofas. The Governor of the State having been presented, General Lafayette, Judge Peters, and George Washington Lafayette were introduced, the company all standing. The Mayor of the city then welcomed the Guest, in the following address:—

"General—The citizens of Philadelphia welcome to their homes, the Patriot who has long been dear to their hearts.

"Grateful at all times for the enjoyment of a free government, they are, on this occasion, peculiarly anxious, but unable to express a deep felt sentiment of pure affection towards those venerated men, whose martial and civil virtues, under providence, have conferred upon themselves and their descendants, this mighty blessing.

"Forty-eight years ago, in this city, and in this hallowed Hall, which may emphatically be called the *Birth-place of Independence*, a convention of men, such as the world has rarely seen, pre-eminent for talents and patriotism, solemnly declared their determination to assume for themselves the right of self-government, and that they and their posterity should thenceforth assert their just rank among the nations of the earth. A small, but cherished band of those who breasted the storm and sustained the principles thus promulgated to the world, still remains.—In the front rank of these worthies, history will find, and we now delight to honour, General Lafayette, whose whole life has been devoted to the cause of freedom, and to the support of the unalienable rights of man.

"General—Many of your co-patriots have passed away, but the remembrance of their virtues and their services shall never pass from the minds of this people; theirs is an imperishable fame, the property of ages yet to come. But we turn from the fond recollection of the illustrious dead, to hail with heart-felt joy the illustrious living, and again bid welcome, most kindly and affectionately welcome, to the Guest of the Nation, the Patriot Lafayette."

To which the General replied as follows :—

"Sir—My entrance into this fair and great city, amidst the most solemn and affecting recollections, and under all the circumstances of a welcome, which no expression could adequately acknowledge, has excited emotions in my heart, in which are mingled the feelings of nearly fifty years.

"Here, Sir, within these sacred walls, by a council of wise and devoted patriots, and in a style worthy of the deed itself, was boldly declared the independence of these vast United States, which, while it anticipated the independence, and I hope, the *republican* independence of the whole American Hemisphere, has begun for the civilized world, the era of a new and of the only true social order, founded on the unalienable rights of man, the practicability and advantage of which, are every day admirably demonstrated by the happiness and prosperity of your populous city.

"Here, Sir, was planned the formation of our virtuous, brave, revolutionary army, and the providential inspiration received, that gave the command of it to our beloved, matchless, Washington. But these and many other remembrances are mingled with a deep regret for the numerous cotemporaries, for the great and good men, whose loss we have remained to mourn. —It is to their services, Sir, to your regard for their memory, to your knowledge of the friendships I have enjoyed, that I refer the greater part of honours, here and elsewhere received, much superior to my individual merit.

"It is also under the auspices of their venerated names, as well as under the impulse of my own sentiments, that I beg you, Mr. Mayor, you gentlemen of both Councils, and all the citizens of Philadelphia, to accept the tribute of my affectionate respect and profound gratitude."

The arches were very numerous, and extremely beautiful, tasty, and ingenious—uniting high moral feeling, with ardent patriotism. Some idea may be formed of them by the following description of the one in Chesnut-street :—

It was constructed of frame work, covered with canvass, and painted in perfect imitation of stone, after the plan of the triumphal Arch of *Septimus Severus*, at Rome. Its front 45 feet, depth 12, embracing a basement story of the Doric order, from which the Arch sprung to the height of 24 feet from the pavement.

The spandals on each front were decorated with figures of *Fame*, painted in *basso relievo*, having their arms extended and holding a civic crown over the key stone. The wings of the Ionic order, were decorated with statues of *Liberty*, *Victory*, *Independence*, and *Plenty*, with suitable mottos. The whole surmounted by an entablature 30 feet, and supporting a flight of steps; in the centre were the Arms of the city, executed by Mr. SULLY; on each side of the Arms were placed statues of *Wisdom* and *Justice*, sculptured by Mr. RUSH, with appropriate emblems. This splendid work of Art was designed by Mr. STRICKLAND, and executed by Messrs. WARREN, DARLEY, and JEFFERSON, scene painters. The superficial surface of painted canvass exceeded 3000 square feet.

The Governor of Louisiana and many strangers and citizens were introduced. Among others, the General recognised an old friend in Colonel FERRET, and embraced him. The Colonel burst into a flood of tears, and was so completely overwhelmed with emotion, as to be compelled to retire. He commanded a regiment in the revolutionary war, was wounded and knocked off his horse.

At five o'clock, the General left the Hall, accompanied by the City Authorities, resumed his barouche, and was escorted by six companies, under Colonel WILLIAMS, to the Mansion-House. In the evening he paid visits to Mrs. MORRIS, and several other distinguished Ladies of his former acquaintance.

In the evening the City was illuminated. Numerous transparencies were exhibited, which displayed exquisite taste and elegance. A slight shower of rain, threw a damp over the buoyant spirits for a short time, but it was soon over. Windows were arrayed with beautiful marble and alabaster, and decorated with the fairest contents of the green houses. The United States Bank was a perfect anomaly in illumination. The lights were so arranged as not to be seen, and the doors being thrown open so as to discover the interior, the whole building presented the appearance of a palace of transparent marble.

On Wednesday the General held a levee at the Hall of the State House, and thousands shook his hand. At this levee he received no less than fourteen Addresses, from the aged Soldiers; the Clergy, presented by Bishop White; the Philosophical and Bible Societies; the University; the Chamber of Commerce; the Bar; the Young Men; the French Citizens; the Washington Grays; the Lafayette Association; the Revolutionary Officers, and the Young Ladies of several Schools. His answer to each was peculiarly pertinent. He afterwards dined with the corporation. The following was his toast on the occasion:—

"The City of Philadelphia, where American Independence was first proclaimed, and where the Holy Alliance of public order with popular institutions is every day happily demonstrated."

In the evening he visited General CADWALLADER, and received all the officers of the late parade.

On Thursday he dined with his family; and in the evening called on Doctor Griffith; was at Mr. Huerta's Concert; and afterwards waited on Mrs. Powell.

On Friday he dined with Governor Shultze; and before dinner called on Judge Peters, and Mrs. (Major) Jackson. After dinner he called on the widow and daughter of Colonel Tousard, then visited Mrs. Nicklin, the daughter of the late General M'Pherson.

In the evening he visited the Philosophical Society, and spent the remainder at the house of Mrs. N. Biddle.

On Saturday he visited the Navy Yard, attended by the Governor and citizens of the first distinction, escorted by the United States Marines, a regiment of Militia, several independent companies, and a long civic procession. His arrival at the Yard was announced by a salute, from the John Adams, commanded by Captain Dallas. He first alighted at Major Gamble's quarters, where he received an address from the Corporation of Southwalk. As he passed the green a number of children chanted suitable pieces of music in honour of the Hero. He was then received by Commodore Barron and his officers, was addressed by the former, and took a view of the ships of war, &c. A collation was provided in the Mould room by the officers of the station, at which over 500 Ladies and 200 Gentlemen were present. After refreshment the Commodore introduced the Ladies separately to the General, who took each by the hand, receiving from them very agreeable tokens of affection and admiration. The John Adams was beautifully decorated and manned on the occasion. The reception of the General by Mrs. Gamble was universally praised.

After returning from the Navy Yard, the General dined with

upwards of 400 Brethren of the Fraternity, at the Masonic Hall. The scene was brilliant and munificent.

Of the Masons present were Brothers George Washington Lafayette, La Vasseur, Commodore Stewart, Major Gamble, General Porter, and Colonel Victor Dupont, of Delaware, former aid to Brother Lafayette.

In the evening he paid a visit to Joseph Reed, Esq. attended the Concert at the Washington Saloon, and spent the remainder of the evening at the house of General Cadwallader, in company with Mr. Adams, Secretary of State, and other distinguished citizens.

On the Sabbath he attended divine worship at Christ Church, and heard a sermon from the venerable Bishop White. He afterwards dined at the country residence of Judge Peters, in company with Mr. John Quincy Adams, Mr. Forseth, Mr. Breck, General Cadwallader, General Barnard, Major Gamble, and many others.

The Grand Civic Ball given in honour of General Lafayette, on Monday evening, at the New Theatre, exceeded in magnificence and beauty any thing of the kind ever witnessed. Between fifteen and seventeen hundred ladies and gentlemen were present, exhibiting an unrivalled galaxy of fashion, elegance, and splendour. The company assembled early, and were nearly all present at 9 o'clock, when the General arrived, forming for his reception a most imposing group and avenue. The details of this brilliant entertainment it is not in our power to give.

Of the company present were Mrs. (Robert) Morris, the Misses Bollman, daughters of Doctor Bollman, who attempted with Colonel Huger to secure Lafayette from Olmutz, Governor Shultze, Governor Williamson, John Quincy Adams, Esq., General Barnard, and distinguished citizens from many of the States, the whole amounting to nearly 200. Several thousand persons were present.

Over 2000 pupils of the Schools of both sexes, were arranged on Tuesday morning in the State House yard to receive and address General Lafayette.—The spectacle was beautiful and interesting.

On the 5th of October, Lafayette left Philadelphia. He passed the Brandywine, and entered Wilmington, the capital of Delaware, on the 6th about noon. He was received with demonstrations of lively gratitude and joy; and a sumptuous repast was provided for him. He then proceeded to Newcastle in that State, and was present at the marriage of Colonel V Dupont, formerly one of his aids in France. From this place he proceeded to Frenchtown.

Agreeably to arrangement, the steam-boat United States, captain Edward Trippe, left Baltimore for Frenchtown on Wednesday morning at 9 o'clock, with the committee from the corporation of that city, the military committee, and other gentlemen, who went with the committee by invitation. This deputation was accompanied by a most interesting member, Mr. Du Boismarten, a venerable Frenchman, whose head is whitened with 83 cold winters, many of them he had found not only cold, but cheerless and bleak. He is the personage who procured and commanded the vessel that first landed Lafayette upon our soil. At 3 o'clock the company partook of an excellent dinner provided for the occasion.

The boat arrived at Frenchtown about half past 4 in the afternoon. The Governor's Aids accompanied by a squadron of Cavalry, under the command of Captain Jacob Hollingsworth, proceeded immediately to the Delaware line, to escort the General to Frenchtown.

At about 8 o'clock in the evening, the Hon. John Quincy Adams arrived at Frenchtown, in the Union Line, on his way to Washington. The Deputation waited upon him and informed him that he had been invited to be present at Baltimore to participate in the reception of General Lafayette, and desired him to come on board of the steam-boat United States. He thanked them kindly for this mark of respect and attention, and accepted the invitation. He was then conducted into the cabin and introduced to all present.

The General, having been detained till very late at the nuptial party of his friend, Mr. Victor Dupont, did not arrive at the Maryland line till after 1 o'clock in the morning. He was there presented by Louis M'Lane, Esq. Chairman of the Delaware Committee, to the Aids of the Governor of Maryland. The first aid announced to the General in very appropriate and warm terms, in behalf of his Excellency Governor Stevens, a cordial welcome to the State of Maryland; and informed him that they were ready to escort him to head quarters which were established at Fort M'Henry. The General arrived at Frenchtown a little after 2 o'clock, to which place the Delaware Committee accompanied him. Mr. M'Lane there, on parting, made a most feeling and elegant address, and in behalf of himself and associates, took a most affectionate leave. The Aids of the Governor then conducted the General on board the steam-boat, where the Deputations received him upon the deck. Mr. Morris, President of the First Branch of the City Council, and Chairman of the Committee, advanced to the Guest and addressed him in a manner that evinced at once that he felt what he spoke from the bottom of his heart—it was as follows:—

"General—The immortal Franklin, dwelling with rapture on the high destination which his matchless and prophetic mind foresaw awaited his country—ever alive for the success of its untried institutions, imagined the happiness of it would afford a patriot of the revolution who had been summoned from this world, could he, at a distant period, be allowed to return and see fulfilled all his fond hopes in relation to this our beloved country.

"Illustrious Sir—That which appeared but the offspring of the musings and reveries of our Patriot Father, has substantially been realized in you. The distinguished part which you acted during the war of our Independence, and the sequel of your life, furnish abundant evidence of the intense interest which you have entertained for our welfare—your chivalric exertions, in our behalf, having been crowned with peace, you gave a distinguished proof that no sordid or selfish motive impelled your actions. You returned to the land of your fathers! —blessings on your name and work proclaimed from every tongue. Between that and the present time, is an era in which has occurred the most extraordinary events recorded in history—when the empires of the Old World have been convulsed to their foundations, and thrones dashed one against another. During the same period there has arisen in this our New World, a confederate Republic, which had its origin with, and is acted upon and kept in motion by the people, to whom this invaluable right belongs—a principle which the whole tenor of your consistent political life has shown dear to you. Its fitfulness to conduce to our happiness in peace, and protection in war, and every other object of legitimate government, has been confirmed by every variety of event that could illustrate its wisdom and test its durability. It has pleased Divine Providence to have spared and protracted your eventful life, that you might contrast the origin with the present elevated station which this country has assumed among the nations of the earth; and to realize the blessings enjoyed by ten millions of people, "who sitting under their own vine and fig-tree," with our country's friend, and the *Friend of Mankind!*

"The Corporation of Baltimore, uniting with our common country, in the joy that swells every bosom, as the organ of public sentiment, have deputed us to advance, to receive and welcome you, and, as heralds, proclaim the lively and distinguished pleasure our community holds in reserve, at the prospect of our city being again honoured by your presence, and to assure you, that could their sensations towards you bear any additional excitement, they would derive renewed strength from the gratifying manner, that you have recurred to an event in the revolutionary history, which affords an assurance, they have maintained a place in your recollection. Although time has diminished the number of those who personally knew you, and their survivers but a chosen few, who breasted the same storm, who mingled their blood with yours, in the same glorious strife. Nevertheless, there has arisen a new generation, who are restless and impatient to survey the features of a man, whose talents, whose energies, whose virtues, whose disinterested services in the cause of Liberty, have long since roused in their bosoms the raptures of enthusiasm; and who delight to repeat the never dying name of Lafayette."

The General having but just left his Delaware friends, and meeting so suddenly this reception, it affected him most sensibly—he pressed his hand to his heart, and said, *I am grateful.* He was then introduced by Mr. Morris to the gentlemen of the Corporation—then to General Harper, who delivered a feeling address.

General Smith and Colonel Bentalou stepped forward and announced to him the object of their mission, and the joy they felt in meeting him again. The General embraced them in the warmest and most affectionate manner, and inquired particularly after his old friends and associates.—The meeting of the General with the amiable, retiring, and venerable Mons. Du Boismartin, was of a most touching character to the sensitive mind—they held each other by the hand and conversed together in French for a considerable time. After the introductions were gone through, Captain Trippe announced that he had an entertainment ready for the company. They all followed the General to the cabin, and a little after 3 o'clock the General repaired to the ladies cabin, prepared for his lodging room, and invited Mr. Adams to accompany him. The company then retired to their births. During the night, particularly the early part of it, the rain poured down in torrents, in which the Cavalry and the Governor's Aids were drenched, but they heeded it not.

Just as the steam-boat entered the Patapsco, the threatening clouds dispersed, the morning sun shone forth in its brightest effulgence, and seemed to bid "*Welcome to Lafayette.*" During the night the company were apprehensive the day would be unpropitious to Baltimore, but as "the bright sun shone out," their hearts leaped for joy. On approaching the fort, the steam-boats Maryland, Virginia, Philadelphia, and Eagle, all beautifully dressed with flags and streamers flying, came down the river, full of anxious citizens, to meet the United States, and passed transversely around her—as they passed, the people on board waved their hats, and gave the most hearty, enlivening, and oft repeated cheering. The five boats, in regular order, the *United States* leading the van, proceeded for the fort, during which they came along-side, alternately, and the passengers saluted the General, which he received, uncovered, in the most cordial manner. The whole scene was most interesting.

The landing was a very interesting scene. The barge, commanded by Captain Gardner, and manned by some of our most respectable ship masters, was the first that made for the shore—it contained General Lafayette, Mr. Secretary Adams, General Smith, Mr. Du Boismartin, and Mr. Morris. In the second boat, George Washington Lafayette, Mons. La Vaiseur, Colonel Paul Bentalou, Mr. Patterson, and the Governor's Aids, and the other members of the Deputation followed in succession. The General was received at the platform at Fort M'Henry, by Col. Hindman, of the army of the U. States, and Edward G. Woodyear, Esq. a member of the committee of arrangement. The officers of the Army and Navy in Baltimore, the Citizen Volunteers of Fort M'Henry, during the bombardment, the Committee of Vigilance and Safety of 1814, and the officers of the late 36th and 38th United States regiments of Infantry, had their stations, and the General passed through their line on his march up to the "star fort." Upon entering the gate the troops of the garrison presented arms—then opened to the right and left, which brought to his view the tent of Washington. Upon which His Excellency Governor

Stevens advanced from the tent, and greeted him with the following address :—

"General—In bidding you a hearty welcome to the State of Maryland, whilst I gratify the honest feelings of my own heart, I express, but feebly, those of the people, whom it is my pride and pleasure on this occasion to represent.

"Beneath this venerable canopy, many a time and oft have you grasped the friendly hand of our illustrious Washington, aided his council with your animating voice, or shared with him the hardy soldier's meal. The incidents which the association so forcibly recalls, however inspiring, it were needless to dwell upon. The recollection of them fills the mind with gratitude, a full measure of which is justly due to you, as the generous companion of our fathers, the gallant and disinterested soldier of liberty.

"May the sentiments of gratitude towards the author of the blessings we enjoy, never be weakened in the bosoms of my countrymen.

"On this very ground, scarce ten years are past since our brave fellow citizens, have proved that they knew how to defend the liberty, which you nobly assisted them to achieve. Ten times an hundred years shall elapse, and the glorious example shall not be lost upon them.

"You are about, General, to enter the city of Baltimore, which you have known in other days. In her growth and embellishment, you will behold a symbol of our national prosperity, under popular Institutions, and a purely Representative Government. Her monuments aptly illustrate the feelings of my fellow citizens.

"In the column which has been reared to the blessed memory of Washington, we have an evidence of the veneration and permanency with which they cherish the memory of your compatriots, the heroes of the revolution. In the column of latter date, you will discern the gratitude of freemen, for the services of those who devote themselves to the cause of liberty.

"Welcome, thrice welcome, General, to the soil of Maryland. Nothing that we can do, can too strongly express to you the affection and respect which we entertain for your person and your principles, or the joy with which we receive you among us, as a long absent Father upon a visit to his children."

The Governor then conducted him to the Tent, where he found the Society of the Cincinnati, the patriarchs of the revolution—here he was received and embraced by all of them—the scene was one of the most impressive and heart-touching, that was ever witnessed—all were convulsed into tears, but they were tears of the most heart-felt joy and gratulation.

Colonel John E. Howard, the hero of Cowpens, and President of the Cincinnati Society, when the first emotion had subsided, addressed the General in the name of the Society, who in his reply, declared that "language could not express his feelings with meeting with his brothers in arms, in the Tent of their common friend, the beloved Washington." He then most affectionately embraced his old friends, Charles Carroll, of Carrollton, one of the signers of the Declaration of Independence, General Beeson, General Stricker, Colonel Howard, and all the aged members of the association, while tears rolled down their venerable cheeks. He shook hands with the younger members in the most cordial manner, looked frequently with an inquiring eye round the Tent, and seemed deeply affected. On discovering part of Washington's camp equipage, he said in an under voice, "I remember!" There was not a dry eye in the Tent.

The General and invited guests then retired to an adjoining Marquee, to an excellent breakfast prepared for the occasion, when many recollections of former days were brought forcibly to mind; and when this repast closed, the General was conducted to his barouche, accompanied as before by all the civil and military authorities present. When he had taken his seat, Charles Carroll, General Smith, and Colonel Howard, were handed into the same barouche, which was followed by another containing George Washington Lafayette, whose warm reception we should have noticed before, Colonel Bentalou, and two other gentlemen, and other carriages followed.

The General's barouche exceeds in beauty any thing of the kind in America; it was built expressly for the purpose, by Curlet & Co. of this city. When the carriage drove from the outer gate of the fort, the General was received by about one thousand cavalry, who formed his escort into the city, followed by thousands of citizens.

On passing Federal Hill, a salute of twenty-four guns was fired, to denote the number of States composing the Union, on the return of the General to America.

Descending Federal Hill, the procession passed under a beautiful arch at the head of Forest-street. The crowd of citizens hailing him here, was extremely great, and the increase continued every step till he reached the magnificent arch at the head of Market-street, where his friends descended from the barouche, and he alone proceeded down the line of military, which extended far into Old Town, and from this fact it may be collected that ten thousand troops were present. The appearance of Market-street was splendid and animating—every house-top, every door was filled with spectators; and of the multitudes of female beauty and fashion that crowded all the windows, and every street, it would be no easy task to give a description.

The streets were also thronged, but the greatest order prevailed, and the Nation's Guest passed along the vast line, cheered by a hundred thousand voices, and by the waving of handkerchiefs and flags. Having passed through a splendid arch at Market-street bridge, he proceeded to Fell's Point, and returning by Pratt and Gay-streets, he descended at the Exchange, and entering the great hall, was received by the Mayor and Councils. The Mayor delivered an appropriate address, to which the General made an affectionate reply, and after the usual ceremonies, he returned to his barouche, and proceeded to Light-street, across which, at the entrance into Market-street, an elegant pavilion had been erected, into which he was conducted, accompanied by a number of distinguished persons; and here he received the passing salute of one of the finest assemblages of military men ever seen in any American city; language would fail in describing the interest and splendour of this ceremony which occupied two hours.

At 5 o'clock, the General sat down to a very splendid dinner, at which the Mayor presided, supported by William Patterson and John B. Morris, Esquires, as Vice Presidents. The room was elegantly illuminated, the glare of light thrown on the furniture, and the numerous portraits of Revolutionary Heroes, produced the finest effect—And the company was regaled by the music of a band, next to none perhaps in this country. The Governor of Maryland and his aids—John Quincy Adams, Secretary of State, General Macomb, of the Army of the United States, Colonel Howard, General Samuel Smith, Mr. Curtis of Arlington, Generals Stricker, Stuart, Reed, Benson, Harper, Stansbury, M'Donald, and the Colonels commanding regiments from the country and in the city, and a great number of others were present.

The standard of the brave Count Pulaski, who fell at the assault upon Savannah, was proudly borne in the ranks of the corps of volunteers, fastened to one of the spears belonging to the Legion, entwined with Pulaski's sword and cross belt, now owned by Colonel Bentalou, as a pledge of affectionate remembrance, of his departed friend.

In the evening the city illumination was splendid; the Exchange and the Banks exhibited a blaze of light. The Dispensary, Theatre, Museum, the Arches, the Pyramids of fire near the Bridge on Market-street, and the brilliant revolving star, three feet in diameter, all had an imposing effect beyond the power of language to express. The whole scene was interspersed with transparencies, mottos, and devices, all peculiarly appropriate to the occasion.

At 12 o'clock on Friday, the General was addressed at the Exchange by Major General Harper, in behalf of the third division, and the officers were all presented to him. The General next received the attentions of the citizens generally, who shook him most cordially by the hand.

About half past 7 the General arrived at the Masonic Hall, which was most splendidly illuminated, and decorated for the occasion. The M. W. G. Master delivered a feeling and appropriate address; to which the General returned a cordial and affectionate reply. More than 700 brethren were present, splendidly decorated in all the costume of the craft.

From the Masonic Hall the General repaired to the Ball Room, which for taste, elegance, and beauty, exceeded all the powers of description. This splendid Ball Room was no less than the theatre, specially fitted up for the occasion. The reception of the General was also sublime and imposing beyond the powers of conception, and his introduction to this splendid circle of ladies was a scene most truly interesting. This ceremony being closed, a signal was given by a flourish of bugles, and instantly the dance began. This also was a brilliant scene, which continued until half past seven, when supper was announced. General Lafayette led the way, escorted by the managers, and the supper room exhibited a scene as splendid and imposing as the Ball Room. The cheerful conviviality exhibited in the supper room, the appropriate toasts that were drank, and the cordial hilarity of the guests, when taken collectively, may be considered as the finishing touch to this magnificent fete at Baltimore.

General Lafayette left Baltimore on Monday for Washington, accompanied by the Mayor, the Committee of Arrangements, the Aids of the Governor, and an escort of cavalry to Rossburg, where he lodged on Monday night, and breakfasted on Tuesday morning. After which he was accompanied and escorted as before to the line of the District of Columbia, where he was met by a committee, introduced to a superb barouche, escorted by a military cortege, and a cavalcade, and received a national salute of artillery. Here a brilliant Procession was formed, which was preceded by a corps of cavalry, and brought up by a cavalcade of citizens, the whole extending over two miles; while the entire way-sides were thronged with citizens who made the air again resound with the shouts of welcome. He was thus conducted to the Capitol square, and passed under a Civic Arch, elegantly decorated and enlivened with appropriate inscriptions. Under the Arch were 25 young Ladies (representing the 24 States, and the District of Columbia,) dressed in white, with blue scarfs and wreaths of roses, and each bearing a banner designating the State and District she represented. They had been escorted to the Arch by some Juvenile companies. As soon as the General arrived, Miss S. W. Watterston, representing the District, and only eleven years old, advanced, and presented a very appropriate address. It is needless to express the feeling which the Guest manifested at the scene. He shook hands with each of the interesting group. After receiving the welcome of another group of young Ladies from Georgetown, he entered the Capitol, passed through the rotunda, and entered the Tent of Washington. Here he was met by the Mayor, and other Authorities, Officers, Clergy, &c. &c. To an address from the Mayor, full of fine feeling, the General made the following reply :—

"The kind and flattering reception with which I am honoured by the citizens of Washington, excite the most lively feelings of gratitude; those grateful feelings, Sir, at every step of my happy visit to the United States, could not but enhance the inexpressible delight I have enjoyed at the sight of the immense and wonderful improvements, so far beyond even the fondest anticipations of a warm American heart; and which, in the space of forty years, have so gloriously evinced the superiority of popular institutions and self-government, over the too imperfect state of political civilization, found in every part of the other hemisphere. In this august place, which bears the most venerable of all ancient and modern names, I have, Sir, the pleasure to contemplate, not only a centre of that constitutional Union so necessary to these States, so important to the interests of mankind, but also a great political school where attentive observers from other parts of the world may be taught the practical science of true social order.

"Among the circumstances of my life to which you have been pleased to allude, none can afford me such dear recollections as my having been early adopted as an American soldier, so there is not a circumstance of my reception in which I take so much pride, as in sharing those honours with my beloved companions in arms. Happy I am to feel that the marks of affection and esteem bestowed on me, bear testimony to my perseverance in the American principles I received under the tent of Washington, and of which I shall, to my last breath, prove myself a devoted disciple. I beg you, Mr. Mayor, and the gentlemen of the Corporation, to accept my respectful acknowledgments to you and to the citizens of Washington."

After the customary introductions, the General reviewed the military, amounting to 1600, and received a grand salute. The General accompanied by the Mayor, and attended by General Brown, and Commodore Tingey, proceeded to the President's House. The streets were lined with spectators, and the windows filled with ladies, all repeating benedictions on the beloved Guest, and waving their handkerchiefs in token of their happiness.

On alighting, the General was received by the Marshal of the District, and supported by General Brown and Commodore Tingey, of the Committtee of Arrangements, and conducted to the Drawing Room, where the President advanced to him and gave him a cordial and affectionate reception. The President had on his right hand the Secretary of State and Secretary of the Treasury, and on his left the Secretary of the Army and Secretary of the Navy; while the Attorney General, General Jesup, Colonel Gibson, Colonel Towson, Major Nourse, and Doctor Lovell, of the Army, Captains Rodgers, Chauncey, Porter, Jones, and Morris, of the Navy, the Post-Master General, the Comptrollers, Auditors, and other high Officers of the Government, were arranged on each side of the room, to the number of 50 or 60. The interview was impressive, and occasioned many grateful recollections. After an interchange of courtesies, and spending about 20 minutes in delightful converse, during which liberal refreshments were passed round, the General took his leave and rejoined his escort. He then passed in review the whole body of troops, and retired to his quarters at Gadsby's Hotel. After some time spent in his private room, a great number of Officers, Citizens, &c. were introduced to him.

After the ceremony of the procession, &c. a public dinner was provided, at which the Mayor of Washington presided, assisted by the Presidents of the boards of Aldermen and the Common Council; and at which were present the heads of departments, revolutionary officers, military and naval officers of the United States, members of the City Council, and many distinguished characters from different parts of the nation.

His reception by Mr. Monroe President of the United States, was most cordial and honourable. He called on the President, the day of his arrival in Washington, as before mentioned. The next day he was with Mr. Monroe both at breakfast and dinner, and on Thursday, the President gave a public dinner in honour of Lafayette, at which were present, the Heads of Departments, many distinguished public characters from various parts of the United States, and the principal officers of the army and navy. While in Washington, he also visited the Secretaries of State, of the Treasury, and of War, and Major General Brown, of the United States army.

General Lafayette rode over to Georgetown on Thursday, having been earnestly invited by the Mayor and corporation to visit that city; and the citizens demonstrated their gratitude and joy on the occasion, by a military escort, and a respectable procession. But the most acceptable offering was such as he had received in all other places, the spontaneous and cordial sautations of the whole people. On Friday, he visited the navy yard, by invitation of the veteran Commodore Tingey. His reception here was remarkably brilliant and impressive; he was accompanied by many distinguished citizens and public functionaries; and the attentions of the naval veteran were honourable to himself and highly gratifying to General Lafayette. He dined again on Friday with President Monroe; and on Saturday proceeded on his proposed visit to Alexandria, and York-Town. He was accompanied as far as the Potomac by the Mayor and committee of arrangements from Washington, escorted by the Georgetown cavalry. On the south side of the river, he was received by the deputation of Alexandria, attended by many other citizens, and several officers of the army and navy of the United States.

He entered the Ancient Dominion at Alexandria, at noon, on the 16th, every where accompanied, escorted, and welcomed with the offerings of all hearts, hands, and voices. The parade of military exceeded 1500. In the procession was a car with the tent of Washington. The procession passed through thronged streets, by crowded houses, under splendid arches, and amidst the roar of welcome, and shouts of transport. On the apex of a magnificent arch was perched a live mountain Eagle, of extraordinary size, who spread his wings when the General passed, and seemed to unite in their welcome. On his way he was met by another of those interesting and affecting sights—a body of two hundred young boys and misses, who, while one of the latter chanted a beautiful pæan, strewed flowers in his path. He was here addressed by the Mayor, the Common Council, his brother Masons, and others. Salutes of artillery were fired at intervals. At the public dinner given to him, Mr. Secretary Adams, Commodores Rodgers and Porter, General Macomb and other distinguished citizens, were guests. The toasts were good and the volunteers numerous. "Our distinguished Guest—the People's prisoner," was one of them. The General held a levee in the evening. The public buildings and many private houses were brilliantly illuminated.

On the Sabbath General Lafayette proceeded to Mount Vernon, and visited the tomb of Washington, his revered Father and Friend. While here, he was presented, by Mr. Custis, with a ring containing a portion of the hair of the Sainted Hero, together with the masonic sash and jewel formerly belonging to the Great Mason, accompanied with the following address:—

"Last of the Generals of the army of Independence! At this awful and impressive moment, when, forgetting the splendour of a triumph greater than Roman consul ever had, you bend with reverence over the remains of Washington, the child of Mount Vernon presents you with this token, containing the hair of him, whom while living you loved, and to whose honoured grave you now pay the manly and affecting tribute of a patriots and a soldier's tear.

"The ring has ever been an emblem of the union of hearts from the earliest ages of the world; and *this* will unite the affections of all the Americans to the person and posterity of Lafayette, now and hereafter. And when your descendants of a distant day shall behold this valued relic, it will remind them of the heroic virtues of their illustrious sire, who received it, not in the palaces of princes, or amid the pomp and vanities of life, but at the laurelled grave of Washington.

"Do you ask—Is this the Mausoleum befitting the ashes of a Marcus Aurelius, or the good Antonius? I tell you, that the father of his country lies buried in the hearts of his countrymen; and in those of the brave, the good, the free, of all ages and nations. Do you seek for the tablets which are to convey his fame to immortality? They have long been written in the freedom and happiness of their country. These are the monumental trophies of Washington the great; and will endure when the proudest works of art have "dissolved and left not a wreck behind."

"Venerable man! Will you never tire in the cause of freedom and human happiness? Is it not time that you should rest from your labours, and repose on the bosom of a country, which delights to love and honour you, and will teach her children's children to bless your name and memory? Surely, where liberty dwells, there must be the country of Lafayette.

"Our fathers witnessed the dawn of your glory, partook of its meridian splendour; and oh, let their children enjoy the benign radiance of your setting sun. And when it shall sink in the horizon of nature, *here*, here with pious duty, we will form your sepulchre; and, united in death as in life, by the side of the great chief you will rest in peace, till the last trump awakes the slumbering world, and calls your virtues to their great reward.

"The joyous shouts of millions of freemen hailed your returning foot-print on our sands. The arms of millions are opened wide to take you to their grateful hearts; and the prayers of millions ascend to the throne of the Eternal, that the choicest blessings of Heaven may cheer the latest days of Lafayette."

General Lafayette having received the ring, pressed it to his bosom, and replied:—

"The feelings, which at this awful moment oppress my heart, do not leave the power of utterance. I can only thank you, my dear Custis, for your precious gift. I pay a silent homage to the tomb of the greatest and best of men, my paternal friend."

On Monday, the General proceeded down the Potomac for

York-Town, in the steam-boat Petersburgh, accompanied by two other steam-boats.

The steam-boat Virginia left York the same day at 11 o'clock, and proceeded down the river, followed by the steam-boat United States from Baltimore, and Virginia from Richmond—at 12, at the mouth of the river, met the steam-boat Petersburgh, with General Lafayette on board, followed by the steam-boats Potomac and Richmond, the former from Alexandria, the latter from Norfolk. The General, according to previous arrangement, debarked from the Petersburgh, and came on board the Virginia, where he was met by the Committee of arrangements; the Virginia firing at the time a salute of 15 guns. After the General and his suite, who were accompanied by the Secretary of War, and several officers of distinction, both of the army and navy, had entered on board the Virginia, she returned to York followed by the steam-boats Petersburgh and Richmond on the larboard side, and the Potomac and the United States on the starboard; the Virginia following in the rear in the centre, thus forming, as it were, an ellipsis, when they moved up in a very handsome style, the bands on board playing very appropriate airs, while the heights were thronged with troops and spectators, anxious to see, and pay their respects to the man whose career of life has never been equalled, and such a man will probably never exist again.—The feelings of all present were more or less excited when the General came on board the Virginia; but when he was addressed by B. W. Leigh, Esq. in behalf of the State; the manner in which the address was delivered, as well as the style in which it was written, together with the circumstances which gave rise to such an address *on this spot*, all manifested an appearance such as cannot be described. On the General's landing he was supported by Colonels Bassett, Harvie, Peyton, and Jones, who introduced him to the Governor of the State; the latter received him with the following address:—

"General Lafayette—

"Sir—In behalf of the people of Virginia, I tender to you a most cordial and hearty welcome to our state.

"In you we recognise the early, the steadfast, the consistent friend. Whilst the United States in general owe you so large a debt of gratitude for the liberal tender of your purse, your person, and your blood, in their behalf, the State of Virginia, is, if possible, still more deeply indebted to you. You were her defender in the hour of her greatest trial. At the early age of twenty-four years, with an army greatly inferior in numbers, and still more in equipments and discipline, you conducted your military movements with so much judgment, that the ablest officer of the British army could never obtain the slightest advantage over you; and whilst that officer spent his time in harassing our distressed state, you manœuvred before him with the most unceasing caution and vigilance, with a steady eye, to that grand result, which brought the war to a crisis on the plains of York.

"Forty-three years from that period, we have the happiness to find you in our country, the vast improvement of which is the most conclusive evidence of the correctness of the principles for which you contended by the side of Washington.

"I will conclude, Sir, by the expression of a sentiment, which I believe to be strictly true;—It is, that no man, at any time has ever received the effusions of a nation's feelings, which have come so directly from the heart."

The General advanced, and grasping the Governor's hand, said,—"I am gratified, Sir, most highly gratified, by the reception you have given me on the part of the State of Virginia. The happy conduct and the successful termination of the decisive campaign, in which you have the goodness to ascribe to me so large a part, were attributable much more to the constituted authorities and people of Virginia, than to the General who was honoured with the chief military command. I have the liveliest recollection of all the scenes of my services in this State, and of all the men with whom it was my happiness and honour to serve—and happy as I was to assist and witness the accomplishment of American liberty and independence, I have been yet happier in the assurance that the blessings which have flowed from that great event, have exceeded the fondest and most sanguine expectations."

The procession formed, and the "Nation's Guest," in an elegant barouche, drawn by four beautiful gray horses, moved up into the town. The General dined with a select company of some 20 or 30, consisting of the revolutionary officers, &c. At night, some transparencies were exhibited over the door of his house, and under the Richmond marquee.

On this day, Monday 18th, the reception was purely civic, not a soldier appeared under arms. But on the 19th the military spectacle was imposing and brilliant. Soon after breakfast, Lafayette walked from his quarters, to the *tent of Washing-*

ton surrounded by the Committee of Arrangements and others Numbers were then introduced to him—many ladies, the veteran soldiers of the revolution, citizens from other states, and all quarters of Virginia. The classic ground of York-Town was converted into a camp; and the harbour was filled with vessels, steam-boats, &c. In the midst of the camp the *tent of Washington* had a conspicuous situation, near the house where its illustrious owner had his Head Quarters in 1782.—To this the General repaired, and received the visits of the Ladies, strangers, &c.—after which he was introduced to Colonel Wm. I. Lewis, of Campbell, who delivered an address suitable to the occasion.

Leaving this he passed under a splendid triumphal arch, erected on the spot where once stood the redoubt, which Lafayette stormed, and which bore the names of Lafayette, Hamilton, and Laurens. The other redoubt stormed by the French troops, bore an Obelisk, bearing the names of Viomenil, Dupont, Dumas, De Novilles, Rochambeau, and De Grasse. On every part of the battle ground were to be found balls, shells, and fragments of bombs, the interesting evidences of the ardour and peril with which the capture of York was characterized. —The General, in his splendid barouche, accompanied by the Governor of Virginia, Chief Justice Marshal, and Mr. Secretary Calhoun, proceeded to the arch, where he was received by General Taylor, and addressed as follows:—

"General—On behalf of my comrades, I bid you welcome They come to greet you, with no pageantry, intended to surprise by its novelty, or dazzle by its splendour. But they bring you, General, an offering which wealth could not purchase, nor power constrain. On this day, associated with so many thrilling recollections; on this spot, consecrated by successful valour, they come to offer you this willing homage of their hearts.

"Judge, General, of their feelings at this moment by your own. Every thing around them speaks alike to their senses and sensibilities. These plains, where the peaceful ploughshare has not yet effaced the traces of military operations; these half decayed ramparts, this ruined village, in which the bomb's havoc is still every where visible, tell us of past warfare: and remind us of that long, arduous, and doubtful struggle, on the issue of which depended the emancipation of our country.

"On yonder hillock, the last scene of blood was closed by the surrender of an army; and the liberty of our nation permanently secured. With what resistless eloquence does it persuade our gratitude and admiration for the gallant heroes, to whose noble exertions we owe the countless blessings which our free institutions have conferred upon us?

"The spot on which we stand, was once a redoubt occupied by our enemy. With how rapid a pencil does imagination present the blooming chieftain, by whom it was wrested from his grasp. Can we be here, and forget that superior to the prejudices which then enchained even noble minds, he perceived in the first and almost hopeless struggles of a distant and obscure colony, the movement of that moral power, which was destined to give a new direction and character to political institutions, and to improve human happiness. Can we forget, that, deaf to the solicitations of power, of rank, and of pleasure, with a noble prodigality, he gave to our country his sword, his treasure, and the influence of his example.

"And when in the aged warrior who stands before us, we recognise that youthful chieftain, with what rapidity does memory retrace the incidents of his eventful life? With what pleasure do we see his manhood realize the promise of his youth? In senates or in camps, in the palaces of kings, or in their *dungeons*, we behold the same erect and manly spirit. At one time tempering the licentiousness of popular feeling; at another restraining the extravagance of power, and always regardless of every thing but the great object of his life, the moral and political improvement of mankind.

"General—In the brightest days of antiquity, no artificial stimulus of rank, or power, or wealth, was required to excite noble minds to acts of generous daring. A wreath of laurel, or of oak, was at once the proof and the reward of illustrious merit. For this, statesmen meditated, warriors bled, and eloquence soared to its sublimest heights. The prize was invaluable; for, it was won only by merit. It detracted, however somewhat from its worth, that it was conferred by the partiality of compatriots, and in the fervour of admiration, inspired by recent success.

"Your life, General, illustrious throughout, in this also is distinguished.—Time, which dims the lustre of ordinary merit has rendered yours more brilliant. After a lapse of nearly half a century, your triumph is decreed by the sons of those who witnessed your exploits.

"Deign then, General, to accept the simple but expressive

token of their gratitude and admiration. Suffer their leader to place upon your veteran brow, the only crown it would not disdain to wear, the blended emblems of civic worth and martial prowess. It will not pain you, General, to perceive some scattered sprigs of melancholy cypress, intermingled with the blended leaves of laurel and oak. Your heart would turn from us with generous indignation, if on an occasion like this, amid the joyous acclamations which greet you every where, were heard no sighs of grateful recollection for those gallant men who shared your battles, but do not, cannot, share your triumph. The wreath which our gratitude has woven, to testify our love for you, will lose nothing of its fragrance, or its verdure, though time hang upon its leaves some tears of pious recollection of the friend of your early youth: in war the avenger, in peace the father of his country.

"In behalf then, of all the chivalry of Virginia; on this redoubt, which his valour wrested from the enemy at the point of the bayonet; I place on the head of Major General Lafayette, this wreath of double triumph:—won by numerous and illustrious acts of martial prowess, and by a life devoted to the happiness of the human race. In their names, I proclaim him alike victorious in arms and acts of civil polity. In bannered fields, a hero—in civil life, the benefactor of mankind."

Lafayette was deeply affected. There was a solemn earnestness in his manners, a touching sensibility in his whole countenance, which most deeply impressed every observer. Many wept—all were moved. When General Taylor had closed his address, he was about to fix the civic wreath upon the General's head. But the considerate veteran, always himself, always attentive to the slightest proprieties of word and action, caught the hovering wreath as it approached his brow, with his right hand, and respectfully bowing, dropped it to his side, when he thus replied:—

"I most cordially thank you, my dear General, and your companions in arms, for your affectionate welcome, your kind recollections, and the flattering expressions of your friendship. Happy I am to receive them on these already ancient lines, where the united arms of America and France have been gloriously engaged in a holy alliance, to support the rights of American Independence, and the sacred principle of the sovereignty of the people. Happy also to be so welcomed on the particular spot where my dear Light Infantry comrades acquired one of their honourable claims to public love and esteem. You know, Sir, that in this business of storming redoubts, with unloaded arms and fixed bayonets, the merit of the deed is in the soldiers who execute it; and to each of them, I am anxious to acknowledge their equal share of honour. Let me, however, with affection and gratitude, pay a special tribute to the gallant name of Hamilton, who commanded the attack, to the three field officers who seconded him, Gimat, Laurens, and Fish, the only surviving one, my friend now near me. In their name, my dear General, in the name of the Light Infantry, those we have lost, as well as those who survive, and only in common with them, I accept the crown with which you are pleased to honour us, and I offer you the return of the most grateful acknowledgments."

The General was not apprized of the address or the offering of the wreath; but with his never ceasing readiness he turned round, and drawing Colonel Fish to the front, said, "*Here, half of this wreath belongs to you.*" "No, Sir," replied the Colonel, "it is all your own." "Then," rejoined Lafayette, putting it into the Colonel's hand, "take it, and preserve it as *our common property.*" The whole scene was strongly marked with the moral sublime.

After this ceremony, the line passed and paid the Guest military honours; and the General then resumed his barouche, and the military, in line of march, took up the escort. On a platform and gallery erected on the field, were seated nearly 1200 ladies, and by their presence, gave additional delight and splendour to the scene.—The General's attention was early arrested by this fair assemblage, and requesting the escort to halt, he directed the barouche to leave the line and drive up to the platform, where, stopping at intervals, he expressed the gratification and pleasure these marks of attention were peculiarly calculated to afford. He resumed his place in the line, amidst the cheerings of the citizens and strangers, and the waving of handkerchiefs, and the procession then escorted him to his quarters in the town.

The dinner which followed was sumptuous, and the toasts were excellent. In the evening there was a splendid display of fire-works.

On Wednesday, the 20th, the General partook of a miltary breakfast in the *tent of Washington*, where all the officers and soldiers in the field, were introduced. The most interesting of these interviews were with the soldiers of the revolution. One of them advanced, seized the General by the hand, exclaiming, "I was with you at York-Town. I entered yonder redoubt at your side. I too was at the side of the gallant De Kalb, your associate in arms, when he fell in the field." The tears streamed from the veteran's eyes; and Lafayette showed by his countenance the sympathy he felt. "Yes, my brave soldier, I am happy to have lived, to meet you once more."

After a short time, Lafayette, respecting that inestimable spirit of equality which pervades all free institutions, went forth to salute the crowd of citizens who stood in the street. He was stationed at the gate, and the long line of gratified spectators passed by him. Each person seized his hand as he passed him. To all Lafayette extended some mark of kindness and consideration. The spectacle was deeply impressive. The variety of manners in the different spectators, was singularly striking. Some, as they approached, fixed their eyes on his face, and lingered after they had passed, as if to drink in the last expression of its countenance. Others advanced with the deepest feelings of awe, with their eyes cast upon the earth.

General Lafayette, after the sublime scenes of York-Town were closed, visited Williamsburg, Norfolk, Petersburgh, and Richmond, by special invitations, where he was received with all that magnificent parade, and those splendid decorations, as well as civic feasts that have marked the whole progress of his tour, from his first landing upon the shores of America. The limits of this work will not admit of a particular detail. Suffice it to say that the offerings of American hearts in this glorious cause, are every where the same, whether expressed by addresses, triumphal arches, military parades, civic feasts, splendid balls, and illuminations, the smiles of the fair sex, or the sympathetic tear of the old heroes of the revolution. All these, and much more that cannot be expressed, were displayed to their full extent in Virginia.

General Lafayette left Richmond on Tuesday, November 2d, on a visit to his illustrious friend Mr. Jefferson, agreeable to invitation, and arrived at Monticello on Thursday, November 4th, where he was received by Mr. Jefferson in a most feeling and affectionate manner. They flew into the arms of each other, by a most cordial impulse, and remained locked in a silent embrace for several minutes, before their feelings could find utterance. Language cannot express the affectionate salutations that followed. Mr. Jefferson presented his friend to his family and friends, who all gave him a cordial and affectionate welcome. The whole scene was peculiarly interesting and touching.

General Lafayette passed a week at Monticello, to enjoy the repose of that beautiful seat, under the courteous hospitality of his beloved friend, which also afforded him some leisure to reply to his numerous correspondents.*

The General closed his most agreeable visit at Monticello; took leave of that classic ground, and his ever dear and venerable friend, and departed for Montpelier, agreeable to his engagements, to meet the welcome congratulations of his much esteemed friend, Mr. Madison. Here he was also received with open arms, and made welcome to the bosom of a family, whose every heart cheered him with a most cordial reception. His visit at Montpelier, as at Monticello, was peculiarly interesting and gratifying, but his stay was necessarily short, on account of his engagements to be at Washington. He tore himself away from this happy family, and again commenced his journey for the seat of government, where he arrived on Tuesday, the 23d of November, and was received with the highest testimonials of affectionate respect. He dined with the President on the same day, in company with the principal officers of the government and city. On Wednesday, he set out for Baltimore, accompanied by his Son and Secretary, the Hon. James Barbour, of Virginia, and other gentlemen of the first respectability. He was received at Baltimore with unabated cordiality; attended the great Cattle Show, &c. and was complimented with the delivery of the premiums. In the evening he attended the theatre, and returned the next day to Washington.

Upon the return of General Lafayette to Washington, both Houses of Congress, upon the report of committees, specially appointed to recommend a suitable manner of receiving General Lafayette, resolved as follows:—

"In Senate Resolved, That the President of the Senate invite General Lafayette to take a seat in the Senate Chamber, agreeable to his wishes; that the committee deliver the invitation to the General, and introduce him into the Senate Chamber, and that the members receive him standing."

Upon the report of a special Committee, the House passed the following resolution:—

*It is said that his unanswered letters exceeded 400.

"Resolved, That General Lafayette be invited by the Committee to attend the House on Friday next, at 1 o'clock; and that he be introduced by the Committee, and received by the Members standing, and addressed by the Speaker in behalf of the House.

"Committee of invitation to consist of 24 members, a representation of each State."

On Thursday, December 9th, at 1 o'clock, General Lafayette entered the Chamber of the Senate, accompanied by a Committee of that body. On entering the bar, Mr. Barbour, Chairman of the Committee, announced the presence of the General in the following words: "We introduce General Lafayette to the Senate of the United States;" whereupon the President of the Senate and the Senators, rose from their seats, and the General advancing towards the Chair of the Senate, was invited by the President to take a seat prepared for him on the right of the Chair.

Soon after the General was seated, Mr. Barbour moved that the Senate adjourn.

Mr. Lloyd of Massachusetts concurred in the wish for the Senate to adjourn, to afford the Members an opportunity of paying their individual respects to General Lafayette.

The Senate then adjourned, and the Senators individually beginning with the President of the Senate, tendered him their respects, which were cordially and feelingly reciprocated.

On Friday, December 10th, the House Resolved, "That a messenger be sent to the Senate of the United States, requesting that body to attend in the Chamber of Representatives, this day, at 1 o'clock; seats were ordered for the Senate, and that body shortly after entered, and took their seats accordingly.

At 1 o'clock, according to previous arrangement, General Lafayette appeared, attended by the committee of 24 members of the House of Representatives, and was introduced to the House by Mr. Mitchell, Chairman of the Committee.

On the General's entry, the members and persons admitted on the floor of the House, rose, and remained standing, uncovered.

Mr. Speaker then rose, and, in behalf of the House, addressed the Nation's Guest, in the following eloquent strain, adorned by those graces of oratory, for which he is distinguished :—

"General—The House of Representatives of the United

States, impelled alike by its own feelings, and by those of the whole American people, could not have assigned to me a more gratifying duty, than that of being its organ to present to you cordial congratulations upon the occasion of your recent arrival in the United States, in compliance with the wishes of Congress, and to assure you of the very high satisfaction which your presence affords on this early theatre of your glory and renown. Although but few of the members who compose this body, shared with you in the war of the Revolution, all have a knowledge, from impartial history, or from faithful tradition, of the perils, the sufferings, and the sacrifices, which you have voluntarily encountered, and the signal services in America and in Europe, which you performed for an infant, a distant, and an alien people; and all feel and own the very great extent of the obligations under which you have placed our country. But the relations in which you have ever stood to the United States, interesting and important as they have been, do not constitute the only motive of the respect and admiration which this House entertains for you. Your consistency of character, your uniform devotion to regulated liberty, in all the vicissitudes of a long and arduous life, also commands its highest admiration. During all the recent convulsions of Europe, amidst, as after the dispersion of, every political storm, the people of the United States have ever beheld you true to your old principles, firm and erect, cheering and animating, with your well known voice, the votaries of liberty, its faithful and fearless champion, ready to shed the last drop of that blood, which here you so freely and nobly spilt in the same holy cause.

"The vain wish has been sometimes indulged, that Providence would allow the Patriot, after death, to return to his country, and to contemplate the intermediate changes which had taken place—to view the forests felled, the cities built, the mountains levelled, the canals cut, the highways constructed, the progress of the arts, the advancement of learning, and the increase of population. General, your present visit to the United States is the realization of the consoling object of that wish. You are in the midst of posterity! Every where you must have been struck with the great changes, physical and moral, which have occurred since you left us. Even this very city bearing a venerated name, alike endeared to you and to us, has since emerged from the forest which then covered its site. In one respect, you behold us unaltered, and that is in this sentiment of continued devotion to liberty, and of ardent affection and profound gratitude to your departed friend, the father of his country, and to your illustrious associates, in the field and in the Cabinet, for the multiplied blessings which surround us, and for the very privilege of addressing you, which I now exercise. This sentiment, now fondly cherished by more than ten millions of people, will be transmitted, with unabated vigour, down the tide of time, through the countless millions who are destined to inhabit this continent, to the latest posterity."

To which address, General Lafayette replied, in a tone in which energy of character and sensibility of feeling were most interestingly blended, to the following effect:—

"*Mr. Speaker, and*

"*Gentlemen of the House of Representatives*:—

"While the people of the United States, and their honourable Representatives in Congress have deigned to make choice of me, one of the American veterans, to signify in his person, their esteem for our joint services and their attachment to the principles for which we have had the honour to fight and bleed, I am proud and happy to share those extraordinary favours with my dear revolutionary companions—yet, it would be, on my part, uncandid and ungrateful not to acknowledge my personal share in those testimonies of kindness, as they excite in my breast emotions which no adequate words could express.

"My obligations to the United States, Sir, far exceed any merit I might claim. They date from the time when I had the happiness to be adopted as a young soldier, a favoured son of America.—They have been continued to me during almost half a century of constant affection and confidence, and now, Sir, thanks to your most gratifying invitation, I find myself greeted by a series of welcomes, one hour of which would more than compensate for the public exertions and sufferings of a whole life.

"The approbation of the American people and their Representatives, for my conduct during the vicissitudes of the European Revolution, is the highest reward I could receive. Well may I stand, "firm and erect," when, in their names, and by you, Mr. Speaker, I am declared to have, in every instance, been faithful to those American principles of liberty, equality, and true social order, the devotion to which, as it has been from my earliest youth, so shall it continue to be to my latest breath.

"You have been pleased, Mr. Speaker, to allude to the peculiar felicity of my situation, when, after so long an absence, I am called to witness the immense improvements, the admira ble communications, the prodigious creations of which we find an example in this city, whose name itself is a venerated palladium; n a word, all the grandeur and prosperity of these happy United States, which, at the same time they nobly secure the complete assertion of American Independence, reflect on every part of the world the light of a far superior political civilization.

"What better pledge can be given of a persevering national love of liberty, when those blessings are evidently the result of a virtuous resistance to oppression, and the institutions founded on the rights of man and the Republican principle of self-government. No, Mr. Speaker, posterity has not begun for me —since in the sons of my companions and friends, I find the same public feelings, and permit me to add, the same feelings in my behalf, which I have had the happiness to experience in their fathers.

"Sir, I have been allowed, forty years ago, before a Committee of a Congress of thirteen States, to express the fond wishes of an American heart.—On this day I have the honour, and enjoy the delight, to congratulate the Representatives of the Union, so vastly enlarged, on the realization of those wishes, even beyond every human expectation, and upon the almost infinite prospects we can with certainty anticipate.

"Permit me, Mr. Speaker, and gentlemen of the House of Representatives, to join, to the expression of those sentiments, a tribute of my lively gratitude, affectionate devotion, and profound respect."

After the General and the Members had resumed their seats and a short pause ensued, Mr. Mitchell, the organ of the Committee of reception, moved an adjournment.

The motion was agreed to, and the House was adjourned to Monday.

The Speaker then descended from the Chair, and most affectionately saluted the General. His example was followed by the Members of the House, individually, and some time was spent in this agreeable manner before the General retired.

The sublime and touching realities of this whole scene surpass the powers of imagination; every eye, every ear, and every heart, were wholly engrossed by the magnitude of the object before them. Nothing is to be found in the whole field of Grecian or Roman story, as a parallel to this. Of all the proud triumphs through which the veteran hero has passed since he first landed upon the shores of America, this was not only the most glorious, but must have been the most interesting to his feelings.

The scene in the Senate was not less interesting and imposing than that of the House; and it is well understood, that General Lafayette is the only *public character* that has ever been received by the Senate of the United States. This virgin honour was reserved for the man who was truly the most deserving.

On Monday, December 20th, Mr. Hayne, from the committee to whom was referred the subject of making provision for General Lafayette, reported to the senate a bill, providing, that the sum of 200,000 dollars be granted to Major General Lafayette; also, one complete and entire township of land, to be located upon any of the public lands that remain unsold.

On Tuesday, December 21st, this bill passed the Senate, and on Wednesday, December 22d, the bill passed the House of Representatives.

Some slight objections were made to the bill while under discussion in Congress, which were remarks by way of inquiry for information, rather than serious opposition, which led one of the members, in a conversation with General Lafayette, to offer a delicate apology; but the General with great *naivete* interrupted him, by adding—"*I too, Sir, am of the opposition.* The gift is so munificent, so far exceeding the services of the individual, that had I been a member of Congress, I must have voted against it."

CHAPTER IV.

A SUMMARY OF THE SOUTHERN AND WESTERN TOUR OF GENERAL LAFAYETTE.

General Lafayette commenced his tour from Washington, through the southern and western states, about the first of March. In his course he visited the principal towns in the states of North and South Carolina, Georgia, Alabama, Louisiana, Mississippi,

Tennessee, Missouri, Kentucky,* Illinois, Indiana, and Ohio. He visited Pittsburg, and returned to Albany, by the way of Buffalo and the western canal. From Albany he proceeded directly to Boston, through Springfield, where he arrived on the 16th of June.

The author regrets extremely that the limits of this work will not permit him to give a particular description of the interesting scenes that awaited the General throughout this whole tour. It must, however, be remembered, that descriptions of scenes the most interesting, of feelings the most sublime and touching, and of characters the most exalted, lose their intended effect, by being too minutely dwelt upon, or too often repeated, and become irksome and tedious. A general sameness necessarily prevails throughout the whole; as in the Atlantic so in the western tour of General Lafayette, all classes of citizens vied with each other in expressing the grateful emotions of their hearts to the guest of the nation, the veteran hero, and the patriot benefactor of America.

The orators of the country, the surviving heroes of the revolution, the patriots and sages, the fair daughters of Columbia,

* Extract of a letter from General Lafayette to a gentleman of Philadelphia, dated

Louisville, May 12.

"In the night of the 8th and 9th inst. we ran foul of a snag, which lay concealed two feet under water, and so well *infiladed* our steam-boat, that it pierced through our upper deck, and sunk the boat in a few minutes. We had time, however, to come out of the ladies' cabin, before the water had penetrated through the partition, and all landed safely without any life being lost. The Paragon, which was descending the river in the morning, was good enough to take us on board and bring us to this place This accident is not imputable to any one; the conduct of the captain of the Mechanic was such as to entitle him to the thanks which you will see in the St. Louis Gazette.

"You will find in another part of that newspaper, an error, which I wish much to be corrected. It is, that I have only lost my carriage and my hat, the latter was most obligingly replaced by a manufacturer of Louisville. But amongst the lost trunks is that which contained all the papers which I had preserved during my journey—all my letters to be answered—and a great number of answers which I had prepared during twelve days navigation. This loss throws all my correspondence into confusion—I have not saved a single memorandum—and as to every thing anterior to the shipwreck, I must rely on the indulgence of my friends. [One of the trunks has since been found and is on the way to its owner.]

"I expect to be on the 28th or 29th of this month at Pittsburg, and arrive at Boston on the 16th of June, by the way of Albany. I hope to be at New-York on the 4th of July, thence go to Washington, taking Philadelphia in my way, to take leave of several respected friends, and embark for France on the 15th of August."

with their numerous offspring, and the whole mass of citizens, all with one acclaim welcomed the man whom their united hearts delight to honour. The same military parades, civic feasts, cordial and affectionate addresses, triumphal arches, splendid balls, and soldiers tears, that showed the joys of kindred souls, greeted the arrival of Lafayette in every place he visited, throughout this extensive route, from Washington to Charleston, to New-Orleans, to St. Louis, to Cincinnati, to Pittsburg, to Buffalo, to Albany, and to Boston, a distance of more than 4000 miles.

These were not the momentary triumphs of a conqueror, who returns flushed with some recent victory; but the triumphs of the hearts of other generations, who rise up to bless the patriot hero of their country, who took their fathers by the hand, led them to victory and glory; and when he had given them an exalted rank among the nations of the earth, stepped aside, and left them to pursue their enjoyments of freedom, happiness, and honour. Again, after a lapse of nearly fifty years, he comes, at the united voice of more than 10,000,000 of people, as free, as happy, and as independent, as the nature of man can possibly become, to receive the welcome plaudits of the nation.

More than 3000 miles of the western tour of General Lafayette were a pathless desert when he last visited America; now they can proudly boast of nine new and valuable states, covered with rich and flourishing cities, towns, and villages; possessing a free, a virtuous, and an intelligent population; richly enjoying all that is essential to the happiness of man. Throughout this vast interior, the forests have bowed to the axe of the wood-man, cities, towns, and villages, roads, canals, manufactures, commerce, and the arts and sciences, have risen into being, as by the wand of the magician; and the all-propelling power of steam has greatly facilitated the social and commercial intercourse throughout the vast circuit of this western route.

The changes throughout the eastern or Atlantic tour, in a period of forty or fifty years, far surpass every thing of the kind, either in ancient or modern story, and must have been almost incredible to the patriot hero; but the changes of the west are far greater, and must have appeared to him like so much of the section of a new creation. The sublime realities of this whole scene, when taken collectively, surpass the powers of the pen or the pencil, and are vast beyond the stretch of imagination.

CHAPTER V.

RECEPTION OF GENERAL LAFAYETTE BY THE LEGISLATURE OF MASSACHUSETTS—PROCEEDINGS AT BUNKER HILL.

On Thursday, June 16th, General Lafayette, agreeable to invitation, met the Governor and Council, the Senate and House of Representatives, in the Representative Chamber. The several branches of the government being assembled, he was introduced by a committee, and seated by the side of the Governor, by the Speaker's desk. The Governor then rose and made the following address:—

"General Lafayette,

"The immediate Representatives of the people of Massachusetts, in the Executive and Legislative departments of the government, have assembled on this occasion to offer you their cordial congratulations, on your return in health and safety to the capital of this Commonwealth, and in the name of their constituents, to repeat to you the assurance of respectful and affectionate interest, with which they shall ever regard your presence among them.

"Your arrival in the country, on this happy visit to your American brethren, was greeted by them with expressions of the liveliest satisfaction and joy. Your own observation since, will bear faithful witness how true are their hearts to the language of salutation, with which they first welcomed you. The population which has crowded your path-way, the prosperity which has smiled along your progress, in your tour through the Union, are but the fruits of events in which you largely and gloriously participated. The remembrance of your early sacrifices in the cause of this country, has excited the deepest sense of public obligation, and the breasts of millions of freemen will never cease to swell with gratitude, in the recognition of your services, most generously and effectually rendered to an oppressed and suffering people. A nation just to itself cannot be indifferent to the fame of its benefactors, and while liberty is dear to the enjoyment of Americans, the names of those who fought in its defence will be associated with every memo rial of the scenes through which it became triumphant.

"In offering to you, General, the congratulations of the Government, upon your present visit, I have the highest personal gratification, in further executing the pleasure of the Legislature, by tendering to you the hospitalities of the Commonwealth during its continuance."

To which General Lafayette made the following reply:—

"Sir—The honour conferred upon me by the immediate Representatives of the State of Massachusetts, in the Executive and Legislative branches, at the same time it fills my heart with the most lively, and the deepest sentiments of gratitude, recalls to my mind recollections equally grateful and endearing; and while I am so kindly welcomed by your Excellency, in this splendid State-House, I remember the remote times when similar favours have been received on the floor of Faneuil Hall—the consecrated cradle of American, and I hope, of universal liberty.

"In the long and happy series of visits through the several parts of the Union, to which you have been pleased to allude, Bunker Hill has ever been my polar star; and I now rejoice to be arrived in time to join, on the grand half century jubilee, with my companions in arms, as being together the representatives of the early and unshaken devotion of our revolutionary army —of the patriotic wishes of such of us as are still on this land —of the dying prayers of those who are no more; and permit me here, Sir, most deeply to mourn the recent loss of my two friends, your respected Predecessors, who had so heartily joined in the late welcome, I have had the happiness after a long absence, to receive from the people of this State, and in this beloved city of Boston, which I never entered without feeling the warmest emotions of affection and gratitude.

"While I have continually to admire the rapid wonders of creation and improvement, that have been the result of independence, freedom, and those republican institutions, which alone are equal to support the weight, and display the faculties of an extensive empire, I have particularly delighted in the sentiments of fellow feelings, and mutual affection, whereby the people of every part of the confederacy are strongly attached to an union, on which resides the safety of these states, and the hopes of mankind.

"I beg, Sir, the gentlemen of the two houses of the legislature, and your Excellency, to accept my respectful thanks, and cordial devotion."

The General was then introduced by the Governor to the members of the Council severally, and by the presiding officers of the two other boards, to the several members who came forward to pay their respects to him.

BUNKER HILL MONUMENT.

The celebration of the *Fiftieth* Anniversary of the memorable battle on Bunker Hill, and the ceremony of laying the *Foundation Stone* of an OBELISK to commemorate that great event, took place on the 17th of June.

The day was temperate and fair;—and all the arrangements made to honour it, were executed with a punctuality and good order, which could only be effected by the entire union of all the hearts and hands in the ceremonies.

The Grand Lodge of Massachusetts, having been requested to assist on the occasion, assembled at an early hour in the morning at their Hall, and soon after were visited by their illustrious Brother, General Lafayette, and their respected brothers George Washington Lafayette and Le Vasseur. The meeting was most interesting. After the fraternal greeting of Grand Master Abbot, the distinguished Guest expressed the great pleasure he felt in meeting his brethren in the beloved city of Boston, on the anniversary of the battle of Bunker Hill, and in the Grand Lodge, whose first Grand Master had, in the true spirit of a Mason, shed his blood in defence of the liberties and institutions of his country, on that ever memorable occasion. The assemblage of the fraternity was very numerous. The Grand Lodges of Maine, New-Hampshire, Rhode-Island, Connecticut, Vermont, and New-Jersey, were represented by their Grand Masters, or other distinguished members; and the Grand Royal Arch Chapters of several States, by their Grand High Priests, and other officers. The distinguished Visiter was attended from and to his residence at Mr. Lloyd's, by a deputation composed of past Grand Masters and Deputies.

The *Grand Procession* was formed near the State House with the utmost precision and regularity, under the superintending direction of Brigadier General Lyman, assisted by a staff, composed of Majors Brimmer and Aspinwall of Boston, Major Edwards of Brighton, Captains Sprague of Salem, Ford of Milton, Talbot of Dedham, and Young of Charlestown, Lieutenant Baxter, and Ensign Gardner, of Boston.

The Military Escort was composed of sixteen companies, and a corps of cavalry commanded by Lieutenant Parker, all volunteers, and in full uniform.

Survivors of the Battle.—Those worthies were in eight barouches and carriages, and were about forty in number.—Each wearing on his breast a badge, "*Bunker Hill, June* 17, 1775," and many bearing the implements of war they used in the fight.

Then followed between one and two hundred Revolutionary Officers and Soldiers, each bearing an appropriate badge. Their appearance was truly venerable.

The Bunker Hill Monument Association, in full numbers, six deep, all wearing the badges, "B. H. M. A."

The Masonic Procession succeeded.—This section of the Procession was very splendid, and exceeded two thousand of the fraternity, with all their jewels and regalia. The Grand Lodge of Massachusetts was fully organized, and bore the implements and vessels used in laying the foundations of ancient edifices. They were followed by the Grand Encampments of the Knights Templars of Rhode-Island, Connecticut, Vermont, Maine, New-Hampshire, and Massachusetts, in full numbers with their banners, implements, and regalia; by the Grand Lodges of the above States; by the Grand Chapters of Royal Arch Masons, and by various subordinate Chapters and Lodges, bearing banners. A full band of music was attached to the Masonic procession. Of the regalia of the Grand Lodge, was a gold Urn, borne by the Deputy Grand Master, containing a relic of our departed Brother George Washington.

Hon. Mr. Webster, President, and other officers of the B. H. M. Association.

The Rev. Dr. Kirkland, the Rev. Mr. Thaxter, (a Revolutionary Chaplain,) and the Rev. Mr. Walker, Chaplains of the day.

Directors and Committees of the Association.

General Lafayette, in a coach and four, accompanied by Lieutenant General Lallemand, of Philadelphia.

Mr. George Washington Lafayette and the General's suite in a carriage.

His Excellency the Governor.

The Hon. Council, Senate, and House of Representatives accompanied by the Adjutant-General, Secretary, Treasurer, &c.

Governor Fenner, the Secretary of War of the United States, and others.

Delegations from the various States.

Delegation from the Pilgrim Society in Plymouth.

Officers of the United States Navy and Army, and the Military in uniform.

Citizens.

In this order the whole proceeded from the State-House, about half past 10, and passed through Park, Common, School, Washington, Union, Hanover, and Prince-streets, to Charlestown River Bridge, and from thence through Maine, Green, and High-streets, in Charlestown, to the Monumental square. The front of the procession had nearly reached the bridge when the rear of it left the Common.

All the streets, the houses to their roofs, and in some instances to chimney-tops, and every situation on which a footing could be obtained for a prospect of the procession, were filled with a condensed mass of well dressed, cheerful looking persons, of all sexes and denominations, many of whom had occupied their stations for several hours; and who, at appropriate places, spontaneously rent the air with joyous and orderly acclamations, while the Ladies displayed their tokens of smiles, and waving handkerchiefs, as the procession passed, particularly when the Guest was in sight.

Arrived at the Monument spot, the various sections of the procession formed a square around it; when the Grand Master of Massachusetts, accompanied by General Lafayette, President Webster, the Past Grand Masters, the District Deputy Grand Master, bearing the Architectural Implements, the Grand Wardens, bearing the *Corn*, *Wine*, and *Oil*, in vases, the Grand Chaplain, Grand Treasurer, and Principal Architect, repaired around the foundation stone, which having been squared, levelled, and plumbed, by the Grand Master, Brother Fayette, and Mr. Webster, and declared to be true and proper, the following deposits were made in the cavity of the Stone :—

1. The official account of the battle of Bunker Hill, by the Provincial Congress of Massachusetts Bay.

2. Official account by General Gage. [*Both written on parchment, and presented by* Mr. John F. Eliot.]

3. All the printed accounts of the battle, viz. by Samuel Sweet, by H. Dearborn, Major General U. S. A.—and by a Bostonian, (Alden Bradford, Esq.)

4. Plan of the battle, and a plan of Charlestown.

5. Circular Letter of Bunker Hill Monument Association, by Edward Everett.

6. Address of Bunker Hill Monument Association, by William Sullivan.

7. Account of the battle of Lexington in an address delivered at Concord, by Edward Everett.

8. Life of Josiah Quincy, jun. containing letters and *fac similies* of the writings of revolutionary characters.

9. Coins of the United States.

10. *Medals* of distinguished persons connected with America, presented by the Hon. Thomas L. Winthrop. *The Medals bore the following inscriptions, viz.*

Comitia Americana
GEORGIO WASHINGTON,
Supremo Duci Exercituum, Adsertori Libertatis. Hostibus Primo Fugatis; Bostonia Recuperatæ,
xvii. Martii MDCCLXXVI.

BENJ. FRANKLIN,
Natus Boston, xvii. Jan. MDCCVI
"Eripuit Cœlo Fulmen, Sceptrumque Tyrannis."

CHRISTOPHORUS COLUMBUS,
Natus An. MCCCCXLII. Cogureti ad Gennam, Obiit in Valle Oleti, Apud Hispanos,
An. MDVI.

Comitia Americana
GULIELMO WASHINGTON,
Legionis Equit: Præfecto.
Qui parva militum manu strenue prosecutus hostes, virtutis ingenitæ præclarum specimen dedit, in Pugna ad Cowpens,
xvii. Jan. MDCCLXXVI.

Comitia Americana
JOH. EGAR HOWARD,
Legionis Peditum Præfecto.
Qui in nutantem hostium aciem subito irruens, præclarum belliceæ virtutis specimen dedit, in Pugna ad Cowpens,
xvii. Jan. MDCCLXXXI.

CPSIA information can be obtained
at www.ICGtesting.com
Printed in the USA
LVHW041629060123
736479LV00001B/202

9 783375 126629